SISTERS OF THE CHOSEN

Printed in Australia

Book cover and character illustrations by Vladimir Shvachko

Title text art by Radovan Zivkovic

Internal design by Book Burrow www.bookburrow.com.au

Images in this book are copyright approved for the author.

First printing: July 2025

Paperback ISBN 978-0-6484-2417-8

eBook ISBN 978-0-6484-2418-5

A catalogue record for this work is available from the National Library of Australia

For encouraging me to become a more confident person,
and removing me from my comfort zone at every opportunity,
I dedicate this story to my good friend,
Sean

Contents

One: No More Strings

Iya

Four cycles ago

It was my 208th birthday. Not that any of my hundreds of brothers and sisters around me cared, let alone remembered. It was hardly a special occasion when I shared it with three others. There were so many of us and our birthdays were so frequent that none of it mattered. Why should I be upset about it?

The dining hall was set up in the usual fashion for dinner: the long tables were covered in elegantly decorated cloth coloured purple and gold, its beauty unappreciated by the masses; the plates were filled with identical food placed in identical positions with identical portions; and an audience of royal servants lined the hall's perimeter, anticipating our every beck and call.

The room's most unique feature – two equally sized lavish thrones on a raised platform – lay in wait for our parents, the emperor and empress, to watch over us as we *enjoyed* yet another pointless celebration.

We had repeated this same scenario for lifetimes, we children never ageing, always looking the same. The only sign of time passing was witnessing our servants age from adults to elderly and then disappearing forever.

The children were hoeing into their food, not caring if it spilled onto their royal garb. After all, it wasn't our job to clean. We didn't have jobs at all. Our only prerogative was to sit in our rooms with all of our countless toys, gifts and outfits, and keep ourselves amused for time everlasting.

'I heard the oceans on Nares turn green this time of cycle,' my sister Arlaus said, trying to spark a conversation.

My brother Eiro sighed. 'Sure would be nice to see.'

I waited for more, but that was it. How typical of the conversational depth we were capable of. Our family had nothing of value to say to each other, having exhausted every possible topic of conversation many cycles ago. Everything that is, and was, had been said, leaving nothing but worthless small talk and extended awkward silences.

Everyone was the same; it was amazing how little diversity there was in my siblings. The girls all wore boring dresses and most had short brown hair like me. The boys on the other hand had to wear a formal suit to every birthday dinner. Unlike the interesting skin colour varieties and possible backstories of our servants and guards, we were all pale and very uninteresting.

We children were all stuck in bodies ranging from toddlers to late teens, I myself looked like I was twelve. My twenty-two-cycle old brother, Mikan, who was still in the body of a toddler, was sitting across from me. Like the others, he was used to the procedures around here: eyes down, talking… pointless, just eat and go back to your room.

He reached for his drink; a task made all the more difficult due to his size. It was the young ones like him I pitied the most for enduring our annual age reductions.

He noticed me studying him. His babyish face forced an uncharacteristic smile. 'It's… it's your birthday today, yeah, Iya?' he said, almost in squeaks.

I might have burst out laughing from the absurdity of his voice if I hadn't been so depressed. I nodded in place of laughter, not that I cared about sparing his feelings. I just nodded.

'Well, I hope you enjoy your presents,' he added, clearly wanting to end the social engagement he forced upon us.

Above us along the vaulted ceiling edges, a troop of royal guards peered over the dark balcony ledges. No, not royal guards, we knew what they really were: assassins and thugs. A private military force of acolytes that protected my parents at all costs. Each was heavily armoured, had arms bigger than Mikan's whole body and wore a foul, despicable look on their face. They all shuffled along the balcony to get a better view of below, it was about to happen.

A crackle echoed throughout the otherwise silent chamber and two clouds of smoke enveloped the thrones. The haze dissipated to reveal my parents, the emperor and empress, as well as their own personal teleporter lackeys. Both my parents wore robes too loose for them. Lackey #1 and #2 stepped away from the thrones. Here we go, another inspiring family chat.

My father, more shrivelled vegetable than man at this point, raised a bony hand to his mouth and cleared his raspy throat. 'Good evening, children. Tonight is a special night.'

I felt like calling him out on his crap. How exactly is any one night considered special if they're *all* special, Father? It's not like he could speak how he really wanted to. All of these birthdays were being watched by billions of people from their homes around Aster and the colonies. Now cue Mother with her 'special' drivel, too.

Our mother managed to raise her sagging, droopy face long enough for a fake smile. 'That's right. We have some birthdays today,' she said, bringing her stick-thin arms together for a soundless clap.

I half-expected her arms to break that time. If my siblings weren't such prudes, I would probably make bets with them as to when her arms would finally snap off. Although, my first bet would be that my father's nose falls off, that thing seemed to be hanging on for dear life.

A light applause filled the room, some rolled their eyes and a few mockingly tried to out-clap each other. As for me, I didn't even bother bringing my hands up, it didn't mean anything anyway.

Father's teleporting lackey assistant knelt and whispered names into his ear. Couldn't they at least *pretend* that they knew whose birthday it was by doing this ahead of time?

Father's eternally baggy eyes scanned the room. 'The birthdays today are for,' he started. The lackey repeated the names into his ear and Father spoke them aloud. 'Saiydi, Eema, Lollan and… Iyra…'

Again. He said my name wrong, *again*. It's Iya, not Iyra. This was the tenth time. I wanted to scream out and correct him. I wanted to tear his withered head off and vomit down his open neck hole.

The four of us stood from our seats and approached the raised platform as the royal servants produced wrapped boxes of varying sizes from a nearby hiding place. One by one, we each received a present from one of the servants, bowed in appreciation, said our thanks along with an exaggerated smile and then returned to our seats.

I placed my present next to my plate, sat back down and sighed. I was thankful that these daily celebrations were the only contact I had with my parents. A shame they put a stop to hugging after one of my elder brothers cracked one of Mother's ribs. That was the best birthday party ever!

Yet again, as I sat there in my seat, I came to the same realisation that had been haunting me most of my life: I had to leave this place, by any means necessary.

Time to sleep again. The children all self-herded along the quiet, square, lattice-like corridors and into their individual rooms like the good zoo animals they were. My door sealed itself once I was inside, and now this large room would be my cell until morning.

I threw myself onto my bolted-down bed and looked up at the ceiling. Over a hundred stuffed toys watched me from all corners. I pretended each one was a person. In a way, they were, as each was a gift from an adoring fan. But I hadn't done anything with my unnaturally long life to deserve their devotion other than being born royal. I had never met a person who wasn't family or staff.

I was nothing but a prisoner here. A prisoner that could have anything she wanted, other than freedom. But that paled in comparison to the age reductions. I wouldn't mind being a prisoner if

I could at least age, because I would have died a long time ago now. Suicide was pointless, too, thanks to resurrection.

Being a royal, I was guaranteed to live as long as possible. My selfish, vile parents wanted to live and rule forever, and the very idea of one of their children usurping them must have been why none of us had a body aged over 18.

Even with the grand powers that acolytes give us, death – something most thought had been made obsolete from our society – still loomed over us. My parents' bodies in particular, having lived for almost 2500 cycles now, appeared to be falling apart. Soon wasn't soon enough. I wanted them dead, *permanently* dead, not just brought back again moments later. I wanted them to suffer like they had made me suffer.

I stared at a doll hanging from the ceiling on a string. It wasn't the only one, of course, but this one was made to look like me, albeit with a smile on her face. I used to think it was cute when I got it, maybe back when I was fifty. But now it just made me angry. That's the girl they wanted me to be. A smiley idiot who just accepts the fate she's given.

I strained the muscles in my wrists and then all over my body. No tears, they won't break you. No tears, they won't control you. It is *you* who will control them! I didn't want to see that stupid toy anymore. I hated it just as much as I did my parents.

While still lying, staring up at it, I raised my hand above my face between the doll and I. I separated my fingers and my thumb, as if I was holding the doll in a giant hand. Then, I pinched my fingers like a claw on its head, hoping to kill it.

What? It moved. The doll… moved. I sat up in my bed and noticed that it was swinging from side to side. Did… *I* do that? I raised my hand above my face and gently pinched the doll a second time. Its head squeezed, staying within my fingers. I moved my hand to the side and the doll followed, ripping it off the string. I released it and watched it drop to the ground in front of me. Interesting.

One cycle later

The same familiar crackle, followed by smoke, although this time things felt different. This was probably the first time I had ever been excited to see my parents. Their lackeys left them, as they always do, and Father started with his idiotic spiel about how 'special' the night was. Soon I would be close enough to strike.

'Evening, children,' he started as his lackey approached again and prepped to tell him the names. 'It's another special night, isn't it?'

Tonight was the night I had been training in secret for. I was giddy, I was finally going to leave this place, or at least… I hoped so. Kids had tried escaping before, but because of their tracking devices, they were brought right back again. No, I was going to do something severe.

'Another wonderful party!' my mother squealed. 'Let's all give the birthday girls and boys a big clap.'

We were lucky we were all test-tube babies, otherwise I couldn't imagine coming out of that horrid woman. We all clapped, even me. I didn't want anyone to stop this from happening, so everything needed to look normal. That way they'll know I'm truly a psychotic child that could snap at *any* time. Yes, I was too dangerous for them to keep.

The lackey bent down and my father wrinkled his entire vegetable-skin face in concentration. 'The… *uh*… it's Saiydi, Eema…, Lollan and Iya.'

Wow, this time you got it right, you bastard? *This* time? Whatever, it was too late, my mind was made up. I stood up like the others and strolled towards the raised platform.

Was I really going to do this? What if they had me permanently executed? Fine then. It didn't matter where I was or what happened to me, *any* fate was better than this.

I glanced up at the assassins stoically watching over me as I walked, and when one locked eyes with me, I quickly looked back down, as if everything was normal. I waited in line with the other three, waiting for my turn to receive my present.

Wait for it, the closer the better. Wait until you're at the front of the line, no one in the way then. Hurry up you stupid… one of my sisters couldn't lift her oversized gift and so another servant walked over and assisted her carrying it back. Come on, come on. The other two took their gifts without incident, good.

My disgusting father and hag mother gazed down at me from their seats of power with their insincere smiles, clearly as impatient as I was for this to soon be over. Well… don't worry you two; I won't keep you for much longer.

I smiled back with the toothiest abomination I could manage. Queue the rehearsed line. 'Mother, Father? I just wanted to say… we kids are *so* lucky to have you perfect parents.'

'What?' my father said smiling through gritted teeth, like I was a waste of his time.

My mother raised a hand to her cheek, surprised. '*Oh?*'

I hadn't seen them, but numerous servants had gathered behind me, ready to haul me away. They stopped when Mother raised her palm at them.

She attempted to smile. 'What else? I want to hear *more* of what you think of us.'

'Suralia,' my father started, bringing a palm to his wrinkly forehead.

'No, Avarut, this is nice,' she replied.

They both looked at me expectantly, as if I was a trained performer.

'I just thought… instead of clapping for the birthday kids, we should all clap for you in appreciation, for a change,' I said, before looking back at the others, who all looked confused. 'Come on, guys.'

Thankfully, my idiot siblings bought it and started an applause. I looked back at my parents and gave them the biggest smile yet. I raised my hands in front of my face and focused my gaze so that they were both between my hands.

Then, with as much ferocity as possible, I clapped my hands together with such force that the two thrones and their occupants rocketed towards each other, merged in a mix of blood and steel, and then burst in a glorious explosion of gore in all directions, showering everyone nearby like a smooshed berry dessert.

My clothes were drenched in red. I glanced back at my siblings; many had already clambered and screamed their way to the chamber's rear. Some unfortunates had been impaled with flying metal throne pieces.

I laughed, quietly at first, then louder until it was all I could hear.

The assassins had jumped, flown and teleported down to me, blocking my view of the carnage. They approached with their various deadly powers already activated, all about to snuff me out. I took one last look at the pulp that was my parents strewn across the room, closed my eyes, and grinned.

Two: Peace

Tau

The present

New Elysia's Refugee Camp

The former royal gardens was filled with activity. Everywhere I turned there were smiles on peoples' faces, each brought joy to my heart. It looked as though everyone was enjoying themselves, and that was exactly what I had hoped for. I couldn't help but beam as I took it all in. I knew this festival had been a good idea.

Every marquee tent hosted a different activity for small wandering audiences: one man juggled colourful painted rocks; poorly costumed performers reenacted recent events through song and dance; lines of children waited to have their faces painted; and vendors offered their sweet and savoury wares, for free of course. The melodies of multiple musicians carried over the constant conversations of the crowd, lending a jovial vibe to the whole place.

As I traversed the path between the tents, I noticed that not many people recognised me. My dress, with its swirling colours, would normally stand out, but today, everyone wore equally festive clothes, so maybe I just blended in. Or maybe I wasn't much of a celebrity anymore.

Whatever it was, I appreciated no one making a fuss over my presence. After all, today wasn't about me, it was about how far we had all come together.

To think, only half a cycle ago we were using these gardens as a makeshift refugee camp. A power of work had been done since then, primarily on housing in the Residential Rim beyond the outer garden walls. There were scaffolds tending to most of the buildings, and although they were a shadow of their former quality, in my eyes they were better than before, for the people inside were no longer living in fear. It was funny how prosperous we were now in peacetime compared to before.

I glanced back at the golden Citadel. With its grand gates now always open, the public were free to explore inside, and even sit in the throne if they so wished. From here I could see hundreds coming and going through the main entrance of the former epicentre of power.

Although we did have numerous elected leaders governing, including my friend Tarsus, we had no need for a singular ruler anymore.

As I looked back, my eyes fell on a smiling Tetsu, my self-appointed bodyguard. He had a large pink flower in his outstretched hand.

'*Oh?*' I began. 'For me?' My cheeks warmed.

He gestured at the massacred bush from which he had procured it, now left with very few flowers. 'If you like it, I can get another?'

I giggled and smelled the sweet, yet musky plant. 'One will do.' I pointed at the people around us. 'Someone else might want one, too.'

He dipped his head in a short bow. 'Always thinking of others. You know, you remind me of my dad, sometimes.'

'Your dad?' I asked with a laugh.

He nodded. 'Yeah, I'm serious. He always wanted to help people, too, but could never work out how. You, on the other hand, are a master.'

Lately, Tetsu had been complimenting me quite a lot. I felt bad for spurning his recent advances, but I knew it had been for the best. It was both incredible and surreal to see so much romance taking root, but I kept remembering back to all the enemies that were still out there, an entire empire's worth. War was coming again, so with all this uncertainty, I didn't think I could risk so much heartbreak when we eventually lost.

If only I could be ignorant of what was inevitable, like the average person here, I might give in to hope. After all, if our world could have this brief glimpse of happiness, why couldn't he and I? He deserved it for being so patient and protective of me. And I deserved it after spending so much time healing and resurrecting others, feeling all that pain as though I had died again and again.

I think I should risk it. This festival was about all of us coming together, after all. I reached out and brushed his fingers with mine. His biggest smile yet appeared, and the two of us strolled through the camp, enjoying the sights and smells of a fleeting peace, hand in hand.

'Do you think Elysia would be proud?' I asked him, gripping him tightly. 'Of what we've all done here?'

'The first queen?' Tetsu replied. 'After all that's happened, we don't even know if she was real.'

I looked down at my flower and frowned. 'You think she never existed?'

Tetsu shook his head. 'Well, I think she *existed*, but what really happened, and what she was really like… might be different to what we've been taught.'

I smiled at several happy children as they ran past. 'I've tried to base my whole life on her principles of healing and kindness. I'd hate to find out she wasn't like that.'

Tetsu pulled on my hand to stop me. 'If she was anything like you, she wouldn't just be proud.' He gestured around with his free hand. 'She'd *love* what you've done, and who you've become.'

I burst forward and hugged him. I nuzzled my head below his chin, closed my eyes and squeezed him. 'Thank you.'

He squeezed back and the two of us embraced in silence for a beautiful moment, one that I didn't want to end.

When I finally opened my eyes, I noticed Marid a couple of tents away.

She was staring at us with a big smile of her own. But her eyes widened when we both acknowledged her presence. '*Oh*, don't stop on my account.'

'It's okay, Mum,' I began, releasing Tetsu and approaching her. 'What's wrong?'

She, too, was dressed in a more casual garb, with her sword securely sheathed in her cane. 'Nothing, actually. I just thought you'd like to know the good news: Kalek has finally been apprehended.'

Tetsu stopped beside me. 'He's the last one, right?'

Marid nodded. 'That we know of, yes. And with the last few territories signing the charter in a few days, Seron will finally be able to say it is at peace.'

I sighed and looked down. 'That's good.'

Marid bent her head down to my level and raised an eyebrow. 'Tau? Isn't this… what you've *always* wanted?'

I nodded and tried to look happier. 'It is, I just wonder if it will bring peace to *everyone*.'

Marid bit her lip in thought. 'If this doesn't bring her some peace, then nothing else can.'

I looked back at Tetsu. 'Let's go visit the Prison Quad. It's time my sister came out of hiding.'

Three: Another Masterpiece

Raumanu

Descending into Seron's atmosphere

The landing craft's cabin shook me awake.

'What?' I said, followed by a raspy cough.

Turbulence. We must have been entering a planet's atmosphere. Surrounded by empty seats, I appeared to be the only one here. Where was I again?

Oh, that's right, I was heading to Seron. If I was given anything close to comfort – a bed, a cushion, even just being allowed to sit down – it was enough to make me fall asleep. It was like I had narcolepsy, but this was the price to be paid for being so old, having a body that was continually on its way out. No amount of resurrection or age reduction could help me anymore.

'Raum, Sir?' a man's voice called out over the intercom. 'Did you say something?'

Who was that? *Oh*, the pilot.

I cleared my throat. 'What did you call me?'

'*Ah*, Raumanu, Sir. Sorry, Sir. We're about to land, Sir.'

I could feel the spacecraft's momentum shift from one side to the other, we were turning. We slowed, and there was another strong shake as we landed.

In the seat to my side was my cane. I unbuckled my straps and leant over to reach it. A sharp pain shot through my back, causing me to groan.

'Sir?'

'I… didn't say anything!'

I fell face-first onto the seat, grabbed my cane and used it to push myself up. I brought my trembling, free hand to the painful throbbing in my lower back.

Alright, one step at a time. I hobbled over to the interior's side, where a whirring hatch slowly opened to the outside world.

'Keep it running,' I called back to the intercom before taking my first step down the ramp, cane first.

The wind howled so loudly that it rung in my ears and flicked my long, white beard into my face. The heat practically seared my cheeks in moments, or at least it felt like it. The sand pelted my wrinkled skin like a hail of stinging needles. There was nothing but featureless dunes in all directions. The star was high above, casting no shade.

I remembered this awful place, Seron. My, my, had it changed. This was the same world where Caelum and I found and tortured the last Chosen, almost 600 cycles ago.

Above me in the sky I spotted something familiar. An L-line, long and white. It had been hanging there since that time, when Lucenia desperately tried to defend this world from us. I remember we toyed with her for so long.

'*Ah*, Lucenia,' I said to myself, 'your handiwork endures. But not as permanently as mine shall.'

Now that another Chosen had been created, two from this same world, it seemed a waste to destroy it. But I would do whatever was needed to get Sacet under control. Had her power been anything other than teleportation, we could have just abducted her as normal. Alas, I had to leave her with no places to run and no holes to hide in.

After descending the steps, my cane dug deeply into the sand. It was useless out here, so I threw it back through the hatch. I shambled farther from the ramp, taking extra care with each step. Every one of my joints ached, as though some phantom opponent was trying to pull my limbs off. I needed to make sure the splash damage didn't hit my craft, but I also needed to be close enough to reach it in time.

Here, this was far enough. I licked my dry lips and stretched my arms. For more centuries than I cared to remember, I had been known as the most powerful Chosen, but it wasn't my raw strength that countless respected and feared. No, it was my intelligence, my creativity, my art that was truly beyond measure. The demise of this world would come from my signature move, yet the amount of power needed for it was very little.

I brought my hands closer to my face, palms to the pale-blue sky. After a few moments of concentrating, a small sparkle of light floated between my fingertips. Only a fraction of what made up this universe was visible to all. The majority of it was an energy that moved and shifted, altered and manipulated the totality of existence. This dark energy was what I was going to fracture.

I carefully bent down and placed the floating particle into the sand, careful not to let it touch my beard or silk robe. The particle was absorbed into the ground like a water droplet, but soon, the sand split as if a miniature seismic force had ripped it apart from below.

The ground shook, I could already feel the chain-reaction under my feet. The particle was cascading towards the planet's core, randomly splitting into millions of paths, forking like a bolt of lightning. It was nothing more than a set of instructions, telling every mote of dark matter it encountered to push away instead of pull. It was a virus that would spread until there was no more to hear the herald of perfect destruction.

I slowly stood, careful not to do any more damage to my back, before heading back to the craft. Now, it was only a matter of time before the entire planet would be ripped apart by dark matter, the very construct that held it together in the first place. No force in the universe could stop what I set in motion here. Another planet destroyed… another masterpiece.

Four: A Prison With No Walls

Sacet

New Elysia's Prison Quadrant

My father, Caelum, sat motionless, hands on his knees, legs apart and eyes closed. He was a large man; his biceps alone were bigger than my head. He had pale skin, black hair and a wide jaw, and having had no access to shaving equipment, now also sported a thick beard.

Noor and I were all too familiar with his sitting pose, which was as though he were constantly meditating. He'd been like this for so many days now, aside from an occasional workout of pushups and sit-ups.

I had been watching him for almost that entire time, with Noor taking over whenever I needed a break. And while Noor and I looked and felt exhausted, he showed tremendous patience and endurance, even with his invincibility inhibited by his prison cell. But I couldn't leave this duty to anyone else. It was possible that any soldiers we posted on prison detail, anyone that we didn't know, could be a spy.

Caelum would consume the basic food and water we passed through to him, but he rejected all other attempts to interact. He was intensely stubborn, but then so was I. Either way, I was glad he never said or did anything. I had no interest in understanding this monster, nor allowing him any opportunity to escape.

I had to make sure he stayed alive, for if he somehow died under my watch, he'd be resurrected elsewhere, as we learned during the war.

His newly modified cell was special, consisting of one-way opaque walls that blocked his sight. The walls were thick, too, making it practically soundproof. From his perspective, he was alone in his well-lit cell.

We in the surrounding dark corridors, on the other hand, could see through the walls from all angles. Not only that, but he couldn't hear us unless we pushed a button by the door. And thanks to devices recording everything he did, any sound he made was also amplified for us to hear.

His cell wasn't the only one, the greater chamber contained fifteen other cells just like it, many of which also housed enemy acolyte spies we had managed to capture alive. There were so many enemies unaccounted for, all those vapourised in the satellite crash, for example, but so long as Caelum was here, I knew we'd be okay.

I had been standing outside his cell for… well, I actually didn't know how long I had been here. At least a hundred days now, maybe more? Noor and I had a bedroll set up nearby for whenever we were tired. And both food and water were regularly brought to us when we needed it.

I knew Tau and the others had things well in hand outside. The last thing they needed was a dealer of death like me out there bringing everyone down again. There was a small part of me that didn't want to leave simply because I couldn't face my many victims.

Surrounded only by reinforced steel walls without windows, time had presumably passed peacefully without our involvement. We'd had plenty of visitors to check in on us, but their visits were becoming less frequent. That was fine; I didn't deserve their kindness.

Tau had visited us the most. Each time she'd heal us both, effectively granting us another day of focus without sleep or sustenance.

Noor, meanwhile, had rarely left my side. His loyalty would be cute if he didn't fall asleep on watch so much. Even now he was lying in the corridor, leaning against our captive's cell, unconscious. His normally imposing physique was curled into a ball and his short brown hair was messy.

The one-way wall slightly reflected my awful condition, with bags under my eyes; frizzled, dirty hair; and grubby, blotchy skin. Even my black-tipped, purple streaks were starting to lose some of their colour. I brushed them back and sighed.

A loud whirr from behind startled me and I spun on the spot. Noor snorted awake, too. The entrance to the prison wing had sprung open and let in a group of soldiers in desert-camo armour escorting a hover-dolly. An enormous man lay upon it, so large that his limbs hung over the edges and dragged along the ground. I recognised the unconscious brute instantly as Kalek.

How did I not sense them coming with my second perception? Was I that out of it?

The soldiers, a mix of several women *and* men, hurried the dolly through the entrance, into the corridor, past Noor and I, and then stopped in front of a neighbouring empty cell. They unlocked and opened the door using the security panel, hovered the body into the cell and dumped him on the floor.

As the soldiers left the cell and the facility, Tau and Tetsu entered.

The four of us exchanged smiles and waves. Noor and Tetsu embraced in a friendly hug, laughing as they did so. I suppose it had been a couple of days since last time. Or maybe a few?

Tau ignited her aura of light-blue flames as she approached, before pointing her hands at both Noor and I. A familiar wave of rejuvenation washed over me, but it again didn't feel as potent as the time before.

'Thanks,' I said, taking a deep breath to collect myself. 'As usual, nothing new to report here.'

'You guys stink,' she replied with a smirk, and Tetsu nodded in agreement. 'You're both way overdue for a shower.'

I shrugged. 'Body odour hasn't stopped me in the past.'

Tau placed a hand on my shoulder. 'And what of your mental health?'

I pushed her hand off and turned back to Caelum. 'We've been over this; I'm *not* leaving him unguarded. It's too much of a risk to trust *anyone* else to do it.'

Out of the corner of my eye I could see Noor look pleadingly at the others.

Tau sighed. 'Sacet, who do you think we have guarding the reactor that powers this place? Or the security grid control stations? All day, every day, we have teams of people we know we can *trust.*'

Noor nodded in agreement. 'You know I love you, but she's right. We both need a break from this.'

I shook my head. 'But I have to do this. This was all because of me.'

Tau grabbed me with both hands. 'Every time I heal you, I can feel you getting weaker. It's like I'm healing someone destined to die.'

My breath came rapidly. 'I'm not leaving! What if he escapes while I'm relaxing? *Huh*?' I hit the reinforced glass with my fist. 'What then? Do you think I'd be able to *live* with myself if this starts all over again?'

Caelum raised an eyebrow, perhaps having heard the thump on his prison wall.

Tau gestured around. 'And this here, you call *this* living?' She turned and made for the door, and Tetsu followed close behind. She paused and looked back one last time. 'At least think about it. Think about the people who *love* you, Sacet. Because we're tired of seeing you here, stuck in your prison.'

The door opened and they both left. I could hear Tau exchanging some words outside, and shortly after Eno entered through the open doorway. My anger instantly faded.

I smiled at my little brother as he approached. 'Eno!' I bent down to hug him tight.

He managed a smile back. 'You reek, Sis.'

I chuckled and let him go. 'So they tell me. Well? What happened on your mission?'

Noor patted Eno on the shoulder. 'I heard you caught Kalek? Very impressive!'

Eno raised his hands. 'Er, there was a whole team of us. I didn't do much.'

I gave him a quick peck on the forehead, and he instinctively reeled back. 'Even so, I'm very proud of you. Mum and Dad would be, too.'

He nodded back. 'Thanks, Sas.' He then looked over my shoulder at Caelum. 'Still hasn't moved?'

I shook my head. 'No, thankfully not.'

Behind me, I heard groans as Kalek slowly regained consciousness. He eventually got to his feet and rammed the cell walls around him. But without his powers, all he did was hurt himself. He thrashed about in a rage, yelling at the top of his lungs.

Eno was distracted by one of our other prisoners farther down the line, Mycol. Eno flashed a grimace, possibly without realising. Even after all this time, my brother's torturer must have still been haunting him. Like Caelum though, Mycol was quite secure here.

'And neither has he,' I assured, and Eno's shoulders relaxed a little.

Shortly after I regrettably melted MDC, Mycol's body was found among the smouldering ashes. Tau explained that while every other person out in the open had been practically vaporised by the sun portal, Mycol's body had begun to reform itself yet again. Now, without powers or souls to eat, what remained of Mycol was a thin, pitiable husk, a gaunt and pale shell of a man.

If there was a way to execute these prisoners permanently, I would. Maybe my brother and I could finally be at peace then? What Eno went through was too much for any kid. That being said, ever since I was reunited with him, he was different. More grown up. He didn't need me anymore.

I placed an arm around him. 'How are your friends? Nadan and Mui, right? I heard you guys hang out a lot.'

Eno crossed his arms. 'They're not my *only* friends.' There was a hint of a smile on his face. 'Why don't you come hang out with us sometime? I told them about that perfect beach we went to as kids, remember that one with the webberfish? You could portal us there?'

My smile faded. 'I… I'm sorry. You know I can't do that, but if you bring the boys here I can send—'

Before I could finish, his face screwed up in frustration, and he turned and stormed out of the facility.

'Eno, wait!' I called out. But I didn't follow, I couldn't.

Noor noticed my reluctance and frowned. 'I'll talk to him.' He also strode out of the facility, leaving me alone with the prisoners.

I understood where they were all coming from, I truly did. But every time I thought about stepping foot outside, I remembered all the people I had killed needlessly. All the burning hate and anger.

Kalek had calmed down now. Not me though, I wanted to break something, to tear something to pieces. My hands shook and my teeth clenched.

Kalek was now in the centre of his cell, pacing from side to side, so I opened a portal above his head and slammed it down. Without invincibility, he squealed in pain as he was forced to the ground.

I wasn't done. I raised the portal again and smacked it down onto his back, making him wail. Next, I made the portal even smaller, like a fist, and launched it into his face several times.

'*Argh…* stop it!' he bellowed. 'Stop!'

I released the portal and stepped back, resting against the corridor wall. My muscles had nothing left to give. I was so tired, I could barely move.

'You little wretch, Sacet!' Kalek screamed. 'When I get out of here, I'm going to crack open your tiny little skull and drink the juices!'

There was a faint rumble and I looked up from my resting position against the corridor wall. What was that?

Most of the prisoners stood and looked around their cells with excited smiles. A couple even cheered.

'There he is,' Caelum said, still not moving.

I jumped up from my slump and stood in front of his cell again.

He opened his eyes and stared at the cell door I was hidden behind. 'Do you hear that, Sacet?'

There was another rumble below my feet, this time causing the metal walls to rattle audibly. What was going on?

He gestured to the floor. 'Do you *feel* it?'

As I watched him, my other perception flew across the city, where it seemed everyone shared my confusion over the quakes. As far as I knew, New Elysia wasn't near a fault line and never experienced quakes like these previously.

I leant forward and pressed his cell's intercom button. 'It's just a quake, it will be over soon.'

Caelum chuckled, stood up and slowly walked to the door. 'Yes, it will *all* be over soon. This *quake*, however, is on a magnitude unlike anything this world has ever seen. But *I* have.'

Another quake, this time the entire corridor shook so fiercely that I tripped and fell onto the ground. I brought myself up and pressed the button again. 'They can rumble the ground all they want, I'm *never* letting you out of here.'

He leant against the door with his arm and forehead as though trying to peer through the glass. 'No one has been able to make me angry like you have in a *long* time. I have stewed here, thinking about all the ways I could make you and your friends suffer.'

His cell vibrated again and one of the cell walls behind him cracked. The one in front of his face splintered, too, but he took no notice, as if still staring right through. His cell lights shorted and went dark, and his eyes locked on me.

His expression remained neutral, unflappable. 'But your torture is over now. You can either let me out and I will capture you peacefully, without violence. Or… we can wait, and I will kill you.'

I stared back at him through the fractured door, unable to respond. He stepped back to the middle of his cell.

Kalek, who now had bloody bruises all over his giant head, looked overjoyed at his warping cell walls. 'Perfect timing, Raum, you legend!'

'Last chance,' Caelum said as the floor rumbled again. 'Open the door.'

The cracks and crumples in the walls worsened as the rumbling intensified.

They weren't going to get him. I raised my hands and opened two halves of a spherical-shaped portal on Caelum's sides. He saw them approaching but didn't move.

'Wrong choice,' he said as I closed the portals around him, trapping him in a perpetual shell again.

The entire building rocked to the side, sending me flying down the corridor. The normally flat floor was now at an incline, and I slid down it. Most of the cell walls shattered, including Caelum's, spraying glass fragments through the air.

I felt one puncture my shoulder. Still sliding, I grabbed my shoulder and cried out. Somehow, I was still able to keep hold of the portal. All light faded in the windowless building and the usual electronic hums powered down into silence. Darkness now filled every corner of the interior. Were the cells still inhibiting the prisoners?

My feet finally hit something and my ankle went sideways. Excruciating pain coursed up my leg. I tried to sense my surroundings, but the now constant quaking and waves of pain were playing havoc with my perception. Another seism, and this time the wall at the front of the prison ripped open. Sunlight poured in and illuminated the collapsing facility wreckage.

Kalek burst out of his powered-down cell with a roar and balanced himself on the sinking metal corridor. He glanced left and right until his gaze locked on me, down the steep corridor. He gripped a large section of his cell wall and ripped it away from the rest of the cell, then threw it towards me. It tumbled and ricocheted off the floor and walls. I raised my uninjured arm and summoned a portal to receive it, sending it outside into the facility's courtyard.

Other prisoners were also escaping, either with their powers or by scrambling over their shattered cell walls. The closest one to me was Mycol, and he spotted me with the light of my portal.

His sickly green aura wreathed around him. 'Feeding time, is it?'

Where were my friends? Why was I alone here?

I closed the portal in front of me, and as I did, another unseen piece of hurtling debris came at me. I couldn't open another portal in time, the steel beam flew into my stomach, impaling and pinning me against the end of the corridor wall. Blood erupted from my mouth and Kalek guffawed.

Immense pain. Each rumble in the ground caused more mind-shattering rips in my flesh. I couldn't hold the other portal open any longer; it dispelled, surely setting Caelum free. Enemies closed in around me, but I only cared about one. I desperately sensed through the mostly dark chambers and spotted Caelum floating out into the corridor.

He looked at Kalek first and nodded approvingly. Kalek gestured towards me, and Caelum followed his stare.

I reached out to the beam that was protruding from my torso with both hands and tried pulling it out, but the agony forced me to stop. I screamed again, this time with less fervour. I was done.

Caelum appeared at my side like an apparition, grabbed the pole with one hand and twisted it, causing me to bawl.

'She's mine,' he said, side-eyeing Mycol before focusing back on me and grabbing my neck. 'You should have let me out.' He squeezed so tightly that I heard a snap.

Five: Apocalypse

The tallest buildings swayed and the concrete beneath us snapped apart like a smashed windowpane. The ground split in a million places at once, some sections travelling higher, exposing sewers and basements, others widening into impassable crevices. The disoriented street-goers screams were drowned out by the continuous and deafening rumbling.

To say they were panicking was an understatement. People fled in and out of buildings, some cowered in cover with their hands braced on their heads, and others, still in the middle of the street, were in complete shock and unable to move.

I ignited my aura, hopefully making me and anyone in my vicinity impervious. Even still, I had no idea what to do, where to go, or who to help first.

The building closest to me moaned, its foundations crumbled, and its total sum tipped in my direction.

Tetsu appeared at my side. 'Brace yourself!' he bellowed, raising his shield just in time for the building to crumble over us.

Some of the hexagons that made up his shield flickered under the colossal mass. Although his energy waned and his arms shook, Tetsu kept his shield firm.

The aftermath of ensuing dust enveloped the shield. It darkened and obscured all outside, but our two powers combined illuminated the inside.

We both recognised the fear in each other's eyes. They had finally come, and our short-lived peace was over.

I gestured around. 'Please protect the others first. I'm fine.'

He smiled back. 'You're no help to anyone if you're buried.'

Once some of the dust cleared, Tetsu lowered his shield. We spotted both Noor and Eno in the thin haze, clambering over the rubble to reach us.

'Noor!' Tetsu shouted. 'Over here!'

When they got to even ground, they sprinted over and Tetsu shielded us all.

Another nearby building collapsed, sending a shockwave and subsequent squall of debris.

'What do we do?' Eno squealed over the constant rumbling and screaming townspeople running for their lives.

I looked through the partially transparent shield, back through the streets that we had come through and saw that most of the buildings had fallen. A plethora of rubble and scrambling citizens blocked us, with no clear path back to the Prison Quad.

'We need to regroup with Sacet,' I yelled, slightly regretting the suggestion. 'We need to get out of here.'

As we looked to the prison, its entrance exploded. Bits of infrastructure launched into the sky, and what looked like a man hurtled up with them. Even from this distance, I knew who it was – Caelum. We all froze.

He floated above the city and glanced all around, analysing the pandemonium. He stared in our direction, perhaps recognising Tetsu's shield from afar, before casually floating towards us with a blasé attitude regarding the destruction below him.

'Don't let him reach us!' I yelled to the boys, intensifying my aura to keep them safe.

Both Noor and Eno raised their arms in his direction. Noor let loose a stream of red-hot energy, which streaked through the sky to its target, but it had no effect. It was noticeably weaker than what I knew he was capable of. Eno fired one telekinetic pulse after another, hoping to push him back, but it did little to slow my father's approach.

Caelum sped up and, in barely an instant, an explosion blasted me off my feet, through the air and sent me crashing into the rubble behind us. My body bounced and rolled on the sharp blocks of cement and rods of steel, finally coming to rest in a patch of dirt.

I glanced back to them and saw Tetsu's shield had come down. Standing where Tetsu had once been, predictably unscathed, was Caelum, veiled by the still-clearing dust. Eno's neck was in his grip and he had clearly just snapped it.

'Take a break,' Caelum said with an amused smirk, before throwing the corpse to lay with the others.

Motionless, Eno had purple bruises on his twisted neck, and his mouth and eyes were locked open in a horrified, silent scream. Noor had a fist-sized cavity in his obliterated chest. Tetsu's head was nowhere to be seen; his decapitated body rested limply in a puddle of sewer water.

Caelum slowly raised a pointed finger at me, sending chills down my spine. 'It is time to collect… *all* your hope!'

Sacet, where are you? I couldn't do anything against this man, why even try? We *needed* you now.

I rose to my feet and realised that my aura had dissipated, my hair had turned back to brown. I reignited it again and I could already see the boys' bodies beginning to heal.

Caelum looked at them, smiled and shook his head. 'No, no. You should let them rest.'

I opened my mouth to reply, but it was immediately filled with Caelum's fist. His lightning-fast punch sent me careening through the air again, down the street and into one of the elevated sections of soil that had been raised by the quakes.

As I slid back down to the ground, I again felt my aura diminish, so I shook myself awake to bring it back.

Caelum had already reached me yet again, floating in front of me. He was holding back, toying with me as he used to with Sacet.

'You can't hurt me!' I screamed at him. 'If you kill me, I'll just come back again.'

He nodded. 'You're right. All the others will be resurrected elsewhere, but you… I'm going to have to take you with me.'

He appeared by my side in another bolt of speed, put his arm around me and pulled me close, before rocketing upwards. The wind howled in my rippling ears as we launched out of the streets, high above the city.

'Enjoy the view while you can,' he yelled out as we ascended into the sky.

I could see the bodies of my friends lying in the street among countless others. Most buildings throughout the city had been demolished or were close to it. Entire city blocks seemed to be on separate giant slabs of rock, and many rose high into the air, turned over, or sunk into the empty canyons the other pieces made vacant.

We ascended higher still, the entire city and the desert beyond was visible. The damage was far more extensive than I imagined. City-sized pieces of land rose and fell on the horizon, many splitting from each other to create fissures of indiscernible depths. Many chasms were dark, but others were lit, as if magma had been coaxed to bubble to the surface. The rumbling could still be heard from here.

Caelum was looking down, too, no longer smiling. We were above the clouds, and it was becoming very cold, so I strained to keep my aura active. The air was thinning out and I choked, but I soon realised I didn't need air. I stopped trying to breathe, letting my healing oxygenate my body instead. We were high in the atmosphere now; the howling wind had quietened and there was almost no sound.

I could see the oceans in the distance, as well as the other territories of the world. All of them were in the same turmoil as New Elysia, the entire planet had streaks across it, webbing in every direction. The contours were bright orange, some amalgamating in centralised oceans of lava, spots so gigantic and calamitous that fire and ash shot into space.

Now high in the atmosphere, we both glowed in searing flame, yet Caelum took no notice, showing no signs of slowing. I, on the other hand, struggled against the heat; it took much of my concentration to stay conscious and not let my aura drop.

Caelum finally stopped, or at least I think he did. We were so far away from everything that it was hard to tell. We instead watched on as the orange ravines of lava slowly grew wider. I watched in horror. A tear formed in my eye but gently flew out into the vacuum.

I didn't want to see this anymore, instead I resorted to hitting and kicking Caelum. He disappeared, and in another instant, was holding me from behind in a headlock. He made me watch as the planet continued to disintegrate. All I could do was weep. Everyone I had ever cared for, their lives were over. Our home, gone. My life and love, gone. My hope, gone.

Large portions of crust came loose from the world, and as if gravity had finally given out, the portions, some larger than entire islands or even continents, were let loose into the void. Everything split into smaller and smaller pieces.

Caelum grabbed me by the waist again and together we hurtled through space, orbiting the dying world. Monolithic pieces of Seron flew past us, and Caelum dodged them.

On the far side of the former world, between us and the moon, a thin, sleek, grey construct hung in the darkness like a shadowy assassin admiring their handiwork. It fired upon the incoming rocks with lasers more powerful than I had ever seen. The gargantuan spacecraft seemed to be the only safe place left and we were heading straight for it.

Six: We Lost

I sat up from the bed in a panic. Tau stood by my side, holding my wrist. Her aura was active, having just healed me. Was I that out of it? Or… no. I remembered now. I was killed by my father. This was resurrection.

She wore plain, grey clothing, which had neon-blue stripes in places. I looked down at my chest and saw that I was wearing the same.

An old man was sitting in a chair in the tiny room's centre. He cleared his throat and leant forward. 'Welcome back to the living, Sacet.'

He had a long, thin white beard and moustache, a balding head with tufts of hair on the sides, sagging skin spotted brown with age, and a big, bulbous nose. He rested on a golden-edged black cane. I had never seen anyone as old as him. He made even Marid look young.

He wore finely-crafted, bluish-grey robes, far more formal and dressier than a nomad would wear. They were decorated with bright stripes along the seams, and glistened in the light.

The grey room, a cell similar to those on the satellite I had destroyed, was but a bed and toilet. The only door was behind the old man, and several armed guards looked at me from outside, wielding lasers and looks of trepidation.

The old man glanced back at them. 'Give us some privacy. I'll be fine with her.'

The guards nodded and dispersed along the hallway.

'Sorry about that,' he continued. 'They didn't want a repeat of last time. That being said, no one will be deactivating your collar this time around.'

I felt around my neck and, as expected, there was an inhibitor collar. I couldn't sense anything with my second perception, so I knew it was working. I leant forward to get up.

The old man raised a hand and smiled. 'Relax, not yet.'

I sat back on the bed's side. 'Prisoner again, let me guess, on one of your satellites?'

Tau had an anxious look on her face. 'Sacet, Seron is…'

'Tau, remember what I said,' the old man interrupted, looking at her, 'no talking. The only reason I allowed *you* to resurrect Sacet and not one of the crew is because I thought it would put Sacet at ease. *I* will explain everything.'

Tau looked down at the tiled, steel floor.

'Then explain,' I said. 'Where am I?'

He cleared his throat again. 'Well, I'm Raumanu by the way, but you can call me Raum. Introductions are always important. I will be watching over you and getting you settled into your new life. You've been through a lot, so I forgive you for being rude.'

'I'm not sorry,' I snapped. 'Now, where am I?'

He smiled. 'You're on the mothership, the Black Dawn, named for its captives that never see the sun of their home worlds again. Its purpose is to resurrect conquered worlds en masse and transport them to Aster.'

I rolled my eyes. 'So, what happens next? You take us to your planet?'

Raumanu nodded. 'Yes. You and your friends are quite the celebrities there, and they haven't even met you yet.'

I folded my arms and scoffed. 'As soon as you take this collar off, I'll just teleport me and my friends back home again.'

Tau cringed, clearly desperate to speak.

The old man chuckled. 'That might be more difficult than you think.' He used his cane to stand with some difficulty and then gestured to the door. 'Well, I think you're sufficiently calm. It's time for a tour. Come.'

I hopped off the bed and followed him out the cell with Tau trailing behind. The three of us entered the hallway, to the left were the guards, eyeing me with apprehension. The ship's interior was sleek, and had circular, reflective surfaces almost everywhere we looked.

Raumanu led us to the right, down the corridor to a door, which opened and revealed a vast open area. We were on a railed catwalk that looked on high over the enormous space. The three of us stopped by the railing and surveyed the sight.

Below were row upon row of roofless laboratories. In each were teams of scientists and doctors wearing lab coats and surgical garb. Each room had an empty operating table, and the doctor closest to it had a light-blue aura of flames, like Tau's but far weaker. The army of healers stretched out their hands, and flesh and bone materialised from thin air over the tables.

'This step can only be performed close to their original location of death,' Raumanu explained, watching Tau and I. 'We stop just short of resurrecting them, and then we transport the bodies home to be resurrected there instead.'

I focused on one table in particular, watching from start to finish as new flesh rippled along the bones, regrowing layer after layer, including the skin and hair. I didn't recognise the naked stranger on the table, but I assumed he was Seronian.

The scientists converged and sealed him in a body bag. They placed the bag on a floating gurney and hovered him to a conveyor belt on the side of the lab. The body bag, among hundreds or even thousands of others, rolled out of sight along the twisting conveyors that branched in every direction throughout the ship.

'It will take *cycles* for them to complete their work here,' Raumanu continued. 'But *eventually*, every Seronian will be brought home.'

'What do you mean *every* Seronian?' I asked. 'What did you do?'

'Or at least,' he continued, ignoring me, 'every Seronian we had a record for will be brought back. There were millions who hid so *well* in caves their whole lives that… Overwatch never even *knew* they existed. Those people can never be returned.'

I turned to my sister. 'Tau? What did they do?'

She was sobbing over the railing, refusing to look at me.

'Tau? Tell me!'

'This way,' Raumanu instructed, gesturing farther down the catwalk. He hobbled along, tapping his cane with each step.

The two of us followed several paces behind in silence.

Was what Raumanu telling me right? Based on Tau's reaction… or… no. Was this some elaborate trick? Was Tau one of Verre's illusions? To what end, though?

'Tau?' I whispered to her. 'Tell me he's lying.'

She eventually summoned the courage to look me in the eyes. 'He's not lying. We lost.'

'This isn't an illusion?' I added, and she shook her head.

'It is very much a reality,' Raumanu answered from the front as he led us over the laboratories and onto a new section of catwalk.

The second area of the ship dwarfed the first in its vastness. So large was the cavernous hangar that it stretched farther than my eyes could see, like a blurry grey tunnel with no end. Huge spacecraft were docked along the sides, and another army of ship personnel were tossing body bags onto even more conveyor belts leading up the craft's ramps.

I shook my head. 'This is… this is…'

Raumanu paused and turned back. 'All this because you, Sacet, were too difficult for us to capture.'

I couldn't move. Everyone I had ever known, their lives ruined, displaced. And millions more that would never return? Such a colossal waste of life, all the innocents punished for no reason…

I glared at him. 'If I… had known *this* would happen, I would have surrendered myself.'

He laughed. 'No, you wouldn't have. You have your father's stubbornness in you. He did the same thing, resisted us. So rather than force him away from his home, I had to take *everything* from him, completely destroy it all, so that he would *finally* see. There is no fighting us.'

'But… I thought he was one of you?'

Raumanu nodded. 'He is *now*. This way.' He gestured to a smaller catwalk off to the side with a door at the end.

We slowly made our way over. Before we reached the door, I looked out at the mass-produced death one last time. Even after all this time, I still couldn't fathom all of this was because of me.

We entered a much smaller, regular-sized room this time. It was darker, filled with cushions and chairs. A lounge? On all sides were large panoramic windows that revealed both the magnificence and bleakness of space from many angles. I followed Raumanu over to the nearest window; he was already admiring the stunning vista of stars. Tau stopped by the door and placed her head in her hands, looking as though she was unable to take another step.

Something was wrong, I couldn't see Seron. There was only a field of slowly spinning rocks, lit by the sun. Millions of them were scattered about, each varying in size all and loosely gathered around a central focal point.

Raumanu pointed at them. 'Behold, Seron. Or what's left of it.'

My jaw dropped and I placed both hands on the window. 'What? You... how did you... how could...'

Tears rolled down my cheeks. My home. I bawled, as every memory, every thought I had turned to sadness.

'Whenever I destroy a world, it takes over a hundred cycles for it to all split up properly.'

'You despicable... BASTARD!' I screamed as I sprinted at him.

Raumanu smirked and gave me his attention.

As I raised my hand to strike, I noticed it was gone. My hand had disappeared leaving only the stub of my wrist, which shot arcing red liquid all over the carpet like a hose.

I stopped charging out of shock, not understanding what had just happened. And then came the pain. It rolled over me like an unstoppable tide. I shrieked and shrieked, the pain so overwhelming that I fell to my knees. Whatever Raumanu did, he hadn't even moved to do it.

Raumanu turned and hobbled towards the door with his cane. 'One day, when the planet is nothing but a fine cloud of dust, perhaps then you will forgive me... for giving you a better life.'

While I continued to wail, Tau had her hands over her mouth, too afraid to say or do anything.

The old man paused next to her. 'Heal her up, the tour isn't over.'

Seven: True Freedom

I sat and rested my feet on the short table, next to the unappetising cafeteria food I hadn't touched. It was brown and paste-like, with small herbs and supplements mixed in. I knew from experience how bad this speckled turd of a meal was. No thank you, Overwatch Dietary Division.

There were hardly any people in the cafe, or wandering around the enormous ship for that matter. This was because the Black Dawn had only just begun resurrecting our agents. I guess I should've counted myself lucky that I was one of the first brought back. Now I'd probably have to sit around for days killing time until we were ready to leave. So boring.

I had a spectacular view of the shattered planet through the wide observation window nearby, too bad I couldn't enjoy it. I couldn't care less about their world's destruction or the Seronians' futures, but what would this mean for *my* future?

It was funny how, when I was first exiled here, all I wanted to do was leave. But now that there was nothing left and I'd have to return to Aster, I was afraid. I had no idea what was going to happen next.

I didn't regret anything I did, of course, not even when I helped

Tau and Tetsu escape the Overwatch satellite. I should be able to do whatever I wanted, with whoever I wanted, *to* whoever I wanted. Still, would I be punished again for that little rebellious act? How were my parents going to react when they learned what I did?

I scrolled through the messages on my Integrated Neural Computer to get my mind off it. After being resurrected this time around, the techs had implanted the newest INC version in my brain, and now that the mission was over, they unlocked all the civilian features, too. It was now much snappier and easier to use, as well as immersive, as if the menus and pictures were floating in front of me like real objects. With this, I had access to so much more information than before, not to mention all the built-in games and videos.

Even now I was watching a clip of Sacet getting impaled by a steel beam on a loop. The trillions of Asterians back home had probably already seen this, too, and were no doubt gushing with excitement over her arrival. A part of me felt sorry for Sacet, not realising how easy it was for us to secretly communicate with each other with these things.

Normally, my parents would never allow one of their children to have an INC. Something about keeping us pure or whatever, but we all knew the real reason: they feared what would happen if we got hacked remotely. They even thought that's what happened to me when I killed them, initially. Ironically, if I had *this* thing back in Arc Royal, I might've not had to kill them... for maybe another ten cycles.

What's this notification? Scroll up... more... more. There, a new message. From the academy? What did *they* want? Open.

'*To Iya,*

Congratulations on a successful mission. Thanks to your efforts and that of your fellow agents on Seron, a new Chosen has been discovered and Harrowed. You should be very proud of your accomplishment.

However, due to Overwatch's initial failure to contain said Chosen, we have been informed that alternative arrangements will be made for the harvest world in question, specifically its demolition. Soon, your team will be liquidated, and you will all come home to Aster for reassignment.

The Royal Envoy has also made us aware that you are no longer exiled in the eyes of our glorious rulers, but also that your royal title is still forfeit.

As you should be aware, enrolment for all acolytes at Arc Academy is mandatory. Therefore, accommodation has been made available to you, should you require it. Living onsite is highly recommended. Please come see the customer service team about your payment options at your earliest convenience.

Again, well done. We are all looking forward to your return.

– Head Chancellor Elysia'

Elysia, that ancient sprite. How dare she meddle in my affairs. Without a wage, I couldn't afford to live at Arc Academy. But then, where was I *supposed* to live?

I'm sure I've got plenty of… friends, right? No. Followers and fans at least? They'd let me stay in their homes for free. No, what if they were psychos or worse… *perverts*? What if they chopped up my body into little pieces and hid them? Or ate them. Or if they watched me while I slept? *Ew, ew, ew.*

No one would ever come looking for me because no one cared anyway. Would I have to resort to living on the streets like a common beggar? Hiding in Aster's polluted depths like vermin? Gross!

Maybe I could speak to Arc Academy and get a loan until I worked something out, money-wise? Surely *someone* would be willing to pay me for this harvest world business. I mean, I know I was sent here as a punishment, but I've got to walk away with *something*. If I could pay for my own place, that would be great. A place to myself with no one to bother me.

You know what, this was a *good* thing. In fact, this was what I had wanted all along: freedom. No more parents pretending like my birthdays were special. No more brain-dead brothers and sisters, surviving only on gossip and gifts from strangers. Wherever I lived, I'd be an individual, a real person. I could age again. So what if I wasn't royalty anymore?

Behind me, Kalek was back at the buffet line for probably the fifth time today, loading up his plate with an assortment of bland foodstuffs. There were a few others throughout the mess I didn't recognise, too. I hated these supposed colleagues of mine; the solace of my room suited me better.

As I was about to stand, Korin and Neva entered the mess. Korin, the fugly brunette with an undeserved air of superiority, and Neva, the pretentious, floozy blonde, with more fake body parts than brain cells.

They scouted for a seat and just before they turned in my direction, I looked back at Seron's remains, hoping they wouldn't engage.

'Iya,' Neva called out joyfully. '*There* you are, girl.'

No, no, no.

They trotted over with wide, fake smiles and sat in the chairs opposite me, their backs to the stars.

I looked at anything but them and sighed. Damn it all.

As I closed the letter on my INC, Neva examined my food from afar and flared her nostrils. 'Don't tell me her royal highness is eating the food of us commoners? How disappointing.'

Yep, get it all out you attention-seeking, glory-hogging, oxygen-thieving snobs. I still haven't forgiven either of you for taking all the credit in Sacet's Harrowing.

Korin elbowed Neva in the side with a grin. 'Careful, Neva, she might have us both executed for comments like that.'

I lowered my feet and rolled my eyes at their verbal diarrhea. 'If only I could.'

Neva put her feet up where mine were previously. 'You're not leaving are you, Iya? We wanted to see how everything was going. Why don't we talk about what we're going to do when we get home? Korin?'

Korin pointed at herself and smiled. '*Oh*, me? Well, apparently, I'm getting a little holiday time, so I'm going to hire a few of these harvest-worlders to keep my house clean. They're basically slaves, so I'm going to kick them around a bit. It'll be like I'm royalty.' She pointed at Neva. 'What about you?'

Neva stared at me and grinned. '*Oh*, I've got plans.'

Kalek passed by our table with a mountain of food on his plate. 'Hey, ladies.'

Korin looked disgusted. 'Get *away* from us, you abominable degenerate.'

This was one thing the girls and I actually agreed on. Kalek's advancements towards us were disgusting. I stared him down with them.

'Right,' he said, defeated. 'Sorry to bother you then.'

'*Ah*, Kalek?' Neva said, raising a hand to stop him. 'I forgot to ask, did you get that promotion?'

Neva was such a tease. We all knew Kalek was worried about not getting promoted, and therefore not getting an age reduction in his bonus.

Kalek beamed. 'Actually, I *did* get the promotion. Caelum must've liked how I took down Sacet for him and—'

'Okay, no one *cares* now,' Korin interrupted, visibly frustrated that they didn't get the response they were after. She flicked her fingers to shoo him away and focused back on me.

Kalek slunk into a booth on the other side of the room, which barely accommodated his huge frame. It was kind of funny how someone so physically powerful could be treated so poorly. All three of them might have been the same age for all I knew, but Korin and Neva were *allowed* to be younger because of their more frequent promotions.

Neva put her feet down and leant forward. 'Hey Princess, isn't it strange how mummy and daddy are letting you come home? Even after what you did?'

Korin smirked. 'Joining Sacet's team like that? I wouldn't forgive you if *I* were them.'

I scrunched up my face. 'I never helped Sacet. I harrowed her more than you two did.'

'Okay, well first off, that's a lie,' Korin replied, 'and second, you helped her friends, which is the same thing. So, it's strange you got off without a punishment, right?'

I shrugged. 'It's strange, sure. What do you want me to say here?'

Neva nodded. 'Yes, strange. Almost as if they weren't told what you did, and those incident reports were falsified.'

My eyes widened. 'Why would you—'

Neva gestured to herself. 'Us? No, *we* wouldn't do that. Right, Korin?'

'No way. Not us,' Korin added. 'But you know what *would* be a believable story?'

Neva grinned. 'That the frustrated former princess did it, to cover up her mistake?'

I couldn't believe it, were they blackmailing me? Neva saw my parents recently when she brought that metal shard to them for another huge promotion. She could have told them what I did, so why didn't she?

'The psychics will see right through you two,' I said.

'They wouldn't care,' Neva said. 'And *why* would you want them to?'

I sighed and leant forward so I could speak quieter. 'What do you want?'

Neva stretched her hand forward and poked my nose. 'I want *you*. You're going to be my little celebrity slave. *Always* at my beck and call. My *very* own royal I can boss around.'

I rolled my eyes at first, assuming this was a joke, but they both stared at me. Was she serious? I couldn't think of anything more humiliating than being a servant, especially to them.

Korin looked around to make sure no one was listening. 'Of course, one of us might eventually put two and two together and realise—'

'Would you two leave her alone?' Kalek shouted from his table.

Korin stood up. 'How dare you speak to a superior officer like that?'

Neva stood up, too. 'And don't defend Iya. How many times have we told you not to hit on her, Kalek? She's just a little kid, it's *disgusting*!'

Korin laughed. 'That's right. She's not old enough to know about men like you.'

I shot up and stomped away from the table. 'Oh, shut up! Both of you, just shut up!'

Both the girls laughed and mocked my anger, pretending they were afraid of me.

Kalek stood. 'Iya, I—'

I sidestepped him. '*Don't* talk to me, you… filth!'

'Awww,' Korin cooed. 'On second thought, they're cute together, in a kind of… mutant protecting his baby way.'

Although I put everything I had into looking tough and unafraid, my muscles shook uncontrollably. I stormed out of the cafe, keeping my back to them to hide my tears.

'Hey, Princess?' Neva called. 'When we get home, don't *make* me come find you.'

The long, sterile corridor was eerily silent. I was far enough away from the cafe now that I doubted anyone followed me. My tiny room wasn't much farther, but I had to stop and collect myself. I reached a corridor intersection and leant against the wall to wipe away my tears.

Who was I kidding? I'd be all alone when I got back. With no money, and now also having to spend all my time tending to that bimbo's whims, where would I live?

'Wait in here,' an elderly voice said around the corner. 'We'll call you when we're ready.'

I peeked and saw Sacet and Tau being led into a room by guards. Two of the guards stationed themselves just outside the door to either side.

Stupid Sacet. She doesn't know how good her life is going to become. She'll have everything handed to her from now on. Endless money and power. She could stay at any age and have as many partners and children as she wanted. Go anywhere, kill *anyone*. True freedom! Like what happened with the other Chosen in the past, she'd already have countless fans back home. *Everyone* would want a piece of her.

As for Tau, she'd eventually be rich, too. Her power was the most desired acolyte ability of all, and constantly in demand.

Wait, this was perfect. Maybe I *did* have a friend who could help me? Tau would still remember that I helped her, right? And she wasn't *bad*, really, not like the others. She said she used to hope we could be friends.

So, if I just apologised to them, I could then sponge off Tau. I had to make it convincing though. I was *kind* of sorry, in a way? And they hated the same people I hated. I could totally relate to that.

Tau was a pushover, she'd forgive me. But Sacet? I mean, if *she* did to *me* what *I* did to *her*, I wouldn't. There was only one way to find out.

I made sure my cheeks were dry and traipsed down the corridor. When I reached the room, the guards exchanged a confused look.

I stared them down. 'I will speak to them.'

Perhaps fearing who I was, they let me pass. When I entered the room, Sacet and Tau were sitting on black leather couches and looking down at the dark-green carpet in an otherwise grey room. They both looked dismal.

Several more armed guards lined the room's edges, their eyes followed me as I approached the girls. At the far end of the room was a set of double doors. Where they led, I didn't know.

Sacet looked up first and scowled. 'You. What do *you* want? Come to gloat?'

I gestured to one of the couches next to them. 'Er, no. Can I sit?'

Sacet shook her head. 'No, but you can leave.'

'I came to… apologise,' I said earnestly, sitting down anyway.

Sacet gave a single laugh. 'Liar. Seriously, go away.'

Tau reached out and brushed Sacet's arm. 'Remember I told you how Iya helped Tetsu and I that one time?'

'Yeah,' Sacet replied, 'and in the end, it made *no* difference.'

Tau narrowed her eyes at her sister. 'It made a difference to *me*, to Tetsu, and also to Eno.'

Sacet gritted her teeth and stared at me. 'Fine, apologise then.'

I closed my eyes briefly and took a breath. 'I'm sorry, Sacet. I didn't—'

'You're *not* forgiven,' Sacet interrupted.

Tau and I both gawked at her stubbornness, but I pressed on. 'I *regret* what I did to you, honestly. I've changed.'

'Really?' Tau asked with a raised eyebrow and copying Sacet's body language. 'How?'

Sacet scoffed. 'It doesn't matter. She tried to kill us.'

I smirked, I had them now. 'So did Noor and Tetsu before you decided to… *come* together. And you even gave that maggot, Colony, a chance. And! In *all* fairness, I *never* killed either of you, but you *both* killed me a couple times… so…'

'You *enjoyed* torturing me,' Sacet interrupted.

I was trying to keep a level head, to be friendly, but Sacet's comments were eating away at my patience. 'That was my job. And you don't know *anything* about what I enjoy.'

Tau nodded at me expectantly. 'Then *enlighten* us, Princess.'

Sacet begrudgingly nodded, too. 'I could use a little humour about now. Tell us the truth, for a change.'

I looked around at all the guards, who still watched me cautiously. 'The truth?' I scratched my head. 'The truth... truth. *Um.*'

My chest felt twisted. Having to expose myself like this was humiliating, but I remembered back to Neva again and knew it could be so much worse if I didn't convince them.

'The truth is I'm two hundred and twelve cycles old.'

Tau gawped. 'Two hundred and twelve?'

'Yeah, thanks to my *insane* parents, I'm stuck in this baby-faced, weak kid's body. I wasn't ever allowed to age or leave my home. I got fed up with them one day and killed them, so they banished me to Seron as a punishment.'

Sacet's curled lips straightened.

'I was angry at everyone,' I continued. 'I... *acknowledge* I wasn't particularly easy to get along with. I saw Sacet as a tool to my freedom and I thought if I could hurry your Harrowing along... I could get home quicker, and be free. So... I'm sorry. Again.'

Tau waited for me to finish and leant forward. 'Before you came in, I could tell you had been crying. That isn't everything, is it?'

She could notice that? This was far harder than I thought it was going to be. I sighed gruffly. 'No, there's more. When we get home, I won't have anywhere to live. And I don't *know* anyone, I have no friends or family back there. And... I know this sounds really, really pathetic but... Tau, you're the only person... *ever* to say that I was your... friend. Or could be your...'

I looked down, avoiding their judgemental gazes. What was I doing? Was I expecting an invitation? No, push through, there's still a chance.

'Sacet,' I continued, 'when we get to Aster, they're going to give you your own special place to live. It'll be a paradise, every luxury you could want. Normally, the other acolytes would all live in Arc Academy, and they'd have to pay. But you can have *anyone* you want to live with you for free.'

Sacet shrugged. 'So, my family? And all my friends, and their families?'

I looked up at the ceiling and let out another frustrated sigh. 'Yes, yes. I'm sure they'll let them *all* in.'

'And you think *you* deserve an invitation, too, is that it?' Sacet asked.

I shook my head and stuttered, not sure how to respond. I stood and turned away. 'W-well just… forget it then.'

Tau looked at me like I was one of her injured patients before giving a pleading look to her sister.

Sacet's eyes narrowed again. 'You're truly pathetic, Iya. You must be *really* desperate to expect any sympathy from me.'

I didn't want to agree with her, but I did feel so low. I folded my arms and stayed silent.

Sacet sighed. 'I'll *never* forgive you. But… if you genuinely help us… and after what you've done, it'd have to be a *lot* of help…'

What? Did it work? Was Sacet conceding? I glanced back at them. 'Yes?'

Before she could finish, the double doors behind the couches opened and Caelum entered with the guards.

He gestured a hand to the door. 'It's time.'

Eight: No More Hate

As we entered the dimly lit room, many eyes focused on me. Another lounge like before, but much more luxurious. The room was meant for entertaining, for there were tables and chairs scattered about, and coloured lights – mostly green – lit the sleek surfaces and edges. More long, wide windows created a panorama in the shape of a semi-circle, showing another depressing view of the debris outside.

There was a bar with countless bottles and glasses atop it. Some of the liquor in the bottles glowed, each a different vibrant colour and some a mix of the others, constantly swirling. Several bartenders and waiters stood quietly along the edges of the room.

A long table was in front of me, and sitting at the far end was Tuloch. This man, who once masqueraded as the Dominion King, now wore plainer attire, a simple black uniform. He sat with his hands clasped and look of aversion towards me.

Farther away, Raumanu was sitting on a couch. He had a drink in front of him with a colourful mixture of blue and purple, which he sipped occasionally. He seemed more engrossed by the debris field outside than us.

Sitting across from him on another couch and separated by a small table was a middle-aged, blonde woman. She also had a dark uniform, although hers was grandly decorated, covered in colourful pins. She noticed me, smiled and made a crying motion with her fingers to mock me.

In the far corner of the room, almost hiding in the shadows, sat a hulking, misshapen monstrosity of a man. I recognised him from his shape alone, Mycol. No longer in captivity, his body had regained its previously bulbous proportions, probably after having gorged on unwilling souls. He was hunched over and watching me.

Guards were posted all around, standing to attention with rifles and electrified batons. Caelum calmly brushed past me and stopped in front of the windows to stargaze.

Tuloch pointed at the numerous free seats at the long table. 'Sit!'

I went first, taking the seat at the close end. Tau followed, sitting next to me. Another pair of guards blocked our exit.

A bartender retrieved two liquor bottles and filled a couple of glasses with some luminous liquid. When finished, he brought the drinks over to our table, placed them in front of us and returned to the bar. The green and white drink churned, looking like clouds in an alien sky.

The old me would assume the drink was spiked. That some sort of trap or trick was about to happen. But they had already taken everything from me, what more could they do? The drink's white swirls slowly faded as they were absorbed into the green.

The room was silent. Tuloch hadn't stopped scowling at me since I entered. I glared back at him and took a deep swig of the drink, downing it in one go. It tasted equal parts sweet, foul and effervescent. When finished, I threw the glass at Caelum by the window. It missed him and smashed nearby, shards covering the carpet. He took no notice, instead standing motionless.

Tau gave a concerned stare before slowly pushing her drink towards me.

Tuloch kept his eyes locked with mine. His black moustache quivered. 'You already know most of us here, but allow me to introduce Overwatch's saviour, the captain of the Black Dawn, Andhera.'

The middle-aged woman on the couch nodded at Tuloch, then eyed me with intrigue. 'A pleasure.'

Tuloch focused back on me. His face reddened, still furious, but trying to contain himself. 'If you hadn't destroyed my satellite, *none* of this would be necessary. Seron would *still* be there, and all of its people could have stayed. But you… *you* had to ruin everything.'

He pointed behind at the debris field through the window. 'You have no place to return to now. Nowhere to portal away to. Nowhere to hide.' He gestured at my neck inhibitor. 'And that device is far more secure this time around. We're not taking any chances, so it won't be removed until long after we've settled you on Aster.

'If you obey the rules this time, you and your friends will have long, full lives. The royal family, the Chosen, the disciples and a select few others are allowed to live indefinitely, so you two should count yourselves lucky.'

I had heard this drivel before. I'd soon be living the good life, they'd say. Of course, there was a catch: I had to fight for a cause I didn't agree with, kill innocent people and sell out my sense of right and wrong, my dignity.

Tuloch pointed at Tau. 'As a disciple, *you* will learn how to reduce someone's age. It's a heavily restricted ability, punished greatly when misused, so only use it when instructed.'

Tau shrugged at me, but I didn't know what a "disciple" was, either. Did he mean healer?

He looked back at me. 'Your acolyte friends will join the Academy and *if* they do well, they'll be rewarded with promotions, which mean reductions in their ages, too.'

He sighed and gestured around at the others. 'This is what we *all* want for you. You being you though, you'll still no doubt find a way to cause trouble.' He smirked and brought his hands together again.

'So, now I'll explain how our justice system works. For those who aren't Chosen, breaking the rules means you will be sent away, exiled onto a harvest world. There you have your memory wiped and your life starts all over again. If you die there, we resurrect you and start again, perhaps on a different world, each more challenging than the last.'

Tuloch looked over to the corner. 'Mycol? Mycol here is also a disciple, a special kind.'

The hideous man stood and staggered over, groaning in pain as he did so. The hunched giant stopped in the centre of the room and tried to stand upright.

Tuloch smiled. 'For more *serious* crimes, the punishment is execution. Normally, disciples could simply resurrect a body, but not when someone like Mycol is through with them.'

Mycol's hands turned green, and flames of energy swirled around his wrists. His aura was similar to Tau's, but far more frightening.

Tau shivered. 'I… I can feel them, they're alive.'

Tuloch laughed. 'No, those souls are in between. Not only can Mycol rip out your soul and absorb it, but if he so chooses, he can crush it instead, stopping it from ever crossing over again.'

Tau shook her head. 'Permanent death… you'd kill us? For what?'

Tuloch stared back at me. 'No, we wouldn't kill *you*. Sacet is a Chosen and healers always hold their value. No, on your first offence, we would start with Eno.'

I shot up, sending my chair flying back. 'Don't you dare touch him! I'll destroy this whole—'

Caelum flashed behind me and grabbed my chair, before forcing me back down into it.

Tuloch's face twisted and bulged. '*Never* speak to me that way again or I *will* bring him out here and kill him in front of you!'

I breathed quickly and heavily. I wanted to jump over the table and strangle him, but Caelum's vice-like hands were gripping my shoulders.

'After Eno, it will be his parents,' Tuloch continued. 'Then Malu, your little boyfriends, all the other nomad scum… and if you *still* couldn't take the hint by then, we would save Tau for last.'

My fists clenched on the table. The flames around Mycol's hands danced around in the corner of my eye, but I refused to look away from Tuloch.

He looked over to the guards on the side of the room. 'Bring her in.'

The guards went through a door and came back shortly after, dragging an old woman in with them by the wrists. Marid. Her hands were bound in cuffs, she wore the same simple outfit as us and she had a neck inhibitor, too. The guards forced her forward with a hard shove.

Tuloch sneered at her. 'Your mother here was *already* a prisoner on Seron, we had a life assigned for her. You girls can hardly be blamed for fighting back, it's what we *wanted* you to do. But Marid? She was offered a chance at freedom, all she had to do was follow our orders. Instead, she sided with you, so I will make an example of her.'

Marid refused to show any emotion to our captors, but when she glanced over at Tau and I, she forced a smile.

Tau shook her head. 'You can't be serious?'

Even though Marid had lied to me from the very beginning, in the end she did the right thing by me, by all of us. Although I had never really thought of her as my true mother, she had always been a wise mentor. But now that she was being threatened with death, a *permanent* death, I felt a shiver down my spine and throughout my body. My heart sank and my already tear-laden eyes felt as though they were about to burst.

I struggled against Caelum's hold, but it was no use. 'You'll pay for this. I'll find a way to kill you, I *swear* it!'

Tuloch's face contorted again. 'And I would be resurrected, unlike your mother. Now, let's begin this lesson in respect.'

Mycol staggered forward and grabbed Marid by the arms, pulling her closer to the centre of the room. Marid was small and frail compared to him, and she almost collapsed because of her closeness to his deathly aura.

'Let her go!' I yelled, continuing to struggle against my father. I kicked the drink in front of me as I squirmed, sending the green, shining liquid down the table.

Tau was oddly quiet. She just stared at Marid, frozen in place.

I glanced at all the others. 'Stop this!'

The guards didn't move, Raumanu sipped his drink and the ship's captain simply smiled, enjoying the show. I locked eyes with my father, who was still keeping me in place. His were cold as always, neutral and without emotion.

I looked at Tau as I thrashed around. 'Do something, Tau!'

'I... I...' she stuttered, still unable to act. Her shaking hands were resting on the table's edge.

Marid shook her head at me as the waves of death rippled through her. 'Sacet, please, don't fight this. They will only keep punishing you.'

Caelum now had both of my arms locked with his, keeping me sitting in the chair. I ceased my defiance and focused on Marid.

She managed another weak smile. 'This can't be stopped. Save that fighting spirit for when it matters most.'

'You don't deserve this,' I started, now sobbing.

'No, I do, I disobeyed. I helped you out of guilt, but I knew this was coming. Sacet, look after your friends and your little brother. Find your *real* parents. And Tau? Look after Sacet, you both need each other now more than ever.'

I glared at Tuloch again. 'If you kill her now, I *will—*'

'No,' Marid interrupted, bringing my attention back. 'No more revenge, no more hate. My stubborn daughter, it is *destroying* you. Focus on change instead, on betterment, and on fixing this *stupid* empire.'

I shook my head, flinging my tears away. 'They can't do this… we need you. *I* need you.'

'Enough,' Tuloch interrupted with a raised hand, before nodding at Mycol. 'Do it!'

The power of Mycol's flames amplified, and Marid fell to her knees. She closed her eyes with a pained look on her face.

'No!' I yelled, struggling yet again.

Tears had formed in Tau's eyes, too, but she stayed still.

Mycol smirked. 'What a waste of delicious energy,' he said, placing his hands around her head.

Marid opened her eyes and looked at me one last time before a particle of green emptied out her mouth and into the air. Her body collapsed in a heap, her eyes and mouth still open.

Mycol rotated his hands, playing with the mist-like energy. For a brief moment, it looked like it was in the shape of Marid. Mycol clenched his fingers and the energy coalesced into a single ball, which he gleefully clasped. He then gritted his teeth and grunted. As his shaking hands squeezed, the energy popped and blasted in puffs of smoke. Streams of it rapidly gust around the room before converging back. When his palms finally joined, the energy brightened like a nova, then exploded outwards, hitting everyone in the room with a cool breeze of green.

Now that it was done, Caelum let go of me and I slumped out of the chair onto my knees.

Tau's breathing picked up; she pushed herself out of her chair and ran to Marid's body. As she knelt, her hair and skin glowed, but not as bright as usual. Her auburn hair turned light grey instead of a bluish white. With a weakened aura, she grasped onto the body and waited, but it didn't move.

At the end of another corridor, the elevator opened its doors. Its walls were transparent, so we could see the horizontal shaft that it would soon travel along.

Raumanu was the first to hobble onto the platform inside, then me, Tau and Iya. I went to the far wall and leant on it with my head and forearm. I didn't want to look at anyone. My tears still hadn't dried, nor had Tau's.

After the execution, Tuloch and his people had permitted us to grieve over Marid's body for a surprisingly long time. It was almost as if they were trying to get some final Harrowing in for good measure.

Other than crying, Tau hadn't said anything since. Maybe it was wrong of me to expect her to somehow save our mother. There wasn't anything either of us could have done, but I was still angry at her for not at least protesting.

When we left that horrible room, Iya was still waiting for us on the couches, and she had been following us around. Was she *still* trying to leech off me, even now?

Tau and Iya both joined my side along the far wall. Several armed guards entered after us and with all of them in here, it was quite cramped. We were pressed up against each other and one of their rifles was driving into my back.

'What did I say about that?' Raumanu said, stomping his cane on the metal floor. 'That is unnecessary.'

I looked back and saw the guard lower his rifle, as did all the others, yet they still didn't break eye contact with me.

Raumanu leant on his cane with one hand and reached for his

lower back with the other. 'Get the door,' he said while closing his eyes, clearly in pain.

One of the guards turned and fiddled with the control panel, awakening the platform. It hummed to life and rocketed sideways, down a blue-lit track. The shaft stretched for what seemed like forever; how *big* was this ship?

We traversed in silence, aside from the hum of the platform and Raumanu's pained groans.

How could I allow this to stand? There must be a way to fight back. Now that Caelum wasn't here, this was my best shot. Maybe I could steal a rifle, somehow shoot my collar off, and portal away. But where would I go? And then what would I do next? How could I possibly—

'Eno would be the first to die, remember, Sacet?' Raumanu interrupted.

He had noticed me staring at the closest rifle. Its owner grimaced and took a step back.

I leant back against the wall and folded my arms. I looked through the transparent walls as we passed the laboratories again, and these so-called disciples recreating all of Raumanu's victims.

'Tau? Sacet?' Iya chirped, breaking my focus. 'I'm sorry about what happened to your mother.'

She was acting so odd, but as kind as she was attempting to be, I still didn't trust her.

I pushed her away. 'If you're trying to convince us to trust you, at least *act* like yourself.'

'I was *trying* to be sincere you obstinate dope!' she seethed through gritted teeth, before turning and looking out the walls like I was.

My lips trembled. I was so close to screeching at the top of my lungs, just to let some anger out.

I gave Raumanu a scathing look. 'So, what horrible thing do you have in store for us next?'

Raumanu frowned. 'Just one more thing. You both need to have an operation. Every Seronian does. And afterwards, we'll put you into stasis for the journey home, where you'll finally be reunited with your closest friends.'

'Stasis?' I asked.

'Put to sleep,' Iya explained, arms folded and still looking away from me. 'It's painless. Space travel takes time.'

'Hopefully, Sacet's power will change that for the empire,' Raumanu suggested.

The hurtling platform slowed, causing some of us to jolt. Eventually, we stopped in front of an entrance to another lab, a massive one that stretched far into the distance like a long, wide corridor. Like the other labs, it was filled with scientists busily working with body bags and equipment.

The platform's transparent doors opened and we disembarked.

Raumanu glanced back at us as we followed in his shambling footsteps. 'This room is dedicated to implanting Integrated Neural Computers into the dead.'

He gestured to a distant conveyor belt that was dropping filled body bags onto the floor. Pair after pair of scientists wandered over to the small mountain of bodies and dragged them over to nearby machines. They sat the bodies in the machines, opened the bags so that their heads were accessible, then closed the machine's doors on them and pressed a few buttons.

What followed next made me want to vomit: a high-pitched, persistent squeal, like a whining drill, accompanied by the sounds of flesh tearing. This revolting noise was coming from every one of these machines.

Raumanu led us towards a pair of operating tables where another team of scientists waited. 'But as for you two, we'll need to be a bit more delicate.' Raumanu reached the first table and patted it, looking at me. 'Sit.'

I stopped in front of one of the tables. 'Why exactly do we need this… computer?'

With her eyes down, Tau walked forward without question and sat on the second table. All eyes except hers were on me.

I felt a prod from behind, again with one of the rifles. 'He told you to sit!' one of the guards barked in my ear.

Raumanu sighed at my hesitance. 'Your INC will make your life easier. We *all* have one.'

I felt another prod in my back and walked forward. There was nothing I could do, there were too many of them. I sat on the table, lay flat and stared up at the white ceiling, tiled with squares.

One of the scientists approached and placed a strange, cold, metal bead on my forehead. Rather than slipping off, it sort of stuck there and gently vibrated. I heard some buttons being pressed nearby. My eyelids became heavy, as though I had been drugged. How could I possibly sleep after all this?

I shook my head, trying to stay awake, but it was useless. Everything was fading. The last thing I saw was Iya's grim stare and Raumanu's smile.

Nine: You Will Be Happy

'Now her,' Raumanu said, pointing at me with his free hand, the other holding his wobbling cane, struggling to stay standing.

The closest doctor attached an inhibitor collar around my neck and activated it. I didn't fight back, I couldn't, not after what they had done to my mother. No more death.

I glanced at Sacet, now unconscious. The scientist had left the little grey bead on her head. She had a depressed expression, even while asleep.

The only thing I could hope for is that when this was all over, what was left of my friends would be together. And maybe that life wouldn't be so bad? It sounded like I would just be healing and helping others for the rest of my life, like I always wanted. Was it too much to ask for a life without everyone suffering?

A team of doctors surrounded Sacet, each wielding a sharp instrument. A tray with even more knives, scalpels and drills was hovered over, and in it was a strange, long metal object smaller than my thumb, this neural computer they were talking about.

I didn't know what sort of life we were going to have on Aster, but one thing was certain, I knew Sacet wasn't going to give up fighting them. I knew my sister well; she would find a way to resist. And that was only going to get the rest of us killed.

'Lie down,' another doctor said to me.

I didn't question him, I rested back onto the cold, metal table. A second tray of instruments hovered over to me. Two cold fingers briefly brushed my forehead before releasing an even colder bead.

I fell back into a deep, spiralling darkness. Time was irrelevant here, as was thought. Who and what was I? Where and why? Whenever I was about to grasp at the answers, it slipped away again. Faces popped in and out, as did places that must have been important to me once.

Bright, utter blinding brightness. A white curtain draped over all. Something new? Were the answers here?

A planet shifted into view. Seron, my home. I felt like I could reach out and hold it in my hands. It began to boil and shatter, but this was not a memory of mine, I was sure of that. There were no stars, still only white. Somehow I knew this was wrong, but I didn't know how I knew.

The planet broke apart in an instant and only dust remained. Each mote of dust was so small, but again, somehow, I just knew that each speck had morphed into a person. They all flew away from the destruction and finally faded, escaping the war-filled planet forever.

The white, void of all things, suddenly had two new actors. Two beings, sitting on grand thrones of equal stature. Who were these extremely old people in front of me? They were so ancient that I thought they were dead at first, until they blinked and looked around, before deciding to stare at me. These living corpses wore colourful, illustrious robes.

One was clearly male, a permanent scowl was pinned on his decaying and sunken visage. Thick brown fingers, gnarled like tree branches, clenched the ends of his armrests.

On the right was a woman. She had makeup on her face, coating her otherwise dried and wrinkly skin, clearly in an attempt to look alive again. Small knobbly knees protruded from under her dress robes. Her hands rested in her lap and needle-like fingers danced up and down, as if she was waiting for me to say something.

I tried to vocalise, but I couldn't feel my mouth, or my body, I couldn't move or look around. I felt the presence of others around me.

No sooner had I realised than they erupted in cheers and roars. I was in the front row of an audience.

'The beautiful Empress Suralia,' a deep voice said over the crowd, who settled into silence.

The woman raised one of her hands and waved, and she tried to smile, but her face just wouldn't physically allow it. Murmurs yammered around me again.

'Isn't she wonderful?' a female voice to my right said.

What? No, of course not. What's so great about her?

'And the magnanimous Emperor Avarut,' the deep voice continued.

The man, still with a scowl, waved, too, but he clearly wasn't into it.

'He's the greatest ruler in recorded history,' another voice said, this time male and on the left. 'May his rule be immortal.'

I don't even know who these people are. What was happening, exactly?

My view spun to the right and revealed some of the audience. I knew these faces, every one of them was someone from my life. There was Malu, Eno, Coleo, Tarsus, and sitting beside me in the row of chairs was Caelum, my father.

He pointed towards the two old people and smiled. 'We must always show respect to our rulers. They know what's best for us.'

I turned to the left and saw more of the audience. Sitting on this side of me was Noor, Tetsu, Amiki, Terel and Marid.

My mother smiled and pointed, too. 'They will provide for us, for our family, our loved ones.'

I looked at her and suddenly was overcome with sadness. Something was very wrong!

'They stand for hope,' someone from behind said.

'For prosperity,' another added.

Everyone in the audience had something to add, all speaking at once, creating a harsh discord.

'They will make you rich.'

'… make you happy.'

'They will help everyone.'

'Their light will guide us to the Chosen path.'

'You'll want for nothing.'

Stop it! Stop! I tried yelling, tried to close my eyes, but I was forced to sit there, subjected to this endless barrage.

The voices grew louder, battering my ears and causing my head to ache. Eventually, the voices merged into one, one I recognised. It was Sacet. She was standing in front of me, between the two old rulers.

'Aster awaits your arrival,' she said. 'Your new life and home are here. Obey our rulers and you will be happy... happy... happy...'

That wasn't something Sacet would ever say. None of this made sense. The caricatures around me faded, the flare blinded my view.

'You will be happy,' Sacet repeated.

Ten: Dawned

I awoke in a panic, lashing my arms to keep them away. 'Get off me, get away!' My back was resting on something soft, unlike the metal table. I was drenched in sweat.

A few people were standing over me, more scientists, and one was holding a metal bead. Did he just take that off my head?

How long had I been out? There was a constant, low drone. Engines. I was still in space. Had it been days, or worse, cycles? I wasn't sure.

The room was small, grey and dim. Eight sheetless beds, including my own, were positioned roughly in a circle. Resting on them were Tau, Eno, Malu, Noor and Tetsu. We all wore the same simplistic grey clothing and inhibitor collars, and all but Tau were still unconscious, with little beads on their foreheads.

Tau was already awake, sitting on her bed. She had taken little notice of my waking, staring down at the ground instead.

One scientist was examining the electronic readouts at the end of our beds. When he was satisfied with mine, he and his group wandered over to Eno.

Raumanu and Caelum weren't here, and neither were any guards.

There was only one door at the end of the room. An opportunity to escape, perhaps?

I got off the bed, stepping onto the tiled floor. 'Tau,' I whispered to her, before silently gesturing to the door with widened eyes. 'Now's our chance.'

It took a moment for her to understand, looking between the scientists and me, but eventually, she got up from her bed. She wandered over and grabbed me with both hands. 'No. Sacet, you need to stop. Don't you remember Mum's dying words?'

'What? Tau, we need to try. I don't know how, but I need to get this collar off, then we can—'

'Then we can what?' Tau interrupted, shaking her head. 'I *told* you, we lost. It's over. There's nowhere left to run.'

The scientists removed Eno's bead and glanced over at us, perhaps overhearing. Eno immediately began to stir.

Tau released me and backed off. 'He would be *next*. Mum was right, we *can't* fight them anymore.'

That's what she took away from what Marid said? I shrugged and let out a frustrated sigh. 'Well, what are we supposed to do?'

'Nothing,' Tau replied, looking down again.

Tau had changed, she wasn't herself. She would normally know the difference between right and wrong, she wouldn't put up with what they were doing to us, or maybe I didn't know her as well as I thought? Maybe… *they* had changed her?

Eno's eyes fluttered open before groggily finding us. 'Sas?'

The scientists moved to both Malu and Noor. Eno rolled out of bed and bolted over to me. As he hugged me, only now did I realise how tall he had gotten. I had wasted so much time as a prison guard that I didn't even notice how much he had grown up without me. I hugged him back tight, not wanting to let go.

'Sas, what's going on? What happened to Caelum?'

'I missed you,' I said, unsure of how to answer yet.

'Missed me?' he replied as he let go. 'I only just saw you?'

I released and looked down. 'It's been… um,' I said, almost about to break down again. 'I-I'm *so* sorry, Eno. I was such an *idiot*. I should've spent more time with you. I just… I didn't—'

'No, I'm sorry I got angry,' Eno replied with a frown. 'I'm totally fine, I was just worried about you.' He looked around, confused by his surroundings. 'So, where are we?'

Both Noor and Malu had their beads removed. They slowly roused, rubbed their eyes and sat on the edge of their beds, disoriented.

It had been a long time since I had seen Malu, and we weren't exactly on good terms the last time I checked. She had given a farewell to pretty much everyone but me before heading out into the desert to search for what was left of her family. I honestly thought I'd never see her again.

'What happened? Where is he?' Noor asked, scanning around before noticing me. Like Eno, he got up, ran over and hugged me, too. 'You're okay, I was *so* worried.'

Malu cleared her throat. 'We're okay as well, Noor.'

Noor let go of me. 'Malu? How did you get here?'

Tetsu was next to be revived. He shook his head awake and sat up. 'That was a *crazy* dream. Really messed up.' When he noticed Tau, he pushed off the bed and embraced her tight. 'Good, you're alright.'

Malu rolled her eyes and folded her arms at the perceived favouritism.

Tau gave an awkward hug back and patted Tetsu's shoulder so he'd release her. 'Yeah, we… we'll all be okay.'

Eno rested against the nearest bed and brought a hand to his head. 'I had a strange dream, too. There were these old people… and all my friends told me to… to be happy?'

Malu stood and joined us. 'I saw the same thing. My family was there… I saw Dad. And Tau, you were there, too, telling me to be happy over and over again.'

The team of scientists picked up their various tools and instruments and made for the door.

One turned back briefly. 'Raumanu will be along shortly.'

They exited, and the door closed, leaving us alone in the dim room.

Eno shrugged. 'Raumanu?'

'It wasn't a dream,' Tau said. 'We *all* saw it.'

I had seen the same old people. That dream I had was unnatural. In it, the planet exploded, and I remembered Tau was in it, too. She told me to obey our new rulers so that I could be happy. It was unlike any dream I'd ever had. And then it dawned on me.

'They were brainwashing us,' I said quietly, bringing a hand to my chin to think. 'I'm immune to it, but you've *all* been brainwashed.'

Noor smiled in doubt. 'No we haven't, I still feel the same as before.'

Tetsu shook his head. 'We would know if we were, right?'

Tau nodded. 'Sacet's right, it *was* brainwashing. We had the same dream because they induced it.' She gestured to her head. 'That's what this INC thing was they put in our brains.'

I nodded back. 'Good, we agree on something,' I said before looking at the others. 'Don't believe anything you experienced.'

At that moment, a bunch of strange digital boxes appeared in my vision. What was going on? They annotated and labelled anything nearby, including my friends. Was this my INC? Stop it! I didn't want this. I blinked and it disappeared, returning my sight to normal. Did it activate just because I was thinking about it?

Tetsu closed his eyes. 'The dream showed me that Seron… was destroyed.' He stared at me expectantly. 'So, it's not true? We're still here, right? On Seron?'

Only Tau and I had seen the resulting total annihilation with our own eyes. How would they take the news?

'Seron is gone,' Tau said without hesitation.

The others stared distantly, processed the news in silence. None shook their heads in disbelief or broke down crying like I expected. It was like they already knew, like they were already prepared for the news.

'And you *should* believe everything else the dream showed you, too,' Tau added.

I gawked at her. 'What?'

She raised a hand at me to stop. 'It will be safer. We should do what they tell us. This has all been about capturing Sacet and, if she doesn't co-operate, they'll kill us one by one until she obeys. They can make death permanent, so no amount of healing from me could bring you back.' She sighed. 'They demonstrated it… on Marid.'

There was another long silence as we all exchanged looks.

'As I told Sacet,' Tau continued sombrely, 'we lost. *Everything* is gone.'

Malu smiled and raised a finger in the air. 'No, it's okay.'

I shook my head at her. 'What's okay about *any* of this?'

She stepped closer to me. 'We all saw them, these glorious rulers? They're good people, they'll help us. Everything is going to be fine.'

Noor nodded and looked at me. 'Yeah, they'll make sure us Seronians are all provided for.'

Tetsu chuckled. 'You're right, wow. I didn't think of it that way but… now that the war is finally over, we can all be happy… on Aster.'

Were they serious, or were they just playing along with Tau's advice? I glared at them, horrified.

Malu's face lit up, ecstatic. 'If they resurrect everyone then… we'll all be reunited with our families. I'll get to see my dad again!'

Tetsu's face seemed just as happy. 'Me, too! And I'll see my mum. I barely remember her face, it's been so long.'

'I'll see mine, too, my whole family,' Noor added, but his excitement quickly changed to anxiety. 'I can apologise to them. For thinking they were traitors.'

'And just like that, all the mistakes I made don't really matter anymore,' Malu continued. Her smile faded as she studied me. 'Sacet, don't you see? They'll forgive me and we can be a family again. That is *why* I fought alongside you in the first place.'

Noor reached out and took my hand. '*Oh*, Sacet. I'm sorry about Marid. We all are.' He looked back at the others. 'She was a good person.' They all nodded in agreement as he squeezed my hand tighter. 'But it's over now. You and Eno can see your parents, your grandfather, your whole village.'

I ripped my hand away from him. 'This isn't how I wanted to see them. None of you have a problem with what they did to us, to my mother? What they did on our world all this time? You can't even see… how brainwashed you all are!'

Malu shook her head, then looked at everyone else while gesturing to me. 'And this is why I *hate* her. She sounds all high and mighty, but what she's really about to do is ruin everything for everyone.'

Eno looked up at me, confused. 'You *do* want to see Mum and Dad again, right?'

My heart took a blow. 'I… of *course* I do, Eno, how could you even ask me that? I love them and you more than *anything*. We'll see them, I promise.'

Tau folded her arms. 'Then why would you risk that by trying to escape?'

The whole room stared at me like I was a stranger.

Malu put her hands on her hips and scoffed. 'Sacet, you're always doing this, it's *never* your fault, is it? You try to inflict your own justice on people, because what you say *always* goes. No one else's opinion matters to the gaslighting queen.'

My lips trembled and I turned away. I shook my head. 'No, I'm trying to save people from being treated like cattle. You're just… saying all this because you're brainwashed.'

'Maybe, maybe not,' she said. 'But *I* believe I'm seeing things clearly. Maybe you just can't stand it when someone you don't know is in control of things?'

I stared at Noor, looking for any kind of support.

He grimaced as if struggling with who to side with. 'I'm sorry, but… maybe she has a point?'

I clenched my fists and scowled at them all. 'Fine, give in to them, then. Be good little puppets. Dominion or Asterians, same thing!'

Multiple people then yelled at once right when the far door opened. Several guards entered, followed by Raumanu. The room hushed and watched him hobble closer with his cane.

Raumanu beamed. 'Good morning, Sacet and friends. All slept well, I trust?'

Our group silenced and exchanged awkward glares.

Raumanu gestured for us to follow. 'Come. Come this way. I have something to show you all.'

Eleven: Landing Party

After entering the corridor, I realised we weren't on the Black Dawn anymore, for this second spacecraft was far smaller. After putting us into stasis, they must have transported us to Aster on a different ship. The corridor had windows on both sides, looking out into space. From this angle, I saw a bright star bathing the planet's edge in light, but that was all. The forward section of the ship obscured my view of the planet.

My friends and I moved only as fast as Raumanu could hobble down the corridor.

'I'm Raumanu, by the way,' he said to them as we dawdled. 'But my friends call me Raum.'

'I'll stick to Raumanu then,' I grumbled, and he chuckled.

We eventually reached the end, where another doorway opened to reveal what I assumed was the bridge. We entered into the larger space and collectively gasped.

An enormous front window wrapped around the front and sides of the bridge, granting an impressive view of the moonless planet. Aster, our new home, was mostly grey, except for one huge patch of colour made up of swirling red, blue and purple. An orange glow surrounded the planet as well. Perhaps that was the colour of its sky?

Even the darker surfaces, untouched by the sun, glowed with speckled light. It took me a moment to realise they were city lights. The entire planet was one vast city. Our jaws dropped. Not even in my wildest dreams could I fathom a city as vast and titanic as this.

'That's Aster?' Tetsu asked. 'It's so… grey.'

Raumanu nodded. 'Yes, there is not one speck of land left. It is so overpopulated that we rely completely on all our colonies to provide for us. We have entire planets dedicated to crops to feed the masses.'

A tiny, unnatural rectangle appeared, a message box from my INC labelling the planet as "Aster". It initially took me off guard, and I tried to swat it away. Yes, obviously it's Aster, thank you, INC. Now, deactivate! The message disappeared immediately.

My friends must have been struggling with their devices as well. Noor was shaking his head as if shooing away an insect, Malu was rubbing her eyes and Tau simply closed them, perhaps hoping it would go away on its own.

Eno moaned in frustration. 'Urgh, I hate this INC thing.'

Raumanu chuckled and reached over to tussle Eno's hair. 'Give it time. Once you've mastered your thoughts, you won't know how you lived without it.'

Control panels lined every wall of the bridge, each staffed by seated crew members. In the centre, several rows of seats awaited, and Raumanu gestured to them before sitting in the front row, closer to the pilots. He groaned as he arched his back. The guards stood at the bridge entrance, watching the rest of us.

'All of you, sit,' one guard instructed.

My friends and I awkwardly looked at each other, unsure who would sit first and where. I sighed and went to the middle seat in the second row.

'Eno?' I said, glancing back at him and gesturing to a chair next to mine.

He hesitated, but eventually sat where I directed.

Noor approached us and looked as if he were about to sit in the chair on my other side.

I raised my hand in front. 'No.'

He gave me a hurt look. 'What? Sacet, I'm sorry...'

Ignoring him, I helped Eno buckle his straps, then my own. I finally looked back at him. 'Until you remember who you are, I don't want you *near* me.'

Tau, Tetsu and Malu had taken seats in the third row and buckled up. They all stared at me, Malu even scowled, clearly repulsed.

Noor scrunched up his face before shaking his head and letting out a frustrated groan. He turned and sat in the fourth row instead. The guards took their seats as well, scattered randomly throughout the rows.

Raumanu glanced over his shoulder to watch us, continuing to smile. Was he enjoying this? Tearing our lives apart? I wanted so badly to punch him in the face, but I knew full well how that would turn out.

'We're taking you straight to your new home, Sacet,' he said. 'Iya told us you and your friends were staying together. Is that correct?'

Malu laughed. 'Count me out, I want to live with *my* family.'

Raumanu shook his head. 'That won't be allowed,' he said, grasping his cane tighter. 'All new acolytes must live in Arc Academy, where you'll receive your training to become operatives for the empire.' He looked forward again. 'The *one* exception is that Sacet may have as many permanent guests as she wishes in her suite atop Arc Sacet.'

'Malu, we should stick together,' Tau said. 'Until we know what's going on, let's support each other, okay?' She looked at us one by one. 'And maybe if this place is big enough, we can move all of our families in, too?'

Malu folded her arms and avoided my gaze. 'I guess that makes sense.'

Eno tilted his head to Raumanu. 'Mister Raum, sir, what's an arc?'

'Short for arcology,' Raumanu explained. 'A giant structure that towers over the rest of the planet. Only the richest, most powerful, and most privileged can live in them. Each one houses more people than any city on Seron ever could.'

Eno's eyes widened, and he leaned forward to point out the window. 'Woah, what are all those colours in the sky there?'

'That's an aurora,' Raumanu continued, gesturing out the window. 'That purple spot is where we're heading. Because of the harsh solar radiation bombarding Aster, we beam a localised artificial magnetosphere over…' He looked back and noticed our confused expressions. 'It's beautiful, isn't it? All the important arcs are there: Arc Royal, Arc Unity, Arc Academy… and all the Chosen arcs, of course. Arc Raumanu, my arc, is… over in that blue patch there.'

From this distance, the planet seemed to have countless spikes, each reaching high above the clouds. We could also see thin, bright, white lines crisscrossing all over the surface. There were thousands of them forming an intricate web, maybe more.

'L lines!' Eno shouted.

Raumanu nodded. 'Very good, Eno. Yes, L lines, created by the last Chosen to be discovered, Lucenia. She was also from Seron. We use her lines for transportation.'

Although we seemed to only be slowly approaching the planet, we were probably going incredibly fast, relatively speaking. As we got closer, it became clear that the spikes protruding up into the sky were actually buildings, each monumental in size, towering over the rest of the world like thick, indestructible spires, thousands of stories tall. These were the arcologies.

These arcs all looked shaped like regular skyscrapers, mostly linear and far taller than they were wide, but I occasionally spotted an odd one. One twisted into the clouds like a helix, and another was like a bulbous collection of spheres all stacked on top of each other.

Annoyingly, my INC reactivated again and labelled a bunch of them: Arc Triumph, Arc Fervour, Arc Inevitable… Clear it off my eyes. *Clear!* The messages disappeared again. Good.

The L lines joined the towering buildings at varying heights and shot off in a myriad of directions, each one like a piece of string tying the arcs together.

Far shorter than the arcs, the rest of the city buildings were all roughly the same height and tightly packed together in city blocks. From this distance, the grid collectively looked like an infinite steel sheet wrapped around the world, broken up by the occasional street. The metal plane reflected the intense sun like a shield.

Our seats shook as we descended, and the view from outside glowed orange as flames enveloped our ship.

Raumanu waited until the rumbling stopped before glancing back at us. 'Now, when we land, there will be a welcoming party for the new Chosen—'

'It's *all* about Sacet,' Malu muttered.

'—and things will go smoother if all the guests love Sacet and her friends.'

Malu scoffed again. 'Good luck with *that.*'

I glared back, sick of her attitude. If she was going to be like this all the time, I didn't want her around me.

'So, what I need to know is,' Raumanu continued, 'am I going to regret turning off your collars? Will you all behave?'

'I'll behave,' Eno said. 'So long as I can see my parents.'

Raumanu nodded. 'You'll see them very soon. And the rest of you?'

'I will, too,' Noor added. Tetsu and Malu both nodded.

'Sacet?' Raumanu asked as he and the others stared at me.

Even with powers, I didn't know how to begin fighting back. And this INC thing probably doubled as a tracking device. I sighed. It was like being captured by the Female Dominion all over again.

I felt Tau's hand on my shoulder, and she gave me a solemn stare. 'Promise us you won't do anything stupid.'

'Yes, fine,' I replied. 'I promise I won't hurt anyone.'

Raumanu smiled again. 'Good.' He narrowed his eyes and his eyelids fluttered as if he was concentrating on something.

I heard a loud click as my collar released from my neck and a wealth of images hit my mind like a rippling shockwave. My second perception had been reactivated, and I was overloaded with many sights simultaneously.

Outside, the purple aurora appeared painted on the otherwise pale, orange sky. The sun's light reflected off the clouds, scattering blinding rays. A massive silhouette parted them, casting our ship in shadow.

Then we all saw it: we were approaching a massive arc that had been designed and constructed to look like me. It was like a mountain-sized statue, but it was a skyscraper like the other arcs, filled with a city's worth of empty rooms and hallways.

The others all gasped repeatedly.

Malu shook her head in disbelief. 'You've got to be kidding me!'

As I held my head in pain, Raumanu took no notice, pointing

out the window with a measure of pride. 'That… is Arc Sacet, a gift from our greatest architects and engineers… to *you*, Sacet. Your new home.'

The thing's vacant expression was as cold as the steel it was made from. It was the most egotistical thing I had ever seen, yet I hadn't even asked for it.

The building wasn't just tall but thick, too. It was so immense, a window for a single room appeared microscopic relative to the number of others. My perception continued to spasm, showing me hundreds of arc interior rooms at once and zipping through them at breakneck speed. The strain in my head was maddening.

'After you enter, so will your most loyal fans and followers,' Raumanu added. 'Over one hundred million of them will live on the floors under you.'

Our craft slowed and lowered next to the arc's peak, giving us an up-close-and-personal look at my building's face. We quickly descended along the curvature of my frame. I didn't even have clothes on! My *special* areas were thankfully not shaped into the construction, but the smoothness everywhere else left little to the imagination. My embarrassment was palpable, knowing that literally millions and billions of people were looking at my dimensions from all angles, judging and obsessing over my giant form.

The city-sized arc had the capacity for millions, just as Raumanu had said. Each floor was convolutedly designed, but mostly comprised of row after row of identical homes filled with luxuries, the purpose of many I couldn't comprehend. There were banquet halls with staff at the ready. Pseudo-natural enclosures contained artificial vegetation, pristine rivers that wound down into hidden pipes and a bevy of peaceful garden creatures.

There were several internal arenas, each with the ability to seat many thousands. The largest stadium was where my stomach would be. A huge cavity of air above the stadium gave the illusion of a night sky, with millions of blinking, star-like ceiling lights.

The L lines I had seen from orbit stretching between each arc were bridges made of light. Their energy was vast and powerful, like those on Seron but more refined, straighter, and denser. On closer inspection I could sense people zipping through the air inside them from one arc to another at ridiculous speeds, completely unharmed.

'Are you okay?' I heard a voice say, but I couldn't work out who.

I thought the city-sized arc was big, but I was quickly humbled when I saw the real city below. To describe it felt impossible, for words like expansive and colossal didn't do it justice. The number of people within my perception's radius was beyond estimation. The city without end was both ordered and chaotic, designed with seemingly random symmetrical and completely choked thoroughfares. It made a Seronian city feel like a quaint cave settlement.

The buildings below, although dwarfed by the arc, were still larger than anything I had seen before. There were hundreds of floors reaching down into the depths of the world, layer upon layer, so deep that I couldn't find a trace of soil or sand. There was only steel residences of the poor, choking in a thick, dark, polluted smog. Most of the lowly dwellers wore masks and other breathing apparatus as they traversed the rickety catwalks and bridges. It was as if whenever these people ran out of room, they just built a newer floor on top of the entire world.

The layers of buildings were periodically broken up with crisscrossing divides. These bottomless streets were like colossal steel canyons, with vertical cliffs bordering an abyss of hazy brown gases below. Innumerable flying vehicles ferried the citizens around at a multitude of heights, buzzing like a hive. It was a wonder none crashed.

'Sacet, wake up!' someone said.

'Is she having a seizure?'

'Good.' That voice was definitely Malu.

I was shaking uncontrollably. My mind jolted around, trying to refocus. Tau was out of her chair and holding my shoulders. Her aura surrounded her; was she healing me? What had happened?

I raised my hands. 'I'm okay, I'm okay,' I said, but it was a lie. My collar was at my feet, unlocked and powered down. My head was still spinning; I felt like I needed to vomit.

'You didn't look okay. You were convulsing,' she said, continuing her aura's presence. 'Now that I think about it, this isn't the first time this has happened.'

'I just… I… it's too much for me,' I said, slurring it out as my watery eyes adjusted. 'I'm just not… used to seeing so much around me.'

'Well, you'd better get used to it quick,' Raumanu called back. 'We're about to land.'

I heaved, almost unleashing the geyser of vomit churning inside me. I covered my mouth before swallowing. I needed to turn my second perception off somehow. Maybe I could work out a way to ignore it? I kept my eyes open so that I had something else to focus on.

We lurched as the craft finally came to a stop on a landing platform. The platform was connected to the base of Arc Sacet. Outside, there was a constant, loud groaning noise from a large crowd of people. I didn't dare focus my view on them for fear of making myself sick again.

Raumanu unbuckled and pushed himself up with his cane. 'Final stop.'

I unbuckled my seat, too, and stood. I raised a hand at him. 'Wait, you said it was my choice who lives with me? Malu is not welcome,' I said as the others sighed in disappointment. 'She has made it clear she has a problem with me, so she can go live with the other acolytes. And if any of you feel the same way, then you can, too.'

There was a silence in the cabin as I stared back at them all, only the crowd outside could be heard. Noor and Tetsu looked down at their feet.

Malu had a hurt look but shook out of it. 'Well, *I* already said I didn't want to live with you, didn't I?'

Tau approached and brushed my shoulder again. 'Sacet, *please* don't split us up. Remember, you said that we were brainwashed, right? Malu didn't mean it.'

Malu laughed. 'No, I meant *every* word. I've felt this way for a long time.'

Raumanu smiled. 'Their minds are made up. Malu, stay here and we'll take you to the academy. The rest of you, disembark with me.'

He and most of the guards made their way to the craft's exit, a slowly lowering ramp. As I strode past Malu to follow, she kept her arms folded and looked away from me. The others gave each other awkward looks again before unbuckling and joining us on the ramp.

'I'll be fine,' I heard Malu say quietly to Tau as she passed.

We descended the ramp onto the landing platform and were all shocked by what we saw. Just below the platform was an enormous courtyard that stretched in every direction except for behind where the arc stood. A crowd filled the courtyard, stretching as far as my eyes could see, an army easily hundreds of thousands strong. When we finally stepped off the ramp, they erupted in applause and cheers.

Beyond the courtyard, tall buildings overlooked our position, many with balconies, and they were all lined with people, too, cheering and waving. There were flags and colourful banners, as well as small explosions of celebratory light going off randomly.

There were women and men, kids and elderly. Many had streaks in their hair, purple with black tips, just like mine had been. Some even had their hair dyed cyan, like Tau's when her aura was activated.

Most wore thick layers of clothing, making them appear fatter than they really were. And not only were their clothes colourful, but they were often decorated with pictures depicting all manner of symbols and graphics, the most common of which was a picture of me pinned against a wall and impaled with a metal beam through my stomach. Were these people happy I died? Happy that my friends and I lost?

Strangest of all, every so often I'd spot someone with a completely different colour of skin, shades I didn't know were even possible. A few oranges were dotted about, some light-blue, others a deep pink. Were they the natural shades Asterians could be born as? Or could these be people from other planets that were assimilated, like the original Seronians had been?

Raumanu hobbled closer to me. 'They love you. You should smile and wave to them. Show them you're *happy* about coming here, they'll appreciate that.'

I looked back at my nervous, brainwashed entourage, then sneered at him. 'What do *I* have to be happy about exactly?'

'It doesn't matter,' he replied, fiddling with his beard. 'It's about keeping *them* happy, keeping the people on your side. They came to see *you*.'

I nodded and slowly raised my hand above me to wave. The crowd roared so loudly that I felt the platform shake.

'Now show them your power,' Raumanu suggested.

I stared at him with widened eyes. 'What? No, I'm not some performer, some… trained animal for them to gawk at.'

He shrugged. 'Fine, be difficult.'

As Tau crept closer, the crowd again surged. 'Mum wanted you to change this empire for the better,' she yelled. 'That would be a lot *easier* if everyone liked you.'

I glanced back at the others again. They all nodded in agreement, waiting for me to do something.

'They've all heard of your exploits,' Raumanu continued. 'They were particularly fond of that portal you made to Seron's star. Why not indulge them? With something non-destructive, of course.'

I really didn't feel like making portals for their entertainment, but what Malu had said to me was eating at the back of my mind, too, and I didn't want to make any more enemies today.

I looked at the bridges of light that connected the arcs. They were like water pipes, every moment transferring hundreds of people through. Careful not to cut through one of the travellers, I opened two portals next to each other inside the bridge with their destinations above the crowd in the courtyard.

At first, it didn't look like I had done anything. But then I stretched the portals along the length of the bridge. As I began to split both pairs of portals, the effect displayed itself. There was now a partial part of the bridge, a segment of it floating in the courtyard, the same piece that was now missing from the bridge above, yet my power did not hinder its flow.

Those in the bridge would travel normally, then through a portal, then along the bridge above the crowd, then portal back to the regular bridge, completely unaffected. The crowd oohed in amazement and whistled at the demonstration, so I repeated the process again and again until several incomplete tubes of light hovered above the crowd. I shifted the courtyard portals, too, which made the displaced bridges rotate on the spot.

Next, looking up at the distant peak of the nearest tall building, I opened a portal above it, with its destination between all the bridges in the courtyard. As I lowered the portal over the peak, I kept the portal in the courtyard still. Next, I stretched my fingers in both hands, growing the portals' diameter. The portal descended on top of the skyscraper and snugly fit around it, which shot the peak of the tower out the destination portal above the courtyard.

The crowd continued to cheer, many making astonished gasps and hollers. As the distant tower shrank, the new tower in the courtyard grew, protruding upwards in the middle of the reality-defying lightshow. I could see people from the upper floors of the tower look out their windows in shock. The tower grew and grew, giving its residents a new view of the surrounding city.

My body was completely relaxed, there was no need to strain. In fact, this was easy. When did I become this powerful?

I had proved my point. In a flash, I rocketed the massive portals skyward and closed them, returning the distant tower to its former glory. The bridge portals were carefully closed in reverse order, never once disrupting their flow.

There was a lull in the crowd before yet another eruption of excitement. Raumanu gave me a congratulatory pat on the shoulder, before turning towards the arc and indicating for us to follow. The arc's entrance was a giant archway between my incomprehensibly large toes.

I took one last look at the crowd. Were these people really on my side, or was I just some gimmick to them? They bayed obsessively. Did they approve of their idol now? Their adored performer?

I was honestly a little sickened by them, celebrating my great loss. These were the same people who had sat by and done nothing as the people of *my* world, a harvest world, were enslaved, tortured and murdered over and over again. *Oh*, I'll change this place for the better alright, Mother. I didn't care how long it was going to take, I'd have my vengeance for what they did to Seron.

Twelve: Love Fades

'Here it is,' Raumanu said as we hopped off the circular elevator panel. 'The penthouse suite of Arc Sacet, your new home.' He grinned and gestured to the grand surroundings.

Tau, Eno, Noor and Tetsu all gasped.

The suite was cavernous, extending the entire width of the arc tower, which admittedly was thinner now that we were on the top floor, the tip of my crown. Still, this was more space than we would ever need. There was so much to see here, where to begin?

To my right was a garden with an artificial Seronian sky built into the ceiling. The illusion of a healthy blue horizon hung over the many plants, flowing streams and bountiful flowers. Small, cute, furry creatures scampered, somehow knowing the boundaries of their own enclosure, for whenever they approached the edges of their garden, they would turn around and run back in. Some of them I recognised and even hunted with Eno when we were younger.

To the left was an enormous swimming pool, half under cover, the other on an outside balcony. The blue water was completely still, as if there was no draught this high up. There were numerous twisting and tubed slides, climbable fake rocks and long, horizontal seats.

My perception sensed that the balcony, which ran along the entire circumference of our circular floor, granted a sweeping view of the planet far below us. We were so high up that we were above a layer of clouds.

Around the other side of the elevator tube in the centre of the tower was what looked like a gym. The exercise equipment looked far better than what I used to use in the New Elysian barracks: larger, shinier, and more varied. There were courts, too, flat, open areas with painted lines on the ground, which I assumed were for sports, not that I understood the rules.

Next to the gym was a large entertainment area, with couches, tables and chairs, a stocked bar and separate, colourful lighting. What I assumed was a futuristic kitchen was next to that, and also an elongated dining room. There was an ornately carved dining table for feasts, able to seat at least fifty people.

In front of us, connecting everything was a living room, along with a stairwell. My second perception sensed many rooms above us on yet another floor, and rooftop access above that. There were plenty of bedrooms, again enough for maybe fifty or so people. Each had its own pristine white bathroom. There were even more rooms than that, with random pieces of furniture and objects, their functions unknown to me.

If asked, I would admit it was all very impressive, but none of it sat right with me. I had lived most of my life in the desert, going from cave to cave, and now my home was bigger than any nomad settlement I could remember.

We all watched as maybe twenty people came down the stairs, their strides almost in sync. The men all wore the same neat suit of purple and grey, and the women had the same colours in identical short dresses. The group stopped, formed a line in front of us and bowed oddly, deep and respectfully. Each of them had an unnaturally large grin, like they were a little *too* happy to be here.

'And these are your personal servants,' Raumanu explained. 'They are sworn to obey you.'

One of the larger men took a step towards me and kneeled. 'Honoured Chosen Sacet, I am Fidèle, your most humble and devoted servant. For as long as we exist, my team and I shall attend to your every whim and desire with unwavering diligence and utmost reverence. As we age, our equally loyal descendants will eventually take our place. We will serve you eternally, guaranteeing that you shall want for nothing.'

He had blue skin and an elegantly shaped gold plate over one of his eyes, which I assumed was some sort of cybernetic implant.

Some of the butlers and maids had similar gadgets. One maid had two extra sets of mechanical arms coming out of her back. One of those arms held a feather duster, whilst the other skillfully balanced a tray of drinks.

'We'll need to leave again soon,' Raumanu said before gesturing to the stairwell. 'Why don't you all find a room for yourselves? Go clean yourselves up and get changed into something formal.'

The boys looked at each other and gave the faintest of grins. Eno ran towards the stairwell and began to climb. Noor and Tetsu gave chase, and some of the servants also calmly followed.

Tau looked at me, disappointed. 'Are we going to talk about what just happened?'

I scoffed and turned away from her. 'No.' I strode to the stairwell, and she and several more servants followed me up.

We climbed the stairs and followed along one of the upstairs corridors. As Tau and I walked, we peeked into the huge, lavish bedrooms.

Noor came out of one of them. 'Sacet, I found a bedroom for us,' he said, gesturing over his shoulder.

Tetsu and Eno came out of their rooms nearby, listening in on the conversation. The servants stopped behind us, too.

I noticed all of them staring at me, so I sighed. 'I think I'll find my own room for now.'

Noor's face drooped as I continued along the corridor.

'Don't worry,' I heard Eno say from behind. 'This area can just be men only.'

As Tau caught up with me, she looked back at the boys and gave them a sympathetic frown. Tetsu was staring at her as though he was about to say something, too, but he remained silent.

The two of us rounded a corner and were met with an even longer corridor with even more bedrooms. One of these would do, far away from the others.

Tau sighed. 'So, you're just going to ignore what happened, then?'

Three servants appeared at our side, and I glared at them. 'A little privacy would be nice?'

Their smiles remained, completely unoffended. 'Of course, Ma'am.' They backed away and returned to the others.

I turned back to Tau. 'I don't want to be near you either. You're brainwashed, too.'

'I'm not,' she replied defensively. 'I don't *think* I am. I don't care about these… *glorious rulers*. Anyway, don't you think you're being a little harsh on all of us? It's not *our* fault this happened.'

I stopped. 'No, it's not your fault, but I'd rather keep my distance until I know *exactly* what they've done to you.'

She shook her head and turned away. 'It'll be easy to keep your distance when you've driven us all away.' She began walking back to the others. 'I'm going to get a room near my friends.'

Whatever. Go ahead and be melodramatic.

There was a bedroom behind me, so I entered it alone. There was an oversized bed, an adjoining bathroom and a walk-in wardrobe in the shape of a semicircle, which looped back to the room. Inside the semicircle on the bedroom side was a small area, sectioned off with a see-through glass wall. On the far side of the room was a window overlooking the balcony and the planet-city below that.

I sat on the bed and looked out the window. There was a faint knocking from behind – it sounded like Raumanu's cane in the corridor. Again, I was far too distracted to notice him coming within my second perception. He shuffled into my room, examining its features.

'This whole floor was designed to remind you of your old home,' he said. 'Do you like it?'

'Sure,' I said, staring out the window.

'The stylings, the garden, even the drinks at the bar have a Seronian twist to…'

'Why did you have to brainwash them?' I interrupted, shooting a scathing look back at him. 'They were my family and friends. You couldn't have made an exception?'

He shook his head. 'They are *still* your family and friends. The only thing that has changed is how they view this world and the last. We woke them up to reality.'

'That should have been a choice for *them* to make. They're just your puppets now.'

Raumanu scowled and hobbled closer. 'What's done is done, Sacet. This whining achieves nothing. Perhaps you should get out there and apologise to them for your behaviour instead of wallowing in pity like a child?'

I looked away again, continuing to seethe.

He relaxed his stance and sighed. 'My destructive tendencies have pushed away many loved ones over the millennia. So, *believe* me when I say that anger fades… but so does love. Which one would you prefer to last longer?'

I took a deep breath and glanced back at him. We shared a moment of silence.

He gestured over at the glass panel area I had seen earlier. 'You see that? That's an auto-fitter; it will clean you and change your clothing, and even allow you to design your own.'

I hesitated, but then stood up and wandered over to it. I looked back at him, confused.

He nodded approvingly. 'Step inside.'

I did as he suggested, stepping through the small doorway. The thin, glass-like walls automatically closed behind me, and suddenly my INC activated with an interface of partially see-through panels and lists, which floated in front of me as though they were really there.

'Try it out,' he continued. 'Choose something nice to wear. Tonight you will be the guest of honour at Arc Royal. You will meet the emperor and empress, and others of great import.'

The interface had numerous buttons, and each had a different kind of clothing. There were buttons for dresses, swimwear, underwear, relaxation, formal, casual, fun, armour… even skydiving gear? Something called a wingsuit? The list went on and on. As I moved my eyes, a cursor hovered over my selection. A message in the top left said 'blink to choose'.

I chose the formal option, and a list of pictures came up, filling the menu. There were navigation buttons, too. A message popped up telling me there were over one hundred million options in this category alone and that I should narrow down my search. I dismissed it, chose one of the dresses, then chose purple for the colour.

The tiny room shuddered, and some mechanisms I didn't see before sprang from the ceiling above me. Like miniature cranes, they hummed and spun around me in a circle. I looked down at my chest and saw that the blue-striped, drab, grey clothing I had been wearing was disintegrating.

'Hey!' I yelled, covering my privates and shooting an angry look back at the old man. 'Don't look!'

But he was already facing away, by the door. The machines continued their work until I was naked, and I kept watching him to make sure he didn't turn around.

The cranes spinning in circles glowed purple. More material appeared on me as fast as my old clothing had disappeared. The dress slowly formed, covering my body. When it finally finished, the machine beeped, and the panel shifted to the side to reveal a mirrored wall.

Raumanu then turned around. 'That looks good. I'm going to check on the others to make sure they're getting ready, too. Unless, of course… you want to go alone?'

I looked at myself in the mirror. I still hated this man; he destroyed my entire world. But he was right, I hadn't treated my friends very well.

'No, they can come,' I replied. 'Close the door on your way out.'

I stared over the balcony at the alien night. Although the sky had darkened from its normally orange haze, the surface of the world was soaked in artificial light, blanketing the inky black in its glow. The stars were invisible and I didn't know why. The aurora continued to churn above in a mix of red, blue and purple, the colours far stronger and more vibrant than they were in the daytime.

'How do I look?' Tau asked from inside, coming down the stairs into the living room behind me.

Tau wore a silk, white dress that reached her knees. Large, but tasteful openings revealed some of her skin. Her hair was straightened, too. Her attire was admittedly quite pretty. She seemed to be making a lot more effort to fit in than me.

I, on the other hand, had chosen a much simpler, less revealing purple dress. I tried incorporating a few items that my people would wear, like a necklace and a leather belt. I had no interest in looking attractive, rather I felt my clothes needed to be functional and show some reverence for my genocided culture.

Tau looked at Tetsu on a nearby couch and posed for him.

He gawped. 'You look… *amazing*.'

She gave a *huge* smile in return, and… was she blushing? She joined Tetsu on the couch, avoiding my gaze. 'That suit looks *great* on you.'

Tetsu wore a grey, pleated suit. The shoulders were black, and he had a silver belt to keep his dark-grey pants up. His shoes were silver, too, shiny and sleek.

Raumanu had been waiting by the elevator, ready to escort us to the party. He must have used an outfitter as well, because now his robes were greenish-grey and elaborately edged. They still didn't seem to be very fancy. Like me, he probably preferred comfort over style.

'Okay, we're coming down,' I heard Noor say from the stairwell.

Both he and Eno strutted down the steps and stopped in front of us. Eno wore a small, black and white suit, simple but effective.

Noor, on the other hand, had slicked-up hair and an intricately layered crimson sequin suit with matching pants. The suit's shoulders were oversized and metallic, like armour. He strutted down with confidence.

Tetsu laughed at the top of his lungs. 'What… is that?' he yelled.

Both Eno and Tau giggled, too.

Noor gestured at his getup. 'What, you don't like it?'

'It's fine,' Raumanu said from the elevator. 'It's time to go.'

Our view through the elevator tube changed to a massive, open area, several storeys high. I believed we were somewhere in my arc's thigh. It was like a hangar, a giant hole was in the side of the arc to let a light bridge enter from outside.

The beginning of the light bridge was just a sheer drop off the edge of the building, but waves of white energy formed a translucent tube that shot out to other arcs. Although the bridge's energy was white, it gave off this sparkling aura, refracting its own light into a spectrum of all colours. It was beautiful, it was hard to imagine something so pure and magical was created for these people.

Thousands of citizens filled this floor, many confidently stepping off the edge of the arc into the energy. Rather than falling, each person hovered for a moment before zipping away at breakneck speed. Somehow, even though so many people were coming and going, there weren't any collisions between them, and none showed any signs of fear.

Our private elevator came to rest and opened its doors. Two lines of guards, perhaps a hundred of them, had formed a clear path from the elevator to the light bridge nearest to us. The guards and their barricades kept two large crowds at bay, one on either side, who cheered in excitement when they noticed us.

Raumanu led us out and through the path, slowly as usual because of his slouching back and cane.

Someone in the crowd had started a chant of my name, which grew and grew. As usual, it seemed as though all eyes were on me.

'Sa… cet! Sa… cet! Sa… cet!'

My perception sensed a man in the crowd wearing a gas mask. He wasn't cheering like the others. Someone who lived in the polluted depths, perhaps? He wasn't the only one, there were several others, all wearing baggy, musty, hooded robes.

Noor gestured to the light bridge as we walked, the light of which reflected off his jacket. 'How does that thing work?'

'All you need to do is think about your destination, and your INC will do the rest,' Raumanu explained. 'But this time we're going to hold hands and go together. As we travel, I want you to think of the words "Arc Royal" and only those words over and over again, got it?'

The others nodded and continued following him, but I froze, still focused on the masked man. He rummaged through his baggy robes and pulled out a stashed rifle.

Without thinking, I created a portal around the gun barrel and forced it over. It spat the weapon out through a small portal in front of me onto the ground. The man's intense stare turned to shock.

'Sacet?' Raumanu called back. 'I thought I told you…'

An explosion detonated outwards from the masked man's chest; a fiery wave rolled over the crowd and guards. Bodies flew. Screams, laserfire. I felt the searing heat; the flames were coming right for us, but just as we were about to be engulfed, they dissipated into nothing, swallowed by some other invisible force.

Raumanu had dropped his cane and outstretched his hands towards us. 'Get under your friend's shield!' he yelled.

The floor beneath me vibrated, and I was hurled into the air towards the others. I landed at Tetsu's feet with a thud and a sliding screech along the metal tiles. Did Raumanu just do that?

A second explosion rocked the station from behind, but before it could reach its fiery potential, the flames reversed course until they were extinguished. A third explosion went off, which was quickly quashed at its origin point.

Was I allowed to help fight back, or would I get into trouble for doing so? And who were these people? Why was this happening? My hesitance overcame me as I lay there on the floor.

Raumanu cast an odious look at us. 'I said make a shield!'

Unsure of what was happening, my panicking friends complied, closing in on Tetsu. He brought up his shield around us and several lucky guards, who continued to fire through it.

More screams. Guards exchanged laserfire with even more masked members of the crowd. It was chaos, we weren't sure who was an enemy and who was just an innocent bystander. The guards didn't seem to care, firing into the throng at anyone who got in the way. Thousands ran for the nearest light bridges, leaping off the edges of the arc and hurtling away to safety. Those freshly arrived at the arc noticed the commotion and jumped back the way they came.

The boys joined the guards in combat, Noor with his devastating red beam slicing through the masked strangers and Eno firing volleys of telekinetic bursts, which sent them flying into walls and screaming over balconies. One man was launched out of the arc into the light bridge, but rather than flying along it, he plummeted through the energy and back down through the sky.

Raumanu was dispatching the fighters with ease, simply waving his hand and disintegrating them with nary a second thought. One of the enemies charged at him from behind, and when he got close, he exploded in another firestorm.

At first, it looked like the old man had been consumed in flame, but soon we saw that, like Tetsu's shield, Raumanu had a spherical shield that made him impervious to damage, although his was invisible. He simply turned to the fire and snuffed it out with a flick of his fingers.

'Who else must be brought into the light?' he calmly shouted at the scrambling crowd.

I had originally thought that Raumanu's ability was invisible, and to our regular eyes, it was indeed, but my second perception could sense it. The space around him was like a wave of popping air, like the oxygen itself was exploding. I could anticipate its movement, its flow. Wherever he directed his gaze, the wave of disintegration streamed like water, ripping apart anything it touched.

What could have been a hundred more enemy fighters appeared from every nook and cranny of the building. A squadron ran along the walls and ceiling as if ignoring gravity. Their boots glowed red with each step. Some wielded metal poles, which they fastened to the walls and ceiling before activating.

'Inhibitors!' Tetsu yelled as his shield came down. Noor and Eno's abilities also stopped firing. My second perception was blinded again. Even the nearby light bridge flickered as if unable to exist in the surprisingly large field.

I gave Noor a fearful, wide-eyed look. In the absence of a proper shield, he crouched over me. I had no idea what was going on, so I did the only thing I could do, which was to sit up and huddle with Noor and my friends.

Thirteen: On Display

One suicide bomber after another assaulted the main area, running out from random positions in the thinning crowd before detonating. Raumanu was still somehow neutralising their efforts, making their deaths meaningless to all but the innocent bystanders. His powers had somehow not been affected. Was he outside the inhibitor field?

A bomber who had been hiding beneath a nearby platform sprung up and ran straight for our group, but met oblivion before reaching us.

It was Raumanu yet again, his power acting as an invisible safeguard. '*Hmph*, amateurs. They know nothing of the art of destruction,' he yelled in a raspy voice.

The enemies on the walls opened fire on our position, but as if Tetsu's shield had still been in place, the projectiles disappeared before they could reach us, each fizzled out into nothingness.

Outside the arc was a small aircraft hovering next to the light bridge. Two turrets protruded from its roof, each manned by a gunner. The turrets spun up before unleashing a hailstorm of bulbous, fizzling projectiles towards us, but they faded away like the others.

Without warning, a large hole appeared through the centre of the craft, allowing us to see the colourful sky behind it. Its engines cut, and it hovered for a moment before exploding, sending the wreckage into the side of the arc.

Raumanu's ability was extremely effective, but occasionally he'd get careless, and an enemy's surroundings would disintegrate along with them, including the walls and innocent fleeing stragglers.

The enemy's number was waning, and those left finally retreated, some into the remaining light bridges, others simply jumping off the side of the arc, their special boots allowing them to run vertically down.

The remaining guards shot at the inhibitor poles, bringing back our powers. My perception scanned the immediate area. I locked onto several of the fleeing fighters. I could easily have teleported them back or killed them if I wanted to, but I didn't.

What had been their plan? What if they had come to save us? I had so many questions.

As if only just realising he didn't have his cane, Raumanu bent over in pain and groaned. '*Argh*, can someone… *ahh*, can someone bring me my cane?'

It was Eno who did so, picking it up from the ground and rushing it over to him.

'Thank you, boy,' Raumanu said, before coming over, his movements slow and deliberate, as if every step required immense effort.

The remaining crowd was reeling, the aftermath saw many dead. Our group looked out at them in shock. For me personally, I was conflicted as to whether or not I should even care.

I shook my head at the old man. 'You… weren't inhibited?'

He smirked. 'There's no matter in existence that can penetrate my art. That includes the electromagnetic fields generated by inhibitors.'

With a grim expression, Tau activated her aura again as she scanned through all the dead.

'No, leave them,' Raumanu said. 'We have a party to get to.' He noticed Tau's increased unease after saying this. 'Don't fret, my dear, they'll all be tended to, even the terrorists.'

'Terrorists?' I asked.

Raumanu shambled past us to the light bridge, which had also returned to normal. 'Yes, they *never* learn.' He reached out and held onto my hand, then indicated for me to grab Tau's. 'I will *not* keep the emperor and empress waiting because of this rabble. Others will clean up this mess. Remember, think only "Arc Royal".'

More people arrived at the platform from the light bridges, bewildered by the carnage before them. Several new aircraft showed up along the side of the arc, piloted by what appeared to be military personnel. Their aircraft were larger, sleeker and filled with troops. More guards funnelled into the arc from various entryways to scour through the debris.

I grabbed Tau's hand, and she held Tetsu's, and so on, until we were linked in a chain. We all stood on the edge of the arc, a sheer cliff by any other understanding. Even at the height of my arc's stomach, we were still so high up compared to the rest of the planet. We looked out at the swirling white energy, waiting for something to happen. Arc Royal, Arc Royal, Arc Royal.

Raumanu raised a foot slowly to demonstrate before teetering off the edge. The rest of us followed, but rather than plummet to the surface of Aster, we rose into the white energy as though we were gliders soaring on the wind.

It was beautiful; it was as if the whole dirty world in front of us had turned pale and clean. We zipped forward through the overwhelmingly white tunnel at tremendous speed, yet there were no forces upon my body. No whistling wind either. It was like I was floating in water without wetness. Arc Royal. Arc Royal.

Rather than stopping at other arcs like I expected, our journey took us through numerous switching stations, thin towers half the height of the arcs that supported the light bridges. I had already lost count of how many other citizens had whizzed past us in the opposite direction, each a near miss.

I glanced back at Tau and the others; each was amazed by the speeding tour, smiling with joy. Had they already forgotten what had just happened? Had they already forgotten what they did to our homeworld?

'What did they want?' I called to Raumanu. 'The terrorists?' My voice echoed and warbled unnaturally, as though partly caught in time.

He kept his eyes forward as we sped over the world. 'Probably to abduct or somehow permanently kill you.'

I furrowed my brow and looked down at the surface. 'Why? What did I do to them?'

Our group shook, and both my hands loosened on the others.

'Sacet, focus on where we're going,' Raumanu directed.

Fine. Arc Royal, Arc Royal, Arc Royal, bloody Arc Royal! My grip on the others strengthened again.

'The unbelievers will try anything to stop the Chosen path,' Raumanu continued. 'Don't worry, they'll be resurrected, scanned by our psychics, then summarily executed.'

Executed, like my mother was? These people must have known about these consequences already, so why were they so desperate to get to me? What was this *Chosen path*?

We must have gone through twenty switching gates already. My perception could not keep up with the amount of information below. The city at night had a kind of beauty in its exterior. Brightly coloured neon signs littered the landscape, just like the cities of Seron, but to an extreme number and scale. The distant droning of music and machines reached skyward.

Other arcs filled the distant skyline, some of which were vaguely person-shaped like mine, but the haze of pollution hid their features. One particularly large silhouette, which I originally thought had been a grey mountain was actually an arc so colossal that it was easily double the size of the others. Arc Royal was taller and wider than any mountain I had ever seen. The entire structure was bathed in light, gold at first, but slowly rotating through the colours of the rainbow like an extravagant light show.

The fortress was surrounded by rings and rings of terraced outer walls, creating an immense zone of dominance, its perimeter reaching beyond the horizon, extending to unknown lengths. There were no citizens here, only high walls of steel, seemingly millions of soldiers patrolling, skyscraper-sized guard towers, countless aircraft in the sky and a swarm of MASU-like flying mechs everywhere I could see, their blinking lights replacing the mostly-absent stars.

Gun emplacements were built on every possible surface, the turrets constantly turning, looking for threats. And high above the smaller aircraft were two enormous floating battleships, giant, slow cruisers that encircled the central arc.

Our light bridge, one of many, led over the walls and up the side of the mountain. I looked down at my gently fluttering dress and remembered why I was here. After all that had happened, I did not feel like celebrating anything.

Raumanu led us through one checkpoint after another; each had guards who scanned every member of our group with all manner of devices before waving us through. Security appeared even thicker and more elite at the arc's peak. Odd ethereal music and the sounds of a schmoozing crowd were behind the next door at the end of the luxuriantly carpeted corridor.

I didn't think it could have been possible, but this arc was even more extravagant than my own in almost every way. Every visible surface had copious levels of intricate details etched and molded along them. The silky-smooth furniture twisted at awkward angles, artful but not practical. The floor was a non-repeating puzzle of uniquely shaped tiles. A myriad of elegant designs were laced into curtains, tapestries, and even the guards' over-the-top uniforms. Grand paintings and statues depicted what I assumed were the planet's tyrants when they were younger, and dare I say beautiful?

My perception scanned what I could of the arc interior to see if it was all as luxurious. Strangely, for every floor of opulence, there was another floor above it, overlooking the royalty from the rafters. These floors consisted of a massive, interconnected labyrinth of service tunnels, rooms and stairwells specifically for the staff and guards. These areas were conversely dark, drab and grey, more like an industrial facility.

Eno and Noor were close behind me, with Tau and Tetsu trailing at the back. Every time Tau and I looked at one another, she'd look away. And likewise, every time Noor tried to smile at me, I'd pretend I didn't see it.

I turned to Raumanu as we approached. 'I don't want to be here. What if someone talks to me and I want them to go away?'

Raumanu chuckled. 'You just *ask* them politely to go away.'

'Before or *after* I teleport them to space?' I replied, and he glared at me.

A pair of guards from the final checkpoint opened the large doors, admitting us into the party. It was a grand terrace, a rooftop event under the vibrant green, aurora-filled sky. In the centre of the area were hundreds of mingling guests.

There were plenty of chairs for them to sit and long tables of food. The banquet of fruits, glazed meats and fluffy desserts were stacked in mountainous lumps. Plenty of beverages flowed, too, brightly glowing and swirling in every possible colour, lighting the guests and their surroundings. Not that they needed any more colour, for their clothing was as varied as the drinks. Their fashion sense was goofy and downright alien to me.

'Noor,' I said, looking down at his red sequin ensemble. 'Something tells me you'll fit right in here.'

'Yeah, I see what you mean,' he replied, noticing some of the kookier outfits.

There were women with dresses that dragged far behind them on the ground, creating a tripping hazard; men with headdresses made of live animals, which calmly slept on their heads despite being petted by passers-by; and probably most ridiculous of all were those who wore hardly anything at all, aside from bright, thinly sheared, practically see-through garments. Trinkets, pins and sparkling jewellery. Badges and broaches, bubbles and baubles. Did they dress strangely purely for the sake of it?

I recognised a few familiar faces throughout the crowd, enemies one and all. It seemed as though everyone from Seron who had tormented us at some point was here.

Kalek was impossible to miss, being so large. He was wearing a ridiculous turquoise suit too tight for his frame and was filling a plate in front of one of the banquet tables, scoffing it down quicker than he could fill it.

My very first torturer, Verre, was by the bar, wearing a silky black dress and downing her entire drink in one go. Were my eyes deceiving me, or did she look younger?

Mycol was near them; he was turned away from the crowd, examining his drink closely. He was even bigger than before, almost comically so, his ballooned proportions even rivalling Kalek's.

A pack of younger girls wearing skimpy dresses had claimed the central area, forming a dance circle. I spotted some of Verre's old colonels amongst them, including Korin and Neva.

Caelum was sitting on one of the chairs near the balcony with a red drink in his hand. He was surrounded by a bevy of more young women, all audibly swooning and vying for a closer position.

Yet for all the attention he was receiving, he appeared wilfully oblivious to the goings on around him, instead staring at the shifting colours in the sky.

'*Oh* no, not her,' Tau said, before I saw that she was looking at Siph, Tau's former science commander. There was an awkward gaze between them before Siph decided to blend back into the crowd.

'I can stab her if it would make you happy,' Tetsu suggested. 'Over and over and over…'

Tau pointed a finger back at him. 'Shut up.'

The boys laughed, even Eno, who was never there in the first place. '*Hahaha*, who are we stabbing?'

Beyond the guests, I could see a raised platform, like a stage, and on it were two thrones, just like those I saw in my failed, dream-like brainwashing. The mostly steel grey cushioned chairs were decorated with draped purple and gold banners.

To the left of the terrace was another elevated platform. Yet more guards were stationed on it, looking down on the partygoers. Most had rifles, and I guessed those who didn't were acolytes. There were even a few mechs up there, pointing their turret arms in our direction. They were similar to the MASU I piloted on Seron, but much larger and decked out with even more weapons and armour plating.

To the right of the terrace was a long balcony, where Tuloch and the captain of the Black Dawn were having a drink together. The sheer drop over the mountainous peak's edge would naturally be fatal. We were so high up, yet there was still somehow no wind.

There were just too many faces I despised. All I wanted to do was get out of here, seeming as I couldn't hurt any of them. Even something as minor as portalling away, though, what sort of punishment would I be dealt for abandoning my duties?

As if collectively all noticing us, the crowd turned in our direction and hushed. Even the music stopped. We stared back at them in silence. Everyone's eyes were upon me.

Some randomly began to clap. The applause caught on, building until it surrounded us. Soon, every partygoer was smiling and cheering. Kalek, still with a meat-covered bone in his mouth, had put his plate down to join in. By the balcony, Verre and Tuloch clapped sarcastically. Caelum seemed to be the only one who wasn't applauding, still staring elsewhere.

Raumanu stepped forward and raised a hand for quiet. 'The new Chosen would love to meet each and every one of you tonight. But let's not overwhelm her all at once. So please, keep celebrating, and she'll be over shortly to introduce herself.'

And with that, the crowd went back to their chatter and chortles.

Raumanu faced me. 'Now, go circulate. *Socialise* with them.'

'No thanks,' I replied. 'I've never met most of these people and I already hate them.'

'Sacet,' Tau interrupted, nudging me. 'Don't you think that's a little selfish of you?' Her eyes subtly signalled to Eno. 'We're here to get along with these people.'

'Look at all that food!' Eno said excitedly, his gaze fixed on the table and not noticing what Tau was hinting at.

'*Whoa,*' Tetsu added, practically salivating. 'Is that formashroom pie?'

'*Ah,* I forgot to feed you,' Raumanu said. 'None of you have eaten since stasis, have you?' He gestured to the copious amounts of colourful and fragrant food. 'By all means.'

Eno had already left as Raumanu was speaking, running towards the banquet and picking up a plate.

Tetsu rushed after him. 'Hey, wait!' He glanced back at Tau as he jogged. 'I'll bring something back for you.'

'I don't need to eat, remember?' Tau replied.

Tetsu glanced back a second time. 'That doesn't mean you can't taste though, right?'

Tau smiled and shrugged. 'I guess not. Alright, maybe a sweet dessert?'

By the banquet, Kalek smiled at the approaching boys and ruffled Eno's hair with his massive hand, before suggesting which food they should try first. It was all so bizarre.

Noor gripped his stomach. Clearly eager to join them, he turned to me. 'Are you hungry? Can I get you something?'

'No,' I lied. 'I permanently lost my appetite when I set foot on this planet.' In truth, I was starving, but I wouldn't give these people the satisfaction of thinking they somehow sustained me. I looked into his eyes and sighed. 'But you go.'

Noor thought for a moment, but wisely left me in peace instead of questioning me further. His constant attempts to look out for me were both cute and annoying.

'Please cheer up, Sacet,' Raumanu said. 'This party is for you. I'll leave you be to enjoy it. Promise me you'll mingle with the guests.'

I sneered. 'I promise I'll exchange some choice words with them.'

He smiled before shuffling away and melding with the sea of faces.

Tau brushed my shoulder. 'Shall we? I know it's hard, but I'll talk for you, if you want? I have a feeling you're going to offend more than charm.'

'She doesn't care who she offends,' I heard a voice say at my side. 'Something we have in common.' It was Iya, wearing a short pink dress. She was clenching three multicoloured drinks and offered them to us. 'You might want to drink something before you go talk to those people. They're all vacuous suck ups, hoping and waiting for the day my parents finally die.'

'Speaking of suck ups,' I said, taking a drink and sipping it. 'Come to try and live with me again?'

Iya rolled her eyes. '*Hmph*, now that you've kicked Malu out, your little club is probably too exclusive for *me*.' She turned to Tau. 'Drink?'

'Thanks,' Tau said as she took one, before eyeing me with contempt. 'Yes, that was definitely a bone-headed move by my sister here.' She then smiled at Iya. 'Should *she* really be drinking?'

Iya shrugged, looked at me and gestured over her shoulder towards the balcony. 'Well, she could always throw her glass at Caelum again.'

'How do you know about that?' I asked. 'You didn't come in with us.'

Her grin widened. 'Because gossip about *you* travels quickly. The empire is *obsessed* with you right now.'

'Great,' I drawled as I glanced around. Although they continued their own conversations, the crowd was still eyeing my every move.

Tau shifted in closer to me so she could speak quieter. 'Sacet, you don't have to be their friend, but at least make connections? You're the most powerful person in this room right now, but not because of your abilities.'

She was right, of course. Using violence to fix all of this wasn't going to work. But talking to them seemed so much harder.

I sighed and nodded. 'Fine.' I focused on Iya again. 'Who are the most important people in this room?'

Iya raised an eyebrow. 'The other Chosen, of course? All six are here tonight.'

'Could you point them out?' Tau asked.

Iya scanned the rooftop and pointed over at the balcony. 'See that guy? The blond in the blue suit?'

The man was leaning against the balcony, shooting a glance in my direction every so often like the others. He had bright orange skin, like some of the alien civilians I had seen in public already. He was tall, thin and looked to be in his early thirties. Like Caelum, he was surrounded by guests hanging off his every word.

'That's Elion,' Iya explained, 'and he's the only cool one, so don't throw your drink at him. He was born on a harvest world, like you. He's almost nine hundred cycles old now, so a bit too old for *you* girls.'

'What?' I asked.

Tau shook her head. 'We *never* said we liked him.'

Iya folded her arms. 'Well, I *do*, so he's *mine…* when I finally get to grow up.'

Tau screwed up her face at the absurdity of the idea. 'Gross.'

'What's his power?' I asked, getting impatient. It would be good to know, in case I needed to kill him later.

'He can create any matter from nothing. Not like… *objects*. But if he wanted to make a mountain of gold or titanium, that would be easy for him. The empire became infinitely rich when he showed up.'

Iya then pointed at a dark-skinned woman on the other side of the terrace. 'See her? Lucenia, she's the one who made all the light bridges. She's from your world, one of the original inhabitants. Then we Asterians came, and she unintentionally destroyed most of Seron's atmosphere defending it. That was about six hundred cycles ago.'

'The start of the Great Gender War...' Tau added.

Iya shrugged. 'After Lucenia was brought here, yes.'

The woman had curly, black hair and wore a sparkling gold dress, hanging from her exposed shoulders by two thin strings. Like Caelum, she was surrounded by fans, potential male suitors, each one trying to be the first to strike up a conversation with her. But unlike Caelum, who ignored his admirers, Lucenia revelled in their devotion.

'And over there, that's Andriel,' Iya continued, now pointing at another woman in the far corner.

Andriel had been staring at us intently from her reclined position on a couch since we arrived, occasionally sipping and swirling her orange drink. She appeared to be in her forties perhaps, but she clearly tried to look younger than she was. Long scarlet-red hair flowed passed her shoulders, and she had several sea-blue items of jewellery. Like most of the women here, she wore an elegant dress, silver with blue lines.

'She was the first Chosen born on a harvest world,' Iya continued. 'She's around fourteen hundred and our most powerful psychic. She can read and control almost every mind on Aster thanks to our INCs.'

As we spoke about her, she got up and meandered to the nearest bar to order a drink.

'Welcome, friends!' I heard a raspy, amplified voice yell. 'Tonight is a *very* special night.'

The emperor and empress had appeared on their thrones, somehow from thin air. I did not even sense them enter the party. The crowd and music faded into silence.

'*Oh* crap,' Iya said, hiding behind Tau. 'Don't let them see me.'

'Tonight, you should all congratulate yourselves,' the emperor said, attempting to smile at the quietening crowd. 'All of *you* made this possible. You have brought home a new Chosen, who will no doubt grow in power with every passing day. So do it, congratulate yourselves!'

The crowd applauded and gathered closer to the thrones.

The empress raised a solitary finger in the air. 'But, do not forget, tonight is not *just* about you, it's about *her*. Where is Sacet?'

The crowd parted and looked back at me.

'*Ah*, there you are,' the emperor said. 'Approach us.'

I didn't want to, but what choice did I have? I walked through the dance floor towards them, my footsteps now making the only noise. The boys put down their food and joined the crowd for a better view. I got closer and closer, stopping in front of the thrones.

The emperor narrowed his gaze through thin slits. 'Sacet, you have been threatened with the exile and *death* of all those you care about. You are powerful, but those ties are the *only* reason you do not run or fight back. I know… what you're *really* thinking.' He leant closer and his smile intensified. 'You want to *kill* us, don't you? Tell me the truth.'

Was this some kind of joke? I kept staring at him, but used my second perception to scan those around me. Everyone was still and silent, unhelpful. Was the emperor expecting me to bend down and kiss his feet? Fat chance of that. He was inspecting me closely, waiting for my answer.

I quietly looked down. 'I know what I'm *supposed* to say. That I would *never* hurt you, or even think about it.' I locked onto his eyes. 'But you are correct; I *want* to kill you.'

The audience gasped at my audacity, then watched for the emperor's reaction intently.

He clasped his hands together in front of him and gently rubbed the top of his hands with his fingers. 'And *how* would you do it? If you had *no* family and friends holding you back, how would you do away with us?'

My perception scanned the other Chosen. Caelum had parted the women around him to watch. Elion, Raumanu and Lucenia all eagerly awaited my answer, too. Andriel shared the emperor's intrigued expression and sipped her drink.

I gave a very faint smile. 'I'd slice your body up and teleport the pieces to different stars, hoping that what's left of your soul was too stretched and mangled to be brought back to life.'

An awkward silence filled the air. I continued to stare, refusing to look away. The emperor's smile faded, but then he burst out in raucous hollering. At first, I thought he was choking, until the party guests joined in with what I now realised was laughter.

The empress smirked. 'She is a spirited one, isn't she?'

He shook his finger at me. 'Very few people are *honest* when they come here against their will. You can hate us… for now. But *one* day, we will be your masters like we are to *all* others.'

He then looked at the crowd. 'Tomorrow, the Chosen shall perform the Unification ceremony, and I have a feeling that with Sacet joining them, we will finally see the light of the Chosen path. All of you, celebrate this night like the *grand* occasion it is. Bring this girl whatever she wants.'

As the audience cheered, two guards came up beside the emperor and empress, held onto their wrists and teleported the rulers away in a puff of smoke, similar to how my mother used to do it. Various members of the crowd approached, offering drinks and patting me on the back.

Unification ceremony?

Fourteen: Party Foul

Practically every guest at the party surrounded her with fake smiles. I was quickly shoved aside to make room for more bootlickers. They swamped the new Chosen, spilling what was left of my drink on the ground.

Sacet's expression further soured from the numerous unwanted advances. Fantastic. And I felt like I was really making some headway with them this time. Whatever, I'd give them some space for now, and just before Sacet blew a forehead vein, I'd swoop back in with some more drinks to rescue her from them.

I meandered back to the bar as the music returned with its thumping beat and distorted synth. I was quickly greeted by the same buxom, pink-skinned bartender who had served me earlier.

'*Oh*, back so soon, Princess? What'll it be?'

'I'm not a Princess anymore,' I said, before pointing at some glowing bottles below the bar. 'Another three Opuntian Tornados.'

As she turned away to fetch my order, I felt two other partygoers brush against me on either side. I glanced at them and groaned. Korin and Neva. Both leered at me, almost lecherously so.

'So, you *did* end up coming after all, Iya?' Neva began. 'Korin didn't think you'd show up. I hope you haven't forgotten about our little discussion?'

Korin grasped my wrist on the bar and held it in place. 'I think she was hiding from us.'

I couldn't let them know the truth, that I had spent all my time back on Aster in the streets like a commoner, unable to secure lodgings for myself. But that also, yes, I was hiding from them.

I took a deep breath and stared forward. 'I didn't forget, and I *wasn't* hiding.'

'Of *course* you weren't,' Neva replied, now turning her back to the bar and nodding towards the crowd around Sacet. 'You've been too busy cosying up to your new friends, right?'

I glanced back and saw exactly what I had anticipated. While Tau was doing her best impression of a spineless socialite, trying to make friends by handing out smiles and compliments like they were going out of fashion, Sacet looked like she was about to punch and strangle her way out of the encirclement.

Tetsu had returned to them with two plates of food, one of which he offered to Tau, who gladly accepted it. Noor attempted the same with Sacet, but she was too distracted to even acknowledge him.

Korin produced a small device and placed it on the bar in front of me. A tiny hologram shot upwards from it, showing a familiar visual. It was me sitting on a couch across from Sacet and Tau. She pressed a button to shut it again and smirked. 'You think we wouldn't find out?'

I shrugged. 'So? What of it? It's *none* of your business.'

As the bartender returned with my drinks, Korin whipped my wrist around so that the three of us were facing Sacet and Tau. Neva placed an arm around me, probably pretending like the three of us were friends to the casual observer.

She leant in closer to whisper. 'You *are* my business, remember? *Poor* baby, you should have *asked* if you needed a place to stay. Tonight, you're coming home with me. I have a penthouse for you to vigorously clean.'

I shook my head. 'I'm *not* doing that.'

Korin looked up at the aurora. 'A shame. I wonder where Iya will be sent next for banishment?'

Neva also looked up in fake thought. '*Hmm*, maybe Orturid? You know, the endless jungle planet where everything is out to kill you? Or that frozen one, Salix. And there's also Cladonia or Calamus…'

I gritted my teeth. 'Alright, enough! Leave me alone now, I want to enjoy my last night.'

They exchanged a nod before they released me.

Neva gestured to the drinks on the bar. 'By all means, little servitor, go play with your friends a *bit* longer.'

I didn't dally, I took the drinks and made for the party's centre.

'And stay where I can see you, young lady,' Neva added loudly, drawing the confused gazes of others and amplifying my embarrassment.

I parted my way through the crowd, careful not to spill the drinks, and eventually reached the inner circle. A tall man was trying to engage Sacet with boasts of his wealth and power. He wore a short skirt and a shiny hat shaped like a star. But Sacet's arms were tightly folded, and her eyebrows were angled like a pouty child.

I cleared my throat to interrupt before passing her a drink. 'Sacet, you asked me to show you that *thing* when it was ready?'

I handed the second drink to a suspicious, but grateful, Tau.

Sacet glared, but her eyes widened when she eventually understood. '*Ah*, yes. I did want to see that… *thing*. You're right.'

As I led her away, a slightly perturbed Tau glanced around at the vexed sycophants, and then focused on the man. '*Umm*, sorry, she'll be right back. So… you were saying your ancestors built this place? That's fascinating…'

Sacet and I reached the banquet tables on the side of the party, where her boyfriend and brother were both horking down various sweetmeats. We went behind the table, circling one of the mountains of fruit, partially hiding us from view.

'I never thought I'd say this,' she began, 'but thanks, Iya.'

Now that we were this close to the food, my stomach rumbled. I realised that I hadn't eaten since I was in space.

'It's fine,' I said, picking up a round, yellow fruit and biting into it. Great, you've got her cornered, and she even *thanked* you. What next? I gestured to the crowd. 'So, being a Chosen… how's that working out?'

She sighed and grabbed her head. 'Awful. My whole planet was murdered, but I'm told I should be happy about it. I wish this never happened to me, that I were normal. I wish… I was still living in a cave with Eno, back when things were simple.'

This whole time I had known her, I was angry at her for having all this undeserved power and adulation, but she didn't even *want* it. Something we had in common.

I inspected the fruit. 'A normal life would be nice. I guess I'd want to be a farmer… or something. You know, something in nature?'

She shrugged. 'You didn't want to take over this place one day? I thought you'd be all about the power.'

I glanced around at all the party guests eyeing us, jealous that I had her all to myself. 'And spend any more time with *these* people? No thanks.'

Sacet also picked up a piece of the same fruit and took a bite. 'Well then, why don't you?'

'Don't I what?'

She tapped her fruit onto mine. 'Be a farmer?'

I glanced over my shoulder to the bar at a smirking Korin and Neva. 'I can't, I'm stuck here like you. Stuck wherever they put me.'

Sacet and I both looked down, briefly contemplating our positions. The rest of the guests were hovering closer and closer to our corner, but I wasn't done with her yet.

I elbowed Sacet and smiled. 'Hey, that was amazing when you told my father how you'd kill him. I had chills.'

She raised an eyebrow. 'Not as good as *actually* killing him, though?'

I took a swig of my drink and washed down the fruit. 'True, but you got to *savour* the humiliation. It was over *too* quick when I did it.'

She gestured to her boyfriend and brother, who had gleefully started a food fight with Kalek. 'Speaking of humiliation.'

They had taken cover on opposite sides of a long table and were hurling food scraps at one another. I knew for a fact that Kalek could throw a lot harder than he was, but had obviously decided to play along. He was difficult for the boys to miss, being so large, and so already had large creamy dessert stains on his suit.

The commotion was grabbing most of the room's attention. A food fight would be considered the height of inappropriateness under normal circumstances, but no one was intervening. It reminded me of when I tried doing the same with my siblings during mealtimes, but whenever we attempted to have actual fun, it was always shut down by the staff.

Sacet and I giggled together and enjoyed the show for a moment. Her smile gave me an idea. I reached forward and balled up some colourful slop, before placing it in her free hand. She looked between it and me, bewildered.

I gestured to the well-dressed crowd and grinned back at her. 'This is *your* party, remember? Enjoy it.'

I quickly balled up another gooey morsel before piffing it randomly into the crowd. My projectile splattered onto one of the more well-dressed guests. The bright-red stain covered what I assumed was a ludicrously convoluted and expensive getup, but the horrified look on the man's face was priceless.

'Which of you nouveau trash did this?' he shouted. 'I'll have your soul crushed! Do you have *any* idea what went into making this ensemble?'

I ducked down and cackled into the tablecloth.

Sacet guffawed, something I didn't think I had ever seen her do before. She laughed so much that she had to lean on the table for support. When she eventually calmed herself, she had a determined look on her face. She downed her drink in one go and threw her food, too. Her sticky slop hit another well-dressed guest harmlessly in the face, ruining her hair for the night.

While most of the revolted guests backed away, some, upon seeing Sacet enjoying the chaos, decided to join in like the posers they were, throwing chunks of food about and their drinks in each other's faces.

An unexpected food ball burst over my cheek. I reeled in surprise and saw that Sacet was the culprit.

She grinned and scooped up some more. 'That's payback!'

'*Oh* yeah?'

We both took cover tableside. I noticed a giant, multitiered cake next to her, so I popped up, brought my fingers up to my eyes around the cake, and telepathically lifted the bulk of it in the air above her. I let it all go and the dessert spluttered over her, completely covering her in goop.

Many of the guests looked over and gasped, as if I had gone too far. Even the music stopped.

After a few moments of frozen shock, Sacet laughed out loud again and pointed at me. 'I'll get you for that!'

The food fighters continued as if nothing had happened.

I grinned back at her malevolently. 'Well? Come on then, cheater!'

As I ducked back in cover again, I took a moment to appreciate the anarchy unfolding around us. The crowd smiled; our energy was infectious. Even the man I had hit grabbed a nearby morsel and flung it. It was as if something in them snapped, and they weren't so stuck up anymore.

I noticed Lucenia being escorted out by a bevy of men shielding her. She cowered away from the food projectiles, disgusted. Elion, too, was making for an exit, accompanied by his own entourage. Unfortunate, I was hoping to get in his good graces tonight as well.

Raum was in the centre of the room, completely untouched. Stray food and drinks were disintegrating when they got close to him. Although he wasn't joining in, he wasn't trying to stop it either. He instead just grinned with mild amusement. Caelum remained in his seat near the balcony, unperturbed.

Sitting in one of the many lounge areas in the far corner of the room was Andriel. She was staring directly at me with a half-smile, also amused. No one dared to throw food at *her*. Her stare lingered on me, so I looked away.

By the bar, even Korin and Neva were grabbing bottles, shaking them up, and spraying them on whoever was closest.

A torrent of liquid gushed down over me, so forcefully that I slid with the current along the floor before eventually screeching to a stop. A portal was closing above where I had been hiding. Sacet popped her head up from behind the next table. The liquid must have been from the drink vats under the bar. We both paused our little battle to laugh and breathe.

This was the best party I had *ever* been to.

As fun as all the food fighting and playful use of our powers had been tonight, I was dreading what was coming next. The party was starting to die down, and most of the guests were leaving.

Even if Sacet had miraculously invited me to live with them, Neva had ordered me to stay with her instead. The bright side was that I at least had a free place to stay now. But I had to serve that rich bimbo until she tired of having me around.

I begrudgingly approached Neva and Korin over by the lounge, stopped in front of them and sighed. 'Alright, I'm ready to go, I guess.'

They both exchanged a confused look.

'What are you talking about, *littlest* Princess?' Korin jested. 'Where would *we* possibly go with little disgraced *you?*'

'Go bother someone else,' Neva added. 'I hear Kalek is looking for a friend to cuddle up to?'

They both tilted their heads back to cackle. What were they playing at this time? Maybe pretending they didn't know what I was on about because they were worried someone would overhear us? That never seemed to worry them before. And thanks to the loud music, we could easily speak here without being overheard.

'Are you still here?' Neva said, before shooing me away.

I turned on the spot and walked away, both confused and relieved. I waited a few moments for what I assumed would be a *just kidding* comment, but nothing came.

Had they truly forgotten? But how? Then it hit me. I glanced to the far end of the lounge and saw Andriel staring at me again with the same half smile.

You're welcome.

The feminine voice echoed in my brain; it was her. But why? Why was she helping me? Andriel leant back in her seat and took another swig of her drink.

Best not to dwell on it.

I… well, thank you? But how… oh. You can hear my thoughts, of course.

You'd best catch them before they leave.

What? Catch who?

Andriel gestured to the centre of the party, where Raum had gathered Sacet and her friends in a circle. Like me, their clothes were covered in all manner of food and drink, and each looked quite proud of themselves.

I quickly gave Andriel an appreciative nod, and she nodded, too, in sync with me. I then ran over to the others and stopped when I noticed them all looking at me.

'*Uhh*, Sacet?' I began. 'Can I have a word?'

Sacet looked at Raum, who took a step back, as though giving permission. While the others waited by Raum, Sacet approached me.

'I… *ummm*… I was going to ask…'

'If I let you stay, are you going to do anything stupid?' she interrupted.

I shook my head. 'No. You won't even know I'm there.'

Sacet looked back at the others, who were all smiling in approval, Tau in particular.

Sacet focused back on me. 'You can spend the night; we'll see how it goes from there.'

I did the smallest bow possible. 'Thanks. So, you and I… we're…'

She leant forward and flicked a piece of cake off my shoulder. 'We're not friends yet, if that's what you're wondering. But we're good.'

I managed a smile and nodded.

'It's time to go, Sacet,' Raum called to us.

Sacet and I joined them. She opened a portal between us, and I could see a luxurious room through it. I grinned as one by one, we all stepped through, through to our lives of riches, fame, luxury and security. A life from which I would one day gather enough power to finally have my vengeance on my despot parents.

Fifteen: Master and Disciple

The next morning

Arc Sacet penthouse

The sunrise was stunning, scattering harsh, radiant, golden beams through the polluted atmosphere. Light reflected off the many gleaming steel surfaces. The only shadows cast over the sea of shining steel were the arcs. The world was like a metallic garden, and the arcs like flowers reaching up to the sun, preparing to bloom.

I pulled myself out of the pool and sat on the edge, before reaching for my towel. I heard a noise coming from inside; was it another servant trying to check up on me? Or maybe it was one of the many guards they had stationed around us at all times since the attack?

Sacet emerged from the sliding doorway, rubbing her darkened eyes. 'Morning.' She wore a far simpler, mismatched and dishevelled civilian outfit than last night's fancier dress.

I swished my dangling feet in the water. 'Morning, you look terrible. Didn't get much sleep?'

'No.' She came over and sat in a nearby pool chair. 'I couldn't turn my perception off. It was scanning the city below all night. There's just *so* many people.'

As she spoke, I ignited my aura and waved some of my rejuvenating energy towards her. The dark bags under her eyes faded.

'Thanks,' she replied, leaning back and groaning in relief. 'That feels better. How was your sleep?'

'I don't have to sleep anymore,' I explained. 'Or breathe… or eat, or drink. I regenerate everything my body needs, remember?'

'Right, of course.' She stood and approached the balcony to overlook the unnatural yet gorgeous view.

'Something on your mind?' I inquired.

She leant on the balcony's edge. 'It's this ceremony thing today. Whenever my enemies have something planned for me, it's never good.'

I shook my head and hopped out of the pool fully. 'You've *got* to stop calling them enemies.'

'You'll be there today, right?' she said while glancing back, ignoring me.

I nodded as I dried myself off. 'They're sending the rest of us to this Academy first for an induction. But after that, I promise we'll *all* be there.' I wandered over and stood beside her. 'Try to be positive about it, whatever it turns out to be.'

She gruffly scoffed.

'Are you still mad at us?' I continued, thinking this was as good a time as any to bring it up. 'At me?'

Sacet sighed and looked down. 'No. If I can let Iya sleep in my home, then I suppose I have no reason to be angry at the rest of you.'

I put my arm around her shoulders. 'That's good, because even if I *am* brainwashed, I still care about my sister.'

Sacet hugged me back and smiled. 'Thanks… and I never doubted that, but…' Before she could elaborate further, Sacet peered over the balcony again, as if focusing on something.

I looked over, too. Caelum was floating outside the tower, only a few floors below us and rising. We backed away as he arrived at our level. He hovered there with folded arms, expressionless.

I felt a shiver down my spine. Ever since our mother had died, I found the man terrifying. Not because of his power, but his sheer indifference to us. How could anyone be so cold, so callous to their own children?

'Morning, Father,' Sacet said with a hint of venom. 'Where's the other old man?'

His stare was locked with hers. He landed in front of us and gestured to the door. 'It's time for your little friends to leave. Now.'

Not wishing to anger him, I hastily snatched my clothes up and made for the door. 'I'll go gather them up.'

A line of servants had appeared by the sliding door with additional towels, ready to guide me to the others.

'We're not taking the light bridge?' Sacet asked her father.

His eyes narrowed. 'You and I are going the old-fashioned way.' He grabbed her torso with both hands before she could respond. The two of them rocketed into the sky and out of sight.

Our journey to Arc Academy sped us over the endless steel plane through the L line. Like last time, Tetsu, Noor, Eno and I were all holding hands in a chain, with Eno in the middle. Additionally, Iya and several guards were also at the end of that chain.

The particularly nervous Eno had sweaty palms, but I didn't blame him. The boys and I were probably just as scared; we were just putting on braver faces, for Eno's sake.

Each switching gate launched us in a new direction. Even so, our surprisingly gentle ride never resulted in a collision. We narrowly avoided countless people zipping past in the other direction; I don't think I could ever get used to something so anxiety-inducing.

At this lower altitude, the sun was struggling to pierce through the haze of pollution. Not far below, tens of thousands of flying vehicles zipped through the canyon-sized streets and over the rooftops, somehow respecting the boundaries of their routes.

My INC would pop up with messages about our path every so often. The little map, which I assumed the others could see, too, showed exactly where we were going and what turns were coming up. And as we flew over various landmarks, it would label them for us so that we knew what each building was called, or its purpose. Apartment complexes and factories were common, followed by stadiums and shopping districts.

Our destination loomed in the distance. Arc Academy was a colossal eight-sided pyramid that not only towered above, but its base was equally as thick. Unlike the rest of the steel world around it, most of its surfaces gleamed like bright silver glass. It was like a giant buried crystal, with its top sticking out of the ground. Like other arcs, its peak scraped the clouds. No matter what angle we saw it from, the sun's glare would reflect off the shiny construction into our eyes, yet somehow we were not blinded.

As we eventually closed in and saw more details, we noticed the walls were etched with triangles and octagons in a lattice-like formation, each one a clear window into the densely-packed structure within.

Our L line streaked through the pyramid's side, carrying us through many shiny, thick layers into the arc's architecturally impressive heart, comprised of millions of angled beams, slanted windows, and triangular surfaces, often converging into octagonal focal points.

A myriad of murmuring, uniformed people traversed the multileveled walkways and corridors. They were the students and staff of the Academy, and as far as I was aware, each one of them was an acolyte. The arc's interior was a cornucopia of colour, clever design, and purpose. Apartments and food courts, lecture theatres and classrooms; this place had it all. Like the city outside, it too had canyon-like dividers between the larger partitions that acted as streets and allowed us to peer down into the depths below. Level upon level upon level. It left me wondering: what sort of person was at the top?

The L line eventually came to a stop, dropping us at a cavernous intersection of several other lines, another octagonal focal point. All but Iya and the guards in our group were continually gasping in awe, until we were interrupted by hundreds of additional L line student passengers arriving on the platform and shoving us aside to get to their classes.

I was amazed by the multitude of people shifting seamlessly from room to room, each with their own schedules. Almost every acolyte on the planet, from the *entire empire*, trained here.

I didn't envy them, or my friends for that matter. Although I'm sure their training would make them more capable, their future careers would be to enforce the power of the empire. I couldn't imagine Eno becoming an Overwatch agent, for example. To what extent would this place change them, I also wondered?

As for me, it was here that I would be trained as a disciple, whatever *that* entailed. I didn't know what to expect from my training. What mattered most to me was that I became a force for good in this universe.

The guards instructed us to split off, so I farewelled my friends with hugs and a wave. There was a nervous wobble in my steps as I followed my assigned guards along the labyrinthine hallways and up the rapid elevators.

We eventually stopped in front of a set of closed grand double doors, emblazoned with a symbol of swirling fire, painted equal parts cyan and green.

My anxiety stilled. Something about this door had put me at ease, my entire body tingled with a kind of serenity.

The two guards stood to the sides and gestured at the doors. 'Only disciples can enter,' one explained.

Three teen students brushed past me from behind and stood in front of the doors. They activated tiny, flaming auras, two cyan like mine and the other green. The doors groaned and, as if detecting their presence, slowly opened to admit them.

Like how an opening curtain allows the morning sun to transform a dark room, so too was I as an overwhelming, tingling warmth spilled through the doorway.

Inside was an enormous, circular lecture hall with long, stone seats in tall rows surrounding the centre. All of the chamber's lights were off, bar one incredibly bright, tempestuously roaring cyan flame in the centre, observed by a silent audience.

There was another groan as the doors began to close, so I stepped forward and summoned my aura, so strongly that my flames licked the ceiling. The heavy doors burst open again and slammed into the walls on the other side. A loud, metallic bang rang, drawing the attention of all inside.

My eyes widened in embarrassment. Most stared in my direction before turning back to the central bonfire, but some pointed and whispered to each other, my hushed name passing around them. I raised my hands in apology and slowly walked in.

Most of the long stone seats appeared full; hundreds watched the flame spin and dance. I found an empty seat next to a mesmerised young boy, before realising that most in the audience were children and teens. They were all completely engaged by the flame, and when I sat and gave it my full attention, I understood why.

At the base of the flames was a petite woman, probably smaller than I was. The source of the three-storey high flame sat cross-legged, meditating in silence. She was bald, but quite young looking, not much older than I was. She wore plain white robes, functional and humble.

I could feel wave after wave of healing energy wash over me, even from this distance near the back. It was no wonder why everyone was so captivated, it was like we were being bombarded by a soothing drug.

I never knew an aura could be so powerful; if I had *that* kind of power, I could help so many more people. The aura was so dense that at times she was difficult to see.

The fire abruptly ceased, leaving us in darkness momentarily before a swirling hologram of a planetary solar system faded in to take its place. And still sitting there on the centre dais was the woman, her eyes now aflutter as they adjusted. She slowly stood without using her hands before pacing around the dais, inspecting us with purpose.

'I want to start by telling you a *very* old story,' she finally uttered, her voice echoing throughout the hall, 'one that I have told many times. There once was a young girl, born with the power to manipulate the life force in others. Elysia was… the first of her kind. The *first* disciple of the Empyrean.'

Elysia? *The* Elysia? The first queen of the Female Dominion, and the kind healer I had based all my principles, my entire life on?

'She could *pluck* your soul from the afterlife as easily as pulling a loose thread.' She motioned with her fingers, acting it out. 'And just as quickly rip it out again, sending it back to its source.'

As she spoke, the large planetary hologram zoomed in on a brownish planet. Ethereal images of a grey city overlapped our surroundings. I assumed this was Aster, but it seemed far less dense and built up. The skies were far clearer, too, yellow in hue instead of the harsh orange I had become accustomed to.

'At that time, over two and a half thousand cycles ago, it was an empire at war. But with *her* arrival, a new age had begun. Our greatest warriors could fight with reckless abandon, without the fear of long death. And they *worshipped* the girl, almost as much as the kings and queens of old.'

The hologram morphed repeatedly with her words, first showing an image of a teenage girl kneeling in a battlefield, surrounded by the dead. She wasn't alone; hundreds of robed figures bowed at her feet as she ignited her healing aura. The girl looked like the woman in front of me. *She* was Elysia.

'Even so, the march of war did continue, and as the violence grew, so did the empire.'

Now the hologram showed warriors donned in impossibly heavy armour battling against necrolisks and other hideous alien monstrosities. Then, it quickly changed again to a close-up of a handsome man and a beautiful young woman.

'With her unique healing abilities, the young girl never aged, so the fair and just rulers of the time decreed that she would *share* her eternal life with them also.'

The rulers of the time? She meant Avarut and Suralia? They were once so gorgeous, I could hardly believe it.

Elysia raised her hands to the sides in a dramatic pose. 'And so together they did live and rule for millennia, all the while more disciples were born. These disciples dutifully helped the girl, who was no longer young, to bear her burdens by sharing their everlasting life, thus forever securing the glorious future of an indivisible Aster and its immortal empire.'

She paused for effect, entrancing us all. The holograms slowly faded. Elysia grinned. 'If you couldn't tell, I was speaking in the third person.' This elicited politely subdued laughter throughout.

She relaxed her body language from stern to casual. 'I love giving that speech.' She wandered in a circle and locked eyes with numerous students, as though trying to address each and every one of us. 'Welcome, one and all, students of the Empyrean. My word, there sure are a *lot* of you. I'm glad there are so *many* new disciples to help me with my burden.'

The crowd gave another short laugh. I joined in this time. I was still completely in shock, seeing my heroine in the flesh like this. And what was this Empyrean she kept talking about?

She gestured around. 'But really, you may *think* there's a lot of us, but compared to the *trillions* of Asterians, we disciples are but a *tiny* fraction. And then only ten percent of you will remain as elevated disciples, meaning their healing touch will always be in great demand.'

The hologram above her reappeared, showing a great green flame.

Elysia scanned the audience once more, and her gaze stopped on me. She paused before smiling. Did she know who I was?

She looked back up at the flame and sighed. 'The rest of you will unfortunately choose another path. To become a fallen disciple is easy, but I *urge* you all to put up with the pain, to serve others and not yourself. For that is the simple choice that leads us down one of these two paths. Do we focus on selfless duty?' She gestured up to the green flame. 'Or our duty to ourselves?'

Her aura reignited, sending a colossal spire of cyan flames upwards. 'The greatness of your power is a reflection of how pure you are in this choice.' She flung her flames around the green hologram, as if battling it. 'In this sometimes worrisome universe, one would be forgiven for falling into despair and solipsism. But while there is still a chance to lead you to a more *righteous* purpose, *I...* will gladly be your guide.'

The green hologram was shut down, leaving only Elysia's aura to dominate the room's centre.

I had never been more inspired, more affirmed in my life choices. I knew I had done the right thing by helping others and by avoiding violence and anger wherever possible. I couldn't help but smile with glee as I bathed in Elysia's charismatic light.

The guards ushered me through yet another set of ornate double doors before waiting out in the hall again. Headmaster Elysia's office at the peak of Arc Academy was almost as cavernous as the lecture hall we had our class in earlier. It, too, was pyramid-shaped. All eight enormous triangular windows presented the sky, each altering the orange to a different hue of the rainbow.

The spacious office was lavishly furnished, as I had come to expect of all arcs. There was a sunken lounge in the centre, shaped like a flame. Beyond that was a golden desk even bigger than the throne I used to sit on, so large and high that two sets of staircases on either side were required to climb and sit at it.

That's where Elysia was, sitting on a throne above all and interacting with a float screen. She noticed me and looked up from it. 'Ah, Tau, I've been expecting you.'

I wandered down a gentle decline into the lounge. 'Y-you have?'

She stood and went around the back of her desk. 'Yes, please sit.' She descended the stairs and joined me in the lounge. 'It's great to finally meet you.' Noticing my hesitation, she gestured to the many comfortable seats surrounding us. I chose one and we sat together.

'I-I-I'm sorry,' I began, 'I'm actually a little star-struck. You're… you're my *hero*. *Everything* I did on Seron, I asked myself if that's what the first queen would have done.'

She tilted her head and smiled. '*Aww*, thank you, Tau. I'm honoured.'

I compulsively stood again, unable to contain my excitement. 'My friends didn't think you even existed, but I knew you had to be real. I mean, the stories exist for a reason!'

She slowly nodded. 'I did hear about how… your people glorified me in the cycles after I left. But… to be honest, I went to Seron back then as more of an… exotic holiday.'

My wobbling legs crumpled, and I sat again. 'What?'

'Don't get me wrong, my teams and I resurrected countless millions; there was a *lot* of work to do after we had practically genocided their people. But afterwards, Overwatch asked me to act as a queen temporarily, so I saw it as a way to sightsee that world for a bit. I played a role, nothing more.'

I shook my head. 'No, d-don't dismiss what you did. You still healed and helped people, right? You might not have thought it important, but… it shaped my life, and I can never thank you enough for that.'

She nodded in appreciation. 'You're very welcome. *Oh,* how rude of me.' She pointed to a short table nearby, which had compartments underneath with brightly covered drinks inside. 'Can I offer you a beverage?'

'Um, no, that's okay,' I continued, before sitting up straight. 'Elysia, Ma'am, I have to ask, why am I here today? Out of *all* your new students, why did you want to meet *me?*'

She relaxed back in her seat. 'Well, for one, you and your sister are the talk of the empire. And *you,* raised as a soldier in war, yet somehow managing to remain an elevated disciple? *Beyond* impressive.'

I took a deep breath and leant forward. 'Actually, my path *did* falter, Ma'am. I wasn't always faithful to… to your ideals, like you wanted.'

The headmaster gave a knowing smile. 'I'm aware. I've seen the reports… and some less-than-charitable footage you'd probably prefer the whole empire hadn't watched, voyeuristic beast that it is. But what's *important* is that shortly after, you regained your faith where most would have fallen.'

I blushed. 'It was… a really hard time. I *couldn't* have done it without my friends.'

She giggled. 'You're *too* modest, you're an extremely skilled healer. I've actually had your aura measured.'

I cocked an eyebrow. 'Measured?'

She nodded again. 'Yes, aside from me, you have the *purest,* most *potent* aura of any elevated disciple in the empire.'

Both surprise and relief washed over me. 'Well, that's… incredible. I don't even… Ma'am, it means so much to me to hear that.' I gave a long, drawn-out sigh. 'It's hard to feel pure after… what they did to Seron. I feel so bad—'

'An absolute tragedy,' Elysia interrupted, reaching out and grabbing my hand. It was surprisingly cold. 'My teams are working nonstop to bring them all back.'

I dipped my head in thanks. 'Thank you. I can't get the scale of it out of my head. And I've been trying my best to fit into this new life, but I've been worried about Sacet and… I guess you're going to tell me not to worry, that it's all going to be fine?'

Her smile disappeared and her eyes wandered. She let go of me, stood and wandered to the centre of the lounge. 'About that, there is *one* more reason I asked you here, call it an ulterior motive. If I tell you something in confidence, can you keep it a secret?'

I clenched the edge of the couch. 'I want to say yes, but… it depends on whether keeping that secret would endanger my loved ones.'

She closed her eyes and faced away. 'Tau… Sacet, as well as you and all your friends… everyone you've ever cared about are… are…'

I waited for her to finish, but she leaned forward in silence instead. 'Ma'am?' I stood and circled around her. She had a twisted expression, as though in great pain. I grabbed her just as she was about to collapse. 'Headmaster! Ma'am, are you alright?'

I activated my aura instinctively to heal her, but I couldn't feel whatever pain she was experiencing; my power gave her no relief.

After a few deep breaths, she eventually regained her composure and stood again. 'I… I'm sorry, Tau. I can't. Please, forgive me.'

'I don't understand. Were you feeling pain? How is that possible?'

She raised a hand to stop me. 'It's… not your concern. Some burdens cannot be shared, and evidently neither can some truths.' She winced again before turning away.

'What truth?' I said back. 'Are my friends in danger?'

Elysia spun and went back to smiling. 'You and your friends… will be fine. It was lovely meeting you, but unfortunately, it's time for my daily meditation. Now, remember to stay on the elevated path. I look forward to seeing what you can do in our classes.' She then gestured to the door. 'I trust you can find your way out?'

I begrudgingly bowed. 'Alright, Ma'am. Please take care of yourself.' I meandered back to the doors, looking back at her every so often.

She, meanwhile, practically floated up the steps to her golden desk. As she sat on her throne, she caught my gaze from afar. 'Tau, promise me one thing,' she called.

I paused. 'Y-yes, Ma'am?'

'That when the time comes, you'll embrace the unknown.'

'The unknown?'

Her smile faded again. 'You'll know it when you see it.'

I nodded, but didn't understand. 'I… uhhh, I will, Ma'am,' I answered, before turning and leaving.

Sixteen: The Chosen Path

Inside Arc Unity

This arc seemed more for show than function. It was the tallest I had seen so far. From outside, it looked like a red needle piercing the sky. With an already thin bottom, it got progressively thinner as it rose.

Although Caelum had flown me here, a much longer distance than the other arcs had been, Raumanu was now the one at my side wherever we went. I had spent most of the day waiting around for them to set up this silly ceremony, and frankly, I was keen to get it over with.

Raumanu and I were walking down the hundreds of rows of pews either side of us. Filling the seats were thousands of civilians, each dressed in the same white, ceremonial outfit. They all muttered as I passed.

Like Arc Royal, this arc's interior was covered in carvings, paintings and tapestries. It all had a red motif to it, as though the history of the Asterian people was written in blood.

The afternoon sun poured in through the enormous stained-glass windows, and a large assemblage of candelabras was interspersed along the pews' edges.

The view above was amazing. The shaft of the tower was almost completely hollow to the top. As my neck craned up, all I could see was floor upon floor of neon red lighting, and finally, at the very top of the almost infinitely tall tower, was a final red flare, as blinding as the sun.

Outside the arc, my perception sensed millions of people had been permitted access to the city's rooftops through hatches, and were filling the steel plane in all directions. They were all looking up at the arc, for on the side of the building were gigantic live projections of what was happening inside. Because of the city's flatness, no one's view was obstructed.

Raumanu and I moved slowly through the pews. When we reached the sixth row from the front, I looked to the side and noticed my friends. Tau and Eno were closest to the aisle, followed by Noor, Tetsu and Iya. Each gave me their version of support: a big smile, a hopeful thumbs up or a simple nod. All except Tau, who looked far more worried than usual. I gave them a nervous nod back and continued.

At the far end of the aisle, the pews faced a raised marble platform. The other four Chosen were already there, waiting for us. They were standing around a large circle containing a six-pointed star. The inner hexagram had a different colour at each point.

Each of the Chosen was dressed in their own personal style. Raumanu was in his usual well-dressed robes. Caelum had a black battle uniform on, the same that he wore when torturing me on Seron. Andriel wore a shiny crimson leather bodysuit, so smooth it looked as if she, too, were drenched in cascading blood. Elion wore a long, stylish coat, probably the most normal of them all, and Lucenia was in a peculiar, hooded golden robe-dress.

Above the platform was another balcony that looked down on us and the audience. The emperor and empress were there, as always on a pair of thrones. Their usual cadre of guards accompanied them. They all watched on with intrigue as Raumanu joined the others, taking his place at one point of the hex.

I trembled as I ascended the steps to the platform. It was unlike me to be so nervous, but it was the uncertainty of everything. In addition, I was told the event was being broadcast across the entire empire, that at this very moment, *trillions* were watching. Well, they were about to be very disappointed. Nothing was going to happen.

Each of us stepped onto a different coloured point of the circle. Raumanu went on orange and Caelum on blue, opposite one another. Elion went on green and Andriel on red. Lucenia went on yellow, and then finally I stepped on purple.

Raumanu turned to the audience and cleared his throat. 'Hear me, all of you, followers of the Chosen path. All of you, children of the Empyrean. All of you, acolytes of the light.'

He took a moment to pause for dramatic effect. 'Long ago, I discovered that when we Chosen focused our energies together, a bond would form between us. A psychic connection between the otherwise psychically immune. With each new Chosen, that bond grew stronger.'

He gestured to me. 'And now, with the addition of a sixth, it is our hope that the Chosen path will finally unveil its truths to us.' He turned back to them. 'Today, we Chosen shall lead you into the light, and we will all ascend together into eternal greatness and happiness! We will all want for nothing!'

Even though he had explained all of this to me earlier in the morning, a second explanation did nothing to assuage my confusion. What I *did* understand was that all this time, I thought it was only our powers that the Asterians craved. No, it was also this creed that compelled them to create harvest worlds, to commit mass atrocities, all in the hopes that they would «ascend». This made me feel even worse about the whole thing; all of these brainwashed idiots torturing people en masse for something that isn't even real.

We Chosen jointly looked up to the emperor and empress, awaiting their permission to begin.

'Commence the ritual!' the emperor yelled.

I expected the audience to cheer, but they remained almost perfectly silent, every one of them on the edge of their seats.

The five others faced the centre of the circle and brought up their arms, pointing them at the person opposite.

'Close your eyes and clear your mind of all thought,' Raumanu instructed.

I rolled my eyes, knowing that was impossible. I raised my hands like the others and closed my eyes as instructed. How exactly do I clear my mind of thought if my second perception can't be turned off?

Whatever this Chosen path was, I felt dirty for helping them attempt it. But I kept reminding myself of what would happen if I didn't help them, especially now. Would Eno be executed on the spot?

'Sacet, concentrate! Stop thinking,' I heard Raumanu yell.

How did he know? Whatever, fine. Nothing. Nothing. Nothing.

My chest felt unpleasantly warm, like I had churning heartburn deep inside. The warmth grew and spread throughout, reaching my limbs and sneaking up my neck.

Nothing. Nothing. Maybe something *would* happen? What if it was painful? No, stop thinking. Nothing. Nothing. The heat expanded, rising through my neck and into my brain. It felt like my body had been submerged in warm liquid.

Suddenly, my mind was transported. My eyes were closed, and yet I could see flashing images, blurry at first before slowly coming into focus.

There were tens of thousands of people, all filling an open amphitheatre under a beautiful, clear yellow Asterian sky. They all recognised my glory, Raumanu, destroyer of planets, conqueror of species. Wait, no, I was Sacet, what was happening to me? This was a memory, but not my own.

My emperor and empress waved to me from their thrones above. Although not acolytes, they were admired by all. Suralia was the most beautiful woman I had ever seen; her cyclic age reductions had retained her youth. I regret not making her mine when I had the chance.

I raised my hands and the crowd waited with bated breath. 'Another planet, destroyed,' I yelled, my strong voice amplified for the masses. 'Another species… assimilated for the glory of the empire!'

The crowd exploded in praise, shouting my name again and again. My vision went white, another feeling of warmth washed over me, and the crowd faded in place of another.

Thousands of my fur-clothed tribesmen bowed before me, their god-king, Caelum'inat, as I sat in my throne made from the bones of my enemies. My city, made of stone, brick and mortar, had stood for thousands of yarnus in the grey desolation, never to fall, never to be taken from me.

My scantily dressed wives brought horns of mead for me to quench my thirst after the battle, not that I needed them; I just enjoyed the taste.

In the past, every enemy king had been nothing compared to my indestructible might. And every enemy queen had bowed before their new god, lest they be cleaved in two. They used to bring tributes, the heads of their slain husbands, which they would place upon my skull altar. Once they had given themselves over to me, their true king, only *then* did I spare their peoples' lives.

That was long ago, before I had conquered all the known lands. It was before the sky people had come. Wave after wave of their grey-clad, metal-armoured ilk had come to challenge us, but each time I had crushed and ripped them apart like all the other toys at my disposal. Their weapons and tools were impressive; my subjects had still not figured out how they worked, but none ever came close to hurting me. If only I could find their lands, no doubt hidden somewhere in the clouds, then I could lay waste to their sky huts.

There was unrest in the courtyard amongst the rabble. I exited onto my palace balcony and looked up. The clouds in the red sky were parting with a faint rumble. They had come once more.

Another suspiciously smooth, grey metal container descended into my city, shooting fire every which way and slowing to gently land in the courtyard. My cowardly subjects scarpered; I'd have to administer a bone-crunching lesson to them later. But for now, what singular sky person dared to think they could enter my personal domain like this? Who could possibly be so bold, so fearless?

A door slid open, and a thin, bearded man emerged, smiling. He wore the oddest of animal pelts, as the sky people seemed to do – grey robes with a green stripe, smooth and unlike any animal skin I had ever seen.

My vision went white again. The warm, liquid-like trance continued its reveries.

I was now on my knees, staring up at a blood-red moon on a black sky. It hung over the prison yard like a constant omen, an unhealing and bloody wound. My family and I, a line of permanently muzzled, silent children, knelt before our faceless executioners; their helmets hiding any similarities they might've had to us.

One of the overseers pulled my short, brown hair. I couldn't scream or vocalise anything, for the electronic muzzles suppressed any rebellious action or thought. I could not protest at the way these men treated us.

Every night I wished they'd just mercy kill us and leave us dead instead of bringing us back to repeat it every day. The torture *never* stopped. I wanted to reach out and end this somehow, to control their whips and spears, but no matter how hard I strained, we would never be free.

We were nothing in their eyes, I knew that. There were no words I could share. I had no name, no memory of how I came to this place, only pain and suffering. I vowed to myself I would kill every single one of them given the opportunity. I would make my pain theirs, over and over, until time stopped. Their spears thrust forward, impaling us once again.

Another blinding flash of white, the clouds cleared and morphed into snow-capped mountains all around me. The weak sun no longer provided warmth to our cold, bitter world. Even our blue sky was whitening, as though frosting over. It was only a matter of time before all life here was extinguished, that we were sure of.

My village hadn't seen food in some time. The bodies in the treacherous gullies had long since frozen. Chances of survival were getting slimmer by the day. I hoped my uncles – the tall, blonde and proud Y'lions that they were – would return with food soon and save our village. If they didn't, we'd have to resort to cannibalism.

Another burst of white filled my view, and now I could see Seron. There were fertile, grassy fields, crops and a distant treeline. A river nearby for running water and rain clouds in the blue sky. It was a perfect world. Unlike the Seron I thought I knew, this place was filled with life and lush beauty, yet somehow I knew this was the same place.

The scene suddenly lit ablaze, explosions everywhere. The villagers working in the fields fell dead. I was on my knees over my husband's burnt corpse, lifting him in my arms, but it was no use; he was gone forever. Even the sky itself was on fire, my white streaks of energy fizzled in the atmosphere, the by-products of my attempts to destroy our enemies and defend my people.

My husband's killers approached through the licking flames, impervious to the heat. These light-skinned invaders had tortured my people for too long. The cane-wielding old man and the hulking, indestructible juggernaut both eyed me from across the blazing fields, waiting for me to make my next move. Not only that, but more enemy sky-boats burst through the cloud cover, another wave of their kind.

They had killed *everyone* I knew. I could tell they had been toying with me, too; there were so many times they could have finished me off. Why keep me alive? Why any of this?

I propelled myself into the air with streams of light coming from my feet. The two men both rose, floating in their own ways. I fired several white lines at them, but they dodged. My power sliced into the fiery fields below.

I couldn't stop shaking, but my fear didn't overtake me; if anything, it spurred me on. I didn't care how powerful they were. I'd find a way to kill them, for you, Masoyi. I screamed and fired in all directions, hoping to annihilate every last one of them.

A veil of white surged again, this time revealing a familiar sight; it was one of *my* memories, replaying in my head. Somehow, I knew I was sharing it with the others; they were experiencing my fear of that day, the day I got my powers.

Everything was in slow motion. I popped up from the sand and peeked over a boulder to look at the smouldering wreckage of our FD craft. The fuselage had been torn open, and Tau was inside, alive. The other children were sprawled in the sand, and some were still strapped in their seats. The nomads who had shot us down were going from child to child, finishing off any still moving. They reached Tau, and I cried out.

I shook my head and broke out of the hallucination, as did the other Chosen. We were back inside Arc Unity, still in circle formation as though we had never left.

I couldn't control my hands, it was as if they were stuck in place, forced to continue pointing at the centre of the hexagram. Beams of light shot from all our fingertips, coalescing into a bright sphere of many colours. Our eyes widened in shock, and the audience all gasped. After a few panicked, uncertain moments, the beams of light stopped, and our hands were released.

The orb of light, which was now as tall as a person, turned completely opaque white and floated there in the centre of the circle. It was giving off a gentle hum. It reminded me of my portals, but I could see no destination through it.

The crowd continued their amazed susurrations, and the emperor stood from his throne to get a closer look.

'What is it?' he called down. 'Someone tell me.'

'We don't know, my emperor,' Raumanu answered before focusing back on the orb.

Caelum glared at me. 'What is it? What did you do?'

'*Me*? *I* didn't do any… I just did what you told me to do!' I answered.

'That's clearly some sort of… portal,' Elion added. 'Where does it go?'

I couldn't help but look stunned. I shrugged. 'I honestly don't know what it is. Why don't you ask Lucenia? Those beams of light coming from our fingers, those were like *her* powers, right?'

While the others looked at her accusatorily, I shifted my second perception over to the orb, but it could not penetrate inside it.

Raumanu shifted closer to it. 'I believe with the addition of Sacet, that… this is *indeed* a portal. We should enter it.'

'What?' Elion and Lucenia said simultaneously.

'This *is* the light that will lead us to the Chosen path,' Raumanu explained.

The crowd murmured again, and the other Chosen eventually all nodded in agreement.

The emperor pointed at me. 'Make *her* enter first!'

They all looked at me expectantly before huddling closer.

Caelum reached me first. He grabbed my wrist and pulled me towards the orb.

'Get off me!' I yelled, trying to shake him free. 'Fine, let me do it myself!'

He let go and folded his arms. The others watched in silence as I cautiously approached the floating white orb. I reached out to it with my palm and gently touched it; it felt cold, but pleasant.

I looked back at the others to let them know that it was safe, but as I tried pulling my hand away, it jerked back. It was stuck, as if my hand were submerged under it. I kept yanking, but with every jolt, my hand sank deeper into the orb.

I had no choice now. I held my breath and gave in, leaning forward and entering the sphere head-first. Soon after, my whole body was consumed by it. Like the memories from earlier, my vision was clouded with white, but when I came to, it was not a memory that I saw.

I was standing on a floating white platform of an unknown, solid material, perhaps marble. The platform was large, and it hung high above the surface of an unfamiliar world.

The ground far, far below was a brightly lit, seemingly infinite flat plane of white that stretched in all directions, making the true horizon indiscernible from the sky. It was like a desert in its emptiness, void of all things.

The sky was totally obscured by a storm that also stretched infinitely. Its tempestuous green clouds were constantly swirling and mixing, yet there was no rain. Something about this place was so familiar, but I couldn't remember.

The platform was broken up into sections; the first of which I was standing on had nothing on it, as though it was a landing area. The portal I had travelled through was nowhere to be seen.

On the far side of the platform, the second section connected to the first with a thin bridge. The far section had a huge grey orb slowly spinning in its centre. Eight reflective chrome-like columns surrounded the orb in a big circle. The orb gave a constant eerie buzz, as though beckoning me closer.

Scariest of all, wherever this place was, my powers wouldn't work here. I couldn't sense anything around me, nor could I create portals. There was no way out.

Seventeen: The Empyrean

Another flash of white to my side. I shielded my eyes, and when the light subsided, it left another orb portal. Initially taller than I was, the orb shrank and disappeared, revealing a perplexed Raumanu.

He fell to the ground despite his walking stick, which clattered nearby. '*Argh*!'

One by one, four more portals flashed and shrank, bringing the remaining Chosen here, too. While the others helped Raumanu up, I explored, heading for the thin bridge that connected the two platform sections.

'Wait,' Raumanu said, looking down at his body. 'I feel… no pain? That fall should have broken my hip.' He dropped his cane and stretched his back, causing it to audibly crack. 'It feels… good.'

'What *is* this place?' Lucenia asked, bending down and feeling the smooth, white platform surface.

As I headed over the bridge, I carefully leaned over the edge and looked down. I couldn't see any sign of the platform's shadow below, or any shadows at all for that matter. It was almost impossible to tell how high we were. I realised that with the cloud cover, there were no stars and no sun to shine.

I tried activating my INC's display, but a simple dialogue box appeared saying "Signal Lost", prohibiting me from doing anything further.

'Did we… teleport to another world?' Elion said in wonder.

'This is no world,' Raumanu explained. 'This place… is what seers have had visions of for millennia.'

Once the others had gotten over their awe, they followed my lead over the bridge to the second section.

Andriel walked alongside Raumanu. 'You mean the ethereal plane, don't you? You're saying this is the actual Empyrean? That thing you've been prattling on about for centuries?'

Raumanu gestured at the clouds with open arms. 'Behold above, the source of all acolyte and Chosen power. The Soulstorm is where all souls go upon death, and where we extract them for resurrection.'

We all stopped to look up. The green storm clouds had countless waves of sparkling particles, each swimming through the sky of their own accord. Could each be a soul of the dead? A former person or lifeform, waiting to be brought back to life, or possibly to be born?

'Where everyone who has been and will be,' Raumanu continued.

Lucenia pulled at her hair nervously. 'How can you be sure?'

Raumanu glanced back at her. 'Because I've been studying the seers' visions long before *any* of you were born.'

'I know, I know,' Lucenia answered.

Elion leered. 'And what if those fortune-tellers are wrong, old man?'

'They are *not* fortune-tellers!' Raumanu shouted back, almost growling. 'It is not the future they see, but this… realm of impossibility. It is the Empyrean. Do you have a better explanation? It is right here in front of you all!'

Our group reached the larger orb in the centre of the second platform, and we stopped to stare at it. The silver ball slowly rotated constantly. Its shell was partially transparent and gently shifted, almost like liquid. Inside it, more energies, like those above in the storm, perpetually bounced inside.

Elion chuckled. 'And what do your precious seers say this is, Raum?'

Raumanu approached the orb, jaw dropped and trying to look inside. 'The seers made no mention of this. It is… fascinating.'

Andriel scanned the platform around us. 'Well, it's the only thing here, so it *must* be important.'

Caelum glanced up at the Soulstorm. 'Whatever you're going to do, make it fast. I don't trust this place.'

Andriel laughed. 'Is the *god-king* afraid?'

'I agree with Caelum,' Lucenia said, wandering closer to Raumanu. 'We should leave.'

I pointed back at the first platform. 'In case you didn't notice, there are no portals to take us back, and our powers don't work here.'

Lucenia's eyes widened. 'What?' She threw her hands up, attempting to fire her ability, but nothing came out. Her breathing audibly quickened as she paced back and forth. 'No, we need to leave. We should *definitely* leave.'

Odd, Lucenia's memory that was shared with us depicted her to be a brave warrior. Like me, she fought against Raumanu and Caelum's incursions. Is this what life on Aster would do to me, too? Turn me into a coward?

'Calm down!' Raumanu roared back at her. 'We are in the light of the Chosen path; it has never shone on us so brightly. We are in no danger here.' He seemed so sure.

Still wary of his surroundings, Caelum strode closer to us. 'That being said, I want to get this over with. Sacet, touch the orb.'

'Me again?' I shrieked. 'No, one of *you* do it. This is *your* «Chosen path», not mine.'

Caelum smirked and approached, before jumping forward and grabbing onto my shoulders. 'I may not have my powers here, but I'm still stronger than you.'

He tightened his grip and dragged me closer to the orb, so I resisted, kicking and screaming. 'Let go of me!'

For once, I was actually proving difficult for Caelum to control. He looked at the others. 'Elion, get her legs!'

The other man joined my father, and together they forced me to the orb, despite my best efforts to struggle, squirm and kick. The others watched on in silence. The men held my palm out to make contact with the orb's liquid-like surface.

We waited as my hand rested on the cold substance, but nothing happened. Caelum and Elion eventually let go of me, and I slid back to the ground.

'You arseholes!' I yelled.

'Well, now what?' Elion asked, ignoring me.

Raumanu stroked his beard. 'Perhaps we perform the ritual again?'

I stood up and stamped past all of them, then looked back. 'You can forget about it; I'm not helping any of you. Why should I when you're so willing to sacrifice me the first chance you get?'

All their eyes were upon me, and they could not see what was happening behind them. The orb was quietly spinning faster than before, and it had turned green. Long strands of silent, watery tentacles sprouted from the object, flailing and feeling about, as if blindly searching its surroundings. I took a few more steps back.

'As the newest member, it's your duty, Sacet,' Lucenia said. 'I'm just glad it's not *me* anymore.'

As if the tentacles heard her, they all turned in her direction and slithered closer. They rose, preparing to strike. I said nothing, but my mouth was agape, and my gaze was fixed upon them. The others noticed my slack-jawed stare and turned.

A tentacle shot forward and wrapped itself around Lucenia, then several more did the same. She screamed and cried while the other Chosen looked on in shock. She desperately clawed at the ground in vain.

'*Ahh!* Help, help me!'

Caelum and Elion launched forward to her aid.

'Stop!' Raumanu commanded, and the confused men did so. 'It is the will of the light. Do not assist her!'

'What?' I shouted.

'Help me!' Lucenia continued to scream. '*Ahhhhhhhhhhhh!*'

As Lucenia was slowly dragged closer to the orb, the rest of us backed away to the outside columns. She gave out one last scream before she was sucked into the green liquid. Like a scared child, she locked eyes with all of us, as if still begging to be saved. The entire orb changed to white, obscuring her from our sight.

The platform we were on lightly quaked. My fingers felt odd, so I looked down and saw that they were melting away like confetti. Each finger broke away, turned white and faded into nothing. The other

Chosen were fading away, too, examining their extremities closely with equal parts intrigue and horror.

Elion ran over to the others. 'How do we stop it? Are we… dying?'

Even Caelum seemed perturbed. But Raumanu was not worried; he actually smiled.

My wrists faded next, then my arms. The disintegration, though painless, was terrifying. It travelled all the way to our torsos and heads. My eyes broke away with the rest of the particles, and all I could see was white yet again.

I became nothing, but as soon as I had fully disintegrated, my body reconstituted in the same way, piece by piece, reforming back in Arc Unity where we had started. The thousands in the crowd gasped at our return.

When Raumanu reformed, he had no walking stick to lean on, so he fell to the ground and groaned in pain. Servants from the sidelines rushed over to assist him.

'Where is Lucenia?' the emperor bellowed, noticing her absence.

We Chosen all exchanged concerned looks. Well, this wasn't my fault; one of *them* could break the bad news.

'Sire, *ack*,' Raumanu began, grunting as he was helped to his feet by the servants. 'Lucenia made the ultimate sacrifice for the Chosen path. Has anything changed here?'

'Hey,' a voice yelled from the crowd. 'Hey, look at me!'

One of the civilians was floating in the air. Beneath his feet, white streams of energy, similar to what Lucenia could create, were firing downwards to keep him level. He was having a lot of trouble with his balance and quickly tumbled forward into the pews again.

'I have powers!' another yelled out.

Several more members of the crowd floated up, mimicking Lucenia's power in the same way. Had these regular people just become acolytes? Some fired their newfound abilities upwards. Although their power was weaker than what Lucenia was capable of, each person who exhibited it was overjoyed.

The emperor, who had been observing the scene from his throne, stood and examined his hands, as if he felt it, too. He waved his hands about, and another stream of energy shot out of them. His expression turned to pure ecstasy.

We remaining five Chosen gathered in a cordoned-off room, somewhere at the back of Arc Unity and away from prying eyes. We sat in well-furnished surroundings, yet we were anything but comfortable. It had taken some time, but each of us Chosen had also received Lucenia's power. Aside from Raumanu, no one seemed happy about what had just happened.

Elion was staring at the exquisitely decorated carpet. His knee bounced up and down incessantly. 'I can't believe she's gone.'

Caelum looked at his hands as white energy danced on his fingertips. Before that, he had been impatiently floating back and forth. Raumanu, the only one who was calm, was sitting forward in his chair and leaning on a new cane.

Andriel was sitting in the corner seat of the room with her hand on her head. She had told us not to bother her while she did "damage control", whatever that meant. Assumedly, she and all the other psychics were controlling the world's population somehow.

Elion shook his head and looked at me. 'Are you sure you don't know *anything* about that portal? *You* were the one who made it; you've probably been there before, and you *knew* what was going to happen. Tell us the truth!'

I folded my arms. 'I told you already, I have no idea what's going on.'

'Elion,' Raumanu interrupted. 'Do not despair for Lucenia, she is in the light now. Sacet is not to blame. This was *fated* to happen.'

There was a loud cackling from behind as a stream of white energy burst through the tall, double doors. It was the emperor, flying in with his new powers. As he hovered, he laughed with glee, firing torrents of energy at any inanimate object that caught his eye: chairs, tables, vases. No object was safe.

'Yes! This is perfect,' he yelled, his words echoing off the vaulted ceiling.

The empress and a smattering of guards followed him through.

Suralia flicked her fingers and fired her ability off, too, also amused by it. The emperor flew around the room and circled above our heads while the others took seats all around us.

Andriel broke away from her meditation and stood. 'My emperor, billions of people now have Lucenia's powers. I've lost count now, and it continues to grow.' She dipped her head. 'But unfortunately, when she was sacrificed, all L lines disappeared with her. Those people who in transit at the time plummeted to their deaths. I have every disciple I can get working to revive them, but it will take time.'

The emperor landed in the centre of the room. '*Bah*, why do you bother me with these... these *trivial* matters, Andriel? By all means, make our people rebuild the bridges. Just take care of it.'

She smiled back at him. 'At once, my emperor.'

The emperor turned on the spot, searching the room. 'Raumanu, where are you?'

Raumanu leant forward off his chair to stand. 'Here, Your Grace.'

The emperor's eyes widened like an excited child. 'My oldest, most *trusted* adviser, tell me, what does this all mean? Is this the Chosen path?'

Raumanu looked around at everyone. 'I believe so, Your Majesty. It is almost time to ascend.'

'Yes,' the emperor slowly nodded. 'Perhaps... perhaps this ceremony can be repeated on *all* of you. Perhaps when all of your powers are sacrificed and given to Aster...'

Raumanu nodded back and smiled. 'The path is right in front of us, Your Grace.'

No, this wasn't right. If the Chosen were going to be sacrificed to that orb one by one, it was obvious who would be next: me.

I stood and gave a pleading look to anyone who would listen. 'But... shouldn't we at least *study* the effects this has had? Something this wide-reaching...'

'No!' the emperor roared, with such ferocity that he sprayed spit. 'You will perform the ceremony again!'

With shaking, widened eyes, Elion gestured to me. 'She *could* be right, what if something goes wrong?' He noticed Avarut's hateful glower, so he averted his eyes. 'Sire, can't we... can't we at least have some time to get our affairs in order?'

The others also exchanged worried looks. I stayed silent, fearful for how the old man might react.

The empress slinked forward and pointed at Caelum and Andriel. 'Do you both agree? Has your loyalty wavered at the mention of self-sacrifice?'

Caelum faced away, clearly attempting to contain what he truly thought.

Andriel sighed. 'I agree that we should study this before blindly jumping forward like we did with soul grafting.'

'And what say you, Raumanu?' the emperor asked. 'Do you agree with the cowards?'

Raumanu inspected the others before looking back at the emperor. 'I say give them one day, Sire. Let them be with their families one last time. But after that… *no one* stops the Chosen path.'

'Very well,' the emperor gruffly conceded. 'We have waited this long, what's *one* more day?'

Eighteen: Goodbye

That night

Arc Sacet penthouse balcony

The aurora was even more beautiful than last night. Now, in addition to the swirling colours, there were millions of little white lights dancing in the sky. They were the people of Aster who had been gifted Lucenia's power, and decided to fly freely through the night sky. Each left a surprisingly long trail, which eventually dissipated.

Although from here they appeared merely as lines of light, I could feel their joy of discovering flight for the first time. It looked like so much fun. Rather than each person flying in a random direction, independent of others, many chose to fly together. The formations they made swirled playfully.

'Beautiful, isn't it?' I heard a voice from inside say. It was Raumanu. He ambled over to the balcony I was leaning against.

I groaned. 'Leave me alone, Raumanu.'

He grinned. 'You know you *can* call me Raum, if you'd like. It's a privilege I give to those I consider equals or colleagues.' He kept looking at me, so I turned away. 'I hope you don't mind, but I'll be spending the night again.'

I faced him and clenched my fists. 'Why? I've had enough of Chosen matters today.'

His eyes narrowed. 'You know why.'

I certainly did. I knew that tomorrow when we attempted the ceremony again, the others were going to gang up on me for the sacrifice. He was here to make sure I didn't try to escape in the night.

'But it's not all doom and gloom,' he continued. 'You have a surprise waiting for you inside. Come.'

Raumanu hobbled back inside. I reluctantly followed through the doors. We wound our way along a couple of corridors before arriving in the sitting room.

Everyone was waiting there for me, sprawled out on the couches. Iya looked the most relaxed, whilst Tau seemed on edge. The three boys all shared one couch. Several of our servants lined the walls, ready to fetch whatever we wished.

'Wait here,' Raumanu said, now tapping away towards the main area.

'Sacet?' Noor chirped. 'Are you… okay? You've been out there since we got home.'

He looked quite unsure of himself, as though he thought I was going to attack him for speaking up.

'I… I'm…' I began, but I trailed off and looked at my feet. How could I tell them that I was going to die tomorrow and never come back?

'Tetsu?' someone said to my side. 'Tetsu!'

Standing in the doorway were an older man and woman, both with elated expressions. Where did they come from?

Tetsu took a few moments to realise what was happening before his relaxed expression exploded in surprise. 'Dad? Mum!'

He launched off the couch and sprinted towards his parents. The three of them met in the middle of the room and embraced tightly. They joyously cried and laughed, as did the rest of us around the room. Even Iya and our servants couldn't help but smile.

'Son! We've been waiting for you for so long,' the father said. 'I'm sorry… I'm sorry I wasn't there for you. We wanted so badly to come back.'

The mother brushed Tetsu's cheeks. 'Such a strong, handsome man you've turned into. My lovely boy. I missed you *so* much.'

'Is this the right room?' another voice to my side said. 'Noor!'

More strangers appeared in the doorway, two men, one older and one younger. Noor jumped up from the couch, too. He was completely lost for words, instead looking at them in staggered confusion. They strode past me and, like Tetsu's family, hugged Noor in a sweet reunion.

I saw tears streaming from Noor's eyes. 'It's… you. I'm *so* sorry,' he began. 'I'm sorry, *please* forgive me.'

'What are you sorry for, Bro?' the younger man asked, who I now assumed was the older brother he had told me about.

'I gave up on you,' Noor continued, almost bawling. 'For most of my life I… I thought you betrayed me; I spent so many cycles hating you. I'm so, *so* sorry.'

The older, bearded man grabbed Noor by the shoulders and locked eyes with him. 'No, Noor. *I'm* the one who should be sorry. You were right to hate me… I let you down.'

While Noor's family kept reassuring and consoling him, Tetsu's family were already reminiscing about their past.

Iya sat up from her relaxed position and watched them with a sort of bemused grin. Eno was on the edge of his seat, looking around anxiously. Tau was smiling at him and then at me, before gesturing to the door.

And there they were. My adoptive parents stood in the doorway, Azua and Enni. Two faces I thought I had long since forgotten, but it all came flooding back to me. Dad had short, black hair, and Mum had long, flowing blonde locks that reached her lower back. Her eyes were blue and his were bluish grey.

'Dad!' Eno practically screamed.

'Mum!' I screamed, too.

'Kids!' Mum screeched back.

The four of us all ran and squeezed each other so tightly that I was momentarily choked.

'My boy!' Dad roared, picking up Eno under the armpits and flinging him around, laughing.

Mum placed both her hands on my shoulders and looked me up

and down. 'Look at you, all grown up, and so, *so* strong.' Her lip quivered as though she were about to break down into tears.

We switched over, Dad now hugging around my neck. 'We missed you, kiddo. Look at you! A warrior after all, aye? Even *with* our meddling.'

Mum kissed Eno's forehead over and over. 'My cute, sweet little boy, you've grown even more than your sister has. You're so handsome!' Eno initially squirmed, but eventually smiled and went along with it.

Both Mum and I had tears, as did a few others in the room. As I hugged Mum again, I looked over her shoulder and saw a smiling Raumanu standing behind them by the door. Had *he* organised this?

It had been great reuniting with my family. We'd spent most of the night swapping stories in the sitting room of our time apart. Every time I tried sharing a story of my own, chances were they had already heard it secondhand from the Asterian media.

Tetsu's mother was called Kekasih, and his father was called Matay. The resemblance to both was very strong. Noor's father and brother were named Kashif and Ahkim respectively.

Like everyone else who had died on Seron in the past, they had been brought here, given a basic home in the depths, and left to fend for themselves. Every story they had of finding work and barely surviving quietly infuriated me, yet they somehow all had a positive outlook about it all.

We hadn't really spoken much about the aftermath of today's ceremony thankfully, other than a few mentions of all the chaos going on outside. Apparently, it was a worldwide celebration out there, with almost every Asterian cavorting in the streets and walkways at the discovery of their new powers.

We had been so focused on everything else that no one had brought up what was painfully obvious to me – that the ceremonies were going to continue, and that *I* was next.

I was bent down behind the bar, getting some drinks for Mum

and Dad. I could have had a servant do it, but I felt this required a personal touch. The problem was I didn't really know anything about alcohol, so I just grabbed whatever was the most colourful.

As I stood back up, I was surprised to see Raum on the other side of the bar, staring at me with concern. 'You haven't told them yet… have you?'

I shook my head. 'No.'

'It's getting late, and you and I will be leaving in the morning. You might not get another chance.'

I looked into the next room where all our families were relaxing on couches in a big circle. I went around the bar and stood next to Raum, and we watched the families from afar. Servants were bringing in food and drinks, and everyone was laughing and having a good time. I wished I could preserve this night forever.

I knew that if I went in there and told them the bad news, I'd bring everyone down like I always do. I'd make them want to fight with me, or rather *for* me. I finally understood what Malu was trying to say, in her own rude way: that just by being around me, their lives would be upended.

I glanced back at Raum. 'I'm not going to tell them, and I don't want you to either. Look at how happy they are. Why should I ruin that?'

Raum shrugged. 'If that is your wish. But I'm sure they'd like to say goodbye if they knew.'

I sighed. 'It's better this way. I'll say my goodbyes without them knowing. Just promise me one more thing: that they'll all be taken care of when I… you know.'

He gave a solemn nod back. 'As we speak in Arc Lucenia, all of her descendants are grieving for her loss. But no matter what happens, that will *always* be their home. They'll be looked after, I assure you.'

I took a deep breath. 'Thank you. You know, you're not so bad… when you're not destroying planets.'

Raum smirked. 'So they say.' He leant over the bar and grabbed a bright-purple bottle. 'You know, maybe you're getting ahead of yourself? It could just as easily be *me* chucked in tomorrow. All you youngins might gang up on an old man?'

I chuckled, but instantly regretted it. The monster had killed over a billion people when he destroyed Seron, and probably far more than that in his time. With drinks in hand, I headed back to my family, leaving Raum behind.

Kashif was in the middle of explaining something to Noor. 'It's not like that. I helped your mother escape. I loved her but… she *despised* me.'

'Well, can't we track her down?' Noor asked, looking not just at his father but his brother and the nearby servants. 'I want to meet her, too.'

The head servant, Fidèle, nodded. 'I will make the arrangements, Sir.'

'Welcome back, sweetie,' Mum said when she noticed I had entered the room. 'Just after you left, we were all talking about plans for tomorrow.'

I passed her and Dad their drinks and sat with them. '*Oh*? What plans?' Everyone in the room seemed excited about it.

Dad took a sip of his drink and winced, probably because I made it too strong. Then he leant over to Mum and hugged her. 'Seeing as your friends don't have classes tomorrow, we thought we'd all go on a little excursion together. We'll show you all the hot spots of Aster. Places for fun, the best restaurants… and also the best *romantic* spots.'

He glanced over to Noor, then back to me. As both our families grinned, Noor and I blushed a little at the embarrassment.

Mum rolled her eyes and shook her head. 'More importantly, sweetheart, you and your friends have *lots* more family to meet in the depths.'

I shook my head in bewilderment. 'You live in the depths?'

Dad nodded. 'Most families new to Aster have to start somewhere.'

Kekasih nudged Tetsu. 'You have your grandparents, your three aunties and your five cousins still to meet.'

Matay laughed. 'And that's just on your *mother's* side.'

Eno was staring at me with wide eyes. 'We can see Grandpa, and we'll get to meet Grandma for the *first* time ever.'

I sensed Raum enter the room behind me.

'That's great,' I began, 'I wish I had the time to meet them all, but I… *uhhh*… I have Chosen duties tomorrow.'

My family's faces drooped a little. Tau eyed me with concern.

I forced a smile for them. 'But all of you go without me, please. You deserve some time off.'

'Can't you just meet up with them after you're done?' Iya asked from the side of the room.

She and Tau had been mostly keeping to themselves, probably to give us more bonding time with our families.

'She'll be indisposed most days, unfortunately,' Raum interrupted, perhaps sensing my awkwardness. 'She has media interviews, press conferences, legal documentation to sign, financial deals to make…'

I looked into Eno's quivering eyes. 'It sounds like I'm going to be busy for a *long* time, little brother. So, Mum and Dad will have to look out for you again, like it was always *meant* to be.'

Eno looked down at his feet. 'I was really hoping you could come, but… I *guess* I understand.'

'It's okay,' Dad said, hugging Mum even tighter. 'You'll get time off eventually. And when you do, we'll take you.'

'I have a better idea,' I replied, before beckoning Fidèle over. 'I want to officially invite all the family that's here to live with us. And I want to *extend* that invitation to any other relatives or close friends that they nominate.'

He leant closer to my ear. 'Madam, are you sure?' he whispered. 'That could end up being *quite* a lot of people, and the penthouse is only so big.'

'Make it happen,' I said aloud, not caring about his concerns.

He gave a short bow. 'Of course, Madam. It will take a few days to push through, but it *will* be done.'

The families' smiles returned. The parents hugged, and numerous people thanked me.

My mother gave me a warm smile. 'That's *very* kind of you, sweetheart.'

Dad gave a familiar, toothy smile. 'Guess we lucked out when we saved you as a kid, huh?'

Mum gave him a gentle punch in the arm. That smile… it reminded me of someone else.

Before Fidèle had a chance to leave, I reached out to him again. 'And I also want to invite our friends Pilgrim and Sabikah, hopefully they're on Aster by now.'

The servant pulled out a small electronic pad from his pocket to write on. 'Understood, Ma'am.'

Noor raised a hand. 'Pilgrim might be listed as Saladire.'

The other servants raised an eyebrow at one another, no doubt because I was increasing their workloads considerably.

I surveyed the room, eventually focusing on Tau. I remembered she had her own friends that she was probably worried about, and she also wasn't happy with how I had left things with Malu. This was probably my last chance to set things right.

'I want you to reinvite Malu and her family. And Tau's friends: Coleo and Tarsus.'

Tau gave me one of the warmest smiles I'd ever seen her do. 'Thank you, Sacet. Thank you.'

I then saw Eno. 'My brother has some friends he'd probably want to invite, too.'

Eno nodded fervently and started to count on his fingers. 'Oran, Mui, Nadan, Keenu…'

Fidèle was struggling to keep up with writing each name, and I could see his eyes widening in surprise. Raum chuckled from behind.

I looked over at Iya. 'And as for you…'

Iya had been leaning on the wall, but she now propped herself up. Her breathing visibly increased. I didn't know what it was about her, but she had completely changed since Seron.

'While I'm not around, you're going to protect my family,' I explained. 'You go where they go, and you will watch out for them. *That's* how you earn a place here. Understood?'

Iya looked relieved. She dipped her head and did a tiny bow. 'I can do that. I… I will.'

'And if any of my family *ever* want her gone,' I continued, looking between my family and Fidèle, 'then she's no longer welcome.'

Everyone was in the upstairs corridors, finding one of the many rooms to settle down for the night. My parents were giving me one last hug before retiring to their room.

'We're so proud of you,' Mum said, giving me numerous kisses on the cheek.

'Make sure you say goodbye in the morning, okay?' Dad added.

I squeezed them tight. 'I will. And Mum? Dad? I missed you both. I missed seeing your faces. Hearing your voices. I'm glad we're together again.'

'We are, too,' Dad replied. 'Goodnight, Sacet.'

'Goodnight, sweetie,' Mum added.

They both released and took one last look at me before heading off to find Eno.

Tau had been skulking around the corner, and now that I was free, she came around it. 'Are you okay, Sacet? With these "*Chosen duties*", I mean? I think I should come with you tomorrow.'

Tau had been acting odd all day. In the morning, she wanted me to relax and be positive, but then ever since we got home, she had been nervously staring at me off and on, as if she knew how I was really feeling. I supposed that if anyone could see through my lies, it would be her or Eno.

I shook my head. 'No, I'll be fine. *Please* stay with the others.'

'You think they'll be in danger?' she asked.

I narrowed my eyes. 'What? No, I just think you'll have a more interesting day with them. What is with you anyway?'

She gave an exasperated sigh and looked up and down the corridor. 'I'm sorry, I guess I'm a little… overwhelmed.'

'It's fine,' I said, before reaching out for a hug. 'Come here. Promise me you'll look after everyone.'

Tau reciprocated, hugging me back for a short while. 'I will, but you promise *me* something, too.'

I let her go. 'Anything.'

She gripped my shoulder firmly. 'If you're *ever* in trouble, you let me know, okay?'

'I will,' I lied. 'Goodnight, Tau.'

'Goodnight.' She went towards her room, glancing back at me a couple more times.

The corridor was finally empty, so I gave a great big sigh of my own. I went into my room, before closing and locking the door with a button press.

My second perception scanned the rooms and saw everyone bunking down. Noor had finished with his goodnights to his family and was getting changed out of his clothes.

I had been too harsh on him; none of this was his fault. He had been so loyal to me, even though I upended his life like all the others. I had spurned so many of his attempts to be romantic with me. I had wasted so much time we could have spent in each other's arms instead fighting and being on guard. But tonight, none of that mattered anymore, my guard was thoroughly down. This night, one more night, one more chance to be with the people I loved. He deserved that, *I* deserved that.

I opened a portal underneath his feet, dropping him onto my bed.

He bounced and initially shouted in surprise, before jumping up from the bed and looking around for danger. 'Sacet, what's wrong? Are you okay?'

'No, but you can help me,' I replied as I casually walked up to him.

I gently pulled him in for a kiss. Adrenaline pumping, he fought it at first, but then went along with it. His lips were warm and massaged mine softly.

He broke away and reeled back. 'I thought you were still angry with me?'

'Not anymore,' I said, before shoving him back onto the bed.

He didn't react, still in shock over what was happening.

If this was my last night alive, I wanted this to be perfect. I looked around at the room and activated my INC. I closed the enormous window blinds and dimmed the lights with a few simple thoughts. Then I changed the colour of the lighting to a gentle pinkish purple and even pushed out the scent of sweet Seronian flowers through the vents.

What's *this* submenu? Music? Okay, is there anything romantic… *oh*, there is? Of course there is. Sure, how about this one? A gentle beat began, accompanied by soothing plucks and tones.

Noor inspected the evolving room, and as if *finally* understanding, he coyly grinned up at me.

I attempted an alluring grin of my own before slowly shifting closer and climbing on top of him. When our faces met, I gave him another passionate kiss.

Nineteen: Home, Sweet Home

The next morning

The rusty hoverbus creaked whenever we turned, as though the flimsy metal structure were about to tear any moment. Not only that, but it rattled when our speed changed, too. We thankfully had the bus to ourselves, besides our driver. Everyone from last night, except for Sacet, had come along for our excursion to the depths, filling the back rows of double seats.

Being down here was far scarier than what the parents had made it seem. As our bus hovered past the cold, dark alleys and streets, I saw horrendous things that made my skin crawl.

There were motionless people lying along the narrow catwalks and in garbage piles, possibly dead. Vagrants would follow our bus briefly, shouting gibberish about the end of days. Neon-drenched alleys were filled with hooded figures hiding in the shadows, many of whom would scatter when they saw us.

'Are we *sure* this is the right way?' I asked to anyone.

Azua grinned back as the bus went around another sharp, shaky turn. 'Definitely, you'll *love* it there.'

'That's right,' Kekasih added. 'Home, sweet home is just a *little* deeper.'

I found that hard to believe. Although I trusted my friends' families, something told me our destination was far from "sweet". What was even stranger was that all three families lived in the same place, along with all of their extended relatives. Even *if* they had gotten to know each other because of the events surrounding Sacet, as they had said last night, why would they all now be *living* together? It made no sense.

As the bus lowered through even more tunnels and gaps, the brown haze of pollution thickened. Far above the layered city, the harsh daylight was no doubt cooking the steel rooves, but down here it may as well have been perpetual night. Cold and dark, it was lit only by flickering, poorly-placed neon strips.

The bus driver leaned forward to a microphone. 'Masks,' he gruffly instructed.

The driver and my friends' families brought their gas masks up from under their seats and put them on, tightening various straps and seals. My friends did the same with the masks that had been purchased for us. I had refused the gift, seeing as I didn't need to breathe anymore. Now with their masks on, all I could see of everyone's faces were their eyes.

We continued to lower until it was so dark and smoggy that we could barely see the other side of the street. We eventually parked next to some kind of station.

'Disembark,' the driver instructed gruffly.

The families stood, so my friends and I did, too. We all shuffled along the centre aisle until we reached the door and disembarked. The driver pulled a lever, closing the door, before abandoning us to ascend back up through the haze.

Now left on an eerily quiet platform alone, my friends looked to their respective families for guidance. Iya stayed by my side, looking just as afraid as I was.

'Everyone, hold hands,' Kashif called. 'Just trust in us, we'll get you there.'

'Have you ever been this deep before?' I whispered to Iya.

'Are you kidding?' she whispered back, which was muffled through her mask. 'This is rock bottom. No *sane* person comes here.'

We all linked hands, with Noor's family leading and Tetsu's

bringing up the rear to make sure no one got lost. Ahead of me, holding my left hand was Iya, and immediately ahead of her was Eno, then Enni. Behind me, holding the other hand was Tetsu. I felt a tug forward and went along with the group.

I could just make out Kashif, who now held a sparking torch above his head, as did Matay at the back. The lanterns fizzled constantly, but thankfully stayed lit.

'Well, what a… *charming* neighbourhood?' Tetsu lied, eliciting a laugh from his parents at the back.

We wound our way through several narrow alleyways choked with smog and litter. Although I didn't need to breathe the toxicity in, it was still getting in my eyes. I activated my aura, not only to aid myself, but to better penetrate the dim haze with my light.

I felt my left hand get squeezed.

'I'm not sure about this,' Iya whispered back. 'I'm supposed to be *protecting* you, but this is the *last* place I'd ever take you.'

'Then it's just as well you're not taking us,' Enni called back, clearly overhearing her, '*we're* taking *you.*'

I hadn't really noticed until now, but the alleyway had gradually been getting narrower and more primitive. Less metal and more cobbled stone. There were no doors or windows anymore, no structures of any kind. This place was ancient.

My feet submerged in something wet, and I looked down to see that the tunnel had turned into a sewer.

Eno pulled on his mother's hand to stop her. 'Do we *have* to go this way? It's getting a little…'

She pulled on Azua's hand ahead of her to pause the group, before bending over and hugging her son. 'I promise it's not much farther. And you're safe with us.' Whatever assuring smile she probably had was covered by her dirty mask.

Kashif pointed into the tunnel. 'Stay on the path and you'll be fine.'

Small, drier paths thankfully lined the edges. We all followed Kashif into the dark tunnel. The pollution was still thick in here, too. It felt like we were descending into a forgotten tomb.

A dark, furry, chattering creature skittered past on the other side of the passage.

Both Eno and Iya let out yelps.

'What's *that* thing?' Eno screeched.

There was more laughter among the adults. The creature had several eyes and a maw filled with teeth, but it kept to itself.

'It's just a jwigeomi,' Ahkim called back. 'Don't touch them and you'll be fine.'

Tetsu leant over my shoulder and looked at Iya. 'You alright there, bodyguard?'

'Shut up!' Iya shouted at him. 'It could have been anything. It just surprised me, is all.'

We pressed on and after several more winding passages and seemingly random turns, we stopped in front of a huge circular iron door.

'Here,' Ahkim said. 'Clean air and hot meals inside.'

Azua and Kashif fiddled with the latch mechanism before heaving it open together. The old metal whined, the noise of which echoed down the passageways.

Eno tilted his head to get a better look inside. 'You live… *here?*'

It was a dark, empty metal chamber, which thankfully wasn't polluted. We all headed inside and stopped, inspecting the dead end. As the circular door closed behind us with a thunderous thwomp, everyone took off their masks and breathed deeply.

'Where next?' Tetsu asked.

Azua had a confused expression. 'This doesn't make sense, where's the entry hall, and the kitchen?'

Eno tugged on his mother's clothes. 'Mum, what *is* this place?'

'Dad?' Noor asked, too. 'Where have you led us?'

Kashif and the other adults looked bewildered, as though they had gotten lost. And then, as if someone turned off a switch, their eyes rolled into the backs of their heads, and their bodies fell into a heap simultaneously. My friends gasped and screamed in surprise, but moments later, they *also* fell over, unconscious.

I amplified my aura and filled the chamber with cyan flames. Although horrified, I couldn't allow anything to happen to them. I knelt by Enni and Eno to heal them, but they wouldn't wake. It was like they were perfectly healthy already.

'Stop this!' I screeched, hoping that someone could hear me.

The wall in front of me rumbled and slowly rolled sideways to open, letting in a blindingly bright light from the long corridor behind it. A group of twenty or so armed strangers entered the room and looked at me with surprise.

What I guessed was their leader was a blue-skinned, bald man in a long, dark coat. His head was tremendously large, specifically the top of his skull, which bulged up and back. His hand was pointed towards me. Had he used some kind of power on my friends?

'That's not Sacet,' one of his armoured guards asked. 'Why is she still up?'

The young woman had pale skin, blue eyes and long, blonde hair. She wore a gas mask which only covered her mouth, as well as dark body armour, all striped with green. She was carrying a crackling, electrified baton.

'I don't care *who* you people are,' I shouted, keeping my aura strong, 'just release my friends, *now*.'

'Impossible, I can't sense her,' the blue-skinned man said to the guards. He lowered his hand as a look of realisation washed over him. 'My powers have no effect, which means...'

'If *you* can't put her down, *I* will,' the woman interrupted.

Other than healing, there was nothing I could do to fight them off. Wait, no. I probably had Lucenia's power now, too, right? I hadn't even tried it yet; I didn't know *how*. All I could do was try to throw my hands at them and hope for the best.

The woman stowed her baton over her back in a sheath, then strode into the chamber towards me, stepping over my friends. The other strangers, some guards and some dressed as civilians, pushed in hovering dollies and began loading them up with my unconscious friends.

'Hey!' I yelled. 'I'm *warning* you, I'll—'

'You'll what, *Elevated Disciple*?' the woman interrupted, her maniacal eyes flashing me an intimidating stare. 'Heal their poisoned lungs? Cure their cataracts?'

Some of the guards were right next to me within my aura's range, but they ignored me. As planned, I threw my hands towards them, but no projectiles came out, only more of my healing aura.

There was a strong smack to my side, which launched me into the far wall with a crash. It was *her;* she had blindsided me with an L line while I was distracted.

The last of the guards had loaded and hovered my remaining friends away, back into the corridor from where they had come.

'Don't kill her,' the blue man said from behind her. 'We *need* her.'

'I know my limits,' the woman replied.

'This changes everything…' the blue man muttered to himself, before turning and heading back down the corridor, leaving the two of us alone.

I sprang back up and got into a fighting stance. 'Good luck putting me down.' Hopefully, she'd fall for my bluff, because I was actually the weakest combatant back in FD basic training. 'Now, get out of my way.'

Her steadfast demeanour didn't change. 'You can either come with me quietly, or I can knock you out and drag you like the others.'

My friends had already been taken around a corner and out of sight. I needed to help them, this instant. I had to be strong, for their sake.

I clenched my fists. 'Knock me out? Try it.'

'Very well.'

The woman raised her arms to the side, and her glare intensified. Green flames erupted from her body in all directions. I couldn't believe it; she was a fallen disciple.

Her aura amplified even larger than mine, filling the chamber and then some. Our auras joined in the centre of the room, partially blending into white. I felt a drain on my powers, as well as a dizzying sickness.

The green flames roared, and she took a few steps forward. The overwhelming power forced me back against the wall. I fell to my knees and was unable to stand again. I tried to summon more strength from within, but it kept failing me.

What *was* this raw power? My life was draining away. Was I going to die? I could see the pure hatred in her eyes. My flames lessened and lessened.

'Please, enough!' I voiced weakly.

'You had your chance,' she replied, before taking another step forward.

I cowered against the wall, and my aura ceased. I felt myself slumping to the side as everything went dark.

My closed eyes darted fruitlessly. I was lying on a cold, metal surface. I smelled blood. I opened my eyes and inspected the dingy, tiled room. I was on an operating table. Bloodied medical tools were in a tray beside me.

There were other tables, too. Noor, Tetsu, Eno and Iya were all waking and sitting up, confused and drowsy like I was. I sat up and saw our captors, several people in pale smocks, each covered in what I assumed was our blood.

Leaning against a nearby wall was the blonde woman I had only just seen. She and a few other guards in dark armour were watching over us. She had her gas mask off now and was staring at me with her arms folded. She looked near my age, maybe a bit older.

'This new firmware is a little unpredictable,' an orange-skinned surgeon said. He turned to the woman. 'But they're clean. The disciple was difficult, healing every incision I made.'

Noor jumped up from the table and pointed his hands towards the man. 'Where's my family? What did you do with them? Tell me!'

The surgeon backed away and raised his arms. '*Whoa*! Easy kid, I just did you a favour.'

The other surgeons raised their hands in surrender, too. The rest of my friends and I shot up as well, ready to fight. Meanwhile, the guards were surprisingly calm.

The woman raised her wrist to her mouth. 'Send them in.'

The only door to the tiled chamber slid open and Noor's father rushed in.

'Son, it's okay,' Kashif began, raising his hands for calm. 'Relax. They're the good guys.'

Both Eno and Tetsu's parents also entered after them, and the families reunited once again. Iya gave me a panicked shrug.

The lead surgeon looked to the others around him. 'It's fine, you can all go.'

All of the other surgeons and guards, except for the blonde woman, made for the open door and left, out onto a rusty catwalk.

'What's going on here?' Eno asked.

Azua and Enni gently grabbed Eno's wrist and pulled him to the side of the room towards the blonde woman. Eno had a pleading, confused expression.

'We'd like you to meet someone, sweetie,' Enni said, and she pointed at her. 'This is your sister, Sacet.'

Eno looked at all of them like they were crazy. 'What?!'

The woman shot an angry look at Enni. 'I *told* you… that's *not* my name anymore.'

'Fine then,' Enni replied, gesturing to who was apparently her daughter again. 'This is… Lotus.'

Lotus bent down to Eno's height. 'Good to finally meet you, little brother.'

Eno gave her a sceptical stare. 'My sister? How come I've never heard of you before?'

His parents exchanged saddened frowns.

Enni bit her lip. 'She… she…'

Lotus gave an annoyed huff. 'I was stillborn. I guess you never heard of me because I was our parents' shame.'

The parents looked simultaneously offended and apologetic.

'Our shame? No, of course not!' Enni shouted. 'We loved you *just* as much as Eno.'

'Why would you say something like that?' Azua added. 'Eno was too young to understand at the time anyway.'

'*Excuse* me, insane people?' Iya loudly interrupted, and Lotus shot her a dirty look. 'Sorry to break up the family reunion, but what… is going… on here? Who *are* you people?'

The lead surgeon focused on Iya. 'My name is Hakkari. And that's Lotus, of course. We are your friends, so please… no violence.'

'I feel sick,' Noor said, leaning against his table.

'Me, too,' Tetsu added. 'Feels like my head was crushed by our hoverbus.'

Hakkari cleared his throat. 'Well, we *did* just finish up with your brain surgery. We needed to… shall we say… *upgrade* your INCs.'

My head was hurting, too. 'What *specifically* did you do to us?'

He turned to a nearby table where some sort of computer was humming. After tapping a few buttons, a huge holographic screen filled the entire wall. 'A number of things.' He scrolled through a long list of hard-to-read text. 'An INC acts as a tracking beacon, which thankfully doesn't work this deep.'

I noticed the words 'loyalty and undying love for the emperor and empress'. That and many others had long strikes through them, as if being disabled.

He turned back. 'Those programs allow the psychic network to home in on your location and force you to do... well... *anything* Andriel *wants* you to do.'

'Andriel?' I asked. 'The red-headed Chosen?'

Azua sighed and rested against the nearest table. 'She controls *every* single person on the planet with a hierarchy of psychics, with *her* at the top.'

'Even above the emperor and empress,' Enni clarified. 'Making Andriel the *real* empress.'

Noor's jaw dropped. 'So, Sacet was right, we *were* brainwashed.'

Hakkari nodded rapidly. 'Very much so. There were a whole bunch of subroutines I had to clear out of those noggins. Tell me, how do you all feel about the emperor now?'

Noor shrugged. 'He's a crusty, old creep.'

'Like a rotting corpse,' Tetsu suggested. 'Both of them.'

Noor then gasped in revelation. '*Ah*, no, no, no. So stupid! I said all those *horrible* things to Sacet.'

Tetsu placed his face in his palms. 'Me, too, brother.'

The boys all looked disgusted with themselves, Eno most of all.

'*Ewww*, I can't believe I *thought* that way,' he added.

Hakkari gave a smile to the parents, before looking back at us. 'Without the beacon, they'll have a *much* more difficult time controlling you from afar, let alone tracking you down. But you can *still* be controlled by a psychic if they can *see* you.'

Tetsu held up his hands. 'Wait, wait. Does this mean we *can't* go back up to the surface?'

Hakkari shook his head. 'No, you can go back up. But unfortunately, to maintain your cover, we have to reactivate the beacon when you leave. The good news is now we can turn it off and on, like a flick of a switch.' He tapped a button on the computer twice. '*Flick, flick!*'

'So, you're going to let us go, just like that?' Iya asked with folded arms. She backed away to the far wall. 'What are you terrorists planning on doing with us?'

'We're *freedom fighters*,' Kashif corrected, before focusing back on his son. 'We're called the Setting Sun.'

Enni hugged Eno from behind. 'Because *one* day, the sun will set on these corrupt emperors.'

Tetsu pointed a finger at multiple rebels. 'Was that *your* group that attacked us when we first arrived at Arc Sacet?'

Kekasih shook her head at him. 'No, no, Tetsu, there are *other* rebel groups. Besides, we would *never* attack you.'

Iya laughed, and when the whole room was looking at her, she shook her head in disbelief. 'Rebels have a nasty habit of dying for nothing.' She looked at me pleadingly. 'It's a huge risk being here. We can't be seen associating with them. We *need* to leave.'

Lotus scoffed. 'We thought you, of *all* people, Iya, would want those scum forever dead. Or have you gone soft since they exiled you?'

Iya smirked back. 'More like *smart*. Tell me, how exactly do you expect us to go back up to the surface anyway, now that we *know* all this stuff? Do you think the psychics won't notice knowledge of a terrorist… I'm sorry, "*freedom fighter*" base when they go spelunking in our brain folds?'

Hakkari smiled as he took off his bloody smock and rested it on the table. 'When we sent your families up, our own psychic, Kaxiyan, altered their memories of this place to think it was just an innocent home. We gave them a subliminal compulsion to return with our targets. Then, when they came back, we returned their memories to normal.'

Iya shook her head. 'There's no such thing as a *rebel* psychic.'

I approached Hakkari and gestured back at the families. 'I'm thankful you freed Sacet's family's minds, and mine too, but Noor's family? And Tetsu's? Bit too much of a coincidence, if you ask me. Unless your goal was to get to Sacet all along?'

Hakkari chuckled and turned the computer off. 'Are our tactics that obvious? Yes, when we heard the news of a new Chosen, we *targeted* your families to become members.'

'What do you want with her?' Noor asked, joining me.

Hakkari raised an eyebrow at him. 'Well, we want her on *our* side so that when the time came, we'd not only have someone on the inside, but someone who could open a back door right into Arc Royal. Plus… we figured Sacet would also want to fight them.'

'It's not too late to bring her here,' Enni said.

Eno looked up at his mother. 'So, we're going to go save her?'

'Yes,' Hakkari continued, 'you'll spend the day here so we don't arouse suspicion. And tonight when you leave, we'll switch your beacons on and alter your memories. You'll remember only a day of fun and family togetherness.

'Then you will return home, find Sacet, and convince her not only to take tomorrow off, but to somehow shake all of the people watching over her. And once she's here, we'll *finally* be ready to strike.'

We were all following Lotus and Hakkari through a dark, cavernous tunnel. The ground was made up of large steel pipes, and we could hear a torrent of something gushing through them. There was rust on every surface, and the place smelled damp from decades, maybe centuries, of structural neglect.

And yet, we could hear the sounds of industry. Over the edge of the pipes were more members of the Setting Sun, tool-carrying engineers. They were banging various pipes with their sledgehammers, and the sounds echoed throughout the cavern. What light they had was dim and red.

Eno had been walking with his reunited family at the front of the pack. 'So, where *exactly* are we?'

'You are in *old* Aster,' Azua answered, gesturing around. 'When the Asterians started building upwards, they forgot about everything below. There's an *entire* world down here to hide in.'

'Where's the hazy pollution gone?' Noor asked from the back.

'It still exists here,' his father replied, 'but these engineers pump it out.'

Lotus placed a hand on Eno's shoulder as they walked. 'It's not so bad. Unlike the people above, we're free here.'

'What made you come down here in the first place?' Eno asked of her.

'I didn't really have a choice. Let's just say I did some silly things in my youth, and now I can never go back.'

Light was pouring in from the end of the tunnel, as were some distant voices, but it wasn't clear what was creating either.

'So, you've been down here this whole time?' Noor asked from behind.

'*Ahuh*,' Lotus called back. 'For most of my life. Although when I eventually *do* go back up, it'll be to execute the rulers of this world.' Her voice quietened. I could hear the same angry intensity she had used on me earlier. 'They *won't* get away with what they've done.'

'How did they… *umm*,' Eno began saying to Lotus, 'how did they resurrect you? If you were stillborn, they wouldn't have had a record of you?'

Lotus shrugged. 'I guess you could say I got lucky. After our parents buried me, they made a tiny headstone, too. Lo and behold, someone from Overwatch found it and brought my little infant corpse back to life, and then to this crappy planet. I lived with Grandma for a bit, but eventually we came down here.'

We reached the end of the tunnel and saw the source of the light. Beyond this first chamber was a second, even more cavernous than the first. The view was so awe-inspiring that I gasped.

There were colossal metal pillars holding up the ceiling, rows and rows of them into the distant darkness. Each pillar reminded me of the arcs far above on the surface. These pillars must've been the foundations of the city planet.

Nestled around, as well as built into one of these pillars was a shantytown, but far larger than anything I had seen on Seron. The little city consisted of thousands of huts built from sheet metal and tarp, whilst the larger buildings that were built into the pillar seemed to be supporting its structural integrity. Each home sparkled with a light in the window.

In the darkness above the town, but beneath the steel ceiling, was what looked like a blanket of stars. I quickly realised that they were people using L lines to fly around. Like everyone up on the surface world, the rebels down here were also celebrating and practising using their new powers.

Hakkari gestured ahead. 'Welcome to your second home, Epiphyte. Or as some call it, the Shifting City.'

The boys gave each other amazed looks, while Iya stared at me anxiously.

Twenty: Nice Knowing You

Arc Unity

Like the last time I was here in Arc Unity, Raum escorted me down the aisle towards the raised platform. The arc seemed even redder than before, the light drenching me in their bloodied beliefs.

The audience was full and loud, each unable to contain their excitement this time around. When they saw me, some jumped up and down, cheering. Most had a creepy smile plastered on their faces. Their demeanour was so different; before, they were calmer, dignified even. Now they were like baying animals, calling for my death.

Having my powers meant that much to them? They couldn't at least pretend it was a sombre occasion until *after* I was dead?

We reached the sixth row where my own family and friends would normally be seated. But of course, it was empty, like I requested. My family weren't informed of the event, and other than Tau, they hadn't suspected a thing. Maybe I had their brainwashing to thank for making them so naive that they didn't even consider this could happen to me.

I paused to look at the seats, imagining that they were all here to strengthen my resolve. My lips trembled, as did my legs. To know

I was about to die and that there was no way to fight back terrified me. I had been powerful and in charge for so long that I had almost forgotten what true fear was like. It was better that they weren't here to see this. I didn't want them to remember me this way.

The platform was set up like before, but this time, of course, one of the Chosen was missing. Raum took his position, as did the others. Caelum, Raum and Andriel were calm, but Elion was visibly panicking even more than I was.

Before we arrived, Raum had told me that Elion attempted to escape in the night. His personal spaceship had been ripped apart by Caelum as it was about to leave orbit.

'Begin!' the emperor barked from the balcony overlooking us.

The others stood to attention, pointed their arms at their neighbours and closed their eyes once more. I felt sick, I wanted to run, portal away from this place, but obviously I couldn't. Defeated, I closed my eyes and joined the others as the audience quietened.

My vision went white as before, straight away this time, too, like the ritual *wanted* to happen.

I was now using matter destruction on the air particles below my feet so that I would stay in the air. I was Raum, floating high above a grey world of savages. The primitive, corpse-filled village smouldered below.

The planet was already breaking apart thanks to my genius, my art form. Rivers of magma could be spotted down the many splitting crevices. Bright-blue lightning cracked the red sky. This barbarian world was done, finished.

Only one remained, and he was the very reason my emperor had ordered this planet's destruction. Word of an undefeatable acolyte had brought me here, one so strong that he rivalled even *my* power.

This Caelum'inat floated across from me, staring me down. Although he was seemingly indestructible and much faster than me, his rage was uncontrolled. He was foolishly predictable. It was almost *too* easy to keep him distracted while our sap squads set up their inhibitor array.

He launched another assault, barrelling through the air like a madman, howling in his foreign tongue, as if *that* would overcome my defences. My invisible shield was impenetrable; no force or form of matter other than light could exist on its cusp without first being exponentially separated into smaller pieces.

When he reached me, he attempted to pummel my shield with his fists. When his seemingly unbreakable skin entered the zone of perfect deconstruction, the two refused to exist in the same space, propelling his arm back from whence it came.

My counterattacks had the same effect as the shield. Every wave of dematerialization I sent at him, rather than dissipating his body like dust in the wind, merely flung him through the sky.

My vision went white again, and this time the scene was familiar. This time I was Caelum, on board a space station, looking out through a window at the remnants of my grey world. All of the people I had ruled over as a god-king were gone. Killed and then taken by these warriors from the heavens. All my conquering was for nothing.

The man, Raumanu as he was called, stood beside me. At first, I thought these sky people did not know how to speak, but when I was brought back here, they must have taught themselves my language. Even so, I did not plan on speaking with any of them, least of all this Raumanu.

He stroked his short, black beard. 'I promise you, you'll still be a king amongst your people.'

I was silent at first, but my anger compelled me to face him. 'You're lying, you would have me bow to the one whom *you* call king. The one who leads *your* people.'

He didn't look away from the leftovers of my world. 'Not one, two. All you need to do is obey two and you will live forever, acting out every dream and fantasy, and gaining *limitless* power.' He glanced at me. 'Your grey world was pathetic, you had *no one* to call your equal, no battle to *truly* test you. I offer you the chance to conquer worlds throughout the universe.'

The far younger Raumanu faded away, as did the space station. I was now looking at a metal pole right in front of my eyes. My hands were bound around it, and I gripped my own knuckles tightly with interlocked fingers, bracing for another thrashing. I was Andriel again.

We had been at it all day in the prison courtyard, my torturer had been whipping me continually with his electrified lash. I was not the only one being punished for nothing; hundreds of others, mostly teenagers, were receiving the same treatment.

I would try to scream out every time he hit me, but I couldn't because of my muzzle. It, too, caused me pain. All I could do was massage the knuckles and fingers of my hands around the pole as if I were being consoled by someone who cared for me. Every day, I swore to get my vengeance, to turn their weapons back on them. I wanted for nothing else.

Then, in a flash of light and a moment of pure clarity, as if the world had stopped moving, I saw into this man's mind: his family, his military career, his childhood. I saw that his purpose here was to turn me, all of us, into something. A weapon... an acolyte. He thought this was all justified, and yet he was partly afraid of me, afraid that if I gained powers, I would make *him* suffer. He was right, it was *his* turn now.

I looked over my bloodied and gashed shoulder at the man, who stopped whipping when we locked eyes. He shook as I unsettled every memory and skill he had ever learned, every synapse in his brain jostled. I ripped his thoughts to pieces, leaving nothing but a jumbled mass of unrepairable organic jelly.

The husk of what was left collapsed, blood spurting from his nostrils, frightening the other torturers. They would all be next, but not before I forced one of them to release me.

The blood morphed into snow; it was all around me, covering the ground. The icy peaks of the mountains were far behind us through the tundra, but it was not far enough. Was there any part of this world that had not yet frozen over? I looked again at the rocky pass.

It was only my father and I left, wearing layer upon layer of animal skins we had pilfered from our dead. The rest of the Y'lions, my family, had frozen to death in the bitter, ceaseless winter, and it was *their* bodies that provided the only food we had left. But we could not stop to mourn or risk the same for ourselves. My father was trailing behind, and unless we found shelter soon, he, too, would die.

A howl carried on the winter's chill. I looked back again, my eyes following our footsteps in the deep white until they lay upon a pack of volks; furry, clawed, brutish creatures that walked on two feet but sprinted on all fours. Their rib cages were visible, for like us, they were starving and desperate, which made them even more dangerous. Their jaws snapped as they gave chase.

My father and I roused what energy we had left, running through the snow, but sinking with each step. He yelled out to me as the volks pounced, together bringing him down, ripping his clothes off and clawing at his exposed flesh. I stopped and yelled back, but he was gone, his lifeless eyes locked on the frosting sky behind me.

I was alone, the last of my family, my village, perhaps even my kind. I would not survive. Our people only wanted to live, to have the bare essentials, the building blocks of life: food, water and shelter. But it was too much to ask in this world.

Once the volks were sure he was dead, they raised their snouts and sniffed in my direction, plotting their second kill. They charged along the crimson snow.

I was not angry; I had accepted this now, kneeling to wait. Yet, a strange sensation rose from the pit of my stomach until it filled my body. A blinding flash. As the volks leapt, I roared upwards and watched as long pillars of stone and steel burst up into the sky, many more grew sideways and impaled the volks, obliterating their fur and flesh into small bits.

As these rumbling pillars finally ceased, more sprouted from the frozen soil in an endless growth, leaving me in its centre. I stopped yelling, panting instead, in awe of my surroundings. Thousands of spikes had formed a forest of needles, each facing outwards from me like a ring of thorns.

Everything changed to white, and a final vision appeared. One of *my* memories again, the time I had created a portal to Seron's sun over the MDC. Caelum had me in a headlock from behind and forced me to watch my shame all over again as an entire city of people was melted by harsh solar rays.

It was like a recurring nightmare, reliving what I had felt when I had erroneously taken out my rage on a mostly innocent population. The guilt was overwhelming, and through our connection, I knew the other Chosen were experiencing that guilt, too.

I shook out of it, as did the others; our visions were over. Again, a stream of white energy shot from my fingertips and formed into another portal in the centre of our circle. The emperor, empress and the Chosen stared at me.

'Let me guess, me first?' I asked.

We had all arrived in the other dimension like before. The surreal surroundings had not changed since our previous visit. There was still a bridge connecting the arrival platform to the one with the silver orb, which actually did appear slightly bigger than before. As we crossed the bridge, I glanced back at the others and caught a few of them quietly nodding to one another. I didn't need to be a psychic to know what was going to happen next.

If I was to survive, I had to be smart about this; whoever was closest to that orb would be sucked in first. It was just a matter of evading the others until that thing had chosen its next victim.

'So, how do we decide who goes next?' Elion asked obliviously.

'Isn't it obvious?' Caelum said before looking at me.

I shook my head, unsurprised. 'You really are the *worst* father ever.'

Without being touched this time, the orb turned green and sprang to life. It silently spun again, eager for a sacrifice. My death seemed fairly certain at this point, but I wasn't going to go down willingly.

'You don't have a choice, Sacet,' Andriel said as they all converged closer.

'You all keep saying that,' I replied, taking a couple of steps back. 'But I'm pretty sure your rulers don't care which one of us is next.'

Caelum continued to shift closer. 'You're outnumbered. And I'm still stronger than you in here.'

'Yeah, but I'm faster,' I replied, before bolting sideways towards the pillars, narrowly avoiding Caelum's grasp.

'Get her!' he yelled, before he and Elion gave chase.

I weaved between the pillars that surrounded the platform's perimeter. Looking back, I saw that both Andriel and Raumanu had receded, hiding behind the pillars. The tentacles around the orb had surfaced, slowly feeling their way in all directions for someone to grab.

Caelum and Elion weren't giving up; they were getting closer to me as we ran around the platform. One of the tentacles whipped at Elion, but he ducked just in time and continued running. Another tentacle, much larger than the others, slapped down between me and the men, stopping them in their tracks. Distracted, I almost tripped on one of the smaller appendages, but managed to jump over instead.

As I was about to reach the bridge again to cross it, I felt a strong smack to my shin. It was Raumanu's cane, he had been hiding behind a column.

I tumbled to the ground, and the others caught up with me. Caelum bent down and grabbed me by the neck in a choke. I looked up at Raumanu with absolute hatred.

'Nice knowing you,' Andriel said, skulking behind a column. 'So short-lived.'

Raumanu leant back on his cane again. 'My apologies, Sacet. You will be with the light in but a moment. Your beautiful power shall live on in all of us.'

Caelum and Elion both handled and heaved me towards a pile of the orb's tentacles. When I landed and felt them squirming around me, I tried throwing them off, but they quickly constricted around my limbs.

A tentacle thrashed me upwards. '*Ahh, ugh*, you'll all regret this!'

Raumanu smiled. 'You will be remembered fondly for your sacrifice. Go now with dignity.'

The tentacles drew me closer and closer until the orb had enveloped my legs.

'I hope you're next, father,' I yelled as my body submerged. 'I curse you. I hope your final death is *slow* and *painful*! This thing will eat you all!'

His unphased expression remained.

My head was drawn under, and a drowning sensation immediately overcame me. My whole body was dead weight, I was unable to move. Everything inside me was sharp and ripping. It felt like I was dying.

I could see the others outside melt away, as did everything else. It faded white again, but there was no warmth inside this time, only cold. No thought or feeling. No time or space.

Twenty-One: Beatdown

The streets of the Shifting City

This "Shifting City" as they had called it was a slum secretly underneath another slum. It must have been hidden so deep that the authorities dared not descend into the toxicity. And yet somehow this shantytown was filled with life, abuzz with activity.

Our group was walking along a street, nothing more than a muddy trail flanked by sheet metal walls. It was slow going, uphill towards the massive foundation pillar that the city surrounded.

Everywhere we looked was a torrent of activity, like a bustling, dirty marketplace to our left, where merchants and rebels haggled over scraps. Oily mechanics fiddled with spare parts to the right, attempting to fix their outdated, corroded rifles and gadgets. Ahead, lines of rebels ran drills with that same rusty equipment. All the while, hundreds more flew overhead using their ill-got L lines.

We received many stares, but they were mostly directed at Hakkari. Most cheered and hollered for him, some even saluted in a strange way I had never seen, with both palms together like a beggar. The street was terraced into multiple walkways above, where more saluted from.

All this attention for a surgeon? What about us?

Lotus rubbed Eno's head as we walked. 'By the way, sorry for knocking you and your friends out, lil' brother.'

'That's okay,' he replied. 'Hey, so… why did you choose the name Lotus?'

'Because it sounded cool.'

Eno shook his head. 'No, I mean…'

'I know what you meant,' Lotus said, before staring intently ahead at their parents.

I had been by Tau's side ever since we got on that damned hoverbus. If the others were going to listen to anyone, it would probably be her. Plus, it felt safer to stand next to the healer.

I chose a moment when I thought others were distracted by the shifting crowds and leant over to whisper in her ear. 'Family or not, we're in grave danger here. And I don't like the idea of being puppeteered by a psychic, above *or* below, do you?'

'I know, I know,' she said back softly, also checking to see if anyone was listening in, 'but what if Sacet is in danger up there? Shouldn't we accept their help to rescue her?'

'Sacet? What about *us*?' I exclaimed, a little louder than I intended. I threw my arms about in frustration. 'If they discover us down here with them, we're *dead*! Do you understand that? We have to get back home right *now*!'

As I threw my hand to the side, a portal suddenly appeared where I unintentionally pointed. We both froze, as did everyone in the group, blocking the narrow street. Through the portal, we could see the luxuriously furnished Arc Sacet penthouse interior. The crowds around us stopped their activities and noticed it, too.

'Did I just…?' I began.

'A portal?' Tau asked. 'But…'

The portal was just like Sacet's. We all stood there, waiting for someone to step through it. But eventually, every one of us had the same look of shock and realisation: Sacet had been sacrificed like Lucenia had.

'No,' Enni started, running over to us. 'No, it can't… it can't be!'

This was it, my chance to escape. I looked into the portal and then at Hakkari, repeatedly back and forth.

'Close it!' Hakkari demanded, noticing my hesitation.

As I was about to leap through, Tau latched onto my wrist. 'Don't!'

'Close it now!'

I conceded with a sigh, flicking my fingers at the portal erratically, but it wasn't closing. Now, how did Sacet close her portals again? Like this? No…

Hakkari stormed over. 'Quickly, before the network detects us!'

After a few more embarrassing attempts, the portal eventually closed.

The street had gone silent. We all stared into each other's eyes, one by one, all thinking the same thing. Sacet was dead. Tears streamed down Enni's cheeks. Eno looked as though someone had ripped out his heart. Noor's lips trembled, and he fell to his knees, roaring upwards. The group's wails echoed off the rusty metal. The city stopped shifting.

After the incident, Hakkari had escorted us double-time to the centrepiece of the city, the colossal pillar. We had gone up and around a giant, wide spiralling staircase, and then through a plain, unassuming doorway into the pillar's interior. Finally, after traversing a maze of cold, poorly lit, unstable rooms and hallways, we were left in a sitting room, of sorts, while Hakkari went off to work out what to do with us.

We had a window overlooking the bleak rebel city outside. Well, a hole in the wall, not a proper window. Somehow, the muddy streets were filled with even more activity than before.

Enni was sitting with Azua and Eno on a metal bench, crying on their shoulders. 'How could they do that to her? She was doing what they wanted, and they *still* took her. Poor Sacet.'

Both Azua and Eno had blank stares, still in shock.

Hakkari had been gone for a while now, having left us with Lotus and a few other guards.

Noor was punching nearby walls in a fit of rage, while Tetsu and Noor's family were attempting and failing to console him. The guards didn't seem to care about the damage, after all, their buildings were already trash-filled messes.

Lotus watched the boys with indifference, seeming instead to be focusing on her parents. She was internally raging, something I was an expert at. To the uninitiated, one might assume that, like Noor, she was upset over Sacet's sacrifice like the others, but I knew better. That look she was giving her parents, she *loathed* them. I knew the feeling all too well.

'I'm going to kill them,' Noor shouted again, 'each and *every* one of them!'

Tetsu kept eyeing Tau with concern, for she was also distraught. She was currently sobbing in a nearby corner. Tetsu left Noor with his family and then joined Tau over in the corner, offering her a hug, which she gladly accepted. She bawled even harder.

What were these rebels going to do with us now that Sacet was gone? What if they didn't let us leave? No, that wouldn't make sense, because if we went missing, the authorities would send search parties. What if they altered my mind to do something I wasn't comfortable with? I wouldn't even be able to explain what happened because I wouldn't have any memory of this.

I only had one choice: to escape, but if I tried it in front of the rebels, I'd be stopped immediately.

I stood up and approached the nearest guard. 'I need to use the bathroom.'

He looked over to Lotus, who narrowed her eyes at me before eventually nodding. The guard gestured for me to follow and turned. He led me along a couple of hallways before we found the toilets.

I retched upon entering. The revolting smell was overpowering. The ancient, mouldy floor had all manner of stains and unknown goop splashed along it. Mildew and other slimy green lichens lined the cracked tiles. Cleaning must have been a foreign concept here. The walls of the bathroom were more stonework, and the rusty partition walls and doors separating the line of toilets were pockmarked with holes.

The guard watched from the entrance as I made for the nearest stall. I pushed open the door with a long, loud creak before entering to inspect the horrifying sight. The toilet itself was just a high concrete step with a hole in it, which dropped into a black void. As nonchalantly as possible, I closed the door and locked the latch.

I took a deep breath and listened out for any movement outside the stall. I think I got away with it. I couldn't believe they just let me walk away from the group and go to the bathroom, after knowing I could portal now. That trust would be their undoing.

I felt a little guilty for escaping on my own, but they'd get over it after they were safe at home. I'd send for help and let them know that Eno and his parents had just been brainwashed by a rogue psychic. Hopefully, after their INCs were restored to normal, I'd still have a place in the penthouse, and maybe even praise for their rescue.

Now, to repeat the same portal as before, but on purpose this time. What would be the safest destination? The same as last time would do, the Arc Sacet penthouse. I closed my eyes and pointed my fingers at the disgusting toilet, then pictured home.

The air pressure around me changed, and a subtle draught blew on my face. When I opened my eyes, I saw it, a viewport directly into the penthouse. It was quiet; no one was inside.

There was a loud crash behind me as my stall door was ripped clean off its hinges by two twisting L lines. The door was hurled away, and I saw Lotus standing there with her arms raised.

I leapt to the portal but jolted midair as one of the tentacle-like L lines wrapped around my waist and tightened. I desperately reached out to the portal. 'No!'

The L line whipped me up into the ceiling, smashing me headfirst into the already crumbling plaster. The painful collision dazed me. I cried out as I was whipped back down again, this time fracturing the tiles with my face.

I groaned as I slowly got up on my knees. Everything was bloody and blurry. I felt infected by this place.

I could just make out the other guard watching by the door, in fact, now there were three of them. The air flow had changed again, for my portal must have closed.

A pair of hands grabbed my back and hauled me up, before slamming me into the nearby wall.

I instinctively brought my hands up to my eyes to use my power, but she quickly snatched one of my wrists and twisted the fingers back with her other hand, farther and farther until I was forced to kneel and scream.

'*Ahhhh*! *Argh*! Stop!'

Snap! Crack!

I continued to scream as searing pain shot through my now broken hand. In my throes of immense pain, I briefly looked up at Lotus.

Her expression was murderous, she took no joy in this. 'You can't make portals with broken hands.'

Hands? Plural? I tried to hide the other behind my back, but screamed again when she darted forward to grab it.

'No, no. NO! Stop! Sto… *ahhhhhhh!*'

Snap! Pop! Snap!

I bawled as the far stronger and more muscular woman treated me like a ragdoll. I slumped to the side as the unforgiving agony drilled through my nerves.

'No more,' I pleaded through blubbering moans.

Lotus wasn't done. She bent down and grabbed my neck with one hand, before lifting and sliding me up the wall in a choke.

She looked me up and down with disgust. 'You know, I used to *idolize* you. You killed the tyrants without fear of consequence… *now* look at you. What a pitiful coward you've become, cutting and running.'

I gargled and strained my throat for air. '*Pl-please…*' I couldn't even reach up to her hand to fight back.

'You escape, then what?' Lotus asked, before gesturing about. 'You turn this *whole* city in for execution? You're just another one of Andriel's puppets.'

I kicked my feet at the wall, desperately trying to push my body up higher to loosen the choke. 'No. That's a lie,' I managed to utter.

She chucked my tiny frame towards the toilet and I smacked into yet another wall.

Lotus' stare intensified. '*I* still follow my convictions without fear of consequence.' Green flames erupted from her back, filling the stall. 'I suppose that'll now have to include *exterminating* you.'

I felt woozy, and everything was getting darker. My very life essence was being drained.

Her flames were growing in strength. 'I *hate* your parents so much, so killing their child should be *cathartic* for me.'

As soon as she mentioned my parents, a fire ignited within me, too.

I returned her hateful stare. '*No one…* hates my parents more than *me*!' I shot up and shoved her back with my open palms. It gave me incredible pain, but I didn't care. 'You think *this* hurts me? It's *nothing* compared to being in a prison of the mind, body and soul for 210 cycles.'

Her narrowed stare remained steady.

'So go ahead,' I continued to shout, 'kill me! Give me the sweet *release* of death. What's the point in living if I can't ever have my revenge?'

One of Lotus' eyebrows raised as her flames lessened. 'You still want it, then? Revenge?'

'Of course I do! Nothing would make me happier.'

Her flames lessened some, but her fists remained clenched. 'We offered you the opportunity to fight them with us, but you chose to run? We could *both* have our revenge on them,' she said as she slammed a fist into the stall wall, 'if you *stopped* being so spineless and *helped* us.'

I gritted my teeth. 'Why bother when you rebels fail and fail and keep FAILING to do what *should* have been done centuries ago, before I was even born?'

'Because now it's different,' she said as she poked me harshly in the forehead. 'You're old, but you clearly still have a *child's* brain.'

'What?' I screeched.

'You have memories of your home. You have *seen* rooms in that place that no one else on the planet has ever been allowed to. With your portals, you could send an army, along with the world's deadliest assassin – *me* – right into Mummy and Daddy's bedchambers. Did this not occur to you?'

I panted now, still reeling in agony. 'I… I…'

'No, it *didn't*,' she continued as her aura ceased. She tilted her head to the side. 'So, are you in? Or do I *actually* have to execute you?'

I groaned, still gritting my teeth from the shooting pains. 'Fine… *argh*… I'm in. Wait, so were you *not* going to execute me?'

Lotus smirked. 'I was, until you decided to make the right choice.' She reached and grabbed me again, before ripping me away from the toilet and back into the bathroom. 'Now head back to Tau to get healed, move!'

She watched as I begrudgingly turned and staggered for the exit.

The other guards parted and led me back along the hallway as Lotus brought up the rear.

'And just so you know,' she continued, 'I hated Sacet, too.'

Twenty-Two: Never-Ending

'Hey!' a distant voice called. 'Hey!'

My eyes fluttered open. All I could see were green clouds tempestuously swirling above. I slowly sat up and took in my surroundings. The terrain was white in all directions on an endless flat plane. The horizon showed no mountains, no points of interest, no difference in colour, just infinite white below and green sky above. I was still here.

Someone was running towards me, but they were still a while off. Was that Lucenia? Yes, she still wore her yellow robe from yesterday's sacrifice. How was she still alive? How was *I* still alive, for that matter?

I groaned in frustration. No, of *course* I was still alive. My fate, it seemed, was to continuously suffer and fight until there was nothing left of me. Even after I had already given up, said my goodbyes, and made peace with the fact that they had won, I still had to wake up to do it all over again.

As Lucenia got closer, she waved her arms about madly. 'Hey, help! Help me!'

I felt drowsy, but I simultaneously felt no pain. It was all coming back to me: the platform, the orb and how the others had sacrificed me. I remembered that the platform was hanging in the sky, far above the white plane. I looked up at the storm, trying to spot it, but it was nowhere to be seen.

When Lucenia got close enough, she stopped far short and gave me a distrustful look. '*Oh*, it's *you*.'

I got to my feet, which surprisingly wasn't difficult. As soon as I stood, the drowsiness faded. But like before, I couldn't sense anything around me with my second perception. I raised my hands and tried to make a portal next to me, but nothing worked.

'I already tried my powers, too,' Lucenia said, playing with the end of her hair. 'Did it take you as well? The orb?'

I sighed and nodded. 'Yeah, it did.'

Lucenia looked as if she could start crying at any moment. 'What happened after it took me? I've been alone here for *so* long.'

'After you were sucked in, the rest of us faded back to Aster,' I explained. 'People everywhere somehow had your power. Billions of them.'

She shook her head, confused. 'Had my power? *My*… power? You all stole it! I…' She paced back and forth. 'No, no, no, no, *NO*! This *can't* be right. I can't be stuck in here now.'

I continued to examine our bleak surroundings. 'Looks to be that way.'

'So, wait, if you all saw me get eaten by it, why'd you all go back again?'

My body drooped at having to recap the depressing events. 'Well, the greedy emperors loved the idea of repeating the ceremony. We waited a day and… the Chosen all turned on me again.'

Her face screwed up. '*Hmph*, good.'

I took a step forward. '*Excuse* me?'

'It should have been *you* in here first, and then I could have talked some sense into the emperors. When it took me, *you* just stood there watching, like the others did. You didn't even *try* to help.'

I folded my arms. 'I was in shock.'

'How convenient for you. You don't think *I* was the one in shock, being dragged into that thing?' She looked away from me and copied my defensive body language.

A tear trickled down her cheek, and her angry façade crumbled.

She fell to her knees and slumped to the side. '*Oh*, what's the use in fighting anymore? We're dead and no one cares.' Tears flowed freely now that she was lying flat. 'Did my family even *grieve* for me, I wonder? Did anyone? I don't deserve this, I have so much more I wanted to do.'

I shook my head. 'You're pathetic.'

She was so self-absorbed that she barely reacted, instead continuing to whine.

I turned away from her. 'You used to be a *great* warrior. That memory you showed us had you facing down both Caelum *and* Raumanu to defend your people. But now? You're so accustomed to your riches and pampering that you... you can't die with dignity.'

I realised the irony of what I said immediately.

She shook her head and cleared her tears with her hand. 'I'm still a warrior.'

I chuckled. 'You haven't been a warrior for *hundreds* of cycles. The entire length of the Seronian war, which you did *nothing* about.'

Lucenia initially creased up her face in anger, but she quickly changed back to sobbing.

I took a deep breath and reaffirmed myself. 'I had given up all my hope, but seeing you like this, wallowing in sadness, it makes me realise I can't give up yet.' I stared back at her. 'I'll find a way out of this place. And when I do, I will permanently end the emperors and *anyone* else that stands in my way.'

I chose a random direction and began marching, leaving Lucenia behind. I didn't look back. I needed to stay resolute. And even if I walked forever and never found anything, I would never give up again.

'Wait! You can't leave me here?' she called out.

I shrugged. 'Then follow?'

After a short stint of marching, I heard Lucenia's footsteps as she ran to catch up, and together we began our long journey across the empty plane.

We had been walking for what seemed like a day, but it was impossible to tell in this unchanging place. Maybe it was far longer, maybe shorter. There was no sun, shadows or any other indication of time passing.

What was the point of this empty place? I just wanted to find something… anything. Anything or anyone at all.

Lucenia trailed far behind, panting and close to collapsing. 'If anyone… is up there… listening to me… please… just let me out of this place,' she said, gasping for air. 'I promise to be… nicer to the commoners… and I promise… I'll try to visit all of my kids… except Jerrod… he knows why.'

I stopped, looked back and shook my head. 'You'd think in a dimension with no pain that you wouldn't be *this* tired. And anyway, you've had *hundreds* of cycles to keep yourself fit. What have you actually been doing in that time?' I remembered when I first saw her at the party, surrounded by suitors. 'Let me guess, you've just been partying and sleeping around?'

'That's *none* of your business,' she replied. 'And anyway, on Aster, an acolyte doesn't need to be fit; they need to be powerful and popular… and beautiful.'

I laughed. 'Well, none of those things matter *here*.'

Lucenia ignored me, instead gazing at something in the distance to our side. 'What is that?'

'What?'

I followed her stare, and far on the horizon was a small, dark dot. Something was out there. Had we kept marching in our current direction, we might have missed it. We looked at each other and nodded before jogging towards it.

It was another agonisingly long walk, especially with Lucenia dawdling behind, but we finally had a clear view of the strange object we saw on the horizon. Even now that we were closer, I still had no idea what it was. I had never seen anything like it before.

I assumed it was a living creature. Its abdomen was like an elongated ball, the shape reminded me of a pulsating heart. It was as big and wide as Caelum, probably bigger. A bright light shone from inside its strange, translucent flesh, like a miniature star. The rest of the flesh had galaxy-like patterns running through it, with swirls of dark reds and blues.

At the top of this singular body piece was something similar to a skull, melded into the abdomen's flesh. It had two empty eye sockets, but no nostril holes, teeth or lower jaw. And instead of the top and back of the skull, five odd limbs were coming out of it in different directions.

The limbs were a collection of braided tentacles that writhed and wriggled endlessly. The sum of them far outsized the body itself. Each was pinkish-red and had a glistening, quivering sheen.

The alien was floating off the ground, and as for which way it was facing, I couldn't say. The entire thing had an ominous red glow around it. As the fleshy sack slowly heaved in and out, perhaps to breathe, it gave odd, deep wheezes.

It wasn't reacting to our presence, so perhaps it was sleeping? I stopped a few paces away and examined it.

'What *is* it?' Lucenia asked, having finally caught up.

The creature stirred, giving a loud groan as its tentacles twisted about. Lucenia's eyes widened as she jumped a couple of steps back. I crept closer, curious, but Lucenia silently waved to me as if suggesting I should stop.

'There's nothing else out here,' I said to her. 'We've come this far; we don't really have a choice.'

Ignoring her further fearful gestures, I approached the creature and placed my hand gently on one of its tentacles. 'Excuse me? Hello?'

The beast's bright light intensified, and its groans grew into a mouthless roar. The tentacles thrashed violently as it raised itself upright, hovering above us. Now that it was vertical, it was a lot larger than I initially thought, at least twice as high as any person.

Freaking out, Lucenia looked around as if planning to run, not that there was anywhere to go or hide behind. Instead, she crouched down as low as possible and brought her hands up to shield herself. I didn't care what this thing was; I stood my ground, waiting for the creature to do something. If it could lead us out of here, I would make it do so.

While continuing its roar, the beast raised its tentacles into the air and summoned an enormous fireball. In only a few moments, the fire grew directly up until it was the size of a mountain, hanging above us like a sun.

Both Lucenia and I shielded ourselves from the inferno's intense light and heat, and yet I felt no pain, no searing on my skin. The rumbling of the ball was almost deafening.

The fire shot up into the sky without warning like a volcanic discharge, leaving a column of smoke and cinders, and when it collided with the clouds, there was a truly mesmerising explosion of epic proportions. The clouds were unmoved. Instead, the fire spread in all directions like an orange ripple on the pond that was the green storm.

The furious creature wasn't done, for no sooner had the fire dissipated than it created streaks of lightning that forked across the sky in another dazzling spectacle. The electricity thundered, splitting the air, reflecting and bouncing off the plane and the storm above. But again, upon contact with the clouds, the bolts did nothing to affect them. If anything, the energy was absorbed.

We couldn't take our eyes off the fascinating, but also *terrifying* monster. It dismissed its elemental tools of destruction, and the plane fell silent again, other than the forever churning storm above. The skull-like tip of its body pointed in our direction, as though it were looking *right* at us.

I edged closer, trying to get its attention. '*Ah*, hello? Do you speak Asterian? Can… can you help us?' I gestured between Lucenia and I, unsure if it could even understand. 'We need to get out of this place. Out of your world.'

As if ignoring us, it turned and slowly levitated both up and away.

'Wait, stop!' I yelled.

'Where are you going?' Lucenia asked, finally showing a little backbone. 'Don't leave us!'

'You have powers here, you can help us, please!' I added, before looking around in desperation, searching for anything to help our case. 'If you take us back to the orb, we can do the rest. Please.'

The creature stopped in place, hovering high above. It turned around to face us again, then stared in silence, perhaps understanding.

The star in its centre amplified once more, making me feel dizzy, like I had left my body. My surroundings spun. Everything disappeared except for the creature's dazzling bright light, which was now as large as the fireball from earlier. It was like a giant eye inspecting me, judging me.

My body seized as a phantom force entered my mind. It walked through my memories, forcing me to relive them all over again at rapid speed. My entire life flitted through my brain, all the while a foreign presence was hanging on my shoulder, experiencing it all with me.

'*Hmmmm*, a Chosen,' an impossibly deep voice boomed, rattling in my mind. The bright light shook. '*Two* of you. So, you are *not* figments of my imagination. Then the end finally draws near.'

There was an upward inflection at the end of the sentence, as though the voice was excited or potentially angry. I wasn't able to respond, or move for that matter. My memories were on autopilot, but they occasionally slowed down during the most important events of my life.

A specific memory from when I was very young played repeatedly. I was a little sister, and the aircraft I was on had been shot down by the nomads. I watched them finish off my sisters again and again, including executing Tau with a bullet to the head.

'*Hrmmm*? A seventh? And eighth?'

My brain then skipped through more memories until it showed the time when Tau resurrected herself in front of me. Kalek was trapped in perpetual freefall to my side, and Tau's ribs were fusing back together.

'*Ah,* so you wish for me to escape,' the voice continued. 'But why would you want *me* out? You must be desperate.'

Another memory played of the time I was with Urias in his village under the mountain. I was standing over the metal shard, which I proceeded to grab. I experienced the pain of receiving the sand powers a second time, an ability that had long since faded.

'Did you lose control? A mistake? No, something interfered.'

I couldn't understand what the voice was talking about. Was it even talking to me? I felt so violated. While connected, I felt its desperation to escape this place, like ours, but far, far greater.

The creature released me from its psychic bind, and I fell to the ground, as did Lucenia behind me. We exchanged looks of shaken bewilderment. Wait, what just happened? I remembered a bright light and then… no, nothing happened.

The creature was right in front of us again. Its tentacles writhed with purpose and grew in length. They tightly wove and braided into thicker columns of flesh. While the faux skull remained at the top, the rest of the sack was wrapped with layer upon layer of tentacles, until eventually it looked like a torso, albeit with the bright light shining out of the chest, like a giant pupil.

Two tree-trunk-like arms sprouted to the sides, with fists at the end like boulders. Other than the mass of loose tentacles below the torso, its body type was similar to Kalek's. Slowly but surely, the tentacles were shaping themselves into something that was vaguely Asterian.

'Who… who are you?' I asked, sitting up.

'*What* are you?' Lucenia added.

'I was once a Chosen like you,' a voice echoed in my head, 'from the universe that preceded yours. And if we do not stop the rituals, then your *entire* universe will be destroyed, just as mine was.'

Twenty-Three: Powered by Feeling

The Shifting City

Inside the pillar

The four rebel guards escorting me were oddly quiet. They had directed my friends and their families to stay put in the sitting room and for me to follow them, and since then they hadn't said anything to me. Tetsu initially protested, but I assured him I'd be fine. The look in his eyes, it hadn't been just the usual loyalty, but genuine care for me.

We were heading down one metal hallway after the next, deeper towards the centre of the pillar. The only people around here were either guards or engineers taking stock, each more silent than the last.

Each room we passed was nothing like the shantytown shacks outside. While those were well-lit and filled with families, these rooms were metallic and cold, falling apart, and devoid of life. Ancient, long forgotten chambers from the previous industrial age.

Many were filled with stockpiles of supplies, like pallets of boxed food or heaps of rusty spare parts. Others had machinery the likes of which I had never seen. The deeper into the pillar we went, the rustier, yet sturdier the walls became.

After what had happened, Sacet being sacrificed, Iya's escape attempt and the subsequent healing I administered, I understood how dangerous the rebels' situation was. Were they going to release us soon? Perhaps we were still waiting until the end of the day, as originally planned? How long would it be until Raumanu sent out search parties for us, I wondered?

I sighed as I reminded myself of Sacet yet again. The families and I had been crying in a circle all morning. We had swapped even more stories about her, each more bittersweet than the last. Both my heart and stomach had felt broken ever since it happened.

I still couldn't get over it. Why would she lie to me like that? To her family, to all of us? She knew she was going to die, that's why she allowed so many people at once to stay in the penthouse. She kept it a secret to do what, to delay our grief? How selfish, it was just so she didn't have to deal with it.

The crippling loss made me both sad and angry, but I also felt incredible guilt. I hadn't tried hard enough to protect her when I *knew* something was going to happen. Well, did I know? Elysia's warning had been cryptic at best. Was Sacet's sacrifice what she was trying to warn me about? Now that she was gone, would helping these rebels make any difference?

There was an iron door ahead, which the guards had to manually unlock and open, producing a long, deep, metal groan. The smell of oil and dust came through, metal shavings rolled out into the corridor.

The enormous chamber beyond was dome-shaped, which echoed every footstep we made back at us. A large, circular opening was in the centre of the ceiling. Resting on the floor and poking up towards the hole was a huge, steel cylinder. It had a pointed top like a missile. The area was mostly dark, aside from the spotlights shining onto the cylinder.

The blue-skinned man was on a metal scaffold above me, with his palm resting on the cylinder. This was their psychic, the man known as Kaxiyan. He appeared alone, but when we came closer, I could hear him muttering something incoherent. Was he talking to himself?

The two guards turned back to leave the way they came and pulled the metal door closed. I heard muffled noises of it locking from the other side. With no other choice, I approached the nearest stairwell and climbed, each footstep rattling on the metal grates.

I briefly craned my neck up at the hole in the ceiling. It was an incredibly high shaft, one that I couldn't see the top of. Perhaps it reached all the way to the surface?

I crossed numerous catwalks until I finally reached Kaxiyan.

He was still talking to himself rapidly, as though his mouth struggled to keep up with his mind. I did pick up a few words here and there though.

'... how they must have felt... space for the first time... you, ignored for millennia...'

I stopped, taken aback by the lack of a proper greeting. I inspected the missile-like object and finally realised what it was: a spacefaring rocket. A very old one, by the looks of it. '*Uhh*. Well, yes, that's very impressive. You wanted to speak to me? Kaxiyan, right? My name is Tau, nice to meet you.'

He patted the spacecraft's gleaming exterior and examined some of its components more closely. '... we both have sat in the dark for too long... the Chosen path's light, only a matter of time now...'

He still hadn't even *looked* at me, so I came closer to get his attention. 'Excuse me, sir? About my friends and I...'

Kaxiyan sighed. '... can't afford patience... before the moment passes...'

I went silent for a moment, not quite sure what he was on about.

Kaxiyan paced, staring at the catwalk and shaking his head. '... can the path be broken? What if Saqiqa was right? This girl... could it be that simple?'

'Which girl?' I said, before intercepting his path and grabbing his arm lightly. 'Who are you talking about?'

Kaxiyan finally looked at me, only now realising I was in the chamber with him. '*Oh*, it's you,' he said in a much slower monotone. Both his body and demeanour stiffened.

'Yes, I'm Tau,' I repeated, looking him up and down. 'Your people brought me here, I assumed you... wanted to speak to me? Are you okay?'

'I'm fine,' he replied. 'I'm in the minds of many people at once. It requires most of my focus to manage my society.'

I raised an eyebrow. 'You're… controlling them? I thought psychics had to visually see them now… because of the INC modifications?'

He tapped his own head and smiled. 'Thanks to Hakkari's tech skills, I'm the exception to that rule.'

I shrugged. 'Then aren't you the same as the psychics above? As her?'

Kaxiyan stomped towards me. 'I am *nothing* like her, I'm not a slave any longer. You have *no* idea how hard it was to escape her network.'

I raised my hands. 'I'm sorry. It's just that you admitted you're still controlling these people.'

He pointed in my face. 'Without me, they'd still be slaves under those tyrants. They have *far* more freedom with me. I give them purpose, a reason to fight!'

I sighed and thought back to his earlier mumblings. 'Like the freedom to… break the Chosen path? What did you mean by that?'

He backed off with a pained expression. 'You heard that, *hmm?* I was referring to our sister group's attempts to execute Sacet. By removing her as a factor, they hoped to stop the path in its tracks.'

I sighed and looked away at hearing her name. 'Well, they died in vain, because in the end she was sacrificed anyway.' I took a deep breath before looking back. 'If it's okay with you, my friends and I would like to go home so we can properly grieve. And no offence to you or your cause, but we're over the fighting.'

Kaxiyan took a step back from me and wrapped his arms around his back. 'None of you are going anywhere.'

I shook my head. 'With respect, I'm putting my foot down.' I turned on the spot and made for the stairs. 'Instruct your slaves to escort my friends, their families and I out. We're done here.'

Kaxiyan made for the railing to look down on me. 'I'm afraid I need your friends for when we retake the surface. And as for you, haven't you worked out why I can't control your mind?'

I stopped midstride, facing away. As soon as he worded it that way, it became obvious. He couldn't enter my mind because…

My eyes widened. 'Because I'm… the seventh Chosen.'

I reminisced on my life, and it sort of made sense. Growing up, while every other soldier around me was easily moulded into killing machines, I had *never* wanted to be violent, aside from a couple of moments I wasn't proud of. There was also the recent brainwashing on our way to Aster. The dream we all had, perhaps programmed in by our INCs. Like Sacet, I never felt any love or admiration for the emperors afterwards, unlike our friends.

Kaxiyan slowly nodded. 'I knew the moment I saw you that everything was about to change. I locked down the settlement, brought our people back. No, my dear Tau, *you* are not going anywhere.'

But why? And how? Out of *trillions* of people, how did two sisters *both* happen to be Chosen? And if Kaxiyan knew right away when he looked at me, why did *Andriel* not notice? Why had all the Dominion brainwashers passed over me all these cycles?

I had another realisation and clasped my hand over my mouth. 'That means if I was sacrificed, everyone could have my power. *Everyone* would be immortal, free from death, sickness and suffering.' I turned back to him. 'Could you imagine it?'

It's what I had always dreamt of, but also assumed had just been a childish fantasy.

Kaxiyan's eyebrows lowered, and he shook his head even harder than before. 'Could I imagine the emperors and Andriel having eternal life rather than eventually wasting away? That will not do.'

I shrugged again. 'So, what, you're expecting me to stay down here, out of sight?'

Kaxiyan's worried face neutralized in a moment of clarity. 'No, the solution is obvious.'

Green flames erupted from the shadowy lower levels. Lotus must have been watching us from afar this whole time. She leapt upwards using two L lines blasting out of her feet. She was thrust high into the air.

I panicked, backing away and bumping into a tray of tools, which fell and clattered loudly. Lotus landed on the catwalk with a loud, reverberating bang. Kaxiyan stood in silence. Lotus straightened up and strode confidently towards me.

I receded even farther, eventually being stopped by the catwalk railing. 'Stay back! I *don't* want to fight you.'

Like Kaxiyan, she ignored my words. She had the same intense, cold stare as last time. I could already feel her powers draining mine.

Yet again, unsure of how to defend myself, I ignited my aura, but realised how futile it was against hers. What could I do? Where could I run? The only door into this place was locked tight.

I had another sudden realisation; my own power wasn't going to save me. I hadn't even tried to use Sacet's power yet, for I thought it would be an insult to her memory, plus I had no idea how. But then, the way Lucenia's power worked… something clicked in my mind.

When I healed others, it was fuelled by my need to care for them, and the less distracted I was by fear or anger, the more powerful I became. Meanwhile, the green version of the aura *required* that anger. That selfish drive. Perhaps every ability was powered by different feelings?

I shook my head at them. 'I just want this to be over… let us go. Free us!'

Looking up again at the shaft, I pictured myself flying up. I wanted freedom. That feeling pervaded me, drifting amongst the clouds, detached from all. I felt a lurch in my stomach as I rose from the ground. It worked! I held onto that feeling, imagining my escape, boosting my ascent.

Lotus craned her neck up and copied me, boosting upwards. I tried to ignore her, focusing on the shaft above, closer and closer. My aura still felt as though it were being drained. Lotus was gaining on me. I flew above the rocket's tip and up the shaft. I passed a series of spotlights which, at this speed, strobed as I passed them. Higher and higher still.

My L lines were different to hers. While mine had a serene, effervescent quality, giving off their own constant rainbow aura and leaving a long trail to their source, hers were just plain white, and like sudden, violent bursts.

The very top of the shaft was still impossible to make out, but more worrying was an upcoming hatch in the process of closing. The mechanism was slow. Did I have enough time to get through? I needed to speed up or I wasn't going to make it. I strained, focusing on myself in the clouds, but it was no use, the door sealed shut long before I could reach it.

In addition to the lights on the sides of the shaft, there were occasional air vents, tiny tunnels just large enough for a person to squeeze through. It was again my only option, so I ceased boosting and snatched at some ladder rungs built into the shaft.

As I successfully stopped and hung off the ladder, Lotus overshot my position and was now above me looking down. I clambered up the ladder to the nearest vent, which thankfully wasn't blocked, before ducking and crawling in.

After a few moments of pulling myself deeper into the dark ventilation duct, I glanced back and saw Lotus level with the shaft. Rather than climb into the vent, she launched in instead. Her body slid and screeched along the steel sides towards me, just as I went around a corner. She slammed into the vent wall, before swiping at me like a monster possessed.

Without the light of our competing auras, the vent would have been pitch black.

'Why are you doing this?' I called back as I frantically crawled. 'I'm no threat to you.'

'*Oh*, but you are,' Lotus said in monotone as she squirmed through the vent after me. 'With your power, do you believe everyone would be as virtuous as you?'

I went around another corner and, thankfully, the duct's ceiling rose, allowing me to stand and sprint. But I felt something whip around my ankle and tighten. She had flung an L line towards me like a coiling rope and was now dragging me back, while also intensifying her sickly green flames.

'Help!' I screamed, hoping anyone would hear. 'Help me!'

'An empire of... *fallen* disciples, like Lotus,' she said, pausing between each heave. 'Consuming the weak... to remain immortal. You'd plunge the empire... into a chaos... that it'd never recover from.'

Now that I was practically underneath her legs, Lotus dismissed her whip and focused her flames. My aura was snuffed out immediately. I shivered as death's embrace slid over me.

No, it was *not* going to end here! I fired two L lines at her torso, which hit and flung her back through the duct. I had hoped my attack would injure her at least, but like how my aura protected me from harm, so did hers.

She eventually stopped sliding and sat up. 'You think Lotus gets her power *purely* from hatred?' she said as she rose again without a scratch on her. 'My pets need to be fed, and I feed her well.'

Lotus marched towards me as I shuffled up and away. As I was about to turn and run, she stopped mid-stride.

She brought her hand to her forehead as her eyes fluttered, looking as though she was in pain, before doubling over and groaning. 'No, get out!' Gone was her usual intense stare, instead replaced with fear. 'She's here.' Her eyes darted about before resting on me. 'Run!'

Was Lotus in control of herself again? I continued retreating back, unsure of what was happening. She contorted violently and after another moment of pained screams, she went silent and motionless. Her gaze looked through me, as if I weren't even there.

A draught of wind picked up in the duct, and a bright light appeared from behind. A portal, I shielded my eyes from the destination's ambient light spilling through.

It was the same chamber I had left my companions in. Noor, Tetsu, Eno and all their respective families were still where I left them, but they also had blank stares. Like robots, they were all frozen in place.

'Come on through, Tau,' I heard a feminine voice call through the portal, but I could not see its source.

I paused. Her. I had never heard her speak, but I knew who it was.

I had repeatedly felt like I had no choice in things, that I was led down paths designed by those more powerful than me. That I was treated like a child, unable to make decisions. Perhaps it was just the taste of this new power, but I still wanted to escape. I glanced behind at the vent I had come from.

'Thinking of leaving?' the voice called. 'Surely you don't want to leave your friends?'

I sighed. Of course I didn't. It wasn't like me to cut and run when people needed my help. Reserved to my fate, I stepped through the portal, as did a completely neutral Lotus. The portal closed, and behind us I saw who had been speaking.

It was Andriel. I had only seen her up close once, at the party. She had a calm, confident smirk, in complete control. She had dyed red hair and wore skimpy, colourful clothes that were wholly impractical for a place like this. She also held a gas mask casually at her side.

She wasn't alone, there was a line of heavily armed and armoured soldiers behind her, motionless. Each was a burly, intimidating behemoth in their own right.

Strangely, I couldn't see Iya anywhere. Had she perhaps escaped in time?

'We haven't been properly introduced,' Andriel began, tilting her head as if examining a quaint curiosity. 'Although, do we really need to? I already know *everything* about you.'

As she spoke, I made my way over to Tetsu and waved my hand in front of his eyes, but there was no response. Then I went to Eno and Noor and tried the same, this time shaking their bodies.

Andriel rolled her eyes. 'There's no point in that, I assure you.' She then gestured to Lotus. 'Seems like I came to the rescue just in time.'

I stopped in place, and she and I stared at one another for a moment. 'You're not here just to rescue us. You're here for *me*, aren't you?'

She nodded. 'Of course.'

'How long have you known?' I asked.

'Since before you became a queen.'

I shook my head. 'And you kept it secret from everyone? Why?'

She shrugged and gestured around at her psychic slaves. 'Because I like to be in control? And because sometimes it's good to keep things a secret. I like to have surprises up my sleeve for when I need them. But now I have plans for you—'

'You're going to sacrifice me,' I finished for her, before looking at my friends, 'and you'll hurt *them* if I don't obey?'

She nodded. '*Very* good, then we understand each other.'

I wandered over to the nearby window and peered out over the now quiet rebel village. There were hundreds of people in the streets below, as well as on the rooftops and floating in the sky. Each one was motionless, blankly staring in my direction.

'Did you enjoy playing with my toys?' she asked as she joined my side to look at them all.

'What will happen to them?' I asked. 'There are innocent people down there, children, families.'

She giggled and sneered at me. '*Oh,* Tau, you're *so* one note.' She pointed out at them. 'They'll stay here and *continue* their work.'

I gave her a confused expression. 'What?'

She smirked. 'I conquered every Asterian mind centuries ago, except for the Chosen. Do you have *any* idea how *boring* it is when there's nothing and no one left to challenge you?'

I thought for a moment, then closed my eyes. 'So, Kaxiyan didn't escape. You… *freed* him.'

Andriel nodded. 'And *many* others. I'm hoping *one* of my toys will work out how to surprise me someday.' She paused and laughed again. 'You know, it's *very* surreal telling you this out loud. I mean, I reveal secrets to my slaves all the time, but I always remove their memories afterwards. But I *can't* with you. I suppose it doesn't matter if I'm going to kill you anyway…'

I sighed and stared at her. 'You can do whatever you want with me, I won't fight back. I only ask for *one* thing.'

She glanced over to the others. 'I already know what it is, and consider it done. They won't come to harm.' She saw my confused look and gave a smug smile. 'I don't need to be a mind reader when you're so predictable.'

One of Andriel's slaves pointed at the empty space in the centre of the room, and a portal appeared shortly after. Its destination was another interior, far brighter than where we were now. It was decorated with colourful lighting, and electronic music buzzed and thumped melodically. The guards closed in and corralled me towards the portal.

Twenty-Four: A Sadistic Loop

Lucenia and I couldn't take our eyes off the tentacled monstrosity. Its heart-shaped body heaved as it waited for us to respond, but neither of us knew how to. The storm thundered above, the booms echoing off the Empyrean's surface and breaking me out of my stupor.

'The… the *entire*… universe?' I finally uttered from my sitting position.

The creature groaned, and another bright light blinded my vision, like before. Then, my mind learned a plethora of things all at once, as if they were being psychically transmitted. Time felt like it had frozen. Similar to when I was experiencing the memories of the other Chosen, I now experienced *this* creature's memories.

'Everyone that lives, everything that exists,' the deep voice rattled as its life unfolded in fast motion. 'No more.' The creature sounded masculine, but there was no telling what genders, if any, its race had.

The creature's name was unpronounceable in our tongue, consisting of an impossible cadence of simultaneous sounds at contradictory pitches. Its new body was still forming, becoming more and more like us, yet still an incredibly poor imitation, a horrific mockery.

'You may call me… Ophan,' it said, sensing my confusion over what to call it. 'I have been here since time immemorial, in this dimension with no pain, death or deterioration of memory.'

I could see a star-filled night sky. I was now on an alien world, with mountains that unnaturally curved and even looped back upon themselves. It had lush forests of blue and red vegetation that twitched and wriggled, as though alive. The soil beneath was dark purple. Everywhere I could see brimmed with strange lifeforms flitting and coiling about in unexpected ways.

'Like yours, our people were prosperous,' Ophan began.

My view zoomed to another place on the planet, a bustling city, or so I assumed. Unlike Asterian buildings which were vertical, these buildings were like multi-pointed stars, the spikes growing in all directions, occasionally crossing over one another. Instead of streets there were spiralling tunnels lit with sparkling light.

I saw more androgynous creatures like Ophan. They did not float but scampered about with their tentacles. Some skittered at ground level, whilst others hung from impressive heights, clambering over the buildings' surfaces with ease.

They differed in colour, and some had more than one light shining in their abdomens. Others had different arrangements of tentacles, fewer or more, thicker or thinner, or sprouting from different places. But one thing remained the same on each, the skull-like shape protruding from the top of the body, perhaps a vestigial leftover from the previous form.

'I and the other Chosen also discovered what you call the Ceremony of Unity,' Ophan continued.

Ophan and five others of his kind were gathered in a circle, surrounded by thousands of onlookers filling a stadium-sized arena, most in traditional seats, but many more hanging from the ceiling. Their collective groans produced a cacophony of ear-splitting noise. The six in the circle raised their tentacles, bringing silence to the crowd. They performed the same ritual that we had, creating an orb-shaped portal in their centre.

'The sacrificed powers led to untold greed, including my own.'

The vision changed, showing Ophan on a cliff's edge at night, overlooking a green ocean. He raised his arms and summoned a column of fire, so large that it practically turned the sky to day.

Hundreds of other columns of fire erupted on the horizon, too. As the blue trees burned, the lower lifeforms scurried from the encroaching fire.

'We sacrificed more.'

The view changed to the orb in the Empyrean, the same exact platform now had a scuffle around it. Ophan and his brethren wrestled another to the ground, before casting them into the orb.

'Until… only *two* of us remained.'

Now, only Ophan and another like him was standing in front of the orb. The other had purple and pink patterns throughout its flesh and tentacles, and instead of one light inside its body, it had two.

'I was… defeated. Like you, I was cast down.'

The two creatures grappled, before eventually the pinkish one got the upper hand and threw a roaring Ophan into the orb.

'After their victory, when only *one* Chosen was left… the storm disappeared.'

Ophan was alone on the infinite plane. The green storm above had calmed and faded to a light cyan, almost like a clear sky on Seron without a cloud in sight.

'Somehow, I *knew* it was all over. That the universe had recycled its energies and began anew. That my place was *here*, to ruminate with my own psyche and struggle with my sanity… in a sadistic loop.'

Ophan brought forth his furious might, using hundreds of different destructive abilities firing into the sky and at the plane to no effect. We fast-forwarded through cycle upon cycle of endless tantrums. Had the plane been destructible, any one of them would have indeed been cataclysmic.

'It took a long time for me to accept the truth, that this was my prison. That there was *no* escape. And that I was alone.'

Another vision showed Ophan floating in the sky just outside the perimeter of the orb platform. Ophan attempted to land on it, but a strange, invisible and impenetrable shield surrounding the entire platform prohibited him. Ophan would instead gaze at the orb for extended periods.

'Although I found the orb, there was *nothing* I could do to interact with it.'

Time moved forward again, and now Ophan was using his powers to create. Mountains rose on the infinite plane. The green oceans poured into existence, and before long, Ophan's lost world returned, albeit lifeless.

'So instead, I crafted my surroundings to ease my suffering.'

As Ophan chose to show with select memories, however, it was not meant to be. Having almost every power it could think of, the one it yearned for most was to die, something far too great a wish for this place.

'The fake world I had created for myself was a lie, a pointless exercise.'

Time could not be measured here, but now that Ophan had access to my own knowledge, it realised that m*illions* of cycles had passed. Tens of millions, since the beginning of the universe.

Whenever Ophan became angry, it would disintegrate its creations down to the white plane beneath the fake soil and start over. All the while the sky above was gradually changing from cyan to green, and wisps of cloud were beginning to appear.

'My overwhelming sorrow was too much to bear. And so, I sought death in a realm without.'

The existential nightmare and the impossibility of a fulfilling eternal life drove Ophan to deliberately put itself into a trance, hoping to never wake again.

The psychic visions finally stopped, and everything returned to normal. It took me a while to shake out of it, to readjust my sight to the infinite white again.

I fell to my knees, dizzy and sick, and slowly looked back at Lucenia. 'Did you… did you see… see… see that?'

Lucenia completely slumped to the ground and hugged her knees into a ball. I was stunned, too, having countless new memories to sift through. What we had learned was beyond imagining, and beyond *horrifying*.

'Why?' Lucenia was reduced to moans and cries, like that of a helpless child. 'Why has this happened to us? What did we do to deserve this?'

I could sense Ophan's confusion, as though I was now tuned into its mind. It raised one of its trunk-like arms straight up, and a crude finger unravelled and pointed at the clouds. 'The Empyrean, as you call it, hungers for the energy it once lent. To begin anew, it must recycle all that exists.'

I eventually composed myself, shedding away any fear or doubt. I had made a promise to myself, and I wasn't going to quit now. I looked directly into Ophan's bright light. 'So, how do we stop it?'

As the three of us flew through the Empyrean sky, it was difficult to tell how fast we were really going without any landmarks below. Ophan had each of our waists grappled with one of its many tentacles.

The storm churned and crackled. Being this close to it gave me an odd feeling deep down. I could hear the voices of the souls above. They were lost, endlessly searching an infinite space.

There in front of us, a dot in the sky. The platform. We appeared next to it in the time it took to blink. The columns and the orb were deserted, but otherwise just as we had left them.

Ophan gently hovered closer, no doubt wary of the shield. 'Reach forward,' it instructed.

We both did, trying to feel for the barrier, but after waving our hands for a few moments and meeting no resistance, we both glanced up at Ophan.

Without warning, Ophan spun in a circle and whipped the two of us through the air. We were effortlessly lobbed above the platform, before gravity quickly reclaimed us.

We plummeted back down onto the solid white marble, Lucenia crashing headfirst and hard, and me able to land with my shoulder and roll. Had pain existed here, we would both have no doubt sustained considerable injuries, but instead we stood without any hassle and looked back.

Ophan reached forward as we had done, attempting to push through the shield, but was quickly met with an abrupt zap. It receded its fizzing tentacle, before balling up a fist and slamming it into the shield in a rage. Similar to Tetsu's shield, the impact's force was evenly distributed along it, lighting a large area up with green energy. When the creature removed its fist, the shield went invisible again.

The orb remained dormant, undisturbed, like it didn't care that we were back here, probably because it had already taken our powers away.

Lucenia placed her palm on one of the pillars in disbelief. 'It worked? It worked! What now?'

'I haven't thought that far ahead yet,' I replied, before approaching the edge and eyeing Ophan. 'Is there anything else you can do to help?'

The creature remained still and silent, floating in place.

'Can you hear us?' Lucenia called.

Ophan's body dipped forward and then straightened again, as if it were nodding.

'But we can't hear you?' I added. 'Because you communicate psychically… the shield is stopping you.'

Ophan nodded again, before backing up and summoning a swath of flame. It unleashed the fiery wave towards us, which collided with the shield, lighting it with orange and green swirls. It then tried lightning, as well as other various explosive energies, but nothing could penetrate.

'It can't interfere,' Lucenia stated.

I strode to the nearest pillar and sat down with my back against it. 'Then we're on our own.'

Lucenia followed and did the same with the neighbouring pillar. 'What are we going to do?' she asked of herself as much as I.

I thought long and hard, trying to think like the other Chosen would.

'Look,' I began, 'the Chosen will be sent in again and again until they're done, right?'

Lucenia nodded. 'Right?'

'Well, what do you think our chances are of actually talking to them and convincing them of Ophan's story?' I gestured over to Ophan. 'Even if they laid eyes on it, do you think that would stop them?'

Lucenia scoffed. 'No. Raumanu is a fanatic, he'll want to see this thing through. And both Andriel and Caelum just want more power.

Elion is probably the only one who'd listen to us.' She looked at me expectantly. 'So then, what do we do when they get here?'

'Nothing,' I replied. 'We don't interfere with the outcome. We hide here, one of them gets sacrificed, and maybe just by being here, we go back, too? Otherwise… they might try to throw us in again.'

We had been waiting on the far side of the platform for far too long. Did the emperors have a change of heart somehow? Did they now not *want* all the powers? No, very doubtful. The thought of those old skeletons using my power to portal around sickened me.

I hadn't noticed before, but two of the pillars had cracks in them. I couldn't remember them being like that when we first arrived, I thought they were all perfect. Did these things age, or had we caused the damage somehow?

Lucenia still had her back to the pillar while I examined the orb more closely. I wanted to know exactly how this thing worked, but perhaps hoping to get my powers back was out of the question.

'That's not a good idea,' she called over to me. 'What if it sucks you in again?'

Agreeing about the potential danger, I backed away to my pillar.

Ophan still hovered in the same position as before. It was understandably *very* good at waiting. But then, Ophan looked around, possibly in a panic, for something had gotten its attention. It lowered itself below the platform and out of sight.

There was a loud whoosh coming from the adjoining platform behind us. Just like when I first arrived in this place, the other Chosen were materialising.

'Hide!' I hoarsely whispered, before darting around and sliding behind my pillar.

'I wonder, I wonder,' I could hear Caelum say, 'who could *possibly* be next?'

I peeked out and saw that all four had returned: Raumanu, Caelum, Andriel and Elion, and they had already crossed the bridge. Caelum wouldn't look away from the orb. Andriel was nervously watching the others, perhaps ready to leap back from them at a moment's notice.

I hid behind the pillar and gestured for Lucenia to do the same.

'Please, we… we should stop this,' I could hear Elion say. 'We shouldn't have to sacrifice ourselves at all. This is complete madness!'

'It is your duty,' Raumanu replied, stomping his cane onto the platform surface, causing an echo among the columns around us. 'The emperor's will is absolute! Not only that, but a greater power is guiding our path, can't you see? Think of the good we do for every Asterian, Elion. Think selflessly for once in your long and lucky life.'

'Alright, fine,' Elion conceded. 'But let's at least be fair about this, let's all stand an equal distance away from the orb and let *it* choose.'

'Are you joking?' Caelum said. 'You'll just run away again.'

I peeked again and saw that they had crossed the bridge and entered the ring of columns, but the orb had still not come to life.

Andriel gave a gruff sigh. 'The emperor is waiting. Plus, I have business to attend to. Can we hurry this along?'

Raumanu chuckled. 'Business, aye? More important than this? Well then, who would you suggest goes next?'

'It should be you, Caelum,' she replied.

'Me?' Caelum yelled back. 'Why? Are you still bitter about me breaking your cold, black heart?'

'No,' Andriel continued. 'It's because without powers, you have an advantage over all three of us here.'

'I agree,' Elion added. 'With your strength, it's clear who is going to come out on top in all this.'

Caelum growled. 'I am the emperor's finest bodyguard, his most *loyal* servant. If any of us should be the last one, it should be *me*.'

As they were distracted by one another, Lucenia and I peeked around the pillar again to see a tense stand-off between the four of them.

'*You*, the most loyal?' Raumanu scoffed. '*Pah*, you and I *both* know serving the empire is rarely your priority. Without me to keep you in line, what's to stop you becoming a 'God-King' all over again?'

There was a strong quake, a rumble so intense that it caused Raumanu to fall over. The orb awakened, turning green, spinning and spreading its tentacles already. While the others were distracted,

Caelum leapt forward, grabbed Andriel by the wrist and flung her towards the orb.

Andriel flew through the air briefly, before crashing down and sliding, stopping well short of the tentacles. Without the aid of his super strength, Caelum's throw had not been strong enough. He starred Andriel down and strode forward, but Elion came up from behind and kicked him in the back, thrusting him to the ground.

Lucenia glanced over at me. 'Are you sure about this? Shouldn't we stop them?'

'Just wait!' I rasped.

'Help!' Elion screamed, drawing our attention back to the fight.

Both Raumanu and Andriel were back on their feet as Caelum and Elion struggled on the ground. Andriel retreated from the orb and stood by Raumanu's side, and then together, they pulled hidden pistols from their robes and pointed them at the other two men.

Andriel smiled at the old man. 'We both had the same plan?'

'So it seems,' he replied, steadying his aim.

With his superior strength, Caelum had overcome Elion, putting him in a choke and lifting him up. When the other two had a clear shot, they fired straight into Caelum's back, but the projectiles did nothing to him. Caelum heaved Elion closer to the mass of writhing tentacles.

'Help me!' Elion continued to yell. 'Stop him!'

Raumanu's forehead wrinkles creased. 'I knew there was no pain here, but why is he still invincible?'

Andriel rolled her eyes, pointed her pistol at Raumanu and fired into his chest. Other than giving him a shock and melting through his robes, the laser did not harm him.

'Because we all are,' Andriel explained, before throwing her pistol onto the ground.

'Let me go!' Elion cried.

Caelum laughed as he waddled closer to the orb. 'I always *hated* you, Elion. Weakling! After I'm done with you, all that's left is an old man and a prissy little stick.'

Caelum threw Elion into the tentacles, which immediately latched on and pulled him into the orb as he wailed. I actually felt sorry for the guy, out of all the Chosen, he seemed to be the least evil. But if someone had to be sacrificed so that I could get out of here, then so be it.

Now that its job was done, the green orb turned white again, and Elion drowned and squirmed silently in its centre. Caelum looked back at Raumanu and Andriel with a smug grin, while they in turn appeared anxious. The three of them then looked down at their hands, which started to disappear, melting away into small white pieces.

I looked down at my fingertips, waiting for the same, but nothing happened; they remained solid. There was no tingling sensation or whiteness.

'It's not working!' Lucenia yelled before running out from the pillars. 'Come on!'

I followed her out, past the satiated orb towards the other Chosen. Caelum had almost completely melted away, his eyes and head were already gone, and so he didn't notice our interruption. But Raumanu and Andriel did. They both looked at us, shocked.

'Stop the rituals!' Lucenia screeched to them. 'You'll destroy the entire universe!'

Both Raumanu and Andriel continued to split into pieces and fade. I caught a glimpse of their final expressions. Andriel's shocked face did not change as she faded away into nothing.

'It's true,' I said to Raumanu in his final moments here. 'You'll kill everyone and everything.'

Only Raumanu's solemn face remained. He smiled back at me. 'So be it.'

He, too, faded away like flaky snow. And then… nothing.

I fell to my knees and punched the floor. 'NO!'

Lucenia collapsed, too, staring up at the tempest. 'We're still stuck here.'

Twenty-Five: My Gift to You

Warmth. Fabric. Blankets surrounding me? The scent of candles and something else pleasant. It was a familiar smell, the aroma of tamaril cake. My favourite food. Was this a dream? I opened my eyes and shot up, wide awake. I was in bed, in a pink room.

No, it couldn't be. It was exactly like my old room in Arc Royal, down to the last detail. The same bed, the same door, the dimensions of the room and the disgusting shade of pink everywhere. And most hauntingly, the dolls… the *hundreds* of dolls hanging from strings above my head!

I threw off the covers and screamed. 'No! No, not *here* again. You can't make me stay, I won't!'

The last thing I remembered was sitting around with Sacet's family and friends, waiting to be released. Had my parents forgiven me? Had their slaves found and rescued me? They needed to know I wasn't responsible for the rebels' stupidity.

I felt something on my neck and quickly realised it was an inhibitor collar. They had the *audacity* to inhibit *my* powers?

I launched out of bed and sprinted for the door, and thankfully, it opened on my approach. Just beyond, I was about to see the long corridor of my siblings' bedrooms. There'd be children bustling about in every direction, frittering away for meaning in their pointless lives. But when the door opened all the way, what I saw was completely different.

It was a grand suite that stretched in all directions, like the peak of Arc Sacet. From this one position I could see the kitchen, an elevator, a balcony and the adjoining outdoor pool. And rather than children, I saw servants everywhere. A few were cooking in the kitchen, the source of the aroma, whilst most stood perfectly still with blank stares.

I strode to the nearest servant. 'You there, where am I?' The servant remained motionless, so I got up in his face. 'Which soon-to-be-dead person brought me here against my will? Answer me!'

'You won't get much out of him,' a woman's voice said from behind, coming down the nearby stairs.

It was Andriel. She confidently descended the steps, followed by a few of her muscular bodyguards. 'These servants' minds were emptied of all individuality *long* ago. Mere husks now.'

My heart immediately skipped a beat. Was she in my mind right now? Could she sense my fears? What was I thinking? Of *course* she could. Having a modified INC at this range was meaningless. Just don't think about sudden movements or anything violent. Just...

I see you still don't quite get the whole mind-reading thing.

'Please, Ma'am,' I began, raising my hands in surrender as she and her crew approached me, 'I didn't mean any offence... I...'

'*You* do not need to beg in my presence, Iya,' she interrupted with a smile. 'And I couldn't be offended by you. Come, we have *much* to discuss.' And with that, she turned and made for another room.

Her silent guards waited and watched me until I eventually did as she instructed and followed her down the passageway.

'To answer your first question, you're in my home, Arc Andriel,' she called back as she disappeared around a corner into another room.

I glanced at the balcony window and saw the aurora-filled night sky outside. There were no other towers visible from this height. 'We're... at the peak?'

'Close enough to,' she replied as I came around the next corner.

We had entered another elegantly decorated room that would give Arc Royal a run for its money in opulence. An unnecessarily long dining table was laid out with a banquet of fine foods. It all smelled so wonderful, and after the day I had, I felt like I could eat it all.

She smiled again and gestured to the food, clearly knowing exactly how hungry I was. 'Only the finest for you, my favourite daughter.'

I stepped forward to grab something off the table but stopped midstride. '*Uhh*, pardon?'

She edged closer until she was basically breathing on me, before bringing up a hand and stroking my cheek. 'I'm *so* proud of you, of what you've become.'

I jumped back, knocking over a dining chair and bumping into one of her bodyguard's armoured, wall-like chests. 'What are you talking about? Daughter? You're… you're trying to control my mind, aren't you? Make me believe a false reality?'

A saddened, sympathetic look came over her, almost like she pitied my naivety. '*Oh*, no, no, my beautiful princess, I could *never* use my power to control *you*, or any of my children. You must believe that.' She gestured to the table again. 'Please, sit with me and I'll explain everything.'

We both took a seat at the table on opposite sides. Although I was famished and food surrounded me, I had somehow suddenly lost my appetite.

'As you may know of me, I was born on a harvest world,' she began, plucking up a small sprinkle-covered cake and examining it. 'The *worst* one of them all. No freedom of any kind, only torture.'

I nodded, for I knew all about her past and how she had received her powers.

She smirked. 'After I was released, the empire *thought* it broke me, but really, it was *I* that broke the empire.' She crushed the cake in her hand before letting it sluice onto the tablecloth. 'It wasn't long before every mind, other than the Chosen, was at my beck and call, like good little puppets.

'I enacted my vengeance *very* methodically. The Asterians that deserved the *biggest* punishment were our so-called *emperors*. I had all of their heirs systematically and permanently killed, forgotten about, and removed from all historical records, then replaced with my own offspring. Every single one of your royal siblings alive today are *mine*.'

My eyes couldn't widen any farther. I was completely frozen in place. 'So, Avarut and Suralia… they're *not* my…'

She shook her head, looking disgusted by the idea. 'Certainly *not*.'

A wave of relief, of sheer happiness washed over me. I couldn't contain it. I gave the biggest smile I could manage. I even felt tears coming, and they soon dripped down my cheeks in an embarrassingly emotional display. I wiped them between quick breaths. 'That's… that's *great*!'

'And that's not even the *best* part,' she continued, almost with a twinkle in her eye. 'Once the rest of my *competition* is out of the way, I will bury those has-beens, leaving me as the sole eternal ruler of Aster, answering to *no one*.'

'Your competition?' I asked. 'You mean the other Chosen?'

She leant back and frowned. 'Yes, and I'm sorry to say that Elion was just sacrificed.'

My heart sank and my jaw convulsed. 'What?!'

'*Oh*, my poor dear, I knew you liked that one. But don't worry, once I'm done, you can have as many lovers as you like, anyone you can think of.' She smirked again. 'Even if they don't want to.'

The prospect of me having the proper royal treatment was enticing. But why me? What *was* I to her, exactly?

She grinned. 'You're special to me, is what you are. I want you to rule by my side.'

'Wait, I thought you already have *hundreds* of family members, *true* heirs? Why me?'

She rolled her eyes. '*Hmph*, those ungrateful reprobates upstairs don't understand me, but *you* do. You understand my *hatred* for the emperors without me having to force you to think that way. You *understand* what it's like to be *imprisoned* by them, but then instead of sitting idly by and accepting it, you fought back.'

I pushed out my seat and shook my head. 'But *you* did that to me? *You* put me there. Put *all* of us there.'

Her expression of pity returned, and she brought both hands to her heart. 'And I am *truly* sorry, but I *needed* a child that understood, and out of hundreds, you were the *only* one to heed my call.'

I brought my own hands to my forehead, struggling to understand.

'Their initial desire was to execute you for what you did,' she added, raising an eyebrow, 'did you know that? And I saw how much you needed an escape from that place, so I made them exile you instead. And I can see that holiday on Seron did *wonders* for your happiness. You can age now, like you've always wanted. You're free to come and go as you please…'

I wanted to be angry, but I knew what sort of person I was in the room with, what she was capable of if I said what I truly felt.

'You *wound* me,' she said, interrupting my thoughts. 'Thinking things like that, of your own mother? We are the *same*, you and I.'

I swiped at all the plates on the table, flinging food everywhere and covering the bodyguards in cake matter. 'This is all because of you!' I yelled, now pointing a finger at her. 'Everything bad that has *ever* happened to me, you orchestrated it for your *petty* revenge fantasy.'

'That is true,' she said, avoiding my gaze. 'Let it all out.'

I gestured to the inhibitor around my neck. 'Even now you inhibit my powers, because I'm *still* your prisoner.'

She attempted another sympathetic smile. 'That was only so you wouldn't leave before I had said what I needed to say. I *promise* I will take it off.'

'*Oh*, well, lucky me?' I shouted. 'What difference does it make when after all this time, I'm just another one of your puppets?'

I picked up the largest cake tray I could find and flung it forward. As it sailed through the air towards her, it collided with a previously unseen shield of energy, which now fizzled as the foodstuff dripped down it to the floor. I glanced at her bodyguards and noticed one had his hands pointed at his master, generating her very own personal shield.

Andriel stood, closed her eyes and dipped her head. 'You're right, and I am sorry. And in time, I hope you will forgive me. Just know that I did what I did out of love for you, to protect you from the unclean, bottom-dwelling filth that is the Asterian race. You and I, we are *far* above them.'

I was completely flabbergasted. Although I did agree that I was a superior breed to most, something about the way *she* said it irked me. And although she apologised, she still did those things to me on purpose.

She gave a coy smile. 'I know what will make you feel better.' She made her way along the table towards another corridor. 'This way.'

I sighed and again noticed the bodyguards giving me expectant stares. I begrudgingly followed her with the guards in tow.

We made our way down the corridor, and Andriel stopped in front of a closed door. 'I think *this* will put you in a better mood.' She placed her hand over a scanner on the side of the door, which beeped and turned green. The door opened and she gestured for me to enter.

After an uncertain pause, I stepped into the darkness. The room was lit only with humming, blinking electrical devices throughout. I could make out a table to my side, and it was covered with surgical tools and various blunt instruments.

A spotlight flicked on, illuminating the far side of the room. Two pitiable figures were restrained against the wall in laser-like, electrified chains. They had inhibitor collars around their necks, too. It took me a moment to realise that the brunette and blonde women in front of me were Korin and Neva.

'Iya!' Korin cried. 'Help us!'

'Where am I?' a much drowsier Neva asked. 'Iya? What is… what's she doing here?'

Both looked completely distraught and drained. Mother entered behind me, and a new fear shone in their eyes.

'No, please,' Korin began, '*please*, Ma'am. We didn't know, we didn't know she was—'

Korin involuntarily bit her own lips as she continued her sentence, which came out as nothing more than muffled, pained gibberish.

Mother smiled, wrapped an arm over my shoulders and guided me closer to the light. Korin continued to beg with a closed mouth, and Neva was actually sobbing. Pathetic.

I remembered everything they had done to me and seethed, going back to when I first met them on Seron. From the moment I had met them, they had never let me forget my shame.

'My gift to you,' Mother said, 'to do with how you see fit.' She turned to them and gave an equally hateful look. 'What do you say to your new master, *filthy* mongrels?'

'We are forever your servants,' they both said in unison, 'your slaves, your playthings.'

'Very good,' Mother said before turning to the nearby table. She grabbed a large, luminous-red dagger and placed it in my hand.

'Now, my *dearest* daughter, I have some other… *guests* to deal with downstairs. I will come check on you soon. Until then, best behaviour, yes?'

I couldn't help but smile. I nodded, eager for her to leave, for I was about to do *unspeakable* things.

Mother stopped at the doorway and turned back. '*Oh*, and Iya?'

I glanced back at her, gripping the dagger tightly.

'Welcome home,' she said with another smile, before leaving and closing the door behind her.

Twenty-Six: What We Do For Others

When we first arrived, Andriel's goons had chained me to the floor and attached an inhibitor collar. They now watched me from all corners. Now I was kneeling in the darkness, my glowing restraints being the only source of light I had. Part metal and part electricity, I'd receive a shock each time I accidentally touched the chains anywhere else on my body.

I had been here for quite some time now. Normally, in a situation like this, I would be fearful for my own life and those I cared about. But I felt oddly calm, knowing that my friends were safe and that my death would bring eternal life to others. The time here allowed me to make peace with what was about to happen. Sacet was dead; there was no changing that, but other lives were hanging in the balance now.

Still, there was one thing that played over and over again in my mind: Elysia's warning. I mean, surely if I made everyone basically immortal, they couldn't be in danger anymore, right? Maybe she also knew what I was? Or had Andriel been talking through her, too? Whatever the truth was, I was resolute. I felt like my whole life had been leading to this point, to this sacrifice I was about to make.

Numerous spotlights flicked on, the returning light temporarily blinding me. When my eyes adjusted, I realised at least twenty heavily armed guards had been in the room with me. Every wall was lined with them, each silent and motionless. The room itself was cold, austere and devoid of actual life.

'Tau, Tau, Tau,' Andriel said as she entered through the only door. 'Sorry for keeping you waiting so long.' She sauntered over with her hands behind her back. 'Very busy day. Sacrificing another useless Chosen, stopping an entire planet's worth of people from accidentally killing themselves with their new powers… and now you. My work is never done.'

I turned properly to face her. 'Which of the Chosen was sacrificed this time?'

She got closer until she was standing over me. 'Elion. It's cute, all the poor are creating mountains of gold and platinum, thinking it will make them rich, but just proving they don't understand basic economics.'

I smiled and looked down. 'It's because they have hope.'

Andriel shrugged. 'I suppose. But without my guidance, they're messy and chaotic beasts. My disciples have been working non-stop to bring them all back to life, but they can't keep this up.'

'Would you say they are… your burden?' I asked.

She gave me a solemn stare. 'My *burden*… yes, that's an accurate way of putting it. Eventually, the dead will outweigh the living, which is why they *need* your healing, Tau.

I slowly brought myself to my feet before taking a deep breath.

'Are you ready, Tau?' she asked.

I took a moment to clear my head before nodding. Andriel looked over at the door, and I followed her gaze. Eno, Noor, Tetsu and Lotus entered.

'I thought you sent them back home?' I shouted as I pulled on my restraints. A jolt of electricity snapped through me until I stopped. 'What are they doing here? You *promised* they wouldn't come to harm!'

Andriel folded her arms. 'Insurance, in case you have a change of heart.'

They silently lined up in front of Andriel and I. Interestingly, none of them had inhibitor collars on, although I supposed that was because Andriel was so confident that they were under her control that they didn't need them.

'Eno, can you hear me?' I said. 'Tetsu?'

Andriel rolled her eyes. 'We've been over this; their brains are essentially *off* currently.'

My shoulders drooped. She was right. They all had glazed looks in their eyes. They watched me, but it was as if they didn't comprehend anything, like simple machines waiting for instructions.

'Now, I'm about to remove your restraints and your inhibitor,' Andriel explained before pointing to Lotus, who took a step back from the others and ignited her green aura of death. 'And if you try to escape, or you try to free anyone, I will instruct this one here to execute whoever's left.'

I sighed. 'I understand.'

She leered at Lotus. 'I could have brought my own fallen in, but I thought it was almost poetic to have *her* be their executioner.'

I thought I had felt so brave in accepting my reality, but now that my friends were here in front of me, my eyes welled. 'Can I say goodbye?'

Andriel narrowed her eyes, but then nodded and blinked. 'There, they can hear your words, and they will remember what happens here today, except for *my* involvement.'

I took another deep breath. 'Eno, Noor… I'm *so* sorry about Sacet. I was warned she might be in danger and… I should have acted.'

Andriel cocked an eyebrow, intrigued, but allowed me to continue.

My lips quivered, and my tears flowed freely. 'I was so sure everything would be peaceful now, but I was wrong. If you're going to blame anyone for her death, blame me. I should have done something… *anything* to save her.'

I tried moving closer to Tetsu, but received another shock. Andriel glanced to her side, and several of her guards approached. Two swiped at my restraints and collar with an electronic card, deactivating them and letting them clang to the floor.

I couldn't stop my blubbering tears now. I rushed over to Tetsu and hugged him, burying my face in his chest. 'Tetsu, you don't have to protect me anymore, I release you from that. But… I still feel guilty about leaving you behind, because… I love you. You and I… we just needed more time, but there was always work to do.'

I shook my head and sighed. 'No, that's a lie. I didn't *make* the time. And I guess I was just too afraid to tell you how I felt, because… I knew we were doomed. I'm sorry I wasted what time we could have had together.'

Surprisingly, his arms slowly rose and gently wrapped around me. I glanced back at Andriel, confused. She nodded and gave a little smile, as though moved by the emotional moment. Although she was a tyrant, there was at least a little bit of good in her. A tear had also formed in Tetsu's eye, and not just for him but the others, too.

'When you wake up, you won't see me,' I continued. 'But just know that I did what I did to protect you, to help everyone, and… maybe to finally bring you all some peace.'

'That's very sweet,' Andriel said, before glancing to the sides again.

The other guards surrounded their master. One grabbed a particularly pointy part of her fashionable clothing and ripped it off. Andriel didn't react, instead continuing to stare at me. What was she making them do?

Another guard opened a metal case on the ground and pulled out some metal clothing. Armour? While he unravelled it, the others undressed Andriel quite rapidly. The whole room of people watched as she was stripped, and I was the only one who averted my eyes for the sake of modesty.

When she was finally bare, the guards held out her new outfit and helped her put it on one legging and sleeve at a time. They sealed her up, and the suit lit with built-in coloured lights.

'The Empyrean takes away our powers while inside,' she explained as she stretched to test the suit's limits. 'But objects are permitted through. When I do away with Raumanu and Caelum, I'll be concealing this powered suit under my clothing. This will be a trial run to make sure it works.'

The door opened behind us, and even more slaves entered. They were dressed in hazmat suits and carried large pieces of strange equipment. Along with the guards, they surrounded the two of us, waving little beeping batons over our bodies, checking Andriel's suit, and setting up the larger equipment around us in a circle.

'Are you sure this will work?' I asked. 'Doesn't the ceremony require *all* the Chosen?'

Andriel shook her head. 'No, but it didn't require *you* previously.'

If I were a coward, I'd fly out the door right now. If I were like Sacet, I'd find some way to fight and save the day. But neither of those options was me, not while my friends' lives were on the line. I activated my aura for a moment to rejuvenate my sore and tired body.

Any trace of emotion had left my face now. 'Alright, just tell me what to do.'

She raised her hands towards me to demonstrate. 'Copy me, like this.'

I did as she instructed, adopting the same stance and mirroring her. Her slaves now formed a proper circle around us and waited.

'Close your eyes and empty your mind,' she continued.

Again, I obliged. In a moment of clarity, of serene selflessness, I knew this was right. In the cosmic plan, I was but one pawn in an ocean of countless other suffering souls. My mind went blank, and I felt a pleasant warmth grow within my abdomen and out towards my limbs.

Whiteness. A vision, not unlike a dream. A steel prison corridor. I knew immediately that I was seeing one of Andriel's memories. A nearby alarm blared, but the noises of the world took second place to all the other things I could hear now, all the hopeless voices.

The cells to my sides were filled with more potential thoughts to steal. More minds for me to control or scramble, whatever took my fancy. My fellow prisoners meant nothing to me, they would only get in the way. I had bigger plans.

The shock-lash gashes on my back still stung, the searing pain travelling to my bare extremities. On the surface, I appeared like any other weak, pitiful prisoner, but now *I* was the one who cracked the whip.

A trio of guards approached from the corridor's far end, raising their guns, like they had a chance. I narrowed my gaze and brought them to their knees with a psychic barrage. They dropped their useless weapons and squirmed on the ground like worms.

I perused through each of the fleshy skull-warmers they called a brain, pilfering any thoughts of value. But unlike the many scientists I had murdered along my path, these soldiers were dim-witted, knowing nothing of importance, so I discarded them, destroying all their thoughts, leaving nothing but three more empty shells.

Another wave of guards tried to flank me from behind, and for their impudence, I decided to have a little fun. I forced all of them to face one another and gun each other down. They fired over and over into limbs and stomachs. I wanted them to feel something before receiving the killshot. I ordered the final surviving guard to turn his weapon upon himself, spraying his grey matter all over the ceiling.

I continued to march to my goal, nothing would slow me down. The next door at the end of the hall was locked. Did they really think this would stop me? I sensed minds on the other side, and I forced the closest one to unlock the entrance. Upon noticing their comrade's odd behaviour, the others jumped into action, attempting to stop him, but their minds were no match for mine either.

The door opened, and at last I had reached the prison's control room. It had windows that overlooked the yard below. The warden and more high-ranking officers all cowered in fear at the sight of me, all but one, an acolyte who stepped forward and raised her arms in my direction.

But I already had my mental claws inside her, and she turned on her superiors, unleashing a blue bolt of electricity that forked throughout the room, bouncing through bodies, computers and other equipment.

Their fleshy sacks fell, sinking in their seats and sprawling over their panels. I had no use for the acolyte, so I reached into her mind and tore it to pieces like the others. Blood spurted from her nostrils and eye sockets.

Although there were plenty more guards and scientists to kill, hiding in various corners of the facility, those who had been orchestrating my torture all this time were finally dead. No, they were also pawns. Just before their deaths, I felt their love for their emperors, the *true* perpetrators. My work wasn't done.

I approached the windows and stared up at the blood-red moon on the black sky. I heard footsteps behind me, and I turned to see a man, a behemoth, toned and imposing, yet with a calm demeanour.

'I couldn't sense you?' I said, confused. 'I can't... I can't read you. But I *know* who you are.'

He smiled. '*Oh*? And who am I?'

I walked to the nearest dead body and pulled its head up from the control panel. 'These weaklings worship you, the immortal man. Caelum.'

He walked closer. 'And what do *you* think I am? Will *you* worship me?'

I mimicked his movements, walking towards him. 'I think you're here to kill me. Why would I worship *you?*'

He stopped and laughed. 'That's what I was told to do, but it's not what I'm *going* to do.'

I approached closer to the point I could touch him and slowly laid my finger on his bulging chest, then my whole hand. 'Almost everything I know I've stolen from other people's minds.' While keeping my hand on his body, I smiled and slowly encircled him. 'I'm not done here, and if you take me away early, I'll forever feel… incomplete.'

He stayed still, only following me with his eyes.

I stopped in front of him again and brought my hand to his cheek. 'I will leave this place… only when all these weaklings are dead.'

Amused, Caelum chuckled. 'Alright, we will leave together when your task is complete. And *I* will help you.'

He disappeared from the spot, smashing through the roof and rocketing into the sky. I ran back to the window and watched as he burst through buildings throughout the facility like a missile. He picked up various guards running through the courtyard and ripped them in two.

I grinned, overjoyed. *Finally*, someone else to relish in the pain of others and perhaps… much more.

Again, my view was consumed with white, the grim scene replaced by that of a loud firing range inside a bright, steel facility. I knew this place… this was one of *my* memories.

A mix of Male Dominion and necrolisk-shaped mock targets whizzed along tracks, some so fast that it was nigh impossible to get a bead on them. I hadn't fired a single shot yet; I was waiting for the perfect opportunity.

No, deep down, I knew I had been hesitating. I thought back to the innocent girl I killed when I was a child. What would happen when these targets were real, too? What if I could never fire again?

'We were worried about you, Tau,' Tarsus said to my side, before rapid-firing her pistol into a target hanging from the ceiling. 'It wouldn't have been the same around here without you.'

Amiki fired next. Even with her wounded right hand, she was still quite accurate shooting with the left. She reloaded awkwardly before placing her weapon on the waist-high barrier in front of us. 'You're lucky to be alive, and also that those portal-nomads wanted to *keep* you alive.'

My other friends, Tarsus and Coleo, were firing nearby. Coleo, in particular, was a crack shot, nailing everything in her lane before it had a chance to move.

I looked down and scuffed my feet on the metal files. 'There was actually just… one portal-nomad. And she was actually—'

'I *know* you, Tau,' Coleo interrupted, turning and giving me her full attention. 'You probably had multiple opportunities to kill your captors, but you're too timid.'

I put down my unfired pistol and averted my eyes from her. 'Is that why you ordered me to jump?'

Corporal Coleo sighed and placed her weapon down as well. 'I wasn't trying to get you killed… or *captured* for that matter. I was trying to give you an opportunity to grow. A little push, that's all! We followed you in afterwards and couldn't find you.'

Amiki gestured to her injuries. 'If that stupid, old man hadn't detonated that bomb, I could've chased those kids down, and none of this would have happened.'

'Corporal's right,' Tarsus yelled over her discharging rifle. 'You haven't made a *single* kill yet, it's embarrassing. You've been dragging the whole squad's overall TAC down. The others are starting to talk, and *we* defend you… but it'd be easier if we didn't have to.'

Coleo grabbed my shoulders to get my attention. 'I'm not saying this as your superior, but as your friend: what if *our* lives depended on you killing an enemy? Could you do it?'

I shook my head. 'If I knew you were in danger, I don't think I… I just don't want to kill anyone if I don't have to. I want to *help* people, not harm them.'

Tarsus was the last to place her weapon down. 'How many times has Amiki saved you now, five?'

I glanced at the other two. Coleo folded her arms.

'Six,' I replied.

Coleo released me with a smile. 'And how many people did she have to kill to reach you?'

I sighed. 'More than I'm worth.'

'We don't see it that way,' Amiki said.

I started towards the nearest door. 'Only because they were men.'

Tarsus reached out to stop me. 'No, you're our sister. No one matters more than your sisters. We're family.'

I kept moving, and the door flew open. 'If only everyone felt like family.'

Whiteness again. When I opened my eyes, I saw that both my hands and Andriel's were glowing. Streams of energy shot out from our fingertips against our will, meeting in the middle and creating a bright, colourful, humming sphere between us.

Those in hazmat suits sprang to action, waving their instruments over the orb, as well as examining the readouts on their equipment, trying to analyse it.

Andriel looked at one of her larger, more imposing guards. Without being asked, he stepped up to the portal and placed his hands upon it. He immediately roared in pain as he was electrocuted, and Andriel gripped the sides of her head as if sharing that pain.

The man's body brightened, the light becoming so intense that he appeared about to explode. He continued to yell as the rest of us backed away and shielded ourselves from the light with our hands.

Then, a mighty blast, the shockwave sending us all off our feet. The man was nowhere to be seen, the only thing remaining of him being white, leaf-like particles gently falling to the floor around us. My eyes widened in shock at the awful end the man was forced to experience.

Andriel sighed as she got to her feet. 'As I suspected, only Chosen can enter.'

One of the slaves approached Andriel and gently passed her a strange metallic object. Andriel's body began to glow, and as she closed her eyes in pain, I realised what the shrapnel was.

It was the shard that Sacet had told me about. The one Urias and his sand acolytes were so desperate to reclaim. It was a piece of wreckage from the aircraft that Sacet and I flew in as children, before it was shot down by the nomads. And somehow, inexplicably, it could temporarily grant the power to control sand to those who touched it.

'Is that…?'

Andriel gestured to the orb and stared at me intently. 'After you.'

Twenty-Seven: Stick to the Plan

Lucenia and I were still leaning against our columns on the Empyrean platform, waiting for the inevitable return of the Chosen. If our new plan didn't work, and they made another sacrifice, there'd only be one final chance to stop them.

'So, go over it again,' I said to her. 'One last time.'

Lucenia groaned but dipped her head and complied. 'If Raumanu or Andriel is first, we tackle them off the platform before the others show up.'

'And if it's Caelum?' I pressed.

'You'll distract him and give me the signal to tackle one of the other two.'

I nodded and looked around, noticing that Ophan had hidden itself again. 'Where has that creature gotten to now?'

Lucenia shuddered. 'That thing creeps me out. I've been thinking,' she said before lowering her voice, 'what if it's lying? If that whole elaborate story was... exactly that, a *story*?'

I shrugged. 'Even if it *is* lying, it wants what we want: to get out of here.'

There was a high-pitched tingling in the air, so we both shot up from the columns.

'They're back,' Lucenia said.

'Into position, quick!' I added.

We sprinted over to the bridge connecting the two platforms and stopped on it. There was a loud whoosh and a flash of white. An orb appeared, which quickly shrank to reveal a feminine figure. She collapsed to the ground.

'Now!' Lucenia yelled.

I reached out and grabbed her. 'Wait!' I couldn't believe what I was seeing. 'Tau?'

I wasn't quite sure at first, for the woman's auburn hair initially could have been confused with Andriel's. But no, it was definitely my sister lying in front of us. How could it be?

Lucenia looked just as confused. 'Your friend? What's she doing here?'

'She's my *sister*, and I don't know. Tau?' I knelt and shook her. 'Tau, can you hear me?'

She came to and looked up at me. 'Sacet?' Overjoyed, she sprang up and hugged me. 'Sacet! I thought you were dead!'

I heard the high-pitched tingling again, so I peeled Tau's arms off and pulled her back. 'Stay behind me.'

'This place,' Tau said from behind, 'it feels so familiar.'

Another flash of light and another orb appeared before us. It again shrank before revealing a woman kneeling on one leg.

Lucenia and I bolted forward as Andriel straightened up. We collided into her at the same time, but rather than getting bowled over by us, she simply put a leg back for support and brought us to a halt.

Andriel was wearing a grey metallic suit, like thin armour, which tightly flexed along the contours of her body. She held us back with ease. There was no way she was normally this strong; her suit must have been augmenting her.

She opened her eyes and smirked before grabbing both our necks, lifting us off the ground, and hurling us back the way we came. We spiralled through the air and landed back on the bridge, narrowly avoiding Tau.

As we sat up, Lucenia glanced over and rolled her eyes. 'So much for the plan.'

Andriel clenched her fists. 'You thought I wouldn't be prepared for you two?' She nodded towards the orb. 'Back up, or I'll *back* you up.'

Lucenia and I exchanged a look. We both knew what the other was thinking. Andriel was too strong for us, so for now, we had no choice but to play along. The only thing we could count on was the orb randomly choosing Andriel over us.

Including Tau, the three of us receded over the bridge, closer to the circle of columns.

Tau was completely awestruck by her surroundings, not realising the peril we were in. 'I feel like I've… been here before.'

Andriel shook her head impatiently. 'That's *wonderful*, but I didn't bring you here for sightseeing.' She grabbed something from over her shoulder, a piece of shrapnel. 'Take this and go to the orb. Now!'

I instantly recognised the object as the shard of the sand nomads. 'What's going on here? Where are the other two?'

Tau ignored Andriel's commands and the orb, instead walking to the nearest edge and peering at the endless plane. 'I remember now, I saw this place in my dreams.'

Something clicked in my mind, and I realised that I, too, had once dreamt of something similar. It was long ago, before being captured by the FD. Tau, Eno and I had been camping along a river. In my dream, I saw the ritual being performed with *six* other silhouettes.

Andriel stomped towards Tau. 'If you delay me any longer, I swear I'll execute… all… of your…'

She trailed off as Ophan, who previously had been out of sight beneath the platform, floated up and stopped just off the edge in front of Tau.

While Andriel was distracted by the alien, Lucenia quietly got my attention. 'New plan?'

I noticed that not only was Andriel distracted, but she was quite close to the edge with Tau. And at the same time, I glanced back and noticed that the orb had spun to life, turning green and preparing its tentacles.

'Same as the old,' I whispered back before gesturing to the edge with my eyes.

'What… what is *that*?' Andriel asked.

'I *know* you,' Tau said to Ophan, slowly treading towards it.

Lucenia and I burst forward a second time. It didn't matter how strong Andriel was, she wasn't expecting us this time. We made contact with her back, thrusting her closer to the precipice. Completely shocked by the surprise attack, she lost her balance and slipped. But like when Ophan had tried to bypass the shield, a green energy field shimmered and prohibited Andriel from *leaving* the platform.

As if being pushed into a wall, she simply righted her footing once more and turned back to us with a malevolent grin. 'Dirty, *very* dirty,' she said as she tightened her grip on the shard. 'You two should have stayed dead.'

Andriel sidestepped away from the edge and closer to the bridge, while Lucenia and I backed up to the columns. The orb's tentacles thwacked the ground behind us.

Tau was right at the platform's edge, unafraid and unflinching, like she was hypnotised by Ophan. And Ophan was drawn to Tau in kind, reaching out a mock arm and placing its boulder-sized fist onto the shield's exterior, causing it to sputter and hiss with energy.

Andriel kept her eyes locked on us. 'Tau, get away from it. You have a job to do.'

This gave Tau pause. I recognised her hesitation, her anxiety.

'Tau,' I interjected, competing for her attention. 'You made me promise to tell you if I was in trouble. Well, I am. We *all* are. Do *not* listen to her.'

'Did you forget about your friends?' Andriel continued, before chucking the shard at Tau's feet. 'I'll kill them *all* unless you do as I say. Now pick that up and sacrifice yourself!'

Tau gave me a pleading look. 'Sacet, our family?'

It seemed Andriel didn't need psychic powers to control Tau. She merely needed to threaten our loved ones.

I pointed back at the orb. 'If all the Chosen are sacrificed, the universe *ends*, along with everyone in it.'

'Listen to us, you stupid girl!' Lucenia barked.

Andriel scoffed. 'That's enough. You two will say *anything* to save yourselves. Tau, remember all the people you'll help by giving up your power.'

Tau stared into my eyes, as if hoping to confirm my story. All I did was nod, knowing that she'd believe me.

'So everyone's in danger no matter what I do,' she said and paused, weighing her options, before turning back to Andriel. 'I'm done being manipulated by you.'

Andriel clenched her fists. 'That peace that you want so badly… it's *right* there in that orb! Wait, what are you doing?'

Tau reached out her hand to Ophan as cyan flames erupted from her back. 'I don't know… but it feels right.' Her hand passed through the shield and joined with one of Ophan's tentacles. An incredibly bright light emanated between them.

Ophan and Tau then roared up to the sky, and the platform rumbled. Bolts of electricity streaked in all directions, blasting the rest of us away. I slammed into a column, and both Lucenia and Andriel fell nearby. But while Lucenia and I got to our feet, unharmed, Andriel's suit continued to fizzle with electricity.

The orb's tentacles had wriggled even closer, now slapping at the back of the columns. This was our chance. I stumbled over to Andriel, bent down and grabbed her shoulders tight.

She tried slapping at my arms, but her strength had been sapped. 'Get off me, you filthy wretch!'

'Help me!' I shouted back at Lucenia. 'Throw her in the orb!'

Lucenia launched forward and tried wrangling Andriel's kicking legs. A lightshow continued to crackle between Ophan and Tau, but all I could do was trust she knew what she was doing.

'Get away!' Andriel continued to protest, thrashing against us both. 'I'll execute Eno. I'll execute Darius!'

She could threaten me all she wanted; I wouldn't stop. I didn't know a Darius, one of Lucenia's loved ones, perhaps?

Little by little, we dragged Andriel closer to the tentacles. She'd occasionally break free from one of us and attempt to dash before the other would snatch at one of her limbs and stop her. Our wrestling devolved into desperation and savagery, all the while lightning was blinding us from the platform's edge.

I could see true fear in Andriel's eyes for the first time. 'Stop it! I can't… I refuse!'

One of the tentacles slithered closer, as if sniffing us out. As it homed in, I forced Andriel to the front, but Lucenia hadn't noticed the tentacle yet.

'Watch out!' I yelled.

The tentacle, as if sensing the vibrations in the air, lashed forward. I ducked, as did Andriel, and as it snapped back, it snared Lucenia's ankle. She screamed, causing several more tentacles to seek us. The first tentacle tugged forcefully, tripping up Lucenia and scraping her along the platform. She continued to scream as more tentacles latched on.

'Sacet, pull me out!' she begged, again being dragged to the orb. 'Please, I'll help you, just get this thing off me!'

I didn't hesitate this time. I let go of Andriel, darted forward, grabbed Lucenia's outstretched hand and pulled with all my might. Although I had slowed the tentacles, they were still too strong, and Lucenia continued to slide towards the orb.

'Don't let go, don't let go, don't let go!' she said.

It was too late; her feet had already submerged into the liquid of the orb. I still didn't give up, continuing to futilely pull on her clammy palm. The mass of tentacles was growing and surrounding us both, and if I didn't retreat now, the orb would take me for seconds.

Already feeling regret, I gave Lucenia a remorseful look. 'I'm sorry.'

'No!' she screamed as I let go of her hand and jumped back over the encroaching appendages, which now wrapped around her outstretched hands.

'I'll find a way to get you out,' I said. 'I promise.'

Lucenia's face was dragged into the green, and her drowned screams cut into my heart, but there was nothing I could do.

I backed away to Andriel, who was slowly getting to her feet. My enemy and I watched the spinning orb, waiting for it to turn white. Strangely though, it didn't. The tentacles continued to slap and thwack at random.

'It's still hungry,' Andriel said, breaking our silence. She slowly backed away to the pillars.

Tau appeared on the edge of my periphery. Her aura was active, and I had never seen it so powerful, so all encompassing. As she wandered between the columns towards the sphere, her flames filled half the platform. I noticed she had the shard in her hand. Ophan was nowhere to be seen.

'What are you doing?' I called. 'Don't!'

Tau's aura then changed into a mix of both green and cyan. With her free hand, she pointed at the sphere and a beam of green energy was drawn out of it to her.

After a few moments of draining, she pointed the same hand at me, and another beam appeared from her to me, this time cyan. My whole body tingled as though I were being healed.

Satisfied, Tau inspected the shard before tossing it towards the sphere. It landed perfectly in the liquid, sticking out of the top. 'Let *that* satiate you.'

Tau's aura fell, and she looked around confused. The shard sank into the liquid, and the orb finally turned white, appeased by the sacrifice. The tentacles retreated and disappeared.

All three of us began to whiten and melt away. First, our extremities disintegrated, then up our limbs to our torsos. Both Tau and I stared Andriel down in silence, and she likewise seethed back. Like leaves caught in a draught, the particles that once made up our bodies flitted away. The effect finally crept up my neck and face, until all I could see was white.

My vision returned, blurry at first, taking some time to adjust to the square chamber. The first thing I noticed was a crowd of heavily-armoured guards and hazmat-wearing scientists surrounding us, at least forty of them surrounding our position.

Tau and Andriel were to my sides, both conscious and eyeing each other with uncertainty. I, meanwhile, realised how volatile this room was. All of the soldiers aimed their weapons at us, preparing to fire.

I grabbed Tau's hand. 'Healing, now.'

A very frightened and bewildered Tau activated her aura as instructed. I felt its warmth surround me. The soldiers opened fire, but their bullets did not affect us now, bouncing off our instantly healing bodies.

I threw a hand at the side of the chamber and opened a portal to the vacuum of space. The star-speckled, inky black appeared through the circle. The wind gushed through the room, whipping most off their feet and dragging them along the steel-tiled floor.

Another soldier suddenly materialised by Andriel's side. He grabbed hold of her and the two of them teleported away.

'Wait, Sacet!' Tau said, her words also ripped by the wind.

It was too late; this was our only way out. I took a deep breath, tightened my grip on Tau's hand and widened the portal. The air flow increased tenfold, sucking each and every person in the room through to the void, including Tau and I.

We spun weightlessly for a moment, surrounded by giant, spinning, still-disintegrating chunks of Seron. The others flailed about, trying to grasp at each other in desperation. There was no sound, only the rumbling of my eardrums. Without oxygen, everyone else was beginning to asphyxiate.

No more people were coming through the portal, and we were moving away from it at tremendous speed, so I closed it. The forty or so people were now alone in the nothing, Tau's fire being like a beacon of light. We were inside the meteor field made up of what was left of Seron. A couple of the bodies collided into a rogue rock, splashing their now-weightless innards like bursting, ripe fruit.

Tau tapped my arm with her free hand and pointed at some of the others. I couldn't believe it, it was Noor, Tetsu and Eno! They had been in the room with us? How careless I was not to notice.

Panicking, I thought back to the only safe place I could think of, the Arc Sacet penthouse, specifically the pool, to give them a gentle landing. Without delay, I opened a portal beneath Eno's feet and threaded him through it. Tetsu was closest to Eno, so I whipped it over to him and did the same.

Then I scanned with my second perception for where Noor had gone in that time. There, behind an enormous brute. Noor's eyes were bulging, and his face had turned completely red. I flung the portal over and saved him, too.

I gave Tau an expectant look to make sure I had got them all, but she gestured at a flailing, armoured blonde girl. I didn't recognise her at all. She was floating amongst so many others. I pointed at her to make sure, and Tau nodded. This girl was our ally, apparently, so I saved her with a penthouse portal, too.

I was now sure there was no one else worth saving here, so I summoned another portal for us. We were flung through to the other side and plunged into the water. I simultaneously released both the portal and my grip on Tau's hand, and the two of us swam up and broke the water's surface.

Eno and Tetsu were poolside, helping pull a still-choking Noor out. As I floated, I briefly locked eyes with the sputtering blonde girl. While she swam to one side, Tau and I paddled to the other and climbed out.

After being exposed to the vacuum of space, everyone but Tau and I was in bad shape. Their skin was reddened from radiation, their muscles were swollen and misshapen, and they were all coughing uncontrollably.

'You're... *hack*... *hrk*! You're alive!' Noor managed to shout while kneeling, before having another coughing fit.

While Tau switched on her aura to bring them back to normal, Noor sprinted over and clumsily embraced me, almost toppling me back into the pool.

'Sas!' Eno said ecstatically, running over, too.

Both hugged me so tightly that I couldn't move. Although I still thought we were in danger, I allowed a brief moment of respite and hugged them back.

I closed my eyes. I was lost for words, so relieved to be back, but also ashamed that my dedication to them had faltered. One thing was certain: I wasn't going to be playing nice with the empire anymore. They were my enemies again. It felt right, but also made me question if this would ever be over.

Tetsu had run over to Tau, too. He reached out and gently took her hands into his. 'I heard what you said... I love you, too.' He pulled her in and kissed her on the lips.

Tau put her arms around him, and when their kiss was over, she smiled and they hugged.

Twenty-Eight: Mouths Shut

There was something strange about how Mother had interrupted my torture session to come get me. It wasn't just the abruptness of it, but also her frazzled behaviour and windswept hair. She and her teleporting servant didn't waste time with explanations, for after arranging ourselves in a triangle and holding hands, we were off. I didn't even have time to ask her why we weren't using Sacet's portals instead.

Now we were rapidly teleporting across the endless city, each stop lasting only a few moments before we disappeared in another blur. Most hops had us briefly pausing in a floating, clear glass-like box overlooking the streets and intersections from above.

Mother was wearing a long, grey coat with cyan lines coiling around it, which covered up every bit of her skin besides her face. It even had a high collar concealing her neck. Its bagginess made her look far heftier than usual, far removed from her usual more-revealing choices.

I spotted countless vehicles and civilians bustling around us on the upper walkways, but we'd zip off to another destination before I could take in any specific sights. It seemed that even the teleporters had their own transportation system. I never knew this form of teleportation had a maximum distance for each jump.

As usual, the servant showed no emotion whatsoever, but Mother had a look of concern, for she knew exactly how close to vomiting I was getting.

'We're… almost… there…' she said, each word at a different location.

My knees buckled, and I slumped. 'No more,' I said as I ripped my hands away from theirs. 'I swear, I'll puke all over you… stop!'

The spinning, warping sensation finally ceased, and just in time, too. In the end, it was lucky I hadn't eaten that cake.

'Easy there, Iya,' Mother began, 'we're here.'

I opened my eyes to mostly dark surroundings. We weren't alone; I spotted several silhouettes. No, it was closer to a hundred others, each standing silently among a crisscrossing network of balconies. We were in an attic-like area, overlooking a larger chamber below, which was the only source of light.

As I stood and took a look over the nearest balcony, I recognised our location. We were in the rafters above the royal throne room, where the emperors' army of bodyguards skulked in shadow. None of them acknowledged our presence.

The throne room was currently deserted, with not even a lowly servant on cleaning duty. Braziers flickered next to the many pillars lining the chamber, bringing a warmth to what I'd consider to be the coldest location in the empire. There were blue rugs and curtains adorning every surface in luxuriant softness, which I also found quite ironic.

I gestured down. 'My parents… I mean the *emperors*… are the *last* people I ever want to see again. Why did you bring me here?'

The teleporter disappeared, and Mother joined me by the edge with her hands behind her back. 'My last appointment didn't go as planned. Right now, you're safer here with me rather than at home.'

'Safer? From what? Who?'

I gawked at her, struggling to understand. She was the most powerful woman in the empire, who could *possibly* present a threat to her?

She sighed. 'Now, now, don't let thoughts like that enter your mind. It's merely a precaution. For now, just remain up here and enjoy the show.'

She turned on the spot just as her teleporter reappeared where we had arrived. The slave had brought another two people with him, Korin and Neva. Their inhibitor collars were gone, but they were predictably under Mother's control, motionless automatons. They were covered in still-dripping cuts and fresh bruises; the results of my own handiwork, for which I had no regrets, although now that Neva had her powers back, her wounds naturally began to recede.

Strangely, however, their mouths were missing. Korin's had been hurriedly and gruesomely stitched shut, and Neva didn't have a mouth at all, only a smooth surface, as though it had never existed. Had she used her shapeshifting to hide it?

Mother nodded at them. 'And here, I've brought you some company. They'll follow your every command. And I've disabled the parts you hated about them, too, like their nasty attitudes, most of their memories…'

'Their individuality?'

Mother leant against the balcony. 'I thought you'd like them *better* this way.'

I approached them and stared into Neva's eyes. 'But… they can't respond?'

Mother shrugged. 'Why would you *want* them to?' She looked over the edge in a panic.

'What is it?' I asked.

He's coming. I need you to be silent from this point on, understood?

I nodded and shifted back to the balcony for a better view.

The teleporter grabbed Mother's hand and the two of them reappeared in the chamber below, right in the centre along the enormous blue rug. The servant poofed away again. She took a few deep breaths before settling into a relaxed pose.

A distant metronomic tapping noise from somewhere below was growing louder.

'Andriel?' a raspy voice called out, echoing up to the rafters.

Then he came into view, Raumanu was practically waddling in from a passageway behind the throne itself. He slowly made his way over to her. 'It's not like you to be early?'

A huge grin slowly spread on Mother's lips. 'Such an important moment *demands* my attention.'

Raumanu scoffed. '*Oh*, I'm *sure* it does. I bet you've been looking forward to seeing Caelum toss me in.'

Mother shook her head. 'On the contrary, it's *him* I want to see gone next. *Neither* of us will stand a chance against him one-on-one, you know that.'

'I suppose I do,' he said with a chuckle, before looking her up and down. 'Interesting attire… for *you*.'

He was referring to my mother's current baggy getup.

'The latest fashion from Qaidur,' she explained with a grin, before gesturing to his robes. 'I wouldn't expect *you* to understand.'

He nodded. 'If you say so. I'm sure this… *fashion* gives us an edge.'

There was a loud bang below, followed by another, and shortly after an explosion of light from somewhere to the side that I couldn't see. It was the throne room doors that had been battered open. One of the doors had ripped off its hinges and was flung down the blue carpet.

The emperor entered my view, coming from the explosion's source, floating towards the others using Lucenia's power under his feet. 'Where… are… my PORTALS?'

I don't think I had ever seen him this angry before, not even when he had banished me. His forehead was red, and once-dormant veins protruded from it. But he didn't scare me anymore, now that I knew how much Mother had toyed with him, he was no emperor to me, just a vegetable sack with a very long expiry date. I very much wanted to vault over this balcony and kill him a second time.

He will get what's coming to him soon enough. Patience…

Accompanying Avarut was Caelum, also floating using his own power, and his eyes narrowed when he saw the other two Chosen. He hovered over and landed next to them.

'Well?' Avarut yelled again, his voice already hoarse with rage.

'I'm sorry, Sire, but I do not know,' Raumanu began, attempting to soothe him. 'I have instructed the Empyreanic Seers to try to find out more. For now, I can't say for sure as to why Sacet's portals have left our people.'

Avarut floated between them towards his throne, gazing at Mother as he passed. 'And how about *you*? I don't suppose you've got anything *useful* to report?'

Remaining calm, Mother shook her head. 'My apologies also, Sire. Nothing.' She briefly glanced at the other two Chosen. '*Perhaps* it is because we are not engaging in the ceremony at its intended speed?'

This caused the other two Chosen to raise an eyebrow incredulously.

Avarut reached his throne and turned slowly. He sat with great difficulty, grunting in pain as his body cracked into place. 'Maybe you are right. Raumanu, your thoughts?'

Realising the invitation Mother had just laid out, Raumanu's scepticism suddenly disappeared. '*Ah*, yes, it *may* be that the Empyrean only gave us a *taste* of the Chosen path, but now wants us to *prove* our commitment. We must follow our path through to the end to reap its *true* rewards.'

Caelum glanced at the other two with a confident, smug smile. 'And when we do, Sire, *I* will be your champion.'

While the men were distracted by Caelum's arrogance, Mother briefly looked up at me and winked.

Iya, I want you to cherish this moment, for it is the last time you see your real father alive. Centuries of patience, and now he will finally receive his comeuppance.

What? My real father?

Mother smiled at Avarut. 'Sire, if I may suggest, it must not be *me* who is sacrificed.'

Caelum's gritted his teeth at her. 'And why not?'

'Think about it,' she replied, 'without me, we would no longer be able to psychically control the world. And if *everyone* were psychic, there would be mass chaos, everyone attempting to control one another, including *you*, Sire.'

Avarut raised his fingers in a pyramid in front of his mouth. 'That *cannot* be allowed to happen.'

Mother then gestured to Raumanu. 'And it cannot be Raumanu, either. Should the rebels gain *his* abilities, even the *smallest* amount of power would permit them to destroy our entire planet before we could finish our ascension. Even a mere child could accidentally bring about Armageddon.' She pointed at Caelum. 'As for him, even if everyone had invincibility and strength, I could *still* control them.'

The three stared at Caelum in obvious agreement.

Him? All this time, *Caelum* was my father? I mean, it made sense, for I obviously came from strong stock, but I was hoping for a father that would actually *care* about me, not someone that was just as callous as Avarut, or as selfish as Suralia.

'You cannot be serious,' Caelum uttered, before approaching the throne. 'Sire, I have *always* been a faithful bodyguard to you. I have protected you for more than a *millennium*, as your impenetrable shield…'

Mother scoffed. 'Wouldn't it make more sense for the emperor himself to be impenetrable?'

Caelum shot her an infuriated look. 'Let our emperor say it for himself, you vile witch! *Centuries* later, and you still hound me with your jealousy.'

Mother smirked and examined her fingernails. 'Pure fantasy. I haven't had personal feelings for *you* for longer than I care to remember. You are simply the next *logical* sacrifice.'

Caelum shook his head and directed his attention back to Avarut with a pleading face. 'Sire, permit *me* to be the final Chosen.' He knelt and drew closer to Avarut's knees. 'I am devout, ready to serve you after we ascend. *They* serve only themselves.'

Raumanu gave a single laugh and shook his head.

From here, I noticed my mother's eyelids flickering briefly. It was subtle, but I had noticed it previously whenever she was making a change.

Avarut leant closer, his face now hovering over Caelum. 'No.'

The colour from Caelum's face drained, and his bottom lip trembled briefly. 'But, Sire?'

Avarut's face contorted in frustration. 'You will sacrifice yourself for the good of all, just like the others. It is your duty to the empire!'

Caelum's usual stoic expression was gone, replaced with anger and a touch of fear. Mother, however, barely contained her amusement.

Both Avarut and Raumanu stared Caelum down. Raumanu tightened his grip on his cane and straightened his back.

Caelum closed his eyes for a moment to compose himself before smiling. 'Very well, then let us do it now.'

Raumanu relaxed his posture a little. 'I'm glad you see it our way.'

Although I had no idea what this *Empyrean* was like, surely the agreement they made here would have no effect on what happens on the other side? These were just words.

Correct, daughter. Which is why immediately after the portal appears, your father is going to get a little surprise. I won't be taking any chances.

The bodyguards up in the rafters with me were stirring. They produced numerous inhibitor collars from under their dark robes and what looked like wrist and ankle restraints. They stealthily positioned themselves above Caelum and teetered over the balcony edges, ready to drop down on him.

'Then let it begin!' Avarut roared, his voice booming all around.

The three Chosen formed a triangle, pointed their hands at one another and closed their eyes. They remained motionless for a few moments while the rest of us eagerly waited. Then a few more moments passed, and still nothing.

'Clear your minds,' Raumanu grumbled.

'What do you *think* I've been doing?' Caelum yelled back.

Silence again, and after more time passed, Avarut grew redder again. 'What's the hold-up?' he growled, smashing his fist down on his armrest. 'Enough stalling!'

Mother slowly shook her head. 'I feel a connection between us, but… something's missing.'

Perplexed like the others, Raumanu gave a contemplative hum. 'It's as though… our path is blocked.'

'No!' Avarut yelled as his palms erupted with white, thrusting him to a standing position. He fired L lines at random pillars and braziers, exploding them into rubble and ash. 'This is *not* how it ends!'

The three Chosen watched his temper tantrum unfold without interfering. After he had destroyed most of the light sources in the room, Mother stepped up to him with a dejected look.

'I think… I think I know *why* it isn't working,' she began.

The men narrowed their gazes on her.

'Sacet's portals are a necessary component,' she continued, 'and we don't have them because… she has *escaped* the Empyrean.'

'What?' Avarut responded.

'Impossible!' Raumanu added.

'Treachery,' Caelum said, before hovering. He bore down on her, stopping only when he was face-to-face. 'How *long* have you known? And when were you planning on telling us? I ought to rip your head clean off and bathe in the resulting fountain.'

Without fear, Mother tilted her head. 'Really, Caelum? Intimidation against *me?*'

'Answer him!' Avarut shouted.

Mother glanced back and forth at each of them. 'It only just happened during our ceremony. The Arc Unity staff spotted her amongst the pews before she portalled away. She's on the run.'

Raumanu paced away with his tapping cane, now deep in thought.

Avarut was seething. 'Then *find* her and sacrifice her again!'

Mother sighed and pushed away from Caelum. She, too, faced away from the group. 'Something... or *someone* has jammed the tracking device inside her INC. Not just her but all her little friends, too. Unless someone spots them, I have *no* idea where they are.'

Caelum's expression creased. 'Rebels...'

'So, his vision was true,' Raumanu said to himself, not realising he was interrupting, 'and there on the plane, I perceived one entity. Only *one*. A dark void tethered to the white below. Hatred in its forever-unblinking eye. Lashes of flesh coiling under the storm. Waiting.'

Mother's eyes widened. I could swear that she looked afraid. What had she realised?

'What are you prattling about?' Caelum asked.

Raumanu glanced back, resolute. 'It is *imperative* we find Sacet quickly. Where is she now?'

Mother brought a palm to her face. 'I *told* you, we *can't* track her. And she has the *perfect* powers to evade escape again and again. As soon as we get close, she'll sense our troops and just teleport to another location.'

Raumanu took a deep breath before nodding. 'Then we inhibit the planet. Activate *every* magnetosphere in the inhibitor net. Flush her out.'

Mother's jaw dropped, and she threw up her hands in frustration. 'Inhibit the... do you have *any* idea how much power that will drain? How much damage it will do to the grid?'

Raumanu continued nodding. 'I do, but our path is more important than the material world. And this is the quickest way to find her and bring her in.'

Mother looked back at the other two for support. 'Once the grid overloads, every power junction could explode. We'll be repairing our infrastructure for *cycles*. And not only that, but if my psychics are inhibited, *my* network will fade. I shouldn't have to explain what'll happen if I have *no* control over…'

'I don't care,' Avarut interrupted, before easing back down into his throne. 'Inhibit *wherever* she may be hiding, other than Arc Royal. And then I want a worldwide search. Mobilize every citizen. Offer grand rewards for information leading to her capture. In fact, Suralia and I will speak to the people ourselves. Make the arrangements.'

The men focused on my mother again, waiting for her to comply.

Initially dumbfounded that her warning was not heeded, her shock eventually dissipated. She gave a short bow. 'At once, Sire.'

Twenty-Nine: No Hesitation

Moments earlier

Arc Sacet penthouse

Countless white lights streaked the orange morning sky beyond the balcony, the Asterians still enjoying Lucenia's power of flight.

What was that strange place? And who, or *what*, was that creature? Upon seeing it, a part of me felt compelled to approach it. But then… what happened *after* that? I couldn't remember, no matter how hard I tried. I had so much to convey to them all, but I didn't know where to begin.

It had taken us a little while to recover, as well as to dry off. We left the pool behind and transitioned inside. All but Sacet and I occasionally closed their eyes and shook their heads to focus, still reeling from both their trip to space and a psychic hangover.

Sacet examined us as we made our way to the nearest couches. 'Are you all *sure* Andriel is not controlling you? You're not just saying what I want to hear?'

Noor shook his head as he took a seat. 'That was Andriel? I feel fine, I'm definitely in control again.' He remained leaning forward, and one of his knees nervously shook. 'And by the way, I *hate* the emperors.'

Sacet still seemed unsure, so I gave her a reassuring touch on the arm. 'The rebels modified our INCs. We're immune to control unless we're up close to a psychic.' I remembered back to both what Kaxiyan and Andriel admitted to me. 'Although now I'm not so sure.'

'Rebels?' Sacet asked. 'The same ones that tried to kill us?'

'No, a different group,' Tetsu said dismissively, leaning back in his seat. 'Our families work for them.'

'Long story,' Noor added, noticing Sacet's growing confusion.

'I'll be right back,' Eno said, disappearing around a corner towards the kitchen. 'I'm *starving*.'

Lotus stopped in front of Sacet. They gave each other a cold stare. Was I about to regret having Sacet save her? She wasn't going to try and attack us again, was she? No, she had been psychically controlled to do those things before. And she was Eno's real sister, so surely she'd be on *our* side.

'So, you're Sacet,' Lotus began, looking her up and down.

Sacet raised a palm to stop her. 'We don't have time for introductions.' She then glanced at the others. 'Nor time for resting, or explanations. We need a place to hide, and it obviously can't be here, this was just the first place I could think of.'

The rest of us exchanged looks of concern.

'So, the Asterians… they're our enemies again?' Tetsu asked.

I gave a solemn nod to support my sister. 'The ones in charge, yes. They always have been.' I took a breath and looked at Sacet. 'I'm sorry I didn't see that until now.'

Eno came back with an arm full of Seronian fruit, along with another piece already in his mouth. He gladly threw a piece to each of us. Not needing to eat, I passed my hapoyo to Tetsu.

Sacet caught one but seemed distracted. She was probably using her second perception. She squeezed the fruit to the point that it squirted onto the floor, perhaps involuntarily, before throwing her hand to the side and opening a portal leading to a dark, foul-smelling interior.

'We should leave, *right* now,' she explained.

The dank air flowed in, smelling of oil and rot. It was clearly a location somewhere in the depths. We all looked through and again gave each other concerned looks.

Sacet sighed, sensing the tension. 'I just need to hide you. Once I know you're all safe, I can work out a way to stop these rituals.'

Waiting for us on the other side of that portal was a life on the run until either we were caught or we somehow defeated the entire empire. It felt like we had only just got here, to this luxurious, peaceful place. But it was all a lie, I knew that now.

I approached Sacet and smiled. 'This isn't just your fight, it's ours, too.'

Eno came over, too. 'It always has been.'

The boys stood and nodded in agreement. Like me, their uncertainty had changed to determination.

'I only just got you back,' Noor said to Sacet. 'I'm not leaving your side.'

Eno folded his arms. 'Neither am I. I have a feeling you're going to need *my* protection, for a change.'

Tetsu shrugged and gave a reassuring grin. 'Let's save the world again, I guess.'

We all turned to Lotus, who simply nodded, before staring through the dark portal.

I walked up to it first, but just as I was about to step through, the portal wobbled. Sacet strained, and it suddenly disappeared.

'What happened?' I asked. 'Are you okay?'

She took a couple of steps to the nearest wall to regain her balance. 'I can't sense any— it's an inhibitor field!'

The others all pointed their hands in different directions, attempting to use their powers, but nothing appeared. I tried summoning my aura, too, but it didn't appear.

'Look,' Eno said, pointing outside at the sky beyond the pool.

We approached the windows and saw that the white lines had disappeared from the sky. Now there were only tiny, falling dark dots. Even those that were flying high above the city had been affected and were now plummeting to their deaths.

'Sacet?' a voice said from behind.

We all turned towards the elevator and saw roughly ten people standing there. It was the Arc Sacet maids and butlers, still wearing their finery and holding cleaning instruments.

'Honoured Chosen Sacet,' Fidèle, the head servant said. 'What are you doing here?'

'Aren't you supposed to be… dead?' another servant asked.

Fidèle shot a look back at her, before awkwardly stepping forward. He attempted to maintain a formal posture. 'What she *means* to say, Madam, is that we thought your ceremony duties had made you… indisposed?'

'They did, but I'm back now,' Sacet answered, before pausing. 'Fidèle, we'd like a vehicle to pick us up. We're taking the rest of the day off and would like to see the sights.'

Although Sacet's words were calm and clever, her body language was still defensive. Realising the situation, I gave a fake smile, as did Eno. Noor and Tetsu's readiness for battle was written all over their faces.

'Of course, Madam,' Fidèle replied. 'I can arrange that for you.'

Each of the servants' eyes looked up and to the left. What were they doing? Were they using their INCs? Their body language changed, like they were on edge. Each servant nervously looked at another.

Fidèle narrowed his gaze on Lotus. His smile disappeared. '*Um*, Honoured Chosen, perhaps you and your… *friends*… would be more comfortable in the sitting room while we send for your hovercar?'

My INC suddenly blipped; a semi-transparent box expanded in my vision's centre. Written on it was a simple message: *Get out now!*

Lotus also appeared to be using her INC. After her eyes stopped twitching, she reached behind her back and pulled out a small baton from a hidden compartment in her armour. 'They know,' she informed us, before whipping the baton to the side, which lengthened and electrified it.

Fidèle responded, reaching behind and under his suit jacket for a pistol, before pointing it at Sacet. 'Kill them!'

We dropped our fruit, and everyone scattered in different directions, most diving for cover behind furniture.

Fidèle fired at Sacet, but thankfully missed. But it wasn't *her* he should have been focusing on, for Lotus was sprinting right at him. In an impressive acrobatic feat, she vaulted over a couch and landed at his side, before sticking him with her baton. It produced a wicked crackle and incapacitated him. He fell to the ground in a heap shortly after.

'Good takedown,' Sacet said to Lotus from behind a couch.

Lotus grunted back. 'Yeah, like I care what *you* think.'

As the other servants were scattering, I grabbed Eno by the wrist and pulled him back through a nearby archway. We took cover behind the wall, and I peeked my head back out. 'Back here, quick!' I said to the others.

Lotus picked up the pistol from the floor before finding cover by the elevator. Sacet and the boys retreated to either side of the archway. Sacet and Noor took the far side, while Tetsu joined Eno and I.

Sacet and I both peeked around our respective corners and saw the remaining servants retrieving stashed weapons from hidden compartments along walls and drawers, from closets, and even from inside formerly inconspicuous household statues. Now armed with pistols and rifles, they reemerged and jointly fired on our position.

Eno was frozen in place. 'What do we do?'

Sacet looked stumped, which was unlike her. She and I surveyed the area for anything we could use, but the only thing nearby was the garden. All the furry animals had scurried into hiding positions behind shrubs and logs.

Lotus was firing back from her position. 'I need a little help here?'

Looking at my now powerless friends, something stirred in me. I couldn't allow my family to be hurt, not again. My usual worries didn't seem important right now. No, I needed to *do* something. Protection of others didn't just mean healing anymore, I needed to attack.

I caught Tetsu's eye and gestured to Eno. 'Guard him.' I continued down the corridor, away from the archway.

'Okay,' he replied, before reaching out to me. 'But wait, what are you going to do?'

A strange feeling spurred me out of his grip and around the corner.

'Tau? Tau!' Tetsu called, but I was gone.

I had the penthouse layout in my mind, and I quietly ran the long way around through the corridors, attempting to flank the servants. I checked each corner as I went, before darting forward to the next piece of cover.

I heard footsteps, so I clung to the next corner and waited. The unsuspecting butler plodded clumsily around, so I stuck my leg out and tripped him. As he tumbled, I leapt onto him and grabbed the wrist holding his pistol.

He fired wildly as we tussled, both trying to control the pistol's direction. I smacked him in the face, stunning him briefly, before peeling his weapon away, turning it on him, and immediately firing. I shot two more times as I got back up to make sure he was dead before continuing to run.

It wasn't long before I had circled behind our enemies, with a view into the main chamber. They each had their backs to me, firing at my friends. Their prime target seemed to be Lotus at the moment, whose cover was practically melting from the repeated projectiles.

Nearby at the bar, a maid was firing her pistol haphazardly, and only when the other servants fired. I could tell she had little to no combat training, just from the way she was holding it.

The next time she ducked, I bolted for the side of the bar and hopped up and over. Now crouching next to her, I shot her in the head before she could react, and she slumped to the side, lifeless.

It all felt like everything was in slow motion. Like all the training I had ever done was paying off, concentrated into this one moment.

I knew the element of surprise wasn't going to last much longer, so I stood and fired at as many of the servants as I could. As though having flashbacks to my time on the firing ranges, I pictured them as targets instead of actual people.

One shot, hit. Two, three, hit, hit. My execution was surgical. One of my targets screamed in pain, the first shot having failed to instantly kill him, so I shot again, this time into his head with pinpoint accuracy.

The remaining four servants spun on the spot, realising what had happened. The jig was now thoroughly up. They each scrambled for safer cover. I could see their mouths moving, shouting out instructions to each other, but I couldn't understand them. All I knew was that they needed to die.

I waited for Lotus to draw their fire before rising again. Realising that one servant's cover was a soft couch, I fired through it repeatedly, and knew I had been successful when the servant's hand rolled out to the side with a pool of blood expanding around it.

Now only three, and I ducked as they sent a hail of laserfire towards the bar. The various bottles and glasses smashed into a rain of shards. The colourful concoctions previously within them now painted every surface.

I heard Tetsu groan and shout.

'Tetsu!' I shouted, before jumping up again and exchanging more laserfire. Lotus did the same, and together we took down another two.

Only one shaking woman remained. She was the one with extra mechanical arms sticking out her back, which she had been using to hold an extra rifle. She dropped both guns and raised all her hands in surrender. 'Please, I've never died before. I don't want the pain. Please don't shoot!'

When the begging girl turned to face me, I fired without hesitation. She crumpled with both fleshy and metallic thuds. Lotus, having seen what I did, raised an eyebrow.

'Tau?' Tetsu yelled.

He appeared from a nearby corridor with bloodstains on his chest, no doubt from killing one of the servants himself. Eno followed him out, unharmed.

'I'm here,' I replied, exiting the bar's safety and joining the others.

Sacet and Noor came out, too, and our group reconvened. They all looked equal parts shocked and impressed.

'They seemed so nice,' Eno said in disbelief.

'Tau… how did you…?' Sacet began.

Lotus quickly counted. 'And here I was thinking you were a wimp like the rest of the elevated.'

Tetsu approached and placed both hands on my shoulders. 'Don't get me wrong, I think you're incredible, but… this isn't going to take you to a dark place again, is it?'

The last time I had been this violent, I could feel my very soul becoming corrupted, filling with hate. I now had a name for that: a fallen disciple. Back then, I had made a vow to myself to never slip back into that hatred, and Tetsu had made a vow to protect me, always.

I looked down and shook my head. 'I don't think so, it's not like then. These people, they were just obstacles… threatening those I cared about.'

Noor shifted to the centre of our group. 'Did anyone else get that warning message?' All of us nodded. 'Who sent it? I thought our INCs were unreachable?'

Sacet had been picking up pistols, and she chucked one to Noor,

Tetsu, and Eno, as well as keeping one for herself. 'No time to wonder.' She gestured to the elevator. 'More will be on the way. We need to go.'

Lotus had her hand on her hip. 'And you expect us to fight our way down the tower? Against thousands of, not servants, but fully armed guards?'

Noor brought his hand to his chin. 'So, we go down the tower in disguise?'

Sacet's eyebrows lowered in thought, and she looked out the window. 'No, we go down the tower… just not on the inside.'

Lotus nodded, realising what she meant. 'I'm assuming someone as rich as you would have unrestricted auto-fitters?'

Sacet made for the nearest staircase. 'This way.'

Lotus gave specific directions for when we entered the fitter, describing which menus and options to choose.

The first piece of clothing we each created was a wingsuit, which was in the 'Skydiving' category. Lotus put one on first, replacing her previous armour, and showed us how it worked. Basically, if we pressed these tiny buttons in our palms, laser-like wings would protrude from our lower backs and allow us to glide.

On top of that, Noor insisted we needed a disguise for the city, so Lotus got each of us to create a simple cloak, complete with hood and oxygen mask.

After each member of our group had been fed through the auto-fitter, we all had the same matching getup. We left the bedroom, headed back downstairs, and assembled again by the pool.

'Masks on,' Lotus instructed, before slipping hers on with ease. 'Once we leave the arc's shield, the air will be too thin to breathe.'

Having some experience with sealed masks in the past, I worked mine out quickly, as did everyone but Eno, so Sacet and I helped him.

'Weapons check,' Lotus continued, examining her pistol.

'Wait,' Eno interrupted, 'we're actually going to… I mean… jump?'

Lotus approached him and placed her hand on his shoulder. 'It's the only way, but I promise you'll be fine, okay?' she said in a rare moment of compassion. 'Follow me as best you can.'

Sacet cocked her head to the side. '*Hmph*, you know somewhere for us to hide?'

'A perfect place not too far from here,' she replied.

I looked out over the balcony to the horizon, below the pointed arcs, upon the endless, reflective steel surfaces that made up the roofs of the upper echelon. I walked to the balcony's railing and climbed it.

After taking a deep breath, I holstered my pistol, then looked over the edge again. The height was even more terrifying now that I was on the precipice. The others all clambered up, too.

'No more hesitation,' I said with feeling. 'We do whatever it takes.'

The others nodded, and Lotus dove headfirst off the edge. Noor and Tetsu followed, then Eno took the plunge with a scream. I nodded at Sacet, who had been waiting for Eno, and the two of us jumped together.

Thirty: Taking the Plunge

The rippling air thrashed at my ears with an endless blast. Eno's terrified screams eventually ceased, whilst Noor and Tetsu spiritedly hooted and hollered. We all eventually got over the initial shock of the jump and followed the blonde's lead, straightening our bodies like plummeting arrows.

We descended parallel to the arc's side, granting us occasional glimpses of life through the windows. A thin layer of clouds was far below, and below that was the infinitely long, mostly flat stretch of city rooftops that made up the planet's upper surface.

It didn't feel like I was falling, but rather flying. For the briefest of moments, I felt free, until the weight of my responsibilities flooded back into my mind. Although our robes billowed uncontrollably, our sleek wingsuits thankfully clung firm, having been designed for this very purpose.

The temperature of the air suddenly became far colder, almost freezing, for we had fallen through the peak's invisible shielding. Thankfully, the river of adrenaline coursing through my veins stopped me from shivering.

The blonde girl leading us occasionally glanced back up to see if we were still in formation. Noor and Tetsu gained on her, and when they were level, they reached out and grabbed each other's hands to help synchronise their rate of descent.

Meanwhile, Eno wasn't keeping his legs and arms in, allowing Tau and I to catch up to him. Just as we were about to overtake, we both reached out with our free hands and grabbed one of his arms, mimicking the formation below. The blonde kept glancing up, specifically at Eno, as if concerned.

Moments before we would drop through the layer of clouds, shining yellow lights pierced through the wispy haze. They rose out of the cover faster than we were falling. They belonged to large, flying, black vehicles. Their headlights beamed towards the arc's peak. We were now close enough to hear their humming engines.

Had they spotted us? I tightened my grip around my pistol and aimed at the nearest oncoming vehicle.

To my relief, they sped past without slowing, continuing their ascent. Several more appeared from the clouds and did the same, and then over a hundred more. They, too, ignored us, perhaps believing us to be some of the many civilians still falling to their deaths.

On closer inspection, each vehicle was heavily armoured, no doubt filled with soldiers sent to apprehend us. It wouldn't be long until they discovered the aftermath of our servants' betrayal. We needed to fall faster.

The smoggy clouds enveloped us, obscuring all. My visibility, already hampered by the mask, was basically now non-existent. I periodically brought my pistol-wielding wrist to my goggles to wipe the condensation away.

Eno's arm squirmed in my other hand, and I realised he was trying to grab me back with his own. He was gazing at me through the dense miasma. When I looked through his goggles, I was expecting to see the same scared little boy I had always known, but instead saw a familiar determination in his eyes, an absence of fear. I quickly brushed my hand down the line of his arm and gripped his hand instead.

We cleared the clouds, and below I spotted a big problem. Whilst Noor, Tetsu and the blonde were a safe distance from the tower, it seemed my group were much closer to the arc windows than before, and I realised why. As we had descended the arc, it was growing wider, with the base at the bottom being the widest part.

The group below noticed this as well; all three were looking up at us and gesturing to the oncoming windows. The blonde freed her hand from Tetsu and faced her palm at each of us, no doubt trying to remind us of her wingsuit instructions.

She carefully flipped back over, her head almost pointing straight down, before demonstrating. She pushed both boys away and then squeezed her glove, making neon pink, buzzing, translucent wings appear from under her loose robes, which parted to accommodate their presence. She immediately zipped above us, having slowed her rate of descent drastically. The rest of us watched her as she effortlessly glided farther from the tower.

We remaining five exchanged nods before also pushing off from one another. Then, almost simultaneously, we all squeezed the buttons in our palms.

Wings shot out from our backs, too, slowing us instantly. My gut dropped, as though someone had a hook in my intestines and was yanking me up. The wind that was previously blasting my eardrums softened considerably.

'*Wooooooooo!*' Tetsu yelled. 'This is amazing!'

The blonde appeared in front of our group again, clearly having more experience with these suits than we had. She pointed at a somewhat distant landmark, an unassuming tower that looked like any other. 'That's our destination,' she shouted back over the howling draught.

Some of the others laughed as they joyously dipped and rolled around in the sky. But I focused on the blonde. Who was this woman, and where was she leading us?

The noise and stench of the city streets permeated our hiding place, a thankfully deserted alleyway. Although comparatively dark, just about everything here in the upper layers was bathed in neon light, leaving very few places to effectively hide.

Hanging above the various businesses and domiciles, screens blared audiovisuals down at us, advertising sleek products I had never heard of. Many of the lights and screens flickered, as though short-circuiting.

If we craned our necks almost directly up, we could still see Arc Sacet looming over us through the narrow gaps between the other rooftops. Thousands of vehicles were now spiralling around the tower in search of us.

I was surprised how easily we made our escape. It seems Andriel had been too reliant on her psychic network. I also remembered back to the warning we each received on our INC screens and realised that perhaps someone else was still aiding us from afar.

Now maskless, we could finally breathe, but as soon as we went on the move again, I was going to instruct everyone to put them back on. With our drab grey robes, we'd hopefully traverse the crowds without unwanted attention.

Out in the streets, shop owners pulled down security gates, roving hooded gangs were ransacking those that were unprepared or too trusting, and an overwhelming sense of anger pervaded the previously calm populace.

Noor gestured at the insanity. 'Looks like they're having trouble keeping everybody under control.'

Tau sighed. 'At least they're free to think for themselves now.'

I gritted my teeth. 'That violence should be directed at the emperors. These people need to know the truth. I wish I could just go tell them. Otherwise, how do we convince them that the rituals need to stop?'

'For now, we hide,' Noor replied, 'we'll work the rest out later.'

I know I had told them we needed a place to hide, but I also knew we needed to act before it was too late. I shook my head, second-guessing myself. 'But what if they continue and it makes things worse?'

Noor pulled me in and hugged me. 'It's just until we come up with a plan. We'll be okay.'

The blonde had been gone for far too long. She had instructed us to stay put as she scouted ahead, but what if, as we waited here, she was reporting us to the guards? Surely she wouldn't immediately betray us after helping us escape? Either way, my suspicion of her was certainly growing, but without her familiarity of the area, we'd be lost.

'So, how do you know this blonde, Tau?' I asked. 'Why did I save her life?'

Eno's eyes pointed down, as if embarrassed.

'She's a member of that rebel group we were telling you about, the Setting Sun,' Tau began, placing her hand on Eno's shoulder comfortingly. 'And Eno's... *biological* sister.'

My stance faltered. '*What?*' I didn't know how to respond, so I stared at Eno, confused. 'Biological sister? I thought you were an only child?'

Tau now avoided eye contact with me. 'Her name's also Sacet...'

'How many times do I need to tell you people?' an echoing voice called from behind. 'I don't go by *that* name anymore.'

Farther down the alley, the blonde had returned. She marched over and, out of everyone, chose to stare specifically at me.

'You're back,' Noor said.

'Good,' Tau said with a sigh of relief. 'So, is this safehouse of yours... safe?'

'It is,' the blonde replied, before focusing back on me.

'I'm sorry,' I began, earnestly, 'I didn't know who you were. It's nice to know we've got more relatives. What do I call you instead?'

She folded her arms. 'It's Lotus now, thanks to you.' Her demeanour was both cold and abrasive, as though she were ready to attack me. It was only now that I noticed she was slightly taller, and definitely stronger, muscle-wise. She was a bit older than me, but not by much.

I squinted and shook my head. '*Um*, what's your problem?'

As if waiting for those words, she took two strong steps forward and stood over me. 'For one, my parents gave *you* the name that was meant for *me*.'

I shrugged and copied her body language. 'Okay? How's that *my* fault? I didn't even know you *existed* until now.'

Tau got between us and tried to separate us with her palms. 'Please, not here. We *need* to get off the streets.'

Lotus brushed Tau aside and got back in my face. 'And second, you dragged *my* brother into every possible danger without a care of the consequences.' She looked me up and down with disgust. 'If *you* never existed, he'd probably be back in the Promised Land on an undestroyed Seron. But you don't *really* care about him, do you? Not compared to yourself.'

I gestured at my brother. 'Of *course* I care about him. What are you talking about? There's no—'

She prodded me in the chest so hard that I had to step back. 'Countless people died when Seron was destroyed, with no chance of resurrection. All so *you* could keep fighting.'

My heart sank. 'If… I had have *known* what Raumanu was going to do—'

Tau gave both of us a stern stare. 'We don't have time for this.'

'Agreed,' said Tetsu, then Noor. Eno nodded, too, looking increasingly awkward.

Lotus clenched her fists, ignoring them. 'You *knew* they were going to keep coming for you. And instead of handing yourself over—'

'*Oh*, so you think *you* could have handled it better?' I interrupted.

'I *am* handling it better,' she corrected. 'I strike the empire from the shadows while you clumsily stumble into every trap they set for you.'

I smirked. 'You sound a lot like a former friend of mine, blaming *me* for everything. I bet you're just jealous that *I* was there for Eno and *you* weren't.'

Lotus' eyes widened with rage, and she pulled back her shoulder, telegraphing a punch. I was ready to dodge, but as her fist came forward, both Noor and Tetsu intercepted it and shoved her back. Meanwhile, Tau placed both hands on my chest to hold me at bay.

'Enough!' Eno cried out, his voice echoing off the alley walls. 'Stop this!'

The energy between the rest of us calmed. Lotus refused to look away from me, but she at least ceased struggling against the boys.

'You're *both* my sisters,' Eno continued, 'and we should be working together, like a family.'

He turned to Lotus. 'Sacet did nothing wrong, and I'm not some helpless kid anymore. I can take care of myself, and I have *her* to thank for that.'

Eno turned to me. 'And she could have left us just now, but didn't, so why are you arguing with her? She's family, and we need her!'

The group went silent. The anger on Lotus' face subsided, as did my own. Eno was right, of course.

A notification box suddenly appeared on my INC, and it maximised without me giving it permission to, taking up most of my vision. It was a visual of the emperor and the empress sitting in their thrones.

'People of Aster, hear me!' the emperor's gravelly voice resounded from all around us.

Out the corner of my eye, I saw my companions were equally affected by the interruption. Not only that, but out in the streets, the visual had appeared on all of the billboards, screens and holographics, too. They were everywhere at once.

'Loyal subjects,' the emperor continued, 'we have invoked our royal right to assume control of every device on Aster to bring you dire tidings.'

'Are you all seeing this?' Noor asked and some of us nodded.

Several people along the street catwalks jeered and threw refuse up at the screens. Then more joined in, and more, until almost all of them were booing.

The empress was stone-faced. 'My dear Avarut and I have come to an important decision: that soon we will abdicate our thrones.'

The six of us stood in a circle, mouths agape. The crowds beyond the alley hushed in disbelief.

'That's right,' Avarut continued, 'because when we have achieved the Chosen path, we will all ascend to greater power. Like the deathless disciples, we will be immortal and beyond the need for rulers.'

Avarut seemed off. His forehead vein protruded even more than usual, and his skin was redder, as though he recently had a tantrum. But his now calm attitude stood in a stark contrast.

Spliced footage flicked by of the rituals taking place, the various Chosen, and even of random civilians enjoying the Chosen powers for themselves.

It changed back to Suralia, who raised an eyebrow. 'There's just *one* problem: the Chosen Sacet and her sister Tau, who we have discovered is also a Chosen, have escaped their sacrificial duties, and are running free somewhere on Aster.'

Both Tau's face and mine now appeared. We glanced at each other with concern. The street crowd also exchanged looks, but these were of intrigue, clearly eager to hear more.

Avarut had his fingers in a pyramid. 'And *that* is why we have activated the global inhibitor net. To give us all a chance to find where they are hiding and capture them, dead or alive!'

Suralia attempted a smile, but it looked unnatural. 'Whomever brings them in will be greatly rewarded with riches beyond their wildest dreams, including ownership of an arc! You will want for nothing!'

Impressed murmurs spread amongst the crowd. Even without being controlled, many were clearly still tempted by their baser instincts and still willing to sacrifice us. Others were not so sure, returning to their former booing.

Avarut's fingers interlocked, and his eyes narrowed. 'Until they are caught, the inhibitors stay on. Without abilities, these girls will not escape you.'

Suralia shook her head with a smirk, as if disappointed by the actions of a small child. 'Now, I know some of you think fondly of them, but what are two sacrifices compared with the eternal happiness we shall all inherit?'

'And the limitless power?' Avarut added. 'Aster, do the right thing, find them and bring them to your nearest authority station, by any means necessary.'

The signal cut, and all the screens in the street returned to their advertisements.

After descending several more city layers, braving the unruly crowds, Lotus had led us through the labyrinthian backstreets to the safehouse's front door. It was tucked away from the main avenues, in another almost deserted alley. The domicile was in a long row of others, all of them practically identical. They were grey and brown, and smelled of mould.

'Wait, wait, wait,' Tetsu said, 'I thought our INCs were modified, but they're still reaching us? Can they track us here?'

'Our INCs still receive the signal,' Lotus answered, 'but it doesn't bounce it back.'

Tau sighed. 'At least not to Andriel.'

Everything here was depressingly dark and damp. We could hear muffled cries and moans from those that lived nearby.

We all huddled around the entrance as Lotus hovered her hand over the front door panel. There was an odd beep, as though the scanner had initially failed, before the door shuddered open with difficulty. Lotus went in first and the rest of us followed. She closed the door and finally we were alone.

It was even darker in here, and somehow the smell was worse. The apartment's rooms were small and pokey. They were furnished, but each piece was shredded and covered in rotting filth. It took a while for me to realise there were windows as well, but they had been blacked out by dust, or possibly soot.

There was a scum-filled kitchen, which had a pile of what I could only assume was faeces in the centre of the tiles. I had seen cleaner food prep areas in nomadic caves.

A corridor to our side no doubt led to the bedrooms, and possibly a bathroom. It was so narrow that it was only able to accommodate the width of one person.

We spread out, but none were game enough to sit down. Lotus went to a window near the entrance, wiped a small circle clean with her wrist, then kept watch through it.

'You're sure this place is safe?' I asked, stepping over a pile of old garbage.

Lotus smirked. 'It's probably the safest place Eno has ever been.'

Noor approached me. 'Alright, so we have some time now. You can bring us up to speed.'

'Yeah, what happened?' Tetsu added. 'I'm so confused.'

I sighed and looked into each of their expectant faces. 'Okay, I'll tell you everything, but you won't believe it.'

Thirty-One: Hanging Dolls

Arc Royal

In the rafters

Mother's last instruction to me was to stay hidden in the staff service tunnels throughout Arc Royal, but the longer I stayed up here, the more alone I felt. None of the guards or staff even acknowledged my presence. It's funny; my whole life, I wanted to be left alone, but now that I was, I felt directionless, hopeless even.

I was currently above the royal children's dorms, which were connected with crisscrossing hallways. Various brainwashed guards were looking down on the kids from steel catwalks in the dark rafters. Directly beneath me was my old, pink bedroom.

My room was untouched since I was last here. Even my cushions and clothes were still laid out exactly as I had left them. The hundred or so dolls still hanging from the ceiling, too.

I hadn't known this before, but the ceilings above all the children's rooms were an illusion. From below, the kids saw a regular ceiling, and could even hang things from it, but from above, it was somehow see-through, allowing the guards and I to watch them all constantly.

Now that I knew I had been watched my whole life, I had never felt so disgusted. This meant every day as I was getting dressed, going to the bathroom, when I thought I was alone, someone could have been watching me.

I shuddered at the thought, although knowing Mother, it was only *her* watching us through the collective guards' eyes. The empty-headed servants probably had no recollection of their duties.

There were no signs of power usage from the kids: no one flying around, no damage to the facility walls, no random piles of created materials. It seemed that sometime after my spat, they had decided to inhibit all of them, just in case.

I could see my brother, Ardo, changing his pants in the neighbouring room to mine. And in another room beyond that, one of my younger sisters, Meridree, was crying. Based on her age, it'd be another ten or so cycles before she went completely dead inside, like I had.

Back in the hallway, many more of my siblings were meandering about, no doubt looking for something to amuse themselves with. I knew the feeling all too well, that nothing would ever change around me. Funny being on this side of things now and still feeling so empty.

Seeing them all still stuck, living in the insanity that had eventually broken me, was opening old wounds. I was reliving those memories all over again, as though I was still down there with them. Meridree's cries grated inside my head, and my eyes welled.

I fell against the catwalk railing, before dropping to my knees and bawling. My cries echoed around the empty, upper chamber, but were ignored.

I suddenly remembered my two slaves, Korin and Neva, were still behind me, following me wherever I went. I glanced back, and we all stared at each other in silence. I wondered if anything of their personalities was left.

'Well?' I began, clearing my eyes. 'Aren't you going to say something hurtful?'

Korin and Neva remained motionless.

'Come on,' I goaded, 'say something, you idiots! Anything!'

Korin pulled out a knife from behind her back and quickly cut open her mouth's stitches. She didn't do it carefully either, slicing into her lips. 'How can I serve you, Master?' she said, spitting blood all over the place.

Neva's sands, meanwhile, shifted with a sprinkling noise, and a mouth reappeared on her face. 'What would you like us to say, Master?'

'Stop it!' I shouted. 'I can't *stand* you two like this. I'm not your *damn* master.' I stood and stomped over. 'Just be yourselves. You're free, okay? Act like you *used* to.'

'Used to?' Neva questioned, glancing at Korin with confusion.

'But... I don't remember... myself,' Korin said with a self-inflicted lisp. 'Act like I *used* to... I don't know what that means?'

'Me either,' Neva added, before looking around, searching for something that made sense. 'That makes me feel sad. Am I allowed to be sad?'

'Yes!' I yelled back with a tear trickling down my cheek. 'You *should* be sad; your brains were wiped of anything that made you... *you*.'

Korin shook her head. 'Why would we say something hurtful to you?'

'Because you were bad people,' I snapped back, wanting to hit them for their stupidity. 'You were always cruel to me.' I sighed. 'I can't believe I *miss* that part of you.'

They exchanged another look, and Neva dipped her head down. 'I am sorry for what my past self did to you.'

'I am, too,' Korin added before shrugging. 'But I still don't understand why you would *want* us to be cruel to you?'

I sighed and turned away. 'I don't know.'

I realised I wasn't the nicest person either. Sometimes I enjoyed being cruel, but I never understood why. I thought back to Sacet's harrowing and all the manipulations I helped orchestrate, just so I could get off that planet and start my life on Aster proper.

All the major players in my life were so selfish. Both my current and former parents, the previous versions of Korin and Neva, pretty much *every* member of Overwatch I had served with... they were *all* looking out for their own self-interest.

Then I realised that Sacet, Tau and I shared the same heartless father. How crazy that they were my sisters, too? All those things I did and said to my relatives... I suddenly felt so dirty. I was just as self-serving as Mother.

'Because maybe I deserve it? Maybe *I'm* bad, too.'

'We don't *have* to be bad?' Neva suggested.

I rolled my eyes at the ridiculous notion. 'It's already *done*.' I focused on Meridree below. 'My sister, Tau, she once told me… if more people like me *chose* to do the right thing, then good would at least stand a chance. But I have made too many bad choices.' They silently exchanged a look while I gestured to the kids. 'Why don't they just fight their way out, like I did?'

They both approached to get a better look from the balcony. Neva gave a warm smile, which I found quite unsettling. 'Maybe they need to be shown how?'

I scoffed. 'Yeah, I already tried.' I closed my eyes. 'They probably think I'm dead somewhere, or that exile is something horrible. But really… I've never been more powerful, freer. They must be afraid to fight… like *I* was… for *so* long.'

It dawned on me like a crashing wave. I pushed off the balcony and excitedly glanced at the other two. 'They're afraid because of what happened to *me*. Do you see? My siblings are just *like* me. I rebelled and was freed, but they don't know that's an option. I have to help them see that.'

'So, we free the children?' Korin suggested.

I raised an eyebrow at her. 'We? I told you already, you're free now. You can do whatever you want.'

Neva stretched, as if limbering up for action. 'Yes, which means we're free to help you.' Some of her sands shifted, and any remaining wounds disappeared.

'It's not like we have anything better to do,' Korin said, before gesturing to the guards. 'Shall I kill them?' She waved at her own blood on the floor. The liquid floated up and flew over to her, before orbiting around her fingers.

I was briefly overcome with doubt. What if my mother stopped us? What if she were in my head right now? Was my INC still modified to block her at this range? I thought about it for a moment and then focused on my siblings. 'No, because if we free them through force, they'll learn nothing. They need to *choose* to fight back.'

Korin nodded at a particularly lethargic child sleeping on a comically large cushion. 'That might take a while.'

'They just need a push,' I suggested, before taking a few steps back. 'You two *really* want to help me? To help *them*?'

They both nodded resolutely.

I turned and made for the nearest service tunnel. 'Then we have a party to prepare for.'

Two floors up

In the dining hall rafters

The servants were setting up for the nightly birthday dinner below us. It was eerier than usual watching them silently and systematically set the long dining tables. Previously, I assumed their synchronicity was because they had done it so often, but now I knew better.

None of my siblings were here yet, nor were Avarut and Suralia. The event itself was still a while off. Only the staff were present, making sure everything was set up correctly.

There were curiously far more guards in the rafters here than there were above my siblings' dorms, and more than usual for the event. Thankfully, they continued to take no notice of the three of us.

I found a spot that overlooked most of the hall below, and Korin and Neva caught up beside me. Now I just had to wait until the dinner started, work out how to shut off the inhibitors, and then watch the chaos unfold.

After looking at the guards more closely, I was taken aback when I noticed Verre up here, too. She must have recently cashed in her rank points for an age-reduction because she looked younger than she did on Seron.

She and several others wearing military uniforms were amongst the guards. They also took no notice of my presence, staring down blankly instead.

Caelum suddenly came into view, too, floating between the tables. He was inspecting the room with his arms behind his back.

My instinctual response was to duck down, but I realised he probably couldn't see me up here in the dark, so I peeked over the edge at him. 'Damn it, what's *he* doing here?'

Caelum floated a little farther away, over to the thrones to inspect them, too. I quickly realised he was performing his nightly bodyguard duty to ensure the area was safe for my former parents.

'Security's tight,' Neva quietly pointed out. 'Are you sure you wouldn't rather free them from their rooms instead?'

'No, it *must* be here,' I whispered back. 'While the whole empire is watching. That way, they can't be dealt with quietly.'

I noticed something strange about the dining hall walls. Metal poles were now built into the architecture that weren't there before. They were interspersed and surrounding everything, excluding the thrones. To the layman, they would probably go unnoticed, but I had spent hundreds of cycles here. They were definitely new. Plus, thanks to my Overwatch experience, I had seen their like before.

'Look, inhibitor pylons,' I muttered.

'They must be off at the moment,' Neva concluded, looking at Caelum as he flew within their proximity.

Korin shrugged. 'Obviously. How about we sabotage them before the kids arrive?'

I smirked at Korin, for it seemed her original, snarky personality was slowly returning. 'No. We let them turn it on, then turn it off again after the vegetable emperors arrive.'

'The… what emperors?' Neva asked.

I pointed at the far end of the rafters. 'There.'

Several of the metal poles at the opposite end to the thrones had cables heading up into the rafters. The cables had been partially concealed behind purple and yellow drapes. They led to a cordoned-off area that acted as a control room.

The technicians in there had a perfect view of everything below as they operated their control panels. I had seen them many times from below, assuming their duties were to manage the event's lighting and sound.

'That's where we disable it from,' I continued, turning to Neva. 'Your job is to spy on the staff over there. Watch them operate the pylons and work out how to disable them. Then wait for my signal.'

'Which is?' she asked.

'I'm going to shout down to my siblings,' I replied, then I pointed at Korin. 'You'll cover Neva from afar, and when you hear me, quietly kill any staff in her way.'

'Got it,' she said with a nod.

I gestured to the guards. 'Then after that, we stop the guards from interfering with my siblings as best we can.'

They both nodded. Korin was about to move, but Neva looked down at my feet.

'What if we fail?' she said. 'You've *already* been exiled.'

Korin raised an eyebrow. 'Are you willing to die for them?'

I doubted my mother would allow me to be executed, but I also didn't know her all that well. I assumed that she would have intervened with my plans by now if she wanted to stop them, but she hadn't, which meant that she either didn't care, or that she was too busy to notice.

I thought for a moment about the possibility of my death, and I realised that the only time I had ever been happy was when I initially rebelled. I felt like I could finally be happy if we were all free, and yes, that was something I was willing to risk my life for.

'I am,' I responded. 'If I wasn't, what point would my life have?'

We stood in silence for a bit before I nodded at them again, and both took off to get into position. Neva disintegrated into her sand form and, attempting to be stealthy, lengthened her cloud out like a rope before quietly trickling up to the ceiling. Korin just walked away as nonchalantly as possible. She kept to the shadows as best she could and found a vantage point with a clear view of the control room.

I, meanwhile, returned my attention to the dining hall. Almost immediately, however, I felt something was off. Where had Caelum gone?

'Last time I checked,' a voice said from behind, 'little Iya was *exiled* from this arc.'

I spun on the spot and saw that he had floated up through one of the gaps in the rafters.

I didn't know how to react. I couldn't run, I couldn't hide.

'And, as I recall,' he continued, now floating closer, 'the last time I saw *little Iya*, she was cosying up to Sacet, a current *fugitive* of the empire.'

My jaw dropped, and I froze in place.

Caelum touched down, choosing to slowly and menacingly stomp towards me. 'Yet here you are, skulking above the scene of your past crime.'

Out of the corner of my eye, I saw that all the guards were now staring in our direction.

Iya, what did you do? I told you to stay hidden!

Mother? I'm sorry, I didn't think he'd see me.

Unaware of the conversation in my mind, Caelum took another step and towered over me. 'Feeling nostalgic? Or maybe you're here to recommit?'

It's okay, I want you to pretend I'm controlling you. Repeat after me: I thought you'd be better at spotting my servants by now, Caelum.

I averted my eyes from the brute. The words were on the tip of my tongue, but they didn't feel right. Was it because I was being told what to say?

Please, my child, do as I say, or he might find out the truth.

Even if you're not controlling me directly, if I say those things, then I am still your puppet. No, I have a better idea. I think it's time that you now trusted me.

I steadied my breath with a newfound confidence and stared back up at my father. 'Why bother lying to you? It sounds like you've worked me out. Yes, I want the emperors to suffer.'

A smile spread on his face as he reached out to my neck. He clasped it entirely with ease.

'And you should, too,' I quickly added while I still could. 'I heard what Avarut said to you.'

This gave him pause. I sensed a flash of uncertainty on his normally stoic face. 'What are you talking about?'

'Avarut wants you to sacrifice yourself,' I continued. 'You served him loyally for *so* many cycles, and *this* is how he rewards you?' I brought my hands up to my neck and gently peeled his now limp fingers away, one by one. 'If you ask me, it's time for a *new* emperor.'

Caelum narrowed his gaze and glanced about. The guards, who had been out of earshot, were all looking away, pretending not to notice the conversation.

I gestured down into the dining hall. 'This place is *your* legacy, after all, not theirs.'

Iya, don't.

'Speak what you mean,' he said, frustrated by my vagueness.

'You're our *real* father,' I explained, edging closer to him, 'all of us royal children. So, wouldn't it make more sense for *you* to be on that throne?'

He remained silent for the longest time, weighing my words and his surroundings. Was my reading of him wrong? How was he going to react?

I know him well; he's trying to work out if this is one of my tricks.

I sighed and turned. 'I thought you'd be stronger than this, but I see you're still his *servant*. I guess, if *you* won't do what you need to, then *I* will.'

Caelum chuckled, quiet at first, and then loud enough for his laughter to echo throughout the hall. 'You've become quite the master manipulator, little Princess.' Then he leant in and grinned. 'Just like your mother.'

What did he say?!

My eyes widened, and I turned back.

He floated up and away. 'Enjoy the party.'

Thirty-Two: The Deepest Recesses

At the safehouse

'And that's everything that happened,' I said as I leant against a grimy wall in the safehouse. 'If we don't find a way to stop the rituals, the universe ends.'

As I recapped all I had experienced, the group grew progressively more silent and shocked. Lotus was still by the window, keeping watch over the alleyway outside, but her focus faltered numerous times. Tau was aghast, now leaning forward on the shredded couch. The boys had been the only ones to ask prodding questions, and when my answers blew their minds, they paced about the living room trying to process it all.

Tau had also added to the story, filling us in on what had happened to her since she was separated from the others down in this Shifting City they were telling me about. There seemed to be a gap in her memory after seeing Ophan, and she was particularly horrified after I told her what she did.

When I heard that Iya had mysteriously disappeared, shortly after being caught by Lotus trying to escape, I wasn't surprised. I would chalk it up to a moment of weakness on my part when I gave her a chance. Never again.

Shortly after arriving, we had ditched our wingsuits in favour of looking more like typical poverty-stricken Asterians. I looked around at my friends, now wearing plainer hooded robes with gas masks at our sides. The one thing this safehouse *did* have that wasn't mouldy and falling apart was a selection of inconspicuous clothing of differing sizes, no doubt to help Lotus' fellow rebels whenever they needed to lay low.

Lotus folded her arms and stared at me.

'You don't believe me?' I asked her.

She scoffed. 'I believe you. It's too *insane* to be a lie.'

Tetsu sat beside Tau. 'So, you're a Chosen, too?' Tau nodded, and Tetsu wrapped his arm over her back and cradled her.

Noor also approached me. 'We're *not* going to let them sacrifice either of you again.'

'That's right,' Eno added. 'They'll have to go through *us* first!'

'*Even* if they threaten to execute us, don't participate in the rituals,' Noor continued, looking between Tau and I. 'Got it?'

I smiled. 'Thanks, guys.' It was good to feel their love again. 'It's not going to come to that, though, they're not going to find you again.'

'But we gotta bring 'em down somehow?' Eno said. 'So… *uhhh*, how do we *do* that?'

The room collectively looked at me, expecting me to have a master plan to undo the bad guys, but I had nothing. '*We* won't do anything. Let me worry about it, okay? As for what I'm going to do, I… don't know.' I looked down in thought before turning and leaving the room.

I went down the corridor towards the dilapidated bathroom, leaving their now muffled conversation behind. This room was probably the filthiest in the entire apartment. All the tiles were either stained, cracked, or missing entirely. Every metal surface was rusted, and every amenity was stained with reddish-brown former fluids. Some sort of dead animal was rotting in the corner, but I didn't care to investigate it further.

The mirror was shattered long ago by an impact, the fist-sized depression visible in the metal behind it. Some fractured shards of glass remained, and I used them to stare into my reflection.

When I saw how pitiful Lucenia had acted in the Empyrean, I knew I had to defeat my enemies by any means. But now that I was out, the reality of how totally and overwhelmingly difficult that goal was struck me to my core. The sheer mountainous size of Arc Royal and its fortifications, the countless armies hunting us down, the powerful and cruel remaining Chosen, all of these and more stood in our way. And meanwhile, here we were, six powerless teenagers.

'Hey,' Noor said from the door. 'You okay?'

I continued to stare into my own eyes and leaned on the basin. 'Not particularly. I'm realising how impossible this task is.'

He wandered in and stopped beside me. 'That's never stopped you before.'

I shook my head and forced a laugh. 'I'm also realising that even if we win, I'll probably still be stuck in this loop of fighting and pain. It just seems like there's always something after me.'

Noor slowly nodded. 'Maybe.' He placed a hand on my shoulder and turned me towards him. 'Or maybe this time it *will* end. Maybe we'll win, and you and I will escape to paradise, lying on a beach somewhere, sipping drinks. We just have to see this through and not give up, no matter the odds against us.' We both smiled, and he raised an eyebrow. 'And you know, it also wouldn't hurt if you and I had more... passionate nights?'

I laughed, and then he laughed, as though he was making sure I approved of the joke. We hugged, and I put my head on his warm chest. We stood in silence, enjoying the closeness.

'That night,' Noor continued as we swayed, 'you didn't... *know* what was going to happen the next day, did you?'

'That I was going to be sacrificed?' I clarified, and he nodded. 'No, I... had no idea...'

Noor's expressions subtly changed, becoming more downtrodden. 'You don't have to lie to me. You wanted to do it alone, didn't you?'

'No,' I started before sighing. 'Yes. Yes, I knew, and yes, I wanted to do it alone. Everything was hopeless, and you were all still brainwashed.' I dipped my head. 'And also, I didn't want to see any of you suffering on my behalf.'

'This loop you've found yourself stuck in,' he continued, avoiding eye contact, 'maybe it'd be easier if you didn't suffer it alone? There's no shame in asking us for help, okay?'

I nodded, but as I hung my head in shame, I noticed what looked to be a tiny picture on the floor, mixed in with the other refuse. I slowly bent down and picked it out, brushing dirt off it with my fingers.

It was faded, probably from having been left here for cycles, but we could clearly see a city with a bright orange sky. Standing in the foreground was an old, dark-haired woman and a blonde girl, about Eno's age or possibly younger. They were hugging and smiling at the camera.

'The previous residents, maybe?' Noor suggested.

'Yes,' I said, recognising the young girl, 'but that looks like Lotus.'

I stormed out of the bathroom and back to the main area where the others were still talking. They all paused when I went right up to Lotus and put the picture in her face.

'Is this you?' I asked. 'Is this your old home?'

She nodded and shrugged. 'What of it?'

I turned and showed it to the others one by one. 'Wasn't she just accusing *me* of putting Eno in danger?' I faced her again. 'I *thought* you said this place was safe.'

All but Eno had equally concerned looks and stared at Lotus expectantly.

She pushed off from the window. 'It *is* safe. If it wasn't already obvious, no one has been here for cycles.'

Noor got in Lotus' face, too. 'You didn't think they'd search old family addresses? How could you be so careless?'

Lotus pushed us both away. 'Back off! I *told* you, we're safe here, it's out *there* you should worry about.'

There was an abrupt rap at the entrance, causing the rest of us to step back. Tau stood, and everyone but Lotus pulled out their weapons and trained them on the door.

I gestured to the corridor, remembering seeing a back window earlier. 'Everyone, stay with me. We're going out the back.'

'Perfect timing,' Lotus said, ignoring me and making for the front door.

'Stop!' numerous of us said at the same time.

She looked back as she fiddled with the panel by the door. 'Only one person knows I used to squat here. The other person in the photo. The only person I trust now.'

The door whooshed up. I prepared to fire, but there wasn't a squad of well-kitted soldiers in the cold alley like I expected, but instead a single old woman. Although she was holding a rifle, it was pointed at the ground.

Like us, she wore a hooded cloak to help hide her sour, wrinkly face.

'Amma!' Lotus said, greeting the old woman with a hug and bringing her inside.

We lowered our weapons and exchanged unsure looks. Lotus must have contacted her when she was *scouting ahead.*

'Jumpy bunch, aren't we?' the woman said as she holstered her rifle behind her back. She gave each of us a bitter stare.

Lotus hurriedly closed the door and joined the rest of us. 'Eno, I'd like you to meet someone. This is your grandmother, Amma. Your *father's* mother.'

'Grandma?'

Amma grinned and gestured for him to approach. 'Grandma, *huh?* I guess that'll have to do. Come here, little one, it's good to finally make your acquaintance.'

The two of them hugged briefly and awkwardly, then Amma looked up at me. '*Ah,* so *this* is Sacet, the weapon all the brown-nosers have been clamouring to get back. I expected you to be taller.'

It certainly wasn't the first time an elderly person had been mean to me. I decided to take it in stride. 'Nice to meet you, too. You remind me of our grandfather.'

'And *you* remind me of a literal *pox,* a walking plague on my family,' she clapped back. 'Stop pretending you're related to us.'

I could see both Eno and Noor take offence on my behalf, but I gave them a subtle shake of the head and they eased.

Lotus was behind Amma, arms crossed and smirking.

This was the woman we saw in the picture, now much older. Her dark hair had turned white, and although she posed with a kind smile in the picture, now I couldn't imagine someone more bitter. Lotus' blind hatred for me suddenly made sense.

Amma nodded at Tau. 'And this is Chosen Tau, *hmmm*? You should hear the rabble out there begging for you to be next, *baying* for your power.'

Tetsu put an arm around a frowning Tau. 'Well, they're not going to *get* it.'

Amma sneered. 'Say that *after* we've got you to a safer location. It's time to move.' She inspected our gear one at a time. 'Good. Good clothing. That pistol is a little rich; keep it concealed. Good.'

Lotus shifted back to the door. 'What's the plan?'

'The same as the old one,' Amma replied, 'we take the weapon to the Setting Sun.'

My friends and I were equally confused, so I shook my head. 'That's hardly a safe…'

'Back to that charlatan?' Lotus interrupted, screwing up her face.

Amma joined her by the door, before gesturing for the rest of us to line up, too. 'Kaxiyan isn't in charge anymore. We need to get back there immediately and take control.'

The rest of us did as we were directed, lining up to leave, although I wasn't happy about it. 'So, we're going underground? And how exactly…'

'Stop talking,' Amma said before grabbing my shoulder and wrenching me to the middle of the line. She did the same to Tau. 'You want me to save your lives? Then just do as Lotus and I say, got it?'

The others nodded, and I remained silent. I hated to admit it, but we needed her help. The sounds of the rioting outside had grown louder and closer.

'Good,' she continued. 'Keep the two Chosen in the centre. Keep your hoods up and masks on. Grab the cloak of the person in front so you don't get separated. Don't speak unless you're trying to warn me of something. When in doubt, do as I do. We have a lot of ground to cover, so let's go.'

Lotus bashed the door control panel to open it, then we quietly exited into the chaos outside.

One alley, one catwalk, one canyonlike street after another, each bustling with thousands of rioters. Claustrophobic walls and towers flanked us wherever we went, many alight with flames. Pure insanity surrounded us. Muggings and robberies, explosions and laserfire, screams and chants, everywhere we turned was a sea of entropy.

'Ignore them,' Amma called back to us as she pushed through another tight crowd, 'unless you have a death wish.'

The normally bright neon lights and billboards had darkened significantly since we started walking, and many flickered like they were about to give out. We were too deep to see the night sky, but if we were topside, we'd no doubt see the beautiful aurora.

While most people fended for themselves, there were also distinct factions forming in the crowd, the most prominent of which was those shouting anti-imperial sentiments. I *very* much wanted to reveal my presence and guide them to Arc Royal, where their ire needed to be directed.

The other common faction halted that idea quite quickly. They were roving gangs of thugs pulling crowds apart to search for me. They ripped down hoods and masks from unsuspecting people, inspected their shocked faces, before moving on to the next group. Amma was expertly avoiding these packs, but I noticed more and more of them as we traversed.

Occasionally, I'd spot some of these hunters wearing huge goggles, surveying and scanning the crowd from afar, for what, exactly, I didn't know. I knew better than to ask out loud.

The hunters weren't the only threats, for the military was scouring the upper levels. Those catwalks were swarming with soldiers going from door to door, smashing them in with battering rams if necessary. Drones and aircraft with flashing lights buzzed way above, too, shining spotlights into random crowds, but did little to dissuade them from their destructive activities. In fact, it seemed like the military didn't care about the crime going on at all; all that mattered to them was finding Tau and me.

Bang!

One of the billboards overhead exploded, raining sparks down on the screaming crowds below. More explosions. More screams. All the lights popped and fizzed out one by one, until the only light left came from the rampaging crowd's personal torches and the unchecked fires they had started.

I reached out to both Eno and Noor's hands instead of just grabbing their cloaks. Both of them squeezed back. Tau and Tetsu did the same.

'What happened to the lights?' Tau asked.

'Quiet!' Lotus snapped.

Amma stopped the group, assessing the situation. 'Their inhibitors have overloaded the grid.'

Although the electricity had gone out, I still didn't feel my powers return. What electricity they did have was clearly prioritising their inhibitors. The empire was so fixated on our capture that their world was going dark.

Lotus shifted closer to Amma. 'We need to get them off the streets, now.'

'The service tunnel is not much farther. Stay close.'

We pressed on, parting through the horde in almost complete darkness. My friends shielded me from most of the crowd, but occasionally I'd brush up against someone, and our masked faces would lock eyes.

The mob slowed, for ahead was a bottleneck in the narrow catwalk, only allowing us to trickle through. More hunters were perched on some nearby crates, scanning everyone who passed.

'Amma?' I said over the din of voices and gesturing to them.

She saw them, then glanced back. The people behind us seemed to only be going one way, forming a wall and boxing us in. We were shoulder to shoulder with others, so I needed to watch what I said. We watched as Amma weighed our options.

'Keep going,' she instructed simply.

I squeezed the boys' hands again. We shuffled forward, little by little, eventually reaching the bottleneck. I could feel the hunters looking directly at us, but I did my best to ignore them.

'INC locked!' I heard one shout. 'Rebels over here! Stop them!'

Hands brushed and snatched at my hood, so I tried to duck and squirm away. They grabbed hold and, with a lucky rip, managed to pull not only my hood but my mask off, too, revealing my face to the gasping crowd. Hands were still shooting out to my companions to do the same.

'It's Sacet!' several onlookers screeched.

'The Chosen!' another bellowed. 'Get her!'

A blast of light. Five people were launched back. An explosion of blood. Amma had fired her rifle into a man's stomach. The crowd reeled, roared and clawed at us, as well as each other, vying to be the one that took us down.

'Run!' Amma shouted back, taking another shot into the crowd.

It seemed like a hundred hands were swiping at me. We were being violently knocked about until my friends and I produced our weapons, too. Some backed away, whilst others simply found something new to snatch at. I fired, as did my friends, repeatedly until we made a hole.

'Get off them!' one man yelled.

'That arc is mine,' another squealed. 'I'll kill all of you!'

Amma darted out of the gap, continuously firing into the crowd regardless of whether they were hostile or not. Lotus reached into our group and pulled Eno out of a woman's grasp. The two of them jumped over the fallen bodies and ran. The rest of us followed with difficulty, having to shoot at numerous grabbers.

I saw Tetsu's pistol ripped away from him, so I targeted the aggressor before he could use it and fired. The hunters on the crates pulled out weapons, too, but shockingly, many in the crowd appeared to be on our side and pulled them off the crates to start savagely beating them.

I hurdled over several bodies with Noor close behind, and Tau and Tetsu brought up the rear. We ducked and weaved through the crowd, which was now fighting itself more than us. Some were even creating blockades for us to pass through.

'Run, Sacet!'

'Get to safety, we'll hold them off.'

One man grabbed hold of my wrist, stopping me in my tracks.

He refused to let go. 'I want your portals, you selfish, little—'

Noor put the barrel of his gun to the man's head and blew his brains all over a nearby wall.

'Please, we need your healing!' one woman called to Tau.

I briefly glanced up and saw the commotion had gotten the attention of the military above, too. Hundreds of onlookers were pointing down and up at us from the other catwalks.

While distracted, I ran straight into a wall. After briefly shaking my head, I looked up and saw that it wasn't a wall, but a man's chest. A hulkish brute the size of Kalek, he was armoured and fierce, towering over all. He brandished a knife bigger than my arm.

His dilated eyes locked onto mine. 'Go, I'll slow them down.'

I didn't argue with the giant; instead, I slinked behind him with the others and continued to run. I glanced back and saw him roar a guttural war cry.

He proceeded to charge into several of our pursuers, each step rumbling the catwalk. He collected them all and flung them off and over the edge to their deaths. He swung his machete clean through a man right down the middle, then cleaved several more in a continued bloodlust.

'Over here!' Eno called from an alleyway before being dragged around the corner by Lotus.

Noor pulled on my wrist, and the four of us sprinted towards the others. No stopping, straight into the pitch-black alley. My pistol was gone, but I couldn't recall when I lost it.

A stream of pursuers had made it through the blockade. Our giant ally was bleeding out on the ground. We rounded a corner and were now hidden from the main thoroughfare. We entered a wall of mist, cold and wet, caused by a water pipe overhead that was about to burst.

The visibility was so poor that it was impossible to see Eno anymore, but we could hear their footsteps on the wet concrete ahead, so we simply followed the noise.

Amassing footsteps resonated from beyond the thin veil of mist. Our pursuers closed in, their lights revealing our path again. Laserfire, the projectiles missed us and fizzled off the walls. They didn't care about taking us in alive.

The dark passage narrowed. Another corner, and another. My wet hands grasped at the cold concrete walls as I twisted and weaved around the corners so as to not lose momentum.

There, ahead of us, a dead end, a single flickering light highlighting our doom. We ran to the end anyway, where we found some stacked crates. Where did Eno go? Had Amma and Lotus taken him and abandoned us? Perhaps there was something we missed? No, there were no other paths from here. Did we take a wrong turn?

Our pursuers' steps grew closer and in greater numbers.

'Eno?' I called out, my voice echoing off the concrete.

'A little help?' Tetsu added.

'Up here,' Lotus called from somewhere above.

Next to the top of the crate stack was a small, easy-to-miss landing, which connected to another catwalk.

'Climb, you idiots!' she instructed, pointing at the crates.

The boys and I pushed Tau forward first. She began to climb just as the hunters rounded the final corner.

'They're not going to make it,' Lotus yelled down the catwalk, no doubt to Amma and Eno, then pulled out her pistol and fired repeatedly into the pack, centre mass.

'Go!' Noor shouted, referring to me, for Tau was almost at the top of the wobbly boxes.

I grabbed the edge of the bottom crate and hoisted myself up, then reached up and did it again. Noor and Tetsu fired back into the crowd, but even their combined shots weren't enough to slow the wave of rabid civilians. The promise of riches and the Chosen path, combined with not having to fear death, spurred this world's residents on like savages possessed.

I heard metallic footsteps overhead. Tau got to the top, stood, and fired, too. Tetsu began to climb. One more crate for me to go. Eno and Amma reached Lotus and joined in dealing out carnage.

'Come on, Noor!' Tau shouted down.

Noor ceased his firing and leapt onto the first crate. I grabbed the lip of the landing and pulled myself up, too, with Tetsu close behind. As I struggled to get onto my knees, a hand appeared, offering to help me up. I took it and was face to face with an armed old man, recognising him instantly.

'Aberym?' I remarked in shock.

'No time for chit-chat,' my grandfather said. After helping me, he took aim with a rifle of his own and fired into the crowd.

Tetsu reached up for the final ledge, so Tau and I bent down to assist him. We grabbed a wrist each and lifted him up. Noor was next, but he was only halfway up the crates, and some of the hunters had made it to the base below him.

'Stand clear!' a voice to our side said.

Farther along the catwalk was a hooded man with a beard, but I couldn't make out his face. He was clutching a small, beeping device. He took aim and chucked the explosive over the edge. It beeped faster as it fell.

Tau and I had just grabbed onto Noor's wrists, but as we pulled, three hunters were grabbing his legs from below. All but Tau and I ducked behind the catwalk railings for cover. I heaved with all my might, as did Tau. The grenade landed amongst the screaming rabble, beeped another distinctive beep, then detonated, melting the alley with a firestorm.

I closed my blinded eyes and continued to pull. The flames washed over me in a searing ripple. Noor was suddenly easier to lift; the force of the explosion launched him up. The three of us rolled on the catwalk, steaming and broiled.

As my eyes adjusted to the alley again, I glanced to the side and saw that all our pursuers had either burst into fiery, ashen corpses or retreated back around the corner. Noor's legs were on fire, but he was putting them out with Tau's help.

The hooded man rose from his cover, approached me and removed his hood. Pilgrim leant down, revealing a wide, toothy grin. 'That look on your faces. Brilliant.'

Thirty-Three: The Fallen One

Traversing Aster's underground tunnels

After the explosion in the alley, we didn't stay to chat, rather we became one with the shadows of Aster's underworld. Any attempts to reconnect had been hushed as we silently descended what felt like hundreds of levels using elevators and staircases hidden in giant, rusty pipes. Down and down and down, until eventually we entered into an ancient, deserted subway system, remarkably still with the lights on. Perhaps it was powered by a separate, but equally-as-ancient power grid.

I was wrong about it being deserted. There were people down here living in cardboard slums, but they were all so disconnected from the world above that they didn't seem to recognise us, let alone care about our presence.

A lone train carriage awaited, which we briskly entered. The carriage interior was filthy, somehow even worse than Lotus' safehouse.

Amma took the controls at the front. She flipped levers and cranked dials until the carriage hummed to life. The doors closed, and we disembarked the lonely station with squealing clickety-clacks.

'Alright, you can talk now,' Amma called back to us.

Tau and I hugged Pilgrim, and the boys greeted him with grins and slaps on the arms. Lotus went to join Amma at the front, and Aberym went to the opposite end of the carriage.

'It's so good to see you, Pilgrim,' I said, and my friends hummed in agreement. 'To be honest, I was worried I'd never see you again.'

He stood his weapon against the carriage wall and grinned. 'What, just because this entire planet wants to kill you, and finding you was harder than finding boobs in the MD? Nah, you weren't getting rid of me that easy.'

Noor, Tau, Tetsu and I found the only remaining unbroken flip-down seats and sat.

Eno stayed by Pilgrim's side. 'You joined the rebellion, too? I *knew* you would.'

Pilgrim chuckled and pointed at Aberym. '*Yeap*, the old man only recruited me yesterday. Before that I was just as brainwashed as all those people up there. I thought the emperor was a guy I'd like to have a drink with. How crazy is that?'

Eno laughed, but the rest of us were in no mood.

After leaving the station, the tunnels were now almost pitch black, with only an occasional flickering lamp. Instead, we relied on the carriages' headlights, which also flickered due to their age.

'So many people defended us back there,' Tau said.

'They're regaining their sanity,' I added.

Pilgrim smiled at her, then at me. 'It's because you're all icons of rebellion. Everyone knows what happened on Seron was the work of absolute monsters. It wasn't a great planet, sure, but it was ours, damn it. Whatever happens next, girls, just know that *everyone* from Seron is behind you.'

Tau reached out from her seat and grabbed his hand. 'Thank you, Pilgrim.'

As we were speaking, I watched Amma and Lotus. They were discussing something, too, though not as quietly as they thought.

'The first thing we do when we get back—' Amma began.

'Is kill Kaxiyan,' Lotus interrupted.

Amma shook her head. 'No, keep him alive, we can't allow yet another psychic back in the enemy's hands. But you also don't want anyone thinking you're in league with him. Make him suffer in front of the others to get them on your side.'

'What do I say?' Lotus asked, looking surprisingly nervous.

I didn't care for these women very much, so instead I focused on Aberym. He was still facing away, hiding a pained expression, as though deeply sad. My reasons for hating him felt so childish and distant now. It had been so long, and so much had happened. A part of me wanted to reconnect and tell him of my adventures that he most likely already knew about.

Noticing I was distracted, Noor grabbed my hand and squeezed. I nuzzled my head into his shoulder and closed my eyes, a brief rest before the loop began again. I opened my eyes and caught Aberym glancing at me, but he quickly looked away.

When I first saw this so-called Shifting City, I was shocked such a large community could live under the empire's noses in what was essentially their sewerage, but after Tau had told us that Andriel allowed these rebels to exist to relieve her own boredom, their society didn't seem so impressive after all.

We were climbing a huge, wide staircase that gradually spiralled around the perimeter of a central, colossal pillar, which seemed to be holding up the world above it. I wondered what would happen if this pillar were to shatter?

There were rooms and alleys between them to our sides. Surely there was a quicker way to get up than this? Thousands of rebels were meandering about the streets and stairs, and when they noticed us, most joined our ever-growing retinue of ascending followers. I made sure my family and friends stayed close to me.

'Come on,' Amma yelled to those huddled along the sides, 'follow us. This way!'

As the mob grew, their excited murmurs did, too, for they knew we were about to confront their disgraced former leader, Kaxiyan. I heard his name spoken with vitriol behind me over and over, as well as their plans for him.

Lotus was at the front, eagerly striding two steps up at a time. She had the same angry look on her face as when she had confronted me. She could be the new rebel leader for all I cared. All these politics were a waste of time.

One rebel, a man with orange skin wearing a variety of technological gizmos, reached his hand out to get my attention as we walked. 'Sacet, a pleasure to meet you. *Um*, if you have a moment, I'd like to go over our plans for...'

'Not now, Hakkari,' Lotus called back to him.

Finally, the top of the stairs. We were met with a giant iron door, currently closed. Another mob chanting for Kaxiyan's death was gathered below it, and our two groups merged into one.

'What's going on here?' Lotus shouted, quietening them.

As they turned, some parted, and we could see that several had brought in mining equipment and blowtorches, attempting to melt through the door.

'Kaxiyan has locked himself in,' one of the women answered.

Lotus stared up at the door. 'That dirty jwigeomi... I bet he's trying to escape in his damn rocket. Keep going, open it!'

'Wait!' Hakkari yelled. 'I think I can override it.' The man pushed through the crowd, approached a panel at the door's side, and tapped at the buttons faster than I thought was possible.

'We already tried that,' one man said. 'We couldn't crack it.'

'Yes,' Hakkari replied as he worked, 'that's because I... *personally* upgraded it... to stop this... exact thing from happening.' He glanced back at our concerned faces. 'Which I now realise I was doing while being controlled. Who put this... *ahhh*, why would you put it in debug mode like that?' The panel beeped several more times. 'Alright, got it, stand back.'

The mob obeyed as the ground began to rumble. Many raised their weapons in anticipation. I glanced back down the staircase and saw that they were full; the mob was thousands strong, all to see this *one* man punished.

Lotus pushed through the crowd, too. 'I want him alive!'

The unoiled, archaic door moaned as it gradually opened, and when the crack was large enough for a person, the crowd trickled through the slowly widening bottleneck. My companions and I were swept through with the surging crowd, whether we wanted to or not.

Through the door was an enormous dome-shaped chamber, with the aforementioned rocket vertically standing in the centre. The rocket was hugged by steel scaffolds, catwalks and staircases. There was a hole in the ceiling, big enough for the rocket to launch through, which I assumed led to Aster's surface.

Up on the highest catwalk was the blue-skinned psychic that Tau had described. He was frantically attempting to fix something on the rocket, but it was too late, for his former comrades were already halfway up the stairs.

Lotus led the charge, and when she reached the top, Kaxiyan screeched in horror before running to the only area of the catwalk not now occupied by rebels.

'This isn't right,' Tau said, looking at each of us, but we blankly stared back. 'We have to stop this.'

'Do we?' Noor asked. 'He tried to execute you.'

Not getting the response she was hoping for, she instead pulled on Tetsu's wrist. 'Just come on.'

We followed her to the base of the stairs with a flood of others and eventually reached the top.

'Please, excuse me,' Tau said as we pushed our way through countless people. 'Pardon me.'

Noticing our slow progress, I intervened: 'Get out of the way! Move!'

We eventually reached the top and discovered Kaxiyan being throttled by Lotus. He was pinned against the catwalk railing, teetering over the edge. The crowd cheered Lotus on.

'How dare you!' Lotus screamed at him as she choked and punched him over and over. 'How could you do that to us? We trusted you…'

'Stop!' Tau shouted, and she ran over to pull Lotus off him.

What had gotten into her? I knew she wanted to always do the moral thing, but she was rarely this forward about it.

Lotus shoved Tau back, and the two of them stared each other down.

'What are you doing?' Lotus yelled before gesturing to the man. 'He needs to pay for what he did to us. Him and all the other psychics!'

Most of the crowd roared in agreement.

'Kill him now!' one yelled, eliciting even more cheers.

Tau raised her hands for silence, but didn't receive any. 'Please listen, I know you're upset with this man, but—'

More boos and jeers.

'What would you know about it?'

'Get her out of here!'

Tau shifted to the railing so she could project. 'If we kill him, we're no better than the empire.'

Kaxiyan slumped to the catwalk floor and raised his hands in surrender. 'I… I… I was a prisoner like… like all of you. Please, show mercy!'

Lotus also approached the railing to address the crowd. 'We're not killing him. If we do, he'll be resurrected and returned to his masters.'

This confused the now muttering crowd.

'We'll keep him locked up,' Lotus continued before smirking. 'That way, each and *every* one here will get the chance to torture him for what he did to you.'

The mob roared in approval again. Lotus smugly smiled down over them. Amma watched her proudly from nearby. Several rebels picked up the weeping Kaxiyan off the grates and led him down the stairs.

It looked as though Tau were going to continue, but Tetsu gently grabbed her sides and pulled her back to us.

Tau fought back, squirming out of his grip. 'Get OFF ME!' Her face had turned red, her fists were clenched, and her shaking eyes locked onto Tetsu in a rage, the kind I had only seen from her once before.

Tetsu released her, taken aback by her behaviour. He looked down at her feet.

As the crowd continued to churn and shout, Tau calmed herself and brought her palm to her forehead, ashamed. 'I… I'm sorry, Tetsu. I don't know why I just said that.'

Tetsu again approached, slower than before. 'I know why.'

They embraced, both on the verge of tears, and our group receded slightly from the railing.

Aberym had caught up to us with Eno in tow. He pointed a gnarled finger at Tau. 'Stupid girl, you have *no* idea what Asterians have gone through with the psychics.'

While Tau was being lectured, Kaxiyan was dragged away, screaming. If my experience on Seron had taught me anything, it was that this level of hatred was never a good thing. But I supposed we'd find something similar no matter who we sided with.

'Everyone, hear me,' Lotus shouted, quietening her people once more, 'I have been on the surface, and it's all true. Our people want change. It's *finally* our moment.' She turned and pointed back at me. 'And now that we finally have our weapon, our ticket inside, it can begin.'

She pointed at various members of the crowd. 'Contact the other cells, the radio silence ends *now*. Tell your families, your friends, your neighbours: break down Arc Royal's walls and burn everything inside. Tonight, the Setting Sun will bring the emperors to their knees, and I will *personally* rip their souls from their bodies and crush them in the palms of my hands!'

The roar this time was so loud that my eardrums were close to shattering, the deafening noise no doubt amplified by the dome-shaped ceiling.

Eno was by my side, and he looked fearfully at his real sister. 'She... she can rip their souls out, like Mycol?'

I sighed. 'Apparently so.'

Yet another door whined open, revealing a stuffy control room. Like everything else in this underground city, the obsolete technology flickered dimly. The room was messy, with cables lying everywhere, some connected to things and others frayed or cut.

Lotus entered first, then Amma, Hakkari, and several other older rebels. Tau and I, being the only two considered important enough from our group to be present for the meeting, entered last. All the other 'drones', as Amma had put it, were expected to prepare for battle.

A guard closed the door from the outside. Tau took a seat next to a control panel and folded her arms, looking disgusted by everyone else in the room.

A long window was on the far side overlooking the Shifting City below, we were quite high up the pillar. The city was a hive of activity, for most citizens were running into their homes, waking their families, retrieving weapons and armour, then returning to the pillar.

Lotus found a central place in the room to address us. 'If it wasn't already clear to you, *I'm* in charge now.'

One of the elders, a bright-pink-skinned old man, shook his head. 'You're just a child, *I've* been here since—'

'You've wasted your entire life achieving *nothing*, old man,' Lotus interrupted with clenched fists. 'Be silent.'

Amma shook her head at him, too. 'My granddaughter has more grit than all of you. *She's* in charge now.' It looked as though she was clutching a pistol underneath her robes.

I shrugged and came in closer. 'So, what's your plan?'

Lotus grinned. '*Huh*, isn't that something?'

Amma smugly smiled, too. 'Sacet actually respecting the hierarchy here? Shocking.'

I rolled my eyes. 'Yeah, yeah. Let's hear your grand plan, because even *if* I had my powers, what would you want me to do? Make a sun portal over Arc Royal?'

Amma shook her head. 'No, we need to attack the emperors directly, otherwise they'll just be evacuated by their teleporters.'

I shrugged. 'Then you'll need to get me eyes on them, I'm not omniscient. Even if I was hiding *in* Arc Royal, I'd need a lot of time to scour through a place that big.'

'Not a problem,' Hakkari said, taking a seat and tapping some keys on a mouldy panel.

One of the old screens came to life, showing a low-quality image of a fancy dining hall. There were hundreds of children sitting at long dining tables. At the end of the hall were two thrones, currently occupied by the emperors.

'Is this… is this live?' I asked.

'Just a recording,' Hakkari replied. 'But it's live every night, and pretty soon, too.'

Tau turned in her chair and squinted at the screen, before looking equally as confused as me. 'What are we looking at?'

Lotus approached the screen. 'It's the royal children's birthday broadcast.' She pointed between the thrones. 'You need to get me *right* there. As soon as I'm through, I execute them, and our assault begins.'

Hakkari raised an eyebrow. 'You think they'll still broadcast tonight, even though the power is out to half the planet? And with everything else going on?'

Amma joined them both and placed a hand on Hakkari's shoulder. 'They are stubborn creatures of habit. They'll do it.'

I sighed and paced. 'Yeah, a pretty good plan. Except that one problem: my powers are still inhibited.'

'So, we wait until the grid fails,' Amma reasoned, turning away from me. 'We'll delay the attack until tomorrow night if need be.'

I groaned. 'We can't wait that long; they'll have tracked us down by then.'

Amma tilted her head mockingly. 'Well then, do you have a *better* idea for getting you out of the inhibitor field? *Every* spaceport is locked down, and ever since Elion tried to escape, APD is shooting down *anything* that tries to launch.'

'Aster Planetary Defence,' Hakkari explained, noticing my continued confusion, before bringing his hand to his chin. 'Although APD is only locking onto ships with modern hyper-magnetic drives, Alcuem drives, or plasma thrusters, which means…'

'We could use the rocket!' Tau proudly finished his thought as she leapt up from her chair. 'Does it fly?'

Hakkari pointed to her. 'What she said. And yes, it will after a few *small* adjustments. It's pretty close to being ready.'

The others raised their eyebrows.

A previously silent man shrugged. 'I thought we converted it to a bomb?'

My eyes widened. 'You want me to fly in a *bomb*?'

Hakkari nodded. 'I'll add the seat back in, you'll be fine.'

We all went silent, exchanging looks and waiting for rebuttals, but there were none.

Amma looked surprised. 'This… could work.'

Tau and I had found the boys back in the silo floor. Surrounding us were hundreds of rebels running back and forth with tools and weapons, preparing for the impending fight. Work had begun on the rocket, and now it was just a matter of waiting until it was ready. Amma's voice periodically came over the facility's loudspeaker, giving orders to large groups.

The boys were reuniting with their families; Mum and Dad were hugging Eno; Noor's father Kashif and his brother Ahkim were introducing other male relatives; and Tetsu's father Matay and his mother Kekasih were doing the same with their own extended family. Rather than interrupt, Tau and I watched from afar with smiles.

Kekasih was pointing at each relative, one at a time. 'This is your aunty, Eedo, and your cousins Ina and Adeer. And this is…'

Tetsu greeted each of his family members with a warm hug.

One of Noor's middle-aged relatives patted him on the back. 'Can't wait to see what you can do, kid. We're gonna' tear those emperors a new one.'

Noor quietly nodded. His interactions with his family were understandably more stilted.

Yet again, I felt uncomfortable knowing they were coming. Not just our families but my friends, too. I wanted to convince them to stay here, but I had no idea how to reasonably do that.

'Sacet, Tau?' a man's voice said to our side. It was Hakkari, carrying a different set of gadgets from last time. He stopped in front of us and gestured to what I assumed was a camera on top of his head. There was a flashing purple light coming from it. 'I had an idea of how to get even more people on our side. Now that we're breaking radio silence, I can really do some damage with cyberattacks. I was thinking I could send a recording out there of you two, telling the people why they need to side with us?'

'Are you recording right now?' I asked.

He nodded, and I looked at Tau.

She shrugged. 'You *did* say the people needed to know the truth?'

I stared into the camera and took a deep breath. 'People of Aster, there's something you need to know.'

I was on the highest catwalk of the rocket scaffold, facing the bomb's peak. An open hatch was in front of me, leading to the cockpit. Thankfully, this thing would be on autopilot, but it wasn't the space launch I was afraid of. In my haste to agree with the rebels' plans, I failed to think of how I would take down Andriel, Caelum *and* Raumanu all at the same time. Perhaps they assumed that if I once could defeat the strongest, most invulnerable man in the empire, that together we'd somehow do the same for all three.

Below the scaffold, now that the rocket was fuelled, hoses and pipes were disconnected, and toolboxes were packed up and taken away. Unnecessary personnel were being evacuated from the silo. I took several deep breaths, nervously waiting for the engineers to give me the thumbs up so I could enter the rocket.

Someone cleared their throat behind me. I turned and saw Aberym.

He had his usual stoic expression. 'Before you leave… *hrmm ahem*, I wanted to talk to you… while I still had the chance.'

I nodded. 'Y-yeah, I… wanted to talk to you, too. Thanks for rescuing us back there.'

He looked puzzled for a moment. 'Thank your grandmother for that. I wanted to say… I'm *sorry* for what I did to you.'

'What?'

He stepped closer and looked down. 'I heard how you performed the nomadic last rites for me, back on Seron?'

He knew about that? The empire truly had spied on *every* moment of my life. How much did he know? Had he heard about how I said he abused me?

I looked down, too. '*Oh*, you heard about that?'

'What you said was true,' he continued, stepping even closer. 'I treated you like an object when I *should* have treated you like family.'

I folded my arms. 'So why didn't you?'

He shook his head. 'Whenever I looked at you, I just saw the enemy. I was a stubborn fool to not see the real you.'

Memories flooded back of our brutal training sessions, and of all the mean things he had said and done to me over the cycles. My eyes welled, but I did my best to hold the tears in. 'Well, I hated you… every night, I wanted to run away, but I didn't want to leave Eno behind.'

He shamefully nodded. 'I know.'

My fists shook. 'Even now I just want to… to *attack* you.' I relaxed and held a hand up. '*But…* all those things you did, they *made* me what I am today. I got my powers from traumatic events, but it was *you* that *pushed* me.' I finally looked at him. 'I'm still angry, but… maybe without that, I wouldn't have been strong enough, *stubborn* enough to get to this point.'

'Well, we're both stubborn then.' He paused, then smirked. 'Remember when you refused to jump in that river?'

I cleared my eyes and laughed. 'I was so afraid that I bit your hand.'

He chuckled, too. '*My* fault for throwing you in, I guess.'

We smiled together a little while longer before remembering where we both were and what was about to happen.

'I heard about your mother,' he said. 'I'm sorry about that, too.'

Images of Marid's final moments flashed. 'You would have liked her. She didn't suffer foolishness, either.'

'I saw her once, when I was younger,' he replied.

'*Huh*? You've met her?'

'Well, I wouldn't say we *met*. Back in the Kuvizia Mountains, my caravan was caught in a crossfire between the Dominions.' He flung his fingers about. 'She was teleporting around the battlefield, decapitating MD goons left and right. We escaped in the confusion, but I remember peering over the cliff and watching her kill three people at the same time. She was… *formidable*.'

I grinned, picturing it in my mind. 'I would have loved to see her in her prime.'

'This was back when I was with your grandmother, and Azua was just a baby.' He brushed my shoulder firmly. 'Anyway, she would have been proud of you. Someone told me she was once a member of one of these rebel groups, too, way before she was on Seron.'

I nodded and sighed. 'That definitely sounds like her. Her last words to me were… to save my fighting spirit until it mattered most.'

He raised an eyebrow. 'Well, I hope you've still got some left?'

I smiled. 'I do. Thanks, Grandpa.'

I heard footsteps farther along the catwalk, behind the rocket. Noor and Eno appeared, then Mum and Dad, and then Tau and Tetsu.

My family and friends accelerated into a run, and all of them crowded around me for a group hug.

I hugged them back. 'I won't be able to talk any of you out of this, will I?'

They all smiled or laughed, and protested simultaneously, shaking their heads.

Mum and Dad released first and joined Grandpa in watching us fondly.

'Thank you for being here for me,' I began, finally letting the tears go, 'all of you.'

Thirty-Four: Surprise!

I was strapped into a tattered, but sturdy cockpit seat, pointing vertically up. There were switches and buttons on almost every surface. The window showed the open shaft above the rocket, an exceptionally tall tunnel that led to the surface.

'Sacet, can you hear me?' Hakkari's voice said from somewhere, and I glanced around to seek it out. 'Relax, I'm patched into your INC. Some good news, your message to Aster went out and… I've gotta say, it's my best work. Over fifty billion views so far, and it's being shared on every platform. I know that doesn't sound impressive to you, but…'

'Are the people *finally* fighting the empire instead of themselves?' I asked.

Hakkari laughed. 'There's currently over a billion people banging on Arc Royal's walls, so yeah, I'd say it had the intended effect. Take a look.'

A screen manifested in front of me, showing the carnage outside the walls. The furious crowds were unlike anything I had ever seen. Countless more soldiers were pushing back on the mob at the gates and entrances.

I smiled and nodded. 'Well, it's about time.'

Throughout the cockpit, all the gadgets, screens and buttons came to life, making humming and beeping noises, and flashing green. Lights swirled in the dome and tunnel, too. My seat was shaking. The rocket was rumbling.

'*Uh*, are you doing this?' I called out.

'Just doing final checks,' Hakkari answered. His voice lowered, as though talking to someone else. 'Any spikes? No? And the temperature values?'

'Nominal,' another voice said.

'Okay, Sacet,' Hakkari continued as my INC screen disappeared, 'just a heads up, without modern gravity-dampeners, you'll be in for a bumpy ride. How are you feeling? You ready?'

I clenched the handles on my seat tighter. 'I was made for this, let's do it.'

The rumbling intensified. The entire cabin rocked.

'Okay, good luck, everyone,' Hakkari answered. 'Launching in 3... 2... 1...'

The engines went from a low hum to a thunderous, distorted explosion of noise. I felt the deafening power of the roaring engines. My stomach jolted, and my heart raced. The brutal acceleration forced me down, squishing me into the seat, like I was being buried alive. All my strained veins felt as though they were filled with iron. Each breath was difficult.

I couldn't make sense of anything. Blurry lights from the shaft whizzed past. Constant shuddering and rattling. Everything was vibrating so violently that I thought it was going to break apart. I screamed and didn't stop, like the almighty groaning propelling me. More lights flew passed. Couldn't make out the chatter through my INC.

I could see colours, the surface was approaching. The hexagon-shaped shaft exit was open, and through it I could see the bright aurora-green sky. *Whoosh!* Right through the narrow window to freedom. The cabin was awash with ambient green.

The buildings passed, the clouds passed, the green sky blackened to star-speckled night, and then the roaring cut, replaced only by the shrill ringing in my ears. The vibrating had stopped, and the craft was adrift, listlessly rotating. I had seen space before, but somehow this was far more beautiful, perhaps because of all the dramatic fear and pumping adrenaline that preceded it.

'Sacet?' a voice said. 'Sacet, do you read?'

I shook out of my trance. 'I hear you.'

'Alright,' Hakkari continued, 'we don't have long. Are your powers back?'

They were indeed. My second perception could sense every panel, every wire and hatch of the spacecraft. 'They're back. Can I move now?' I felt around my straps for the release. 'Get this thing off me.'

'Hold on.'

The straps clicked and loosened, and I floated weightlessly to the ceiling. Up was down, down was up. I rolled in the air and smiled, forgetting our dire circumstances for just a moment.

'Sorry to stop the fun,' Hakkari interrupted, 'but the event has started, streaming it to you now.'

A screen flicked on, displaying a large dining hall coloured purple and gold. Long tables were filling with children, Iya's brothers and sisters. They were all silent, not engaging in conversation or even making eye contact with one another. Soft, classy music played. At the end of the hall were two empty thrones. I took note of their position, focusing on the spot behind them.

'Welcome again to the royal birthday celebrations,' a different male voice said from the screen as the view panned through the audience of sad children. 'As always, we hope the children have a wonderful birthday. We're getting closer to the five hundred and fifty-sixth anniversary since the beginning of the daily event, only three days away now. But interestingly, based on the Imperial Decree earlier tonight, this *might* be the last time we broadcast the occasion.'

'That's right, Mofsar,' a female commentator added. 'With the Chosen path so close to being achieved and all of us about to ascend, there's no guarantee this event will continue.'

The voices trailed off as my INC overlayed thirty partially see-through rectangles in my vision. Although I knew they weren't real, it felt as though they were floating in the cockpit with me. Each miniature screen was colour-coded with a tiny border, half purple and half red. There was a single rectangle with a green border and another with orange. It quickly became apparent that if I focused on any one of these rectangles, it would expand in my vision while minimising the others, allowing for a better look.

'Alright, you should see the portal locations,' Hakkari said.

'I see them.'

I expanded the green one and saw a live feed of a fully-armoured Lotus. She was ready. Our army of Setting Sun rebels was standing behind her, including my family and friends. The purple rectangles showed similar sights, hordes of armed rebels standing in formation, waiting for their portals. These must have been the other rebel factions I was told about.

Meanwhile, the red rectangles showed empire staff and soldiers wandering about in polished military interiors, unaware of the hidden cameras. After sending Lotus and the Setting Sun to the emperors' location, these red areas were where I'd send the rest of the rebels. The single orange rectangle showed an exterior location, supposedly a flying MASU launching platform within Arc Royal's perimeter. This would be the location I'd drop the bomb after I had teleported everyone.

'Any moment now,' Hakkari said, 'be ready.'

I focused on my breathing, trying to clear my mind of doubt. The night side of Aster had come into view through the cockpit window. Huge patches of the planet were blacked out because of the power outages, and entire territories flashed as though about to join them.

I expanded the green rectangle to take up half my vision and watched the birthday screen with the other half. There was activity on the screen a few moments later, the emperors appeared in their thrones with puffs of smoke, being held by their teleporter assistants.

'There they are,' I said. 'Now?'

'Wait until their teleporters leave. All callsigns, standby.'

'And there they are, our glorious emperors,' the male commentator said. 'The empress is looking lovely in her dark-azure dress and gold trappings. And our emperor in his dashing royal blue ceremonial uniform, a favourite of his lately.'

This was it, the most important moment of my life. Time to break the loop, once and for all.

There was commotion on screen, the camera angle switched to the centre of the dining hall. Iya was standing there amongst the tables, pointing accusatorily at the emperors. The music on the broadcast silenced.

'Is that Iya?' Hakkari asked.

'What's she doing?' I added.

'*Oh* my, folks,' the commentator continued, 'there seems to be a party crasher. It's the disgraced princess, Iya. Here to bring further dishonour on herself?'

'These monsters are *not* our parents!' Iya shouted over the feed. 'They have kept you locked in this cage your *whole* life, but you can be free like me. You just have to stand up and fight, right now!'

The emperors' expressions didn't change, and her siblings were staring at their food, as though they hadn't even heard her.

Iya looked increasingly more desperate. 'What are you waiting for? The inhibitors are down, so now's the only time. Come on, stand up for yourselves!' She went from sibling to sibling, trying to inspire them. 'Arlaus, didn't you say you wanted to see the oceans of Nares? Well, now's your chance. And Mikan! Do you want to be a toddler forever? Meridree, what about you? You want out, too, I know it.'

No reactions. Faces of stone. Was Andriel controlling them?

Iya clenched her fists. 'What's wrong with all of you?'

'Portal, now!' Lotus' voice yelled through my INC.

I shook out of it and focused back on the thrones. 'Right.'

The portal opened with little effort, perfectly centred behind the thrones. Lotus sprinted through, wreathed in green flames. The emperors didn't react. With a wicked grin, Lotus pointed her hands at the emperors.

As the Setting Sun members piled through the portal after Lotus, the effect the flames had on the emperors was almost instantaneous. Like when my mother had been executed, their soul energy escaped through their mouths and floated towards Lotus' hands.

'Bring the rest of us through, Sacet,' Hakkari said.

I turned my attention to the other screens. One at a time, I opened a portal between a purple rebel base and a red Arc Royal interior. The same thing happened each time afterwards: rebels piled through, firing with reckless abandon at anything that moved, and the shocked staff on the other side went down.

Another wide portal done. Another, another and another. I kept them all open simultaneously. All thirty were done, already transporting thousands through, but I felt like I was capable of more.

I imagined the outside walls I had just seen, where over a billion civilians had been rioting, then also many locations my perception scanned at random throughout the arc. My energy and muscles fluctuated as I made dozens more portals. A horde of angry citizenry streamed through each.

There was a loud beeping throughout the cockpit. I opened my eyes and saw extra flashing lights, which I assumed weren't supposed to be.

'What's that?' I asked.

'APD,' Hakkari explained, 'get out of there, now!'

I didn't argue. The place I most wanted to be was with my friends and family. I opened a portal to the centre of the dining hall and floated through, landing and rolling with gravity again on the other side. I stood up straight and saw Iya next to me, mouth agape. No time for her.

I looked back through my portal, through the cockpit's front window, and opened another portal in front of the bomb's nose, its destination in the sky just above my memory of the MASU launching platform. As I threaded the bomb through, I closed my escape portal.

Shortly after, the whole room quaked as the bomb had no doubt gone off in the distance. As the loud rumbling persisted, I inspected my surroundings.

The hall was still filling with shouting rebels, many overflowed into the surrounding hallways and stairwells, checking every corner as they went. Many realised their powers had returned, and so stowed their weapons and instead used L lines to fly. They scanned for targets but could only see the completely motionless children at the tables. Many watched Lotus as she was still struggling to execute the emperors, including a galvanising Amma.

Some rebels were pointing their guns at the children and ordering them to raise their hands, but there was no reaction from them. Something was off. My second perception sensed that the children didn't exist, and neither did the emperors. There was disorder above in the rafters, so I craned my neck up.

Many guards were engaged in combat with a bloodied, black-haired woman and a cloud of sand — Korin and Neva. The guards proved to be no match for the formidable pair.

Lotus was still struggling to pull the souls from the emperors. 'I can't… *arrrrr*… they won't die!'

Was that Verre retreating along the catwalk? Korin solidified a needle of blood and flung it at her, piercing into the back of her neck and downing her. The illusions Verre had been controlling, the children and the emperors, faded away.

'No!' Lotus screamed upon realising her quarry was fake, grabbing at the air they once resided in. 'NO! Where are they?'

Iya covered her mouth with her hands and screamed. She cried genuine tears as she backed away from me, towards the hall's entrance. 'How could I have been so stupid?' She turned and ran, exiting through the huge doors.

Some of the guards' bodies fell from the rafters and landed on the now-empty tables beside me. The rebels trained their weapons upwards. Once Korin and Neva noticed Iya leaving, they ducked behind the balconies and fled into some nearby service tunnels. I could easily have stopped them, but I was too perplexed.

Lotus stomped over to me, still with her aura active. 'Where are they? Find them!'

The other rebels, including my family, closed in around me, all equally confused and angry. Meanwhile, hundreds more rebels trickled through the portal, spreading out and filling every nook and cranny of the arc like a flood. Noor stood beside me and stared Lotus down, and Tau meanwhile brought her aura up, too, to counteract Lotus'.

I closed my eyes and allowed my perception to fly free, up and down through the floors of Arc Royal. I spotted several enormous skirmishes taking place between armies of rebels and the arc's militant inhabitants, the noise of which carried through every hall and chamber.

In the centre of the arc was an impossibly huge space that acted as a central hub. From there, I surveyed what I believed to be the most significant facilities and entrances. One of the most intricately designed chambers branching off from the hub appeared to be a throne room, yet the thrones remained unoccupied. Adjacent to it were lavish living rooms, which also sat empty.

Lotus pushed me. 'Well?'

Noor pushed her back. 'Give her some space!'

I sneered at her. 'The throne room is empty, as are all their living rooms. As I said, I need time to—'

'Hakkari?' Lotus called. 'Tell me *you* know where they are.'

'Sorry, no,' he replied in my INC. It looked like we could all collectively hear him.

A message appeared on my INC, almost completely blocking my view. It simply read: 'Have you checked the skies?' The message then disappeared, and all of us looked stunned.

'Did you all see—' a rebel began.

'Hakkari, was that you?' Tau asked.

'Not me,' he responded. We heard him furiously tapping at his end. 'It came from… the network itself?'

'Avarut's Spear,' another rebel realised aloud, 'the battlecruiser flying above us.'

Our army erupted in murmurs and debate as to what to do next.

My perception rocketed up, passed the Arc's peak. A metal behemoth hung in the sky, defying gravity. The giant spaceship was the size of a small city, with hundreds of rooms and maze-like corridors. I didn't know where to begin with the search.

'Silence!' Amma commanded the rabble, before looking at me. 'Get us there.'

I found a large, empty chamber in the heart of the steel beast, and so opened a wide portal to it. Through the portal was the ship interior as expected, dark and metal, with doors leading every which way. Lotus and Amma ran through first, followed by hundreds of rebels, many shouting their battle cries.

Again, my second perception twitched as it spotted something. Floating along a nearby hallway was Raumanu. The very walls warped outwards to accommodate his disintegration field. He was heading this way, dispatching any rebels with his invisible power along the way. They were nothing to him.

My family and friends were looking at me, waiting for me to go through the portal. If they stayed, Raumanu would wipe them out with a wave of his hand. And even if they were resurrected later, that would mean little if we had lost the battle. No, I couldn't allow that.

I remembered back to when we first arrived at Arc Sacet. The rebels attacked us, and Raumanu demonstrated his invisible yet deadly power. Both then and now, my second perception could sense it. It was like a cloud of null space, where not even air could exist. It flowed around him like water wherever he looked. I was the only one who could anticipate his moves; therefore, I was the sole person who stood a chance against him.

I ran to the portal and gestured through it. 'Everyone, go! Find and execute them.'

My family and friends joined the rebels and piled through, all except Noor, who stopped at the entrance with me.

He saw my nervous expression. 'I've got your back.'

The sound of laserfire and explosions echoed down a nearby hallway, followed by horrified screams. Raumanu was getting close. Noor heard the noises and turned to the far hall entrance, as did all the remaining rebels in the room, who pointed their weapons and hands at the huge open doors, ready to fire.

'Noor, go through the portal,' I instructed.

He shook his head. 'What? You should know by now, I'm *not* leaving you.'

I remembered back to when Noor and Malu helped me face down Caelum. Noor's power did nothing to him, and he suffered a vicious death for his efforts.

The rest of my family was waiting through the portal, looking back at us.

'What are they doing?' Eno asked his parents. 'Come on, Sas.'

I stood in front of Noor and gently placed my hands on his chest. 'Execute the emperors. This… this is something I have to do alone.'

Raumanu came around the corner and appeared in the large entry archway, flinging his gaze and his disintegration at several nearby rebels.

Noor's eyes widened. I shoved him towards the portal.

'No!' he yelled as he fell back on the other side. He quickly got up again and reached towards me. 'Sacet, don't!'

'Sacet!' Tau also called.

'I'm sorry,' I said, closing the portal and turning my back on them.

Raumanu landed at one end of the dining hall and laughed. 'I hoped you'd try something like this.'

The remaining hundred or so rebels in the dining hall all had their shaking weapons trained on him, yet none fired.

I glanced at them. 'The rest of you, leave, you're no match for him.'

Raumanu stopped, smiled, and patiently waited. That was good because the more time I could have to keep all the other portals open, the better. The rebels hesitated, but then hurriedly ran for the nearest exits, leaving Raumanu and I alone in the dining hall.

He gestured to me, taking a few steps closer. 'So, no more running, then? No more hiding in dark corners? You've come to finally complete the Chosen path?'

I slowly shook my head. 'The rituals stop here, *Raum*.'

Raumanu mockingly tutted. 'Seems like you're still in the dark, after all.' He raised his hands, curling his fingers like claws. 'Then allow me to bring you into the light.'

Thirty-Five: Hate Grows

Raumanu pointed to me, and I sensed his ability take shape. The invisible cloud of destructive nothingness coiled towards me like a tentacle. I opened a large portal to receive it. The momentum carried the flailing limb through, back into Raumanu's shield from behind. His own power had no effect on itself, other than producing an ear-piercing screech. His supposedly impenetrable shield held.

I portalled myself to another corner of the hall as a precaution. When the portals closed, Raumanu scanned for me, but I was already preparing my next move. I attempted to open a portal inside his shield to get at the frail old man directly, but just like with Tetsu's shield so long ago, something stopped me. It was like my portals needed a clear path to the destination.

'There you are,' Raumanu said, floating up off the floor and flinging three finger-like null lances.

I teleported away to a different corner yet again, before rapid-firing several portals towards him, each leading to hard or sharp destinations. Each met his shield and disintegrated into nothing.

I had to end this fight quickly, and my best chance of doing that was attacking him from afar so he couldn't see it coming.

He again let loose; multiple twisting thorns homed in on me from different angles. No time to think. A portal underneath me to the cavernous central hub. I fell through and closed the portal just as the thorns slammed into the walls above.

The stale air whipped at my robes as I plummeted from the top of the cavernous interior. The artificial chamber was both tremendously long and wide, held up by hundreds of ornate, solid-gold pillars. Although I was speeding to the floor at terminal velocity, I still had plenty of time before I needed to act.

The city-sized hub was mostly dark, as though under a night sky, with occasional floodlights illuminating anything golden. The chamber's volume was so enormous that its most distant sights were veiled with a thin layer of greenish fog.

The heart of the mountainous Arc Royal had numerous levels, was terraced in parts, and had long bridge-like walkways that stretched from one side of the arc to the other, connecting grand structures and spires. The labyrinthine design included spiral staircases and elevators to combat its sickening verticality.

Every building had ancient architectural stylings, more for show than purpose. It was as if this *really* was a historical city, and the steel mountain was built over the top to preserve it.

Countless thousands of people warred below, guards versus rebels and civilians, but they weren't currently my concern. My perception focused back on Raumanu, still in the dining hall.

What was my endgame here? If I killed him, Andriel would most likely have some disciples resurrect him somewhere, and then we'd start over. If I sent him to space and he died, it would be the same situation.

Wait, back when Seron was destroyed, why did the disciples have to be in the planet's former orbit to recreate the bodies? Did resurrection from nothing have a maximum distance? Did being close help with the process or something? So, what if he died in Seronian space instead? That was it, my best chance of beating him.

I remembered back to the remains of my home and opened a portal underneath him to space and wrenched it up. He spotted it immediately and widened several disintegration spikes from his shield, extending his reach beyond the portal's radius. The edge of the portal slammed into the spikes midair.

Was he grabbing the edges of my portal? Not only was he unaffected by the air pressure, but somehow his tentacles had wrapped around my portal and forced it away. I strained my muscles, again attempting to engulf him, but he launched upwards into the dining hall ceiling, smashing through floor after floor, leaving my portal behind.

I needed my proper footing again, so I opened a new portal in my free-falling path, the exit firing me back up towards one of the hub's tower peaks. The reversal of gravity quickly undid my momentum, and I gently landed back onto the tiled roof of the ancient tower.

Keeping up his speed and not caring what he destroyed along his path, Raumanu now looked exactly in my direction, even though we were separated by at least ten walls. I got chills down my spine, having experienced this before with Caelum. He punctured the walls as if they weren't even there, coming straight for me.

'He's seen you,' Hakkari said.

'*Ahuh*, I know,' I replied.

'Looks like he's using a localised sensor net to track your position.'

'Well, disable it then?'

Raumanu crashed through the final wall and sped through the hub's open air. I opened a minefield of portals to Seron in front of him, but he bashed each of them away with his power.

'I'm not all powerful, you know!' Hakkari shouted back.

'Just do it!'

Raumanu was getting too close, so I leapt from the tower and dove into a new portal, this time leading to the aurora-filled sky above Arc Royal. Again, I plummeted, and just in time, too. Raumanu's invisible tentacles ferociously sliced at the top of the tower, removing it from existence. Before I could close the portal, he latched onto it to keep it open. His tentacles shaped into hooked claws, which he used to drag himself through after me.

I briefly took everything in as I fell through the sky. The aurora was intense, somehow a convergence of all colours, as though the magnetosphere had been put into overdrive mode. The arc mountain was far below, and to the side of it was a huge, fiery crater where I had dropped the bomb. The giant spaceship was nearby, where my friends were hopefully executing the emperors. Flaming buildings surrounded the perimeter of Arc Royal's outer perimeter, no doubt the rioters' handiwork. Explosions were going off almost everywhere I could see.

Raumanu again stretched his tentacles towards me, so I opened a diversionary portal to intercept. The tentacles grabbed its edge and effortlessly chucked it aside. He was flying faster than I could fall.

I made a portal directly below, this time to Seronian space again. I took a breath and was blown through into the cold, dark abyss. The meteoroids that once made up my world floated all around me, lit by Seron's distant sun.

My lungs expanded, already feeling like they were on fire, forcing me to exhale. I didn't have long.

Would he take the bait? I watched the hole of light from the darkness to see if he would enter, but he stopped midair, refusing to follow me into the void.

'Nice try,' his rippling, muffled voice called through, the blowing air its medium.

Rather than wait, I closed the portal and pictured the Arc Royal peak, where that party had been thrown for me. I teleported there without delay and landed on solid ground once more.

I collapsed in a choking fit, for even mere moments in the vacuum of space had taken its toll. As my breathing slowly returned to normal, I inspected the radiated burns on my skin. All my muscles now ached and swelled.

Thankfully, I was alone, which made sense, for who would be at a rooftop party at a time like this? I looked over the balcony at the chaos.

Surrounding me was all-out war. Civilians had penetrated the outer walls and were now fighting soldiers and MASU on the ground and above, using L lines both as a weapon and for flight.

Although Avarut's Spear was still the most prominent thing in the sky, it was far from the only aircraft. Many comparatively smaller frigates had entered the arc's airspace to reinforce the defence, firing heavy cannons down into the rising civilian tide indiscriminately.

My perception flew to my previous location, Raumanu was already looking in my direction. Like I had once done to Caelum, I created a pair of portals around him, curved them into hemispheres, before attempting to clasp them around him in an infinite prison. He didn't notice them in time, but when the portals were about to come together, they stopped short.

Perhaps I underestimated his speed, for his spikes again had stretched beyond the portals' radius, creating a thin gap between the clasp. He and I both strained, I to close the gap and he to widen it, but he was far too strong for me. The tentacles peeled the portals apart, allowing him to exit the danger and speed towards me again.

Whatever tactic I chose, I knew now that he wasn't going to fall for a portal that he could see, so I quickly formulated a new plan, teleporting myself to the interior corridor of one of the frigates.

As I stepped through, I saw several crewmembers running about, shouting commands and operating equipment. They collectively noticed me and froze. For this to work, I couldn't have interruptions, so with a portal under each of them, I sent them screaming into the void, including the pilots. It was effortless; killing these people meant nothing to me anymore.

Raumanu was hurtling straight for me again, continuing to track my every move. He disintegrated anything that got in his way, including one of his own frigates, which exploded shortly after he burst through it.

I had time before he arrived, so I figured, why not one more direct attack? In front of the speeding Raumanu I yet again opened a portal to Seronian space, but made it as large as I could, as *rapidly* as I could. Unable to simply go around the ever-expanding disc, he stopped midair and reversed course.

'Look at it, Raumanu!' I screamed. 'Look at what you did to my world!'

I chased him through the sky with it. The portal stretched and stretched, larger and larger, until it surpassed the size of the portal I had once created over MDC. Although I still strained, I noticed the gargantuan portal was easier to create than the last time.

While all the other flying combatants were ripped through the air towards it, Raumanu continued to flee unabated. Several frigates had been swallowed up by the portal already, as had over a hundred MASU and flying soldiers. Even Avarut's Spear was slowly dragging towards it, and the frigate I was inside rocked with turbulence.

Raumanu cleverly flew closer to the ground, dodging and weaving around the tips of spires and turrets. The portal was unable to follow him unless it went over these obstacles. An idea sprang to mind, that being my portal wouldn't crash into things if it didn't have an edge.

While still making the portal pursue the old man, I bent the hole to space, wrapping it along its own edges. Without slowing, Raumanu glanced back at the evolving anomaly with interest.

Gradually, the portal curved completely around on itself, forming a floating black sphere, roughly half the size of the original. I focused all my effort on the portal's speed, which, now that it had no edges, could travel through anything.

Like skittering, fleeing prey, Raumanu zigzagged amongst the sub-arc towers. My black hole pursued, cutting corners directly through those same structures, its reality-warping effects often ripping them apart and sucking them through. Like Raumanu, a similar trail of nothingness was left in its wake, and no matter slowed it down.

His movements remained erratic, making him difficult to pin down. Every time I tried to head him off, he'd notice and choose a new direction. He was simply too fast. Had his cane-wielding, feeble-old-man schtick all been an act?

My sphere had incidentally collected hundreds of his underlings, and although most were military, I realised there were probably innocent civilians in that number, too, so I closed the portal and returned the sky above the arc to normal. Much of the arc's surface was left in ruins.

No longer harassed by my antics, Raumanu looked in the direction of my hiding place on the frigate, which, now that it wasn't being piloted, was slowly descending. I stood alone in the corridor and waited, preparing a portal under my feet, with its destination at the opposite end of the corridor.

When Raumanu reached my frigate, he again broke through the side with ease, and I simultaneously raised my portal over my head to escape and disorient him.

He spun around. 'Blasted child, I will scatter your particles across the astral sea. Submit!'

Like I had done to that Overwatch satellite once, I opened a wide portal outside the windowless frigate, in front of the nose, the destination again being Seronian space. The craft shook with turbulence, stronger than before, causing Raumanu to look back out the hole he came in from.

'You're a madman, *Raum*,' I shouted to get his attention, emphasising his name mockingly. 'You actually *want* the universe to be destroyed?'

He strengthened his pose. 'Of *course* I do. I have yearned for death for so long, but they won't let me die.'

Without using my hands, I began to thread the ship through the portal.

He cackled as he floated closer. 'So, I'm going to take the universe with me. My final *masterpiece* of destruction. Oh, how *perfect* this Chosen path is.'

'Keep him talking,' Hakkari's voice said in my head, 'it's all being shared with the world.'

'What's the point in your masterpiece if no one's alive to appreciate it?'

The portal was in line with his entry hole now. I reached and grabbed a nearby pole for stability. The wind howled as it whipped out of the hole, starting to decompress the chamber. He floated ever closer.

His wide grin returned. 'My service will be *appreciated* by the Empyrean, and my soul energy kept, while yours will be discarded.'

Over three-quarters of the craft was now through. Oxygen was thin. He still hadn't noticed.

I grinned back. 'Who'd want to keep a bitter old man like you?'

Raumanu dashed forward with an infuriated, strained roar. In one quick movement, I portalled back to the Arc Royal peak, but the tips of his claws reached my portal just in time, prohibiting it from closing completely.

By now, the frigate would have teleported fully into Seronian space, trapping him there. The final portal, now the size of my hand and hovering above my head, was widening again, so I tried to close it with all my might.

Raumanu's claws penetrated deeper and wrapped around the portal's edges for a better grip. I saw his furious face on the other side.

I screamed, straining with everything I had. 'Die already! You *and* your Chosen path!'

One of the tentacles suddenly speared forward. I couldn't react in time. It swiped at me through the hole and made contact.

I took two steps back and saw my left arm gone from the elbow down. Blood spurted out of the open wound. It had also grazed my ribs, and my fluids cascaded down like a crimson waterfall. An overwhelming numbness washed over me.

I had lost control over the portal, Raumanu stretched it out and came through. With my last shred of strength, I opened what could very well have been my final portal under my feet to the first location I could think of, the crater on the side of Arc Royal. I fell through and continued to fall as the portal closed. Still falling. Everything went black.

Thirty-Six: Tangled Strings

Earlier

In the service tunnels

I slumped against the austere concrete service tunnel wall and shook my head. Stupid, stupid, stupid! No wonder my siblings didn't respond to me, they were damn illusions.

Guards and staff ran past me through the narrow tunnel, responding to the blaring alarms. They ignored me, as usual. The sounds of battle in the royal corridors echoed down the stark tunnel from both directions.

What were Sacet and Tau doing? They and their companions would have found a way off this planet if they were smart. But now they've guaranteed executions for their friends and families. I told Tau that allying with the rebels was a mistake. Well, at least their entrance detracted from my own embarrassment.

I cleared my tears. I wasn't sad anymore, just angry at myself for being an idiot.

Please don't beat yourself up over it.

I gritted my teeth. 'You…'

I thought what you said was beautiful. I just wish your real sisters and brothers could have heard it.

I punched the concrete, shattering it. 'Why didn't you *stop* me then, before I made a fool of myself?' When I released my hand, I noticed I had unintentionally used an L line, and that there was now a crumbling hole in the wall. 'Were you setting me up to fail?'

Not at all, it was you who insisted on going to the party. The event was bait for the rebels, which they fell for completely. Raumanu's idea. I did offer to kill the guards above the kids' dorms, remember?

'What, how?' I turned around and saw that Korin and Neva were silently standing over me. They had the same absent looks on their faces as when they were first controlled. 'No… no, but I thought—'

That they were free now? No, they became what you needed them to become. Friends, supporters, accomplices. And you didn't trust me, so I acted through them instead.

I bellowed and punched the wall again, demolishing it, then fell to my knees. 'Get out of my head! Get out of *all* our heads!'

Neva placed her hand on my shoulder. 'If you're going to help me rule this empire, you'll need to regrow that thicker skin. You used to think of others as sub-Asterian, so what changed?' She gave a long, drawn-out sigh. 'I truly do love you, but right now, I need the old Iya.'

As I clutched my forehead in my hands, I looked through the hole and saw the Arc Royal centrepiece, a cavernous chamber my siblings and I had been marched through many times. The revered and forever preserved city of Metastus, named after Avarut's father.

There were thousands of Arc Royal guards marching in synchronous units, and bursting from every door, archway and window were countless more screaming rebels. The two armies surged and smashed together along the long bridges and walkways.

The roaring rebels fought savagely, without formation or control. They used L lines to attack and fly, as well as Elion's power to create new weapons from thin air. Meanwhile, the guards relied on their superior weaponry and automated turrets to fight.

One group clasped their hands together and summoned popping chemical concoctions, before hurling them at the guards. The makeshift grenades exploded in blue fire. One currently surrounded rebel breathed a cloud of greenish-yellow gas around her that incapacitated all the nearby guards, but she was gunned down shortly afterwards from afar.

Yet another group of rebels had fashioned themselves golden spears and spiked shields. They recklessly charged the enemy ranks. Several more were somehow shifting the ancient bricks telekinetically and using them as projectiles. Whose power was that?

Although they had such a short time with their new powers, their creativity was admirable. Still, I pitied them all, each of us pawns in this Chosen game.

Neva groaned and stumbled back. She shook her head several times, then looked around at us with confusion. 'Iya? Korin? What is… what's going on?'

'Neva?' I said.

Korin had a similar reawakening, dropping the sphere of blood she was carrying, splattering it everywhere. She examined her wounds before her eyes narrowed on me spitefully. 'What did you do, you little cretin?' She waved her hands at the blood splatter, reforming it into a floating spear, which flew at me, stopping short of my face. 'Why don't I remember anything?'

'It's… hard to explain,' I began, but I was too stunned to elaborate. '*Uhh*, Mother? You there?'

Neva's gaze intensified, too. 'How did we get here? I don't—'

Korin's spear suddenly sloshed back into a floating sphere. They both relaxed their stances and abandoned all emotion, under Mother's control once more.

'I'm sorry, daughter,' Korin said. 'I hate to admit it, but I'm struggling to contain this chaos.'

Neva approached the hole. 'These rebels are getting closer to the dorms.'

Korin gently pulled me back to the hole, too. 'We need to get them to safety.' She pointed to my sibling's dorms, where I was hoping this corridor would eventually lead. 'There's no telling what these animals will do if they reach them.'

The various possibilities entered my mind, each one more disgusting and infuriating than the last. I couldn't allow that to happen. I straightened up with renewed purpose. 'Well, can't you just teleport them out?'

'I'm sorry, I have none to spare,' Korin said, 'but I'm sending you some old friends to help. Keep heading down the corridor.'

Couldn't *spare* them? Fine. 'Just get me there.'

Korin led the way, and Neva pulled me along roughly in the dorm's direction. We followed the corridor around several corners and down flights of stairs until eventually we were faced with a door.

Standing in front of it were several familiar faces, each under her control. They were all Overwatch agents I had served with in the past, each suited up in armour. The most noticeable was Kalek, who was so large that he only barely fit in the corridor. Others of note were Aki, the former FD acolyte who controlled lasers, and Topal, the FD acolyte colonel, a walking power inhibitor.

By the looks of the door, it would lead back into the Arc Royal interior. Kalek charged and smashed through the door like it was paper.

We followed him out and immediately joined the skirmish we had seen from above. There were rebels everywhere, and many turned and spotted us after Kalek's not-so-subtle entrance.

We were on one of the many wide walkways that crisscrossed throughout the cavern. The dorms were at the end of the bridge, where a contingent of guards was keeping a horde of rebels at bay, a horde that we'd have to fight through.

Neva pointed ahead. 'Move!' she instructed as she converted to her cloud form.

Neither side hesitated, immediately going on the attack. Our group moved from cover to cover, warding off attacks from both in front and behind.

Kalek crashed into the architecture the rebels were taking cover behind, pillars and benches, burying them in crumbling steel and concrete. The hail of random rebel counterattacks did nothing to his invulnerable skin. With each charge, he'd collect several rebels with his frame, trampling them or often bowling them off the bridge.

Aki repeatedly redirected laserfire back to their source, including L line projectiles, making the rebels' ranged attacks redundant. She stayed close to me as we moved, acting as my own personal shield. Topal followed closely, pointing at any unarmed rebel, cancelling out their powers before they could even use them.

Korin trailed at the back, sniping any rebel that popped up from cover with her blood-needle projectiles. Neva's sand cloud melted rebel after rebel and spread out like an unnatural smoke screen for cover.

I looked back and saw that two of the other agents had already been killed. I needed to help, or we weren't getting across. I popped out of cover, but found myself unable to attack. These rebels were just like me, trying to kill the tyrannical emperors. Some wore upper-caste clothing, too. These weren't just the poor, the rebels came from all walks of life.

Iya, focus, your sisters and brothers need you!

Damn it, yes, okay. Recalling the painfully long education I had received over the cycles, I thought back to my chemistry lessons. With Elion's power, there were far more powerful tools of destruction than just my telekinesis or L lines.

I sprayed a specific mixture of nitrogen, carbon, hydrogen, and oxygen towards the next group of rebels. They ducked for cover, and so the pale yellow, oily mixture covered the battlements around them instead. Hmm, that didn't work. If memory served, it was highly volatile and needed some sort of—

BOOOOM!!!

There was a massive explosion where I had sprayed, for Kalek had charged into them, bringing the high-energy friction and heat to the fluids I required. At least twenty rebels were blown to bits, as was part of the bridge, the debris of which now rained down everywhere in chunks. Kalek was launched into the sky from the explosion he had set off and careened across the cavern, no longer able to help us.

Korin nodded at me. 'Do it again, I'll shoot it.'

While the remaining agents covered me, I stood and sprayed the next group with the mix before ducking back down. Korin flung a needle as planned, and another bridge-shaking detonation followed.

We shifted forward to the remains of what we had just exploded, then repeated the tactic, again and again. We had almost reached the other end of the bridge, where the dwindling royal guards were still holding fast, protecting the dorm's entrance.

Only a couple more rebel groups remained ahead, but hundreds more enemies were streaming in from behind. Although they were just civilians with little combat experience, their sheer numbers would guarantee them success here.

As my comrades mopped up the rebels that remained ahead, I took cover again, this time from those behind. I sprayed again, with both hands and for a much longer time. I glanced at Korin. 'Do it.'

While the rest of us ran to join the guards, Korin flung another needle back at the trap. The explosion was so enormous that I was blown off my feet, forward onto the guards' platform. The floor rumbled intensely. The deafening quake rang throughout the chamber.

I got to my feet and glanced back to see if my plan had worked. The explosion had destroyed that portion of the bridge, and even better, the rest of the bridge was collapsing, too. But we weren't safe yet, most of the rebels simply flew up using L lines and continued in our direction.

'Come on, keep moving,' Korin and Neva in her Asterian form said in unison, before each collecting me by the arms and spinning me around to the dorms.

My right arm jolted, and I saw Korin fall to the floor. Another laser had found its mark. There was genuine fear in her eyes, as though the real her had managed to break through in her last moments. She used her power to keep her own blood inside her body. I instinctively reached out.

She slapped my hand away. 'Go!'

Neva and I, seemingly all that remained of our group, continued our sprinting and eventually reached the huge entryway, which, as if anticipating our arrival, was slowly opening. We rushed through into the bright dorm corridor, then looked back at where we had just come from. The rebels had overwhelmed what was left of the guards and were flying towards us.

'Close it!' I shouted.

The doors were admittedly already closing automatically, but too slowly, so I tried creating L lines in my hands. Nothing happened. Inhibitors? Of course, because we were inside the dorms.

'Damn it, help me push!'

We both slammed against the closing doors, trying to speed them up. Thankfully, they sealed just in time, and the muffled impacts of weapons and powers could be heard on the other side, which shook the strong doors. I was panting heavily, but we didn't have much time to rest.

I heard mass murmuring behind me, so I turned to inspect the wide, tall hallway. It was filled with my concerned siblings, who had all come out from their bedrooms to see what the commotion was about. These frightened children and teenagers were in their sleepwear. Some were still hiding in their rooms, peaking their brown-eyed faces out from their doorframes, but when they saw us, they came out, curious to see the most interesting thing to ever happen within these halls.

'It's Iya,' one exclaimed, and then the murmurs repeated my name over and over to the back. When I lived here, I was just one more child in the crowd, forgettable, but now they *all* knew my name.

'Iya?' I heard the nearest say. 'What's going on?' It was one of my elder brothers, Mion.

'What's she doing here?' my elder sister Osane asked. Each had similar questions.

There was a loud rumble above, and the ceiling shook, causing many of the children to scream. Another explosion must have gone off. The children looked up, afraid and confused by the disarray, something that was foreign to them.

Still more children had exited their rooms and entered our corridor to see what the fuss was about. The doors behind continued to be blasted. Neva was staring at me, and she gestured to my siblings.

Tell them what you said earlier. Inspire them.

The kids looked increasingly fearful as they focused more now on the rattling doors. I tried to remember all the words I had said earlier, but I knew exactly how desperate they were. They only needed to know one thing.

I pointed over my shoulder. 'You can either stay here and wait for Aster's justice, or come with me to freedom.' And with that, I trudged forward along the hallway centre with Neva in tow.

The children silently parted, and after a few moments of walking between them, there was another loud bang at the entrance, causing another round of screams.

'Okay, everyone follow Iya,' Osane instructed, 'come on, stay together.'

'Make sure the rooms are empty,' Mion added. 'No one gets left behind.'

That's my girl.

The dorms were a place I knew too well, for I had spent the majority of my sad life wandering this lattice of corridors. However, as far as I knew, the entrance we came through was the only way in or out.

I looked at Neva as we walked, keeping my voice low. 'Tell me there's another way out of here?'

Neva shook her head. 'Maybe the false ceiling, but they'd all have to climb up on something.'

'*Hmph*, and all the furniture is bolted down. That's okay, get the guards above to shoot a hole in my room's ceiling.' I turned back to the crowd of kids. 'Everyone, grab an armful of toys or cushions and meet me at my room.'

The confused kids continued to follow and mutter, not understanding.

'You heard her,' Neva yelled, 'get your things!'

As the kids scattered, Neva and I approached my room and entered just as the guards above were shooting down through the ceiling. They fired repeatedly, eventually creating a hole big enough for a person to fit through.

I gestured to the hanging dolls. 'Help me tear these down,' I said before jumping on the bed to reach the closest toy. I ripped it off the string and chucked it underneath the hole, forming the beginning of the pile.

Neva nodded, tearing three down at once and copying me. The other kids were beginning to arrive, each clutching numerous toys as I had instructed.

'Throw them in the pile,' I said, pointing to it, and they complied. 'More, quick!'

I jumped several more times to rip off dolls, but with her height advantage, Neva was much faster. Meanwhile, more and more kids brought in toys for the growing pile. They had formed a line outside, too, streaming in, then leaving to get more.

The bangs at the entryway continued to resound down the corridors. The children went faster, throwing the toys from the doorway.

Eventually, the small mountain of toys was big enough to climb and reach the ceiling.

'You, go!' I yelled at the nearest child. 'And you, get up there.'

Neva helped ferry children up the toy pile, and when the first child reached the top, a masked guard extended his hand for the girl to grab hold of.

'All of you, move,' Neva added as the stream of children made for the hole.

I spotted Mikan enter the doorway, and the surging children didn't notice his tiny toddler body, almost bowling him over. I jumped off my bed and grabbed him up, lest he be trampled, before passing him to one of the older children to carry.

This was taking too long. I pushed through the crowd to get back into the hall, before cupping my hands. 'Everyone, hurry up! Into my room now, or we're leaving you behind.'

Farther down the hall, a fiery explosion engulfed the entryway, ripping the doors off their hinges. There were still hundreds more kids in the hall, who now screamed even louder than before, but my room could only allow so many in at a time.

Dashing silhouettes emerged from the clearing smoke.

'Death to the empire!' one of their voices yelled.

'Make them suffer,' shouted another.

They raised their weapons and hands at us. Were these people serious? How could they possibly think these innocent children were part of the emperors' evil machinations?

Laserfire rained down through the opaque ceiling, directed at the rebels. The counterattack slew the first wave just in time. Hundreds of little holes had now appeared above. As more rebels braved the smoke, the guards above unleashed another volley of death.

Only maybe fifty children left now, and I hurried them along as best I could, pushing against the crowd at the door. Their number eventually trickled through and began the ascent.

The waves of rebels were increasing and firing back with lasers of their own, so I, as hopefully the last child, entered my room and closed the door. One by one we climbed the stack, and when it was finally my turn, it was Neva at the top who reached down her hand to mine.

The rebels had reached my door and besieging it. Thankfully, I was pulled up to the rafters before they could break through. From up here, I could see the rebels flooding every hallway and room other than my own, but thanks to the illusory ceiling, they couldn't see us.

The children were all making their way along the catwalks towards a dark passage.

'Wait, where are you going?'

Neva grabbed my wrist and pulled. 'It's okay, I'll take it from here. I have the perfect place to keep them safe.'

Thirty-Seven: Want for Nothing

Aboard Avarut's Spear

'No!' Noor yelled again, his voice echoing throughout the dark, warehouse-like storage area. He slammed his fist on the metal flooring. 'Why did she do that?'

While the majority of rebels had fanned out, searching the battlecruiser interior, our families and friends had stayed behind to wait for Sacet. But after we were through, she had pushed Noor in and closed the portal on us.

'She can't fight him alone,' Noor continued, kneeling where the portal once was. He kept shaking his head in anger.

Pilgrim helped him to his feet. 'Fight who, lad?'

'Raumanu,' I answered for him, having caught a glimpse of the old man.

Eyes wide and face tense, Noor turned to all of us. 'And it won't be just him. I'm sorry, but I *have* to go back for her.'

There was a brief silence between us, the only noises coming from the rest of the scattering rebels and the ship's humming engines.

Noor's father stepped forward. 'I'm with you, son. Let's rescue this girlfriend of yours.'

Noor's brother and uncles agreed. 'Lead the way, Noor.'

'She needs my help, too,' Eno said resolutely. 'I'm coming.'

Pilgrim patted Eno approvingly on the shoulder. 'And me.'

Azua, Enni and Aberym also exchanged a look. 'And us,' Azua said.

As much as I wanted to protect my sister, I knew we were also so close to ending the emperors once and for all. And they were sure to have strong protection around them. These rebels were going to need my healing.

I smiled at all of these people who were so courageous and loyal. That when the final goal was within reach, they'd turn back at a moment's notice to save their loved one. 'Sacet… is so lucky to have a family as loving as you.'

Noor grabbed my shoulder. 'We're *your* family, too.' He looked at Tetsu. 'Right, brother?'

Tetsu nodded with a smile. 'She certainly is. Now stop talking to us and go get her, you dope!'

I pointed to a nearby corridor, an offshoot of the main chamber. There was a sign on the ceiling that read "Escape Pods".

'That way,' I instructed, before giving each of them an earnest nod. 'Don't worry, the rest of us will make sure these emperors go down.'

'Come on!' Noor said as he glanced back at the others, and their group splintered off down the corridor.

Tetsu turned to me and gestured to his own family. 'We're with you.'

I turned to another sign labelled as "Bridge".

'Let's go.'

We had caught up to the front of the rebel pack, which Lotus and Amma were leading. While some of the rebels had peeled off at various junctions to storm every room and corridor, the bulk of us were heading straight for the bridge. The crowd turned what I hoped was the final corner, and a long, golden corridor was laid out before us, as luxuriously decorated as an arc interior. It was lined with over a hundred golden guards, each heavily armed and facing us.

The rebels all raised their various weapons at them, ready to fire, but to our surprise, the guards all turned sideways and backed away to the walls, as if allowing us through. There was an awkward moment between our two groups. The guards were completely still and silent, and our people looked to our bewildered leaders, waiting for an instruction.

I pushed my way through to the front of the crowd. 'Looks like we're expected.' I strode past Lotus and Amma, down the corridor between the guards, activating my aura just in case I was wrong.

The others were taken aback by my confidence, and eventually followed me slowly.

Tetsu also pushed through to march beside me. 'Could be a trap.' He had his hands up at the ready.

Every guard we passed was motionless, just like all those I had previously seen controlled by Andriel. Our group eyed them nervously as we passed, ready to fire if necessary, but we reached the grand doors at the end of the corridor without incident.

The doors opened into the gargantuan golden bridge of Avarut's Spear. It was even bigger than the control room of the Overwatch satellite I had once been on. There were hundreds of control panels staffed by incessantly tapping officers, who were otherwise quiet. The front windows were wide, granting a superior aerial view of the vibrant sky and the explosive carnage filling it. And most importantly, in the centre of the bridge were two large thrones, facing away from us.

'There they are,' one rebel said.

That was all we needed to charge in together, running through the large chamber straight towards them. Lotus' aura swelled, far larger than mine was, causing our own people to give a wider berth.

The thrones slowly turned, eventually revealing the emperors, as we had hoped. Avarut had his usual cantankerous expression, and Suralia a creepy smile, both unafraid of the roaring, rampaging horde of Setting Sun members.

Previously hidden behind the thrones was Caelum, who stepped out into view, bringing the rebel mob to a sudden, uneasy halt. He stood between the thrones with his arms folded, as though *daring* us to approach any closer. There was still quite the gap between us, one we'd have to cross if we wanted to reach the emperors, but all of us were too hesitant to move.

'Andriel,' Suralia called out, 'we've found that vermin you keep failing to exterminate.'

Every member of the bridge staff stood up straight and turned to silently face us in unison.

Avarut glanced at Caelum at his side. 'Kill them, now!'

Caelum stared coldly at us before locking onto me, specifically.

None of us here had a hope of defeating him; only Sacet ever could. And after what she had told me he did to her, so willing to sacrifice his own daughter to the orb, my chances of convincing him to do the right thing were slim.

I stared at him pleadingly, then looked at Lotus. Although she had stopped like the rest of us, her fingers were clenched in anticipation. Her burning hatred for the emperors was carved on her face. Caelum looked at her, too, then back at his emperor.

'I said kill them, Caelum!' Avarut yelled, his voice echoing in the golden chamber. 'Do your duty!'

Caelum's forehead vein pulsated, and his expression soured. 'My duty... my *duty*. Like the duty you gave me to sacrifice myself?'

Avarut returned Caelum's seething glare with one of his own. 'Your *duty* is to do whatever *we* say forever.'

Caelum visibly shook, looking like he was about to explode. All of the Setting Sun members onboard had finally caught up. All but Caelum were completely still.

The emperor shooed Caelum with his fingers. 'But if you can't handle it, perhaps we need Raumanu back here to put you in your place!'

Caelum bellowed upwards like a wild animal. 'I am *done* being your lackey, old man!' In a flash, Caelum had picked up Avarut by the scruff of the neck and hurled him into the air.

A shocked Avarut sailed towards us before hitting the steel floor and screeching along it, ending up right in front of Lotus and I.

'Avarut!' Suralia squealed, before pointing at him. 'Guards, guards, retrieve him! Protect your emperor.'

None of the crew reacted, instead continuing to silently let the events unfold. Avarut groaned in pain before rolling over to look up at us.

Suralia glanced at the crew one at a time with a stretched, snarling frown. 'What are you waiting for? Help him!'

A highly decorated, female bridge officer stepped forward. 'My puppets no longer take orders from you.'

'Andriel?' Suralia said. 'What have you done?'

The same horrified realisation washed over the emperors at the same time, and their former smugness disappeared. Without even looking, Caelum's hand shot out towards Suralia and scrunched her neck in a choke. She squawked like some pitiful creature as she was lifted and lobbed at us as well.

As she tumbled along the ground with several sharp cracks, no doubt from her brittle bones breaking, Lotus stared at Caelum with a raised eyebrow.

Caelum went back to folding his arms. 'Well? Do it.'

Lotus grinned ecstatically, a new round of bloodlust overcoming her, doubling her aura. Avarut had been attempting to crawl away, so Lotus kicked him over onto his back.

Avarut wailed in pain. 'Caelum, you spineless traitor, if you don't help me *right* now, I'll have Raumanu kill you for your impudence. I'll… I'll have you executed!'

Lotus knelt and straddled on top of the old man, causing him more pain. She brought a finger to his lips and shushed him. 'Silence now. I want this to go exactly as I imagined it.' Her sick smile grew even wider.

I felt Tetsu's hand grab mine, so I squeezed it. The entire chamber watched on.

Lotus grabbed at the air in front of the old man's face, and after a short amount of time, a ball of light appeared from his mouth as he gave his final death rattle. The emperor's eyes turned white, and his skin went pale, even more gaunt than before.

The empress was crying, struggling to crawl away from us, but with so many broken bones, it was a futile endeavour. 'No, no, my love. No, don't let them do this to you. Stop this barbarity!'

Looking at my comrades, I saw they all shared the same resolute expression. We all knew this *had* to be done. I'd like to think I took no pleasure in this, but shamefully, I was eager for it. Such was their evil that my principles were yet again in danger of corruption.

With the emperor's soul now floating in front of Lotus, she clasped both her shaking palms around it and quietly laughed. Her laughter grew into an echoing cackle as she squeezed and fractured the evil soul. What little energy it had inside puffed out from her hands like a putrid green stink bomb, washing over those closest.

Realising only half her job was done, she focused and rose, before standing over the old woman.

Suralia rolled onto her back and raised her hands in surrender. 'Please, young one, *beautiful* young one, spare me and you can have anything you want. *Please, please, please—*'

Lotus stomped on Suralia's chest, producing another croaky screech. 'After I'm done killing you… what's that thing you all say? Ah yes, that's it: I'll want for nothing.'

Suralia already appeared faint, unable to reply. She briefly choked and seized as her life force was exhumed.

The tiny floating ball of light again was embraced by Lotus, who looked down at it like you would a cute baby animal. This was quickly replaced with a manic, toothy grin as she slammed her closed fist down onto the ball, blasting it into shards, the explosion again being far smaller than I anticipated.

The bridge fell deathly silent. Lotus extinguished her aura and wiped away her tears. Then the rebels cheered, hollering loudly and embracing as if the battle was over.

Lotus approached Amma with a look of both great joy and great pain. 'I… I did it. It's over.'

Amma waved her closer in for a hug, and they both closed their eyes. 'The monsters are dead now. I'm so proud of you, my little flower.'

Perhaps they were celebrating prematurely. Just because Caelum had assisted us, and Andriel stayed out of our way, that didn't mean that they were on our side now.

A large screen had appeared on the front window. It showed Raumanu speeding through the air over Arc Royal. Caelum was focused upon it, continuing his spiteful gaze.

The senior bridge officer from earlier approached Caelum's side with a sultry gait, before turning to all of us.

I held up a hand to quieten the crowd. 'We're not done yet.'

'Too right, Tau,' the Andriel proxy said, exhibiting the same air of superiority as the controller. 'So *glad* you rebels could join us in this historic moment. There's just *one* problem.' She directed our attention to the screen. 'If we can't kill Raumanu, none of this will have meant *anything*.'

The rebels, clearly uneasy about the proposition of working with these equally tyrannical Chosen, silently exchanged looks of concern.

I stepped forward. 'Where's Sacet?'

The screen updated, showing a huge smouldering crater. It zoomed in on the rubble and showed Sacet lying on the ground, missing an arm and covered in blood. She wasn't moving. Was she dead?

I realised that even when Caelum or Andriel were going to inevitably betray us, we couldn't beat them here anyway. Sacet, on the other hand, *could* be helped. She was too important to lose now.

I stepped over the former emperors' bodies and stopped in front of Caelum. 'We have to get to her. She can defeat him, but she needs our help.'

Caelum continued to glare at the screen. 'Raumanu... is *mine*.'

The woman gently placed her hand on Caelum's arm. 'The girl is right. You don't have to do this alone, allow the pawns to help.'

Caelum's fist smashed into the woman with such force that her body was obliterated into pieces and sprayed across the room. Without missing a beat, a second female crew member left her post and approached him with the same bravado as the last.

'Okay, ouch? Very well then,' she said, switching to an alluring gaze, circling him like she was performing a bizarre mating ritual. 'Hear me out. Let us send *everything* we have at him. I'll bring down the planet's inhibitors and let the rest of the cattle swarm in.' She stopped in front of him and tiptoed her fingers up his chest. 'And then... once everyone else has proven they're no match, and the *whole* empire is watching, you, the *only* one strong enough, *powerful* enough, will defeat him.'

Caelum smirked, finding the prospect intriguing. He considered her words before floating to Avarut's old throne and sitting. He leant back and brought his hands together in thought. 'Hurry up and die to him then.'

The woman smiled before looking back at us with revulsion, as if only just remembering we existed. 'All of you, get off our ship!'

All of us were stunned, unsure of what was happening.

'Do you want your freedom or not?' she shouted. 'Go down there and kill the last one *loyal* to these fossils!'

'Get to the escape pods,' Amma finally said begrudgingly. Whether she was siding with them or just playing along wasn't clear, but the rebels moved back to the corridor soon after.

While the others left and the crew went back to their stations, regaining some of their independence, I continued to stare at Caelum. He ignored me, instead pressing a button to rotate the thrones back to the front window. His focus was locked on the screen, where Raumanu was searching for my sister.

What a small man my father really was, his pride so intertwined with his power that defeating Raumanu was all that mattered to him.

'Dad—'

'That's *Emperor* to you,' he snapped, his gaze fixed ahead. 'What do you waste my time with, brat?'

'I just wonder… what kind of emperor you'll be?'

He disappeared from his throne and in the next instant was towering over me. His intimidating stare didn't affect me anymore.

I looked directly into his eyes. 'It's not too late to be a good man… and a good father.' With that, I turned and made for the exit, leaving him to stare daggers at the back of my head.

I'm coming, Sacet.

Thirty-Eight: Brought Into the Light

My eyes slowly blinked open, letting in the blurry, chaotic mess around me. Pain, immediate and overwhelming, it took hold of me and wouldn't let go, like a billion little mites biting my nervous system. I couldn't move, or even muster a scream. Wave after wave of agony, the worst I had ever felt.

My second perception spun uncontrollably, but caught a glimpse of some of my guts hanging out of my side. I couldn't sit up to confirm it, but it was likely accurate based on how I felt. Blood gushed out of me at an alarming rate, seeping into the cracks of the rubble.

My eyes finally adjusted enough to see the rest of the blackened crater: mostly demolished concrete and steel, with numerous fires scattered about. Thousands of people using L lines still streamed through the sky, clashing with airborne MASU and guards. There were bright eruptions of energy, fire and colliding steel, with the remnants raining down nearby.

One distant yell stood out amidst the din of war: a furious battle cry. It was coming closer. Slowly, my head turned to the side. On the far edge of the crater, once more speeding towards me with deadly intent, was Raumanu.

I had no energy left to fight, nor to make a portal to escape. If I died here, and if my friends had also failed, then it was over. This was the end.

A tug on my abdomen suddenly amplified my pain. My body was swiftly pulled from the rubble by an unknown force, propelling me into the night sky. I narrowly avoided Raumanu, who crashed into my previous location with tremendous force, disintegrating the entire area upon impact. He craned his head up in surprise.

I glanced along my miraculous flight path and caught sight of a group of rebels soaring through the air. One of them had his hand outstretched toward me. It was Eno, exerting his power from a considerable distance, his telekinesis somehow pulling me instead of pushing. I didn't even know he could do that. I slammed into his embrace midair, and he gripped me tight.

'Got you!' Eno shouted over the blaring wind as the group sped over the crater. 'Told you you'd need my protection.'

I tried to grab back but couldn't lift my only arm. I was starting to slip. Even with the missing body part, I was still too heavy for my brother.

Noor was flying next to us and saw him struggling. 'I'll take her. Here.'

Our group slowed to allow Eno to transfer me into Noor's arms. Mum, Dad, Aberym, Pilgrim and Noor's family were also with us.

'Stay with me this time,' Noor said in my ear.

I simply nodded, unable to summon enough strength to even speak.

Ahkim pointed down at Raumanu. 'He looks mad.'

Raumanu loudly cursed in frustration. His temper and wrinkled, red forehead reminded me of Avarut. He stopped when he realised that the sounds of the battlefield had ceased. The rebels, civilians, and arc guards were no longer clashing in the sky or on the surface. Everything had stopped.

Raumanu glanced about to try and understand, but then appeared relieved. 'You *finally* help me, Andriel?' he shouted. 'Now?'

A bombardment of laserfire from above interrupted him,

obliterating the area and blanketing it with a cloud of dust. I glanced up and identified the source: Avarut's Spear. The battlecruiser was unleashing all its fury upon the old man. The magnitude of the explosions prompted our flying squad to swiftly retreat to a safer distance.

'Take that, geezer!' Pilgrim yelled over the quaking destruction.

The dust, fire and smoke concealed Raumanu's fate, but my perception knew better. The weapons had done nothing to him. After an extended barrage, the battlecruiser eventually stopped firing. A great, black, smouldering plume expanded upwards.

Avarut's Spear wasn't done; it was now in a nosedive, heading straight for Raumanu at high speed, seemingly on purpose.

'It's going to crash,' Noor shouted. 'Get out of its way!'

As our group retreated even farther in the sky, the groaning, steel battlecruiser continued to dive. It made contact with the ground with a deep, droning metal squeal, unlike anything I had ever heard, before detonating, sending a ring-shaped deluge of fire out over the land. The colossal pieces of the ship buckled and crumbled before being blasted into the sky. The crater widened and deepened, rippling with the tremendous shockwave. The enormous blast coated the entire arc in an ambient orange glow. The brutal sound reverberated off the city planet in a cacophony of pure destruction. Everyone's mouths were agape, having never seen an explosion so big.

'He can't have survived that, surely?' Azua said as we slowed to a hover.

'Hopefully not,' one of Noor's uncles replied.

Countless lights appeared on the horizon in every direction all at once, as though someone had flicked a switch. Power had been returned to the city beyond the Arc Royal perimeter. Not only that, but much of the swirling aurora disappeared, returning the sky to inky black. The light pollution of the city hid what stars might have been visible.

As though sensing the lack of stars, millions of white streaks launched from the surface, as though trying to reinforce them. Probably *more* than millions. It was the civilians ascending using L lines again. They were so numerous that their light threatened to turn the night into day. Unlike their slightly random and joyful pathing when they first discovered how to fly, they were all heading directly for the crash site.

Enni smiled in relief. 'Everyone's powers are back.'

'They're on *our* side, right?' Eno asked.

Kashif nodded. 'They're here for retribution, just like us.'

The flaming wreckage of Avarut's Spear was now strewn all across the crater, which had doubled in size. Smoke and fire still filled the centre, and Raumanu was nowhere to be seen.

Noor gestured to the rubble just outside the crash site with his chin. 'Everyone land. If he's alive, he'll have no choice but to surrender now.'

The oncoming civilians' synchronicity was disconcerting. Without modified INCs, couldn't that also mean they were under Andriel's control again? I wanted to protest against Noor's idea, but could only manage a groan in his ear.

'It's okay, I won't drop you,' he said.

We decreased our speed and found a flatter area to land. Noor continued to hold me in his arms. Our group stared into the slowly clearing smoke, trying to spot the old man. The millions of lights drew closer, sparkling like water under sunlight.

The fiery miasma continued to clear, and standing now in a crater within the crater was Raumanu's silhouette. A defined orb and tentacles were visible around him, thanks to the dust being disintegrated upon touching them. He shook his head in disappointment.

I raised a hand and reached out to Noor's face. 'He's… too… strong.'

He looked down and gave me a knowing smirk. 'Only when you fight him alone.' He then focused on Raumanu with steely intensity. 'Let's break the loop, *together.*'

The first wave of the millions of silent civilians arrived, encircling the crash site. Some landed on the crater's rim, whilst the rest remained hovering overhead. There was no space not taken up by them, and each was almost perfectly spaced apart at arm's length. The wall they formed, dome-like in shape, encapsulated both Raumanu and our group, with Raumanu as the focal point. There was no escape.

'Andriel!' Raumanu roared. 'After all this time, you *dare* betray the path?'

'I have chosen a *different* path,' the millions of voices all said at once in a harsh discord, 'one without you.' And with that, at least a thousand or so people who had a direct line of sight pointed their arms at him.

'Get down!' Azua said, wrenching both Eno and Enni to the ground.

Noor collapsed with me and huddled on top. The others did the same, ducking and diving for rocks and other debris for cover.

The psychic army fired long streaks of white energy towards Raumanu. Each line came together and slammed into the centre, creating a blinding bright light, so large that it was probably visible from space. Their streams didn't stop, causing a constant, deafening, distorted buzz.

Although I barely had the wherewithal to remain conscious, I felt Noor clutch me tightly during the pandemonium. This attack eventually ceased as well, as did the ringing in my ears. As expected, Raumanu's surroundings were completely devastated. However, he himself remained unaffected, still floating in the same position.

He laughed at the army. 'You should know better than that, you craven witch. No matter can penetrate my shield.' As he surveyed his opponents, his eyes stopped on me. '*You*, I don't know how you did it, but you've broken everyone's faith in the light.'

'We never had your faith,' a deep voice boomed from above. It was Caelum, floating down from the sky towards the old man. His arms were at his sides, fists clenched. His eyes, wide. His expression, murderous.

Our group remained still, unsure of what was going on. The brainwashed army of civilians eased back in unison.

Raumanu closed his eyes and sighed. 'Caelum...' He turned to face his old enemy, and the two stared each other down. 'So, the barbarian king returns. I knew it was only a matter of time.'

My father cracked his neck, preparing for the impending duel. 'I'm about to finish what you started over a millennia ago. And this time you've no more tricks left. No underlings to get in my way. No inhibitor fields to hide inside of!'

Raumanu shook his head again. 'Did... did Suralia suffer?' His mouth trembled with each word.

Caelum smiled and lowered his eyebrows. 'Why don't you ask your *precious* Empyrean?' He slowly hovered closer. 'Because she is now a permanent resident.'

With each word from my father, Raumanu's sadness slowly morphed into rage. His breathing quickened, and he, too, clenched his fists.

'She *begged* for her life,' Caelum goaded, '*pitiful* end for a worthless creature.'

It was too much for Raumanu. He leant back and roared again, greatly intensifying the reach of his shield. Caelum burst forward and collided with it, the resulting shockwave blew everyone back and off their feet.

Both men launched up. Caelum landed blow upon mighty blow, and although his punches still couldn't get through, Raumanu was pushed back after each hit.

Raumanu, meanwhile, summoned even more tentacles to aid him, which would swipe at Caelum. My father couldn't see the attacks, but most would miss him anyway, for whenever Caelum struck, he'd speed away and strike from another angle.

'You've gotten slower, old man,' Caelum taunted between hits.

The rest of us watched on, unable to keep up with where either would be at any given moment. Their hectic combat spilled outside the dome into the army of motionless, floating civilians, who exploded into red puffs if they got in the way. The men only had eyes for each other, ignoring the eerily silent civilians.

More waves of pain. I was struggling to stay awake, let alone keep track of the fight. I lay back on the rubble and stared straight up. When would this ordeal all be over?

An intensely bright light amongst the sea of others, like a cyan sun amongst stars. Tau descended towards me with the biggest aura I had ever seen. I almost didn't notice Tetsu, his family and the horde of Setting Sun members accompanying her. They all landed next to me, and I could already feel Tau's tingling, healing power coursing through my veins.

Tau's expression twisted as my pain was briefly shared with her, but soon my wounds had healed and my arm had regrown. She and Noor helped me to my feet, and she came face to face with me. 'When I promised to look after everyone, that included *you*.'

Both gave me a hurt, stern look.

I pulled them both in for a hug and closed my eyes. 'I know. I'm so, so sorry. I'll *never* leave any of you behind like that again. I promise, we'll always have each other's backs.'

They embraced me back, and then we all continued to watch the fight. The men battled throughout the sky, through buildings that were demolished soon afterwards, and down underground, cracking the planet asunder.

'Nothing can break through his shield,' I reported aloud. 'I tried everything.'

Noor glanced at me in thought. 'If *nothing* could get through, then not even *light* would. We wouldn't even be able to *see* him if that were true.'

'The light still reaches him…' Tau surmised.

I remembered back to when Noor's laser could be amplified through my portals because it was light and not matter. We all looked at each other, realising the same thing.

Huge explosions continued to sound off in the distance as the men fought in and out of the arc structure. My perception tracked them and saw that neither showed any sign of relenting. They were currently fighting in a now roofless, amphitheatre-like area, similar to the Arc Unity interior.

'I'm ready,' Noor said to me.

I created a portal to the centre of the theatre, amongst the shattered pews. Noor ran through, then me, then the rest of our family and friends. The Setting Sun members followed after, filling the audience rows.

Caelum had just bashed Raumanu down onto an altar, destroying it. Neither of them had noticed the crowd enter, nor Andriel's army in the sky tracking their movements.

'Your shield can't hold forever,' my father shouted.

'The light is my shield,' Raumanu responded. 'As long as I believe, it will *never* falter.'

Noor pointed his palms at him. 'Let's test that theory, shall we?'

As Raumanu glanced over, Noor fired. The red-hot laser instantaneously cut through the dusty chamber like a divine beam of judgment, ignoring Raumanu's shield and slicing through his stomach. What was left of him fell to the ground in two pieces, a top and bottom.

Raumanu's shield had dissipated, and his face displayed equal parts pain and surprise. Caelum's, meanwhile, was overcome with fury.

As Noor's family cheered for him, my father slowly looked over to us and focused on him, too. '*You… you little thief. He was not yours to kill!*'

Caelum disappeared and reappeared in front of us, holding Noor above our heads. Noor squirmed against my furious father.

The rest of us raised our hands at Caelum, either preparing to attack or to convince him to stop. Tau shared her healing aura with Noor, while Lotus attempted to discourage Caelum with hers. While we all bickered, I noticed a bright light over by the altar.

Amma pointed over to it. 'Look!'

One by one, everyone looked over, including Caelum. The light was coming from Raumanu's supposed corpse. His hand was holding the small particle, a pretty blue sparkle that lit all of his surroundings. Raumanu's upper body was still slowly moving, reaching, turning. He gently tipped the sparkle to the side. A small smile grew on his face.

I had never seen him use this power before, but I knew exactly what it was. Glancing up at the sky, I opened a portal under the sparkle just as it was about to reach the ground. I stretched the portal wider and the sparkle, as well as both his upper and lower body were sucked through into space. As soon as he was clear, I closed the portal again.

I craned my neck up, and after a short delay, a bright blue explosion flashed beyond the atmosphere. Everyone else looked up, too. Lines streaked out of the light, zigzagging every which way, forking into countless paths like a lightning bolt in slow motion. It was as if each path were searching for some kind of matter to latch onto.

Soon, the lines had created an intricate design, admittedly quite beautiful, but thankfully, the farther they reached, the more they faded, until finally they stopped.

Noor turned to me with conviction, strode over and embraced me. We eventually broke off, and I noticed that Tetsu had done the same with Tau. But something was wrong; the boys' faces lost all emotion. So had everyone's faces except for Tau, Caelum and I.

'The emperors are dead,' they and the millions of voices surrounding us said at once. 'Raumanu is dead, never to be resurrected. The sun has finally set on their time.'

Tau gasped and jumped back, understanding that all of our companions were also under Andriel's control. Were those kisses from Noor and Tetsu, or did they come from Andriel? The thought of it disgusted me. Tau and I both backed away to Caelum, our only remaining ally, unlikely though he may be.

I looked at Tau. 'I thought you said their INCs were modified?'

Her eyes darted, searching for anyone else still themselves. 'They were!'

Noor approached me and smiled. 'There are very few ways to keep me out, and having your INC modified is *not* one of them. But don't worry, all our enemies are gone.' He came closer until he was almost touching again, so I retreated even farther.

Enni approached Caelum with an amorous walk. 'The empire is ours now. No more fighting is necessary.'

At that exact moment, rays of golden light shot from the distant horizon, lighting the metal lands.

Tetsu tried to rejoin Tau. 'It is a joyous new day for us all. One that we should celebrate together. Come to the throne room and witness a new sun rising.'

Thirty-Nine: Puppet Master

Earlier

In the service tunnels

Neva, or rather my mother, had been leading my siblings and I through the service tunnels *supposedly* to safety. To her credit, we had successfully avoided any more skirmishes with the invaders. However, I recognised the path we had taken from whenever we had caught a glimpse outside the tunnels, and knew that we were being led to the rafters above the throne room, which was hardly a safe place during a coup.

Numerous children in our crowd had been loudly crying the whole way, which echoed along the passage. Stealthy we certainly weren't. Provided we survived the night, I hoped this experience was going to toughen them up, and quick.

Our passage ended and, as expected, we entered the dark rafters. There were no bodyguards above to keep watch. I ran ahead to the nearest balcony and peered down into the throne room. It, too, was deserted, save for two figures in the thrones. No, it couldn't be? The emperors…

Many of the other children joined my side and saw what I saw. Their loud murmurs started up again, and some worriedly ducked to avoid detection. More and more of them filled the rafters, each trying to get a view of below.

If I wanted my siblings to be free from the emperors like I was, they needed to see them like I did, as our enemy. I just hoped they'd follow my lead.

I climbed onto the balcony railing. 'Come on, they're alone. Let's finish them, once and for all.'

I jumped off the balcony and fell two storeys, using a burst of white energy to cushion my landing. Neva also jumped, converting to a cloud midair and back again when she touched down. None of the others joined us, instead watching and waiting.

There was something off about my former parents, they hadn't moved since we got here. They slouched in their thrones, not talking or reacting. Was it another of Verre's illusions?

'It is no illusion,' a voice said from behind, 'that is Avarut and Suralia before you.'

It was Mother, she had just entered the chamber through where the large doors would have been, had they not recently been torn off their hinges. She was beaming, happier than I had ever seen her, and escorted by a collection of acolyte guards, each with their powers at the ready to defend her life.

As she proudly strode along the long, blue carpet, she looked up into the rafters. 'My beautiful children, our troubles are over.' She pointed to the thrones, which I realised had two corpses occupying them. 'The emperors are gone forever, *executed* as they deserved. And I, your *true* mother, will now rule this empire.'

'Mother?' I began, gesturing around. 'I *thought* you said you'd bring us to a safe place?'

She reached me and lovingly brushed my cheek. '*Shh, shh, shoosh,* my princess. Your mother has it all under control now. The rebellion has been defeated.'

There were a few jubilant cheers and sighs of relief above.

Mother gently grabbed my hand and led me to the steps in front of the thrones. 'Come, I want you to see this. I want *all* of you to see.'

Now that we were closer to their bodies, I saw that all colour and life had been drained from the emperors. Screams were petrified on their faces. Every one of my siblings had found a place along the balconies to watch, and many were horrified by what they saw.

'Watch as I dethrone the unworthy.'

Mother ascended the stairs and ripped Avarut out of his throne. His body tumbled down the stairs, stopping in front of me. She did the same to Suralia, in an unnecessary but symbolic gesture of taking power. As Mother sat in Suralia's old throne, an even bigger smile spread on her face.

She gestured to the floor by the side of her chair. 'Come up here, Iya. I told you you'd be by my side, remember?'

I took a deep breath, unsure of myself, before also ascending the stairs and moving to where she had pointed.

She reached out to me and patted me approvingly, before looking forward. 'Now, there is only *one* left who could pose a threat to me, and I'm about to deal with her.'

All her guards, now including Neva, created a symmetrical formation on the stairs. Similar to Tetsu's power, one man manifested a partially visible shield of energy around them all.

A wide portal opened in the centre of the chamber, and through it stepped Sacet. She wasn't alone. Tau followed her through next, and then all her friends and family, too. Caelum surprisingly floated in also, and a deluge of rebels, civilians, guards, and arc staff.

Thousands more entered through the chamber's entrance, all of them in silence. Except for the three Chosen, every single person had the same blank expression, one I now knew quite well.

While the chamber continued to fill, the slaves formed perfectly straight rows and columns, and left a path down the middle for the three Chosen to approach.

'Come closer,' Mother instructed them.

Both Sacet and Tau did so hesitantly, clearly unsure of what was to come next. My father displayed his usual stoicism and floated forward. The three of them stopped in front of the stairs, as I had done. Sacet gave me a look of loathing, perhaps believing I had betrayed her.

Mother stood from her throne and grinned. '*Oh*, Caelum, I misjudged you.' She gestured up at my siblings. 'All this time, you *knew* they were our children. How long have you kept my secret? *Our* secret?'

Sacet and Tau looked up with confusion, probably realising that the royal children were their siblings, too.

My father smirked. 'I've known for over a millennia, since you began. I tested their genetics myself.'

Mother meandered to the bottom of the steps, just shy of the shield wall. 'And yet, you *never* told anyone.' She reached her hands out to him and gestured for him to approach. 'Because deep down, you still love me.'

Father met her at the wall and joined his hands with hers. The shield flickered as it allowed him to enter, before reforming once he was inside.

She hugged his enormous chest. 'Think of it, you and I ruling together. The immortal Emperor Caelum and his beautiful Empress Andriel. We can sacrifice the Tau girl and live forever.'

Shock came over my two sisters, prompting them both to give our father pleading stares.

'Nothing can stop us,' Mother continued as she grabbed Caelum's collar and gently pulled his face down to her own, 'the entire empire is now ours alone.'

They both kissed passionately, holding each other tight.

'Dad,' Sacet said, getting his attention, 'this is wrong, and you know it.'

Mother put her hand on Father's cheek to redirect him back to her. 'Don't listen to the child, she just seeks power for herself.'

Tau was shaking her head. 'I didn't say anything… when you stood by… and allowed my mother to die. But I won't be silent now.' Tau gestured at the motionless crowd. 'Is this empire of robots what you really want to rule over? No free will? Nothing changing, for eternity?'

Mother put a hand on her hip in disbelief. '*Oh*, so now you *don't* want to sacrifice yourself?'

While they argued, I realised the true scope of my mother's deceit. Just by looking at this crowd, I knew she was far more powerful than she let on. She went from having no control over the rebels to having *complete* control. That didn't make sense.

What if she deliberately let me make a fool of myself at the fake party, just so my message could be broadcast to the world, furthering the rebellion? And what if that army of civilians chasing me through the arc earlier were under her influence the whole time? All her underlings died in front of me while I somehow conveniently got to safety? What if the children were never in any actual danger? Would she do something like that, just so she could motivate me? Motivate the others to throw off their oppressors?

She played everyone else, so why not us, too? Even now, my siblings were arranged near the ceiling like little hanging dolls. Tau had almost put it perfectly; they weren't robots, they were her *toys*, and none had a will of their own.

I was sick of this control. Mother was distracted by all the minds under her spell, and by the impudence of my two sisters. I raised my hands in front of my eyes with Mother as my target. My arms pulled back, preparing to kill, and as they came back in, a hand shot out next to me and intercepted my wrist. It was Neva grabbing me.

Andriel turned on the spot and seethed, staggered by my betrayal. 'How... *dare* you, you ungrateful little recreant!'

Neva overpowered me, bending my arm behind my back, and two other guards approached to assist in restraining me. They brought me to my knees and held me in place.

Andriel came up the steps and looked down at me. 'I gave you life. I gave you safety and decadence. I was going to give you power, and *this* is how you repay me?' She was angrier than I had ever seen her.

'You can't keep controlling people!' I shouted back. 'We are not a *commodity* for you to do with as you please.'

'Of course they are!' she screamed in my face. 'Maybe I was wrong about you, Iya. Ever since I gave you your freedom, you've gradually become... like *them*. Perhaps my predecessors were right in wanting to execute you.'

Jeers filled the chamber, and we both realised it was coming from above. My siblings were booing their mother, who in turn was taken aback. Perhaps my actions *had* inspired them after all?

Andriel raised her hands for quiet. 'Children, enough. Quiet down now.'

Father scanned the chamber, looking at his children above and below, as well as all the slaves. He and Tau locked eyes briefly, and she shook her head at him, as though disappointed.

'Be quiet!' Andriel continued to my siblings. 'Your *mother* is talking. I don't want to… don't make me control you. Silence, children.' The kids continued to boo, and Andriel's frustration grew and grew. 'SILENCE!'

The kids all stifled and were silent shortly afterwards, as commanded. 'We're sorry, Mother,' they all said at once.

Andriel sighed and returned to her throne, but didn't sit down yet. She turned to Caelum and gestured to Avarut's old seat. 'Shall we, *Emperor* Caelum? It is the seat you were born to sit in.'

He pondered for a moment before slowly making his way up the stairs. He smirked. 'I agree, the seat I was born to sit in… *alone.*'

His surly expression intensified as he glanced over to her. Andriel's smile disappeared.

A spray of blood all over my face. Caelum's fist had rocketed over and into Andriel's stomach, impaling her. His beady eyes locked with hers. Her mouth was agape and quivering. She reached for his face with trembling hands.

Caelum smirked. 'The people will *choose* to respect and fear my power. *That…* is what *ruling* is.' He relinquished his arm from her body, flicked the blood off it, and then returned to sit on his throne. 'I *never* loved you. The reason I didn't give up our children was so I wouldn't have to share in your shame when they were executed.'

Andriel's legs wobbled, and she fell to her knees. Not a single real ally came to her aid. She coughed and sputtered blood onto her lips, crimson like her dyed hair.

Everyone in the chamber snapped out of her control, including those restraining me, who, in a moment of confusion, now released me. They still all remained where they were, somehow knowing the gravity of the situation, watching my mother slowly die.

Mother slumped backwards, and I caught her in my arms.

She looked up at me and managed a smile, as if regressing to an earlier time before I had betrayed her. 'I… I alway… l-love you,' she whispered. 'My puh… princess.'

No, what have I done? Why did I betray her?

Her whole body stopped moving. Her eyes were still open, so I brought my fingers to her eyelids and closed them myself.

Caelum pointed out to his audience. '*I…* am the emperor now.

If any of you wish to challenge me, step forward now and receive a quick death.' He scanned the silent crowd with wild eyes.

There was chattering throughout, and eventually they all turned to Sacet and Tau, as though expecting them to do something first.

'What about you?' Caelum asked, pointing to Sacet. 'Are you going to stand in my way?' He gestured to his throne. 'Was she right? Do you seek this power?'

The crowd looked back and forth between Caelum and Sacet. She glanced back at them and sighed, before locking eyes with each of her family and friends.

'Do you plan to continue the sacrifices?' she finally answered.

He shook his head. 'No one can have my power. And no one can have Raumanu's or Andriel's powers either. No one should live forever, it is cowardly. And as for *you*… I'm simply *tired* of you.'

Sacet nodded. 'And the harvest worlds?'

Caelum smirked and leant forward. 'There will be no prisoners or slaves in *my* empire, only subjects. And there will be no more need for entire worlds of torture.'

Sacet shrugged, satisfied. 'Well, I'm tired, too, Dad. Tired of fighting. I've done *more* than my fair share of it. So no, I'm *not* going to stand in your way, but I'm not going to serve you either.' A subtle smile appeared on her face. 'I think I'll go to another planet. One with… big green forests, winding rivers, plentiful food, and tall mountains. Live the life I always wanted to.' She looked around. 'And anyone who wants to come with me, who wants this simple life, away from the constant fighting, is welcome to do so.'

She flicked her fingers at the chamber's centre, and a portal opened to a luxurious interior, most likely the Arc Sacet penthouse, before approaching it.

Caelum raised a hand to give her pause. 'Leave if you wish, and take all the weaklings you want, but heed me: you, and anyone who joins you, will no longer be a citizen of my empire.'

Sacet nodded. 'I agree. May we never have to see each other again.' She looked back at her companions and gestured to their exit.

One by one, each of her closest family and friends joined her, all except Tau, who continued to stare at Caelum.

'What kind of emperor will you be, I wonder?' she began.

Caelum raised his fingers together in a triangle. 'The people will be free to wonder that themselves.'

Tau smirked back. 'I hope so. Goodbye, Father.' She then turned to join the others.

Several more from the crowd also decided to quietly make their way to Sacet's portal, and together they piled through.

I looked down at my dead mother, pitying her. She was the only person who ever loved me, loved who I was. What would happen to her after this? Surely Caelum wouldn't leave her dead, risking a disciple somewhere resurrecting her from afar? No, he'd bring both her and Raumanu back, but keep them contained.

I wanted to be there for her, but if I was going to stay, it would be in a position of safety, of power. I had to get on Caelum's good side immediately.

And what about my siblings still above? Surely, they wouldn't want to stay here anymore. Could they even handle living under Caelum's rule? I know he *hated* weakness and generally cared little for his children. Sacet's plan was probably their best chance at a good life.

'Wait!' I called out to Sacet. I gently lowered my mother and stood.

Sacet looked back with aversion, clearly no longer trusting me.

Keenly aware that Caelum was listening in, I pointed to the rafters. 'Take your brothers and sisters with you. They're too weak for my father's new empire.'

Caelum chuckled, hopefully impressed by my lack of caring for them.

Sacet narrowed her eyes. 'Gladly.'

Another portal appeared in the rafters, its light illuminating the darkness. For most of the children, it was an easy choice, they gladly fled without hesitation. But some of the braver kids, perhaps taking issue with my words, glared down at Caelum and I. Eventually, they also took their leave, and once the rafters were bare, Sacet closed the above portal.

Although they continued to murmur, unsure of their futures, no one else in the chamber was moving.

Noor was still standing next to Sacet by the portal. 'Coming this time?'

Sacet locked eyes with her father once more before smiling at

Noor. 'Definitely.' The two of them went through the portal together, hand in hand, and it closed behind them.

Caelum again pointed out to his subjects. 'Now the rest of you, *submit* to your new emperor.'

There was a commotion in the crowd. Lotus was pushing her way through to get to the front. 'I challenge this insanity! *All* of us do.'

An old woman dressed like a rebel had been chasing her, trying to pull her back. 'Stop, Lotus, don't do this. He's *too* powerful.'

Caelum smiled, for he had gotten exactly what he wanted: someone to make an example out of.

'*I* executed the emperors,' Lotus continued, 'and I didn't do it just so *another* tyrant could take their place.' Her powerful green aura exploded out, causing all those around her to back away.

The old woman, realising it was too late to talk her out of it, winced at the impending heartbreak.

Caelum leant forward in his throne. 'So, you want to be empress, do you?'

'I want you to step down, before we all tear you down,' she replied, looking back at the crowd for support. 'Right?' No one responded, so she spun around looking for at least one supporter. 'Right?!'

'Did you know… that you… *immortal* disciples… are very *easy* to kill?' Caelum continued.

Lotus' aura faltered. The rest of the room went dead silent.

Caelum brought up his hand and made a pinching motion with his fingers. 'All I have to do… is *squish…* you into a *tiny* container, one too small for your body to put itself back together in.'

Lotus looked terrified. No one said anything.

Caelum's cruel smile widened again, and he disappeared. In an instant, he had picked her up and rammed her into the throne right next to me. The impact was so great that I was taken off my feet, and I fell down the stairs.

When I came to a stop, I looked up to see a screaming, crying Lotus being held in place in the throne by him. He forced her down deeper and deeper into the metal, warping it.

'Enjoy your throne, Empress!' Emperor Caelum shouted.

With his free hand, he ripped at the sides of the throne, peeling strips of metal up and over Lotus' body, again and again, entombing her. She continued to scream, but her cries became muffled.

Eventually, when Lotus' body was no longer visible, her flames disappeared. Caelum ripped the throne off the floor and rapidly squished it. The screaming stopped, and blood spurted out of any holes it could escape from. He had a maniacal expression as he continued to squeeze and mould it into a rough spherical shape, before holding it up in the palm of one hand, the ball now perhaps a third of its original size.

The old woman was quietly sobbing. The entire chamber was aghast with fear, afraid to act. But I knew what he wanted next.

Our emperor turned to them and displayed the blood-covered metal ball for all to witness, before chucking it over his shoulder to the back corner of the room.

I walked up the stairs, past all the guards, until I was the closest one to him. I gave him a smile, before looking back at the weaklings. 'All hail, Emperor Caelum!' I yelled, then knelt, bowing as one might have to the previous emperors.

Although I couldn't see the people, I heard them all shuffling as they bowed, too. Out of the corner of my eye, I saw that Neva was still gawping at him.

'Bow, idiot!' I whispered, snapping her out of it.

As Neva finally bowed, I looked up at the cruel man. He sat back on his throne and smiled down at me. A new era had begun.

Forty: The Beginning of the End

Sacet's penthouse, huge though it was, was absolutely filled with activity in every room. Our new brothers and sisters, formerly the royal children, were on the floor above searching for bedsheets and spots to hunker down for the night, pushing the penthouse's capacity to its limits.

Numerous rebels had taken over the bar to swap war stories of their individual deeds, the loudest being Pilgrim. Now with unfettered access to the rooms of the rich, they were repeatedly conjuring up feasts and libations with the kitchen synthesisers. Because of all the mind tampering from Andriel, they weren't sure which stories were true, and were drunkenly trying to piece together what really happened.

The servants we had killed earlier in the day were nowhere to be seen, hopefully because their bodies had been taken away, or they had been resurrected and were now too afraid to return to their duties. Replacing them were instead hundreds of civilians, most of whom weren't actually invited in by us, but we didn't have the heart or the energy to tell them to leave. They had turned what Sacet probably had hoped to be a restful night into a never-ending afterparty.

The crowds in the city streets below Arc Sacet were packed, for, thanks to Hakkari, the entire empire had seen and heard everything that transpired during the rebellion. With the power back on, word of the successful rebellion had spread across the empire. The live feed had drawn *billions* of people to the arc in the hopes of coming with Sacet to this new life she had planned.

There were millions of people flying in the sky around the arc, but thankfully, most didn't have a good enough breathing apparatus to reach the height of the penthouse. Occasionally one did, landing on the balcony, almost freezing to death. I'd heal them and begrudgingly let them stay.

I continued to worry about what would become of the people who stayed behind. With my father as emperor, things would probably fall apart. Only time would tell. Like Sacet, I believed I had done my fair share of trying to make the empire a better place. Eventually, I had to accept that people were responsible for their own destinies.

It was good to see everyone else under the one roof now. Though things back inside were loud and chaotic, Azua, Enni, Aberym and Eno had found a nice area in the indoor garden to sit. Their bittersweet moment together probably included mourning for Lotus. Her execution after we left had also been publicly broadcast as a warning to any who dared challenge my father. I felt sorry for her. Was she any different to Sacet not long ago, or to me, had I chosen a different path?

Noor's family members were having a drinking contest in the games room. Noor was finally acting like himself again when they were around. Tetsu's family were kindly helping the children get situated.

Conversely to the many joyous things, it was sad not seeing Malu here with us. What had become of her? Had she perhaps rebelled with the rest of the population? No, knowing her, she would have dedicated her time to finding her family and making amends, perhaps keeping them safe. I hoped she was successful and that I'd see her again someday.

It seemed more and more likely that no one was going to get any sleep tonight. Of course, that didn't matter to me personally. I planned to spend the night on this poolside balcony, looking out at the aurora-filled sky and healing any arriving unplanned guests. It was the only area we had restricted to close friends and family, and thankfully, the others were respecting that rule.

Both Sacet and Noor sat on the edge of the pool, dangling their feet in the water and quietly embracing, trying to finally find some peace together.

I turned and leaned against the balcony. 'Well, that's it then. Tomorrow, no more dealing with the empire.' I smiled at them and gave a congratulatory nod. 'We finally did it.'

Sacet shook her head. 'I think I'll wait until we're on the next shuttle out of here before I agree.'

Noor laughed and kissed her on the temple. 'Me, too.'

I gestured down to Aster's surface. 'How many can we bring with us?'

Sacet shrugged. 'Once we find the perfect new home, I'll open a portal and keep it open as long as possible.'

I nodded excitedly. 'Maybe Hakkari could advertise it for us?'

Sacet nodded back and tred the water.

Noor brought a hand to his chin. 'So, whatever happened to those other two Chosen? Are they still alive?'

I looked down at the water. 'Lucenia and Elion… I imagine they'd still be wandering the Empyrean.'

'And that is where they have to stay,' Sacet added, disturbing the water's surface with a kick. She pointed at me. 'I know what *you're* going to say, that I made a promise to Lucenia, and that we have to try rescuing them or whatever, but if we mess around with this ritual stuff—'

'I agree,' I interrupted, and she raised an eyebrow, 'it could do more damage.'

'Exactly,' she replied. 'You or I might accidentally sacrifice ourselves.' She smiled at Noor. 'And we can't leave the ones we love like that again.'

The cheering and hollering from inside amplified when Tetsu slid open the glass panel door. He entered the pool area brandishing a tray of drinks and a cheesy grin. 'Hey! Pilgrim made some drinks for us, Seronian style. None of that colourful ooze.' He placed the tray on a short table and passed a drink to Sacet and Noor. 'Here you go.'

Sacet gave an exasperated sigh. '*Uhh*, let me guess, bomb juice? I don't think I can. I was just about to convince Noor that we needed to find a bed, while we still could.'

'Yeah, maybe you two should do the same?' Noor added, giving Tetsu a fairly obvious wink that he perhaps thought was subtler.

Tetsu didn't notice and grabbed two more drinks from the tray. He approached me while shaking his head. 'But Tau doesn't need to sleep?'

I giggled and gladly accepted his drink offering. 'Thanks.' I looked back at Sacet. 'Stay up with us, Sacet. Let's keep this celebration going until dawn, I can heal you whenever any of you feel tired, okay?'

She smiled and shrugged. 'Alright, fine. I doubt I would have slept anyway.' She and Noor sipped on their drinks, causing their eyes to water and abruptly coughing.

Tetsu, meanwhile, leant against the railing with me to admire the colourful sky. 'You know, when there aren't so many stressful things going on, it's easy to stop and… appreciate how beautiful things are.' He intentionally glanced at me.

I laughed again. 'How long have you been working on that one?'

He laughed, too. '*Ah*, to be honest, Pilgrim was the one who—'

There was a whoosh of air and a blinding green light as a portal opened next to a wall nearby. We were all taken aback, gasping or dropping our drinks.

Noor jumped up and prepared to fire at it, still dripping wet. 'Was that you?' he asked my sister.

She looked just as perplexed, but also intrigued. 'No…' She placed her drink down, stood, and slowly approached the mystery portal.

The rest of us hesitantly joined her and looked through. Beyond the doorway was a lush, vivid-green forest: thick flora-covered pointed peaks and vast valleys, where a serene mist gently swirled.

'You *sure* it wasn't you?' I asked Sacet.

A notification appeared on my INC, hovering above the portal was a floating message box that read: 'Your new home'. Based on the others' reactions, they had seen it, too.

'Positive,' Sacet replied.

Tetsu tilted his head. '*Hmm*, our mysterious helper strikes again. Who are they?'

Sacet's eyes narrowed, and she stepped into the portal. 'Let's find out.'

'Wait!' Noor called out, but she didn't stop.

Sacet landed on a grassy hillock before turning back and gesturing for us to step through. 'It's okay, it's safe.' She noticed our hesitation. 'If it closes, I'll portal us back myself.'

The three of us gathered our strength before following. It was only after I was through that I took in the immensity of the location's natural beauty.

'This place… it's perfect,' Sacet said, reaching out for Noor's hand and clasping it. 'Look, green forests… winding rivers…' She took a deeply-audible breath. 'Clean air.'

Now that I focused on the valley, I noticed the river curling through the thick growth. And beyond, on the horizon, a long beach stretched on forever. The landing we were on had a precipice ahead, and the sound of raging water was nearby. A waterfall, perhaps?

The cloudless sky was the same as Seron's, a pale blue, but quite oddly, there was no sun. Light seemed to be everywhere with no clear source and no shadows.

'So, who made the portal?' Tetsu asked, looking around for them.

The portal we had come through was identical to Sacet's in every way, and it continued to remain open, humming lightly.

After we all inspected it, we circled to the other side and saw an even more breathtaking sight: a grand temple built into the mountain we were standing on, made entirely of giant crystals. It somehow reflected the world's phantom ambient light with an illustrious sparkle. Entire walls, floors and ceilings of the intriguing crystalline structure were each a different iridescent colour of the rainbow.

Sacet again stepped forward to investigate, before Tetsu protested.

'Everyone, wait. Look, whatever this place is, this sort of feels like a trap to me, you know? Noor, back me up, buddy.'

Noor nodded and gestured to the temple. 'Sacet, what happened to ending the loop? What if this starts a whole new thing for us?'

Sacet grabbed Noor by the wrist and pulled. 'Or what if this is what comes after the loop? A good life in paradise?'

She coaxed us all to continue forward into the exterior temple platforms preceding the main structure.

Even the flagstones beneath our feet were perfectly cut gems that formed intricate swirling patterns. A palace-style garden preceded the temple, which was lined with crystal statues depicting strange lifeforms. Each was more alien than the last, varying in size, number of limbs, and lacking other typical Asterian features like eyes or a discernible head.

One of the largest statues stood out to me, it looked like the creature I had encountered in the Empyrean. Sacet noticed it, too, before locking eyes with me and biting her lip nervously.

The gardens were surprisingly well manicured, burgeoning with plants I didn't recognise. The closer we got to the temple, the more the statues resembled creatures I recognised, until eventually those by the cave-like entrance looked Asterian.

Sacet stopped, looking straight ahead at the temple. 'There's someone in there… alone.'

The rest of us peered into the crystal, pillar-lined tunnel, but quickly realised she was seeing this person with her special perception.

'I'm tired of being messed with,' she continued, before opening a portal next to us, 'it's time for some answers.'

We all saw the person she spoke of through it: a bald, robed woman sitting cross-legged in meditation on a central raised altar. Her aura, a multistorey column of cyan flame spun like a tethered tornado. Elysia.

The four of us stepped into the temple's interior, all eight walls were angled crystals that bounced rays of differing light in a spectacular light show.

'You,' I said, and the others glanced back at me briefly.

'Hello, Tau,' Elysia began, opening her fake eyes and smiling. 'It's good to see you again.'

Suddenly, a memory sprung to mind as though being unlocked. I was standing on the floating platform in the Empyrean again, and there, just over the edge, was the strange creature, a great eye surrounded by sinewy tentacles. Instinctively, I had reached out to it, and our palms met at the barrier.

My power, to transfer soul energy to and from the Empyrean, had siphoned this creature through the barrier and into my body. I had been carrying it inside me all this time. That was my purpose there. I didn't know why I knew that now, but I did. And in that moment, a knock echoed in my brain, like the thing inside was trying to get out. The accompanying migraine wracked my senses.

Elysia's aura was even larger than I remembered and made more impressive by the reflecting crystal chamber. An overwhelming sense of health and good permeated my every fibre, and yet the migraine persisted.

'Tau, you know her?' Noor said, pointing his hands at her. 'Who is this?'

'It's Queen Elysia,' Tetsu answered for me, noticing I was out of it, 'or is it *Head Chancellor* Elysia?'

Elysia laughed before floating off the altar and gently touching back down to stand. 'Either of those is fine.' She dipped her head to my sister. 'Sacet, it's good to finally meet you in person.'

Sacet relaxed her stance before awkwardly dipping her head back. '*Uhhh*, you, too?'

Elysia then gave another courteous bow to the boys. 'Greetings also to you, Noor and Tetsu. Welcome to my world. I would like to invite you and all the other refugees to make new homes here, a new world *away* from the empire.'

I clutched my throbbing forehead. 'You tried to warn me… before the rituals. You… *sent* me in there to retrieve that creature, didn't you?'

Elysia continued smiling and bowed. 'Yes… we needed a powerful ally.'

'You *used* me,' I snapped, and my friends all tensed again, unsure of what was going on.

Sacet looked down in disgust before turning to her with contempt. 'I thought Chosen couldn't be controlled by psychics? What did you do to my sister?'

Elysia smirked. 'I programmed you both a long time ago for this exact purpose. It worked out surprisingly well.'

'What?' Sacet pointed threateningly at the charlatan. 'No more games. Who are you, really?'

Elysia slowly nodded. 'I agree, no more games.'

She floated effortlessly off the gemstone floor. There were no L lines either, as if she were using Caelum's power to hover. Her robes melted away, and her skin parted to unveil the true form beneath: a mass of glowing, writhing pinkish tentacles.

Underneath her disguise, her bulb-like body had a jawless skull-shaped bone protruding from the top, and five pinkish tentacles were sprouting out of it. Her dark, purplish core was like a giant, sideways eye, with two bright pink pupils. The eye's insides appeared as a galaxy, swirling with star-like particulates.

'No more lies,' Elysia's disembodied voice said from all around us, reverberating off the crystal walls.

The boys gawped, unsettled by what must have been a horrifying sight to them, but Sacet and I weren't afraid, having seen her kind before.

Was this alien even a *she* anymore? Elysia's body continued to unravel, reducing to its simplest form. The two bright pink globes intensified.

'We are the victor of the last time the rituals were performed,' its voice echoed. 'As caretaker of this universe, it was our duty not only to help it grow, but also to bring it to an end when the time came. We *chose* you, Tau and Sacet, and the others, but we don't wish to see this universe recycled anymore. Unfortunately, now that the rituals have begun, the universe will *always* be in danger.'

Sacet collapsed to her knees. 'No… NO! *Enough* with the danger. I'm *done* with Asterians and their stupid path. I never wanted to be a part of it. This has to stop!'

'How?' the floating entity responded. 'Did you really think Caelum would leave you alone now? His prideful need for conquest will eat away at him. Eventually, he'll invade whatever place you run to. And although they're in prison for now, how do we deal with Raumanu's suicidal fanaticism or Andriel's hateful control when they finally break free? No, girls. It is the Asterians that will never be done with *you*.'

Tetsu furrowed his brow. 'Then what about Kaxiyan's plan? Can't we just permanently kill them?'

The creature's orbs spiralled. 'A Chosen's soul is indestructible. No Asterian has ever tried to shatter one to confirm that, but we assure you it is true.'

Sacet was shaking her head in her hands.

Noor saw how dejected she was becoming and swatted his arm at Elysia. 'Then we bury them, in an inescapable inhibitor prison deep in an uninhabited planet where they'll never be found!'

Elysia's tentacles swiped back at his torso, thrusting him back. 'And then what? What about the countless beings from distant, undiscovered empires? You have *no* idea the sheer number of lifeforms out there we helped seed. They've just had their technological evolution skipped ahead by thousands of cycles. After tasting these new powers, won't they inevitably come to seek answers, shortly before seeking *more* power?'

The creature rotated to Sacet, its pink orbs softened. 'We're sorry, but the loop you sought to undo will *never* be broken. We must *prepare* for this forever war, together. I will do my best to protect you all from this point on.'

My head had finally stopped pounding. I locked my shaking eyes with Tetsu, and he strode over to me. We hugged tightly. But it wasn't like before when I had been hesitant to share my love. I had no fear of the future, so long as my family was in it.

I smiled. 'As long as we're together—'

'—we'll be okay,' Tetsu finished for me.

Sacet was still on the ground, so Noor approached her and helped her up.

'You didn't think we'd be spending the rest of our lives in paradise, did you?' Noor asked her with an impish grin.

Her eyes flashed at him, hurt, but after a moment, she calmed and scoffed. 'Maybe lying on a beach somewhere, sipping drinks? Yeah, I did.'

'A couple of weapons like us?' he replied, and his grin disappeared. 'I'm so sorry, Sacet.' He went in for a hug. 'Maybe we can find some beach time between all the fighting?'

Sacet hugged him back and managed a smile. 'That would still be paradise to me, so long as it's with you.'

I waved them both over, and we four together embraced in a huddle. I knew what was coming next; we had been fighting its control over us our entire lives. But never again would I stay idle while my family suffered. I was sure they all felt the same. There were tears, but also bittersweet smiles.

After releasing, Sacet again focused on Elysia, stepping closer. Her smile faded, replaced with her signature determined glower. 'What do you want us to do?'

Arc Lucenia

Arc Elion

Arc Academy

Arc Andriel

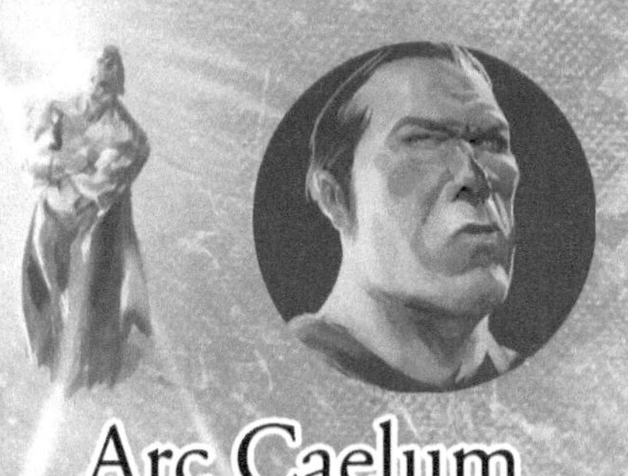

Arc Caelum

Arc Raumanu

Arc Royal

Arc Sacet

ASTERIAN HISTORY

-41 BE
The **Ascension Wars** begins, as the last conglomerate nations of Bracken, Vireya and Waratah clash in a final bid for dominion over the planet Aster and their entire species.

Cycle 0
After Vireyan King Metastus is assassinated, his second son Avarut is coronated along with his beautiful Queen Suralia. They vow to bring a swift end to the **Ascension Wars**. This point in history is considered to be the birth of our great empire. All hail Emperor Avarut and Empress Suralia.

7 ER
A Vireyan orphan girl named Elysia becomes the first Disciple, an acolyte with the ability to heal and resurrect others. Other Disciples are soon born in the following cycles.

-33 BE
Emperor Avarut's birth

-23 BE
Chosen Raumanu's birth

-48 BE
Asterian scientists invent and test the first interstellar warp engine, successfully travelling to the nearest star in only a single day. The royal houses disagree on how the species should move forward, either unified or continuing as separate nations. Tensions rise in a period known as **the Fracture**.

-16 BE
Empress Suralia's birth

-36 BE
As the war rages, the three nations explore nearby systems and discover a bipedal species curiously similar to their own called the Houtan. They are enslaved and forced to fight in the **Ascension Wars** as mercenaries.

9 ER
With a combination of superior leadership and the healing gifts of 1st Disciple Elysia, the Emperors finally conquer their enemies and unite all of Aster under one rule.

BE – Before Emperors
ER – Eternal Reign

742 ER

The lush planet **Orturid** becomes the 417th habitable world claimed by the Asterian Empire. It is home to a savage alien species named the *necrolisk*, a term coined by Chosen Raumanu, then Supreme Commander of the Asterian Carrier Fleet. He explained the endearing name roughly meant *'little death'*. Ironically, the creatures stand twice the height of the average Asterian.

847 ER

A full invasion of Drymar is ordered by Emperor Avarut. However, Chosen Caelum's power is severely underestimated—he repelled every attempted incursion. Raumanu, the empire's most powerful acolyte, is dispatched to deliver the killing blow. Their legendary, days-long battle ends in a stalemate. Our clever Emperor decided that the planet should instead be destroyed, and only its strongest acolytes salvaged. Raumanu obliterates Drymar, killing over 3 billion Drymarians.

806 ER

Chosen Caelum's birth

929 ER

Overwatch's founding

1233 ER

Chosen Andriel's birth

700   800   900   1000   1100   1200   1300

846 ER

The planet Drymar is discovered. A bleak, unforgiving world, it is ruled by Chosen Caelum, known as Caelum'inat by his people, a savage barbarian king and self-proclaimed god.

1021 ER

Over the course of centuries, a team of scientists and acolyte seers, led by Chosen Raumanu, then Supreme Augurant of Truth, proved the existence of the Empyrean. After noticing a spiritual connection through meditation, Raumanu and Caelum realised that they were different from other acolytes. The hunt for more like them began.

925 ER

Prevailing scientific theories of the time finally confirmed that experiencing trauma, particularly in youth, increased the likelihood of becoming an acolyte. Beautiful Empress Suralia approved the creation of the first Harvest World.

1251 ER

After the Emperors almost gave up on the idea of the Chosen, Andriel was discovered on Harvest World Calamus. She established a psychic hierarchy, known as the Network, to bring further order to the Empire.

1605 ER

A paradise world named **Salix** was discovered, home to yet another species genetically compatible with Asterians, albeit with peculiar orange skin. Instead of invading the post-Bronze Age planet, the empire chose to turn it into another Harvest World by experimenting with the climate, triggering an ice age. The hope was that the long-term survival would cause increased trauma.

1977 ER

Another paradise world named **Seron** was discovered. After extended observation, Chosen Lucenia, then Priestess Warrior of the Blood Moon, was found. Both Chosen Raumanu and Caelum were her chief torturers, and in spurring her on to defend her people, caused her to accidentally leave trails of her power all over Seron's sky, later nicknamed L lines.

2010 ER

L lines became such a popular mode of transport on Aster that their negative effects on the ozone layer were ignored. The already weak atmosphere of Aster was letting in even harsher radiation, causing more birth defects and death. A solution was required, and soon.

1660 ER

Chosen Elion's birth

1952 ER

Chosen Lucenia's birth

1682 ER

When the Overwatch crew returned to survey Salix's ice age, they expected total extinction. Instead, they found a sizeable amount of survivors, sustained by Chosen Elion's ability to generate infinite raw materials. The survivors welcomed Overwatch, mistaking them for a strange rescue team. Elion was tortured for an extended period in the hopes his powers would amplify. They did.

1978 ER

Shortly after Lucenia and Seron's defeat, it was decided that the planet would become the Empire's 17th Harvest World. Some of the original population was kept, and any records of their previous civilisation were erased, including their memories.

2136 ER

Powerful artificial magneto-spheres were deployed around most of Aster.

1714 ER

Elion's abilities brought vast resource wealth to the Empire, leading to new economic protocols and safeguards.

2006 ER

Lucenia's L lines were discovered to be burning away Seron's ozone layer over time.

SACET'S FRIENDS & FAMILY

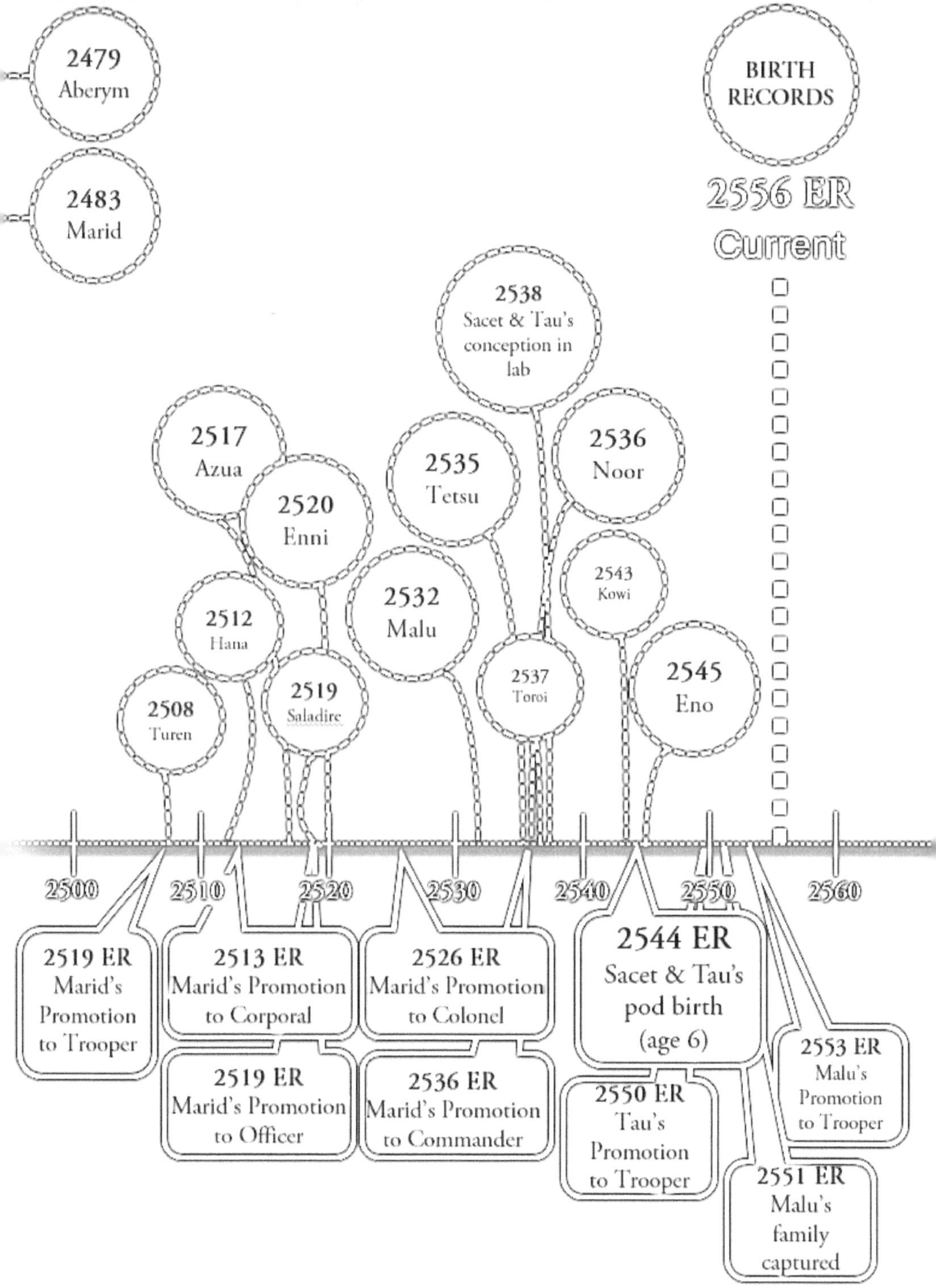

2479
Aberym

2483
Marid

BIRTH RECORDS

2556 ER
Current

2538
Sacet & Tau's conception in lab

2517
Azua

2520
Enni

2535
Tetsu

2536
Noor

2512
Hana

2532
Malu

2543
Kowi

2508
Turen

2519
Saladire

2537
Toroi

2545
Eno

2500
2510
2520
2530
2540
2550
2560

2519 ER
Marid's Promotion to Trooper

2513 ER
Marid's Promotion to Corporal

2526 ER
Marid's Promotion to Colonel

2544 ER
Sacet & Tau's pod birth
(age 6)

2519 ER
Marid's Promotion to Officer

2536 ER
Marid's Promotion to Commander

2550 ER
Tau's Promotion to Trooper

2553 ER
Malu's Promotion to Trooper

2551 ER
Malu's family captured

Note from the Author

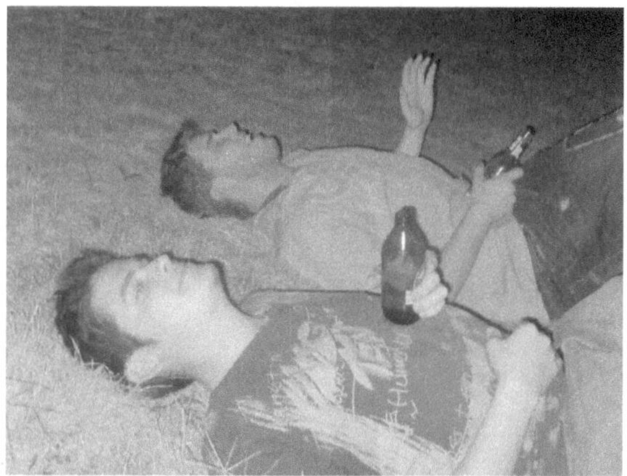

In my youth, I was introverted, even timid at times. That hesitance kept me from the people I wanted to be closer to, experiences I wanted to try, and perhaps even greater career success. I've always wondered how life would have turned out if I had been more charismatic and outgoing.

Thankfully, I've had good friends to regularly pull me out of my shell, sometimes by force. They made me realise that we humans wear lots of masks: sometimes to spare another's feelings, but more often it is to hide our own. I'm still quite introverted to this day, and I always will be, but now, thanks to those friends, I don't wear masks. When opportunities arise, I seize the day.

Believe me when I say no one wants to live with ancient, unfixable regrets, but we all make mistakes. So, when you do find yourself replaying the past in your head, learn to forgive yourself and move on. If you can do that, you can focus on leaving a legacy you and your loved ones can be proud of. Build your empire, whatever form that might take. And never hesitate.

For more confident content and constructive updates from J.B. Villinger's works, contact him directly at jvillinger@live.com.au, or you can also find him on Wattpad @ JamesVillinger.

www.ingramcontent.com/pod-product-compliance
Lightning Source LLC
Chambersburg PA
CBHW020256120726
47904CB00001B/215